King Love

A contemporary sapphic romance

Samantha L. Valentine

Manuscript assessment: Penny Carroll

Copy-edit: Sophia Blackwell

Cover art and design: Samantha Sanderson Marshall

Paperback ISBN: 978-0-9756111-4-2

Ebook ISBN: 978-0-9756111-5-9

Also by Samantha L. Valentine

Novels

Normal Functioning Adult

Meet Me in Berlin

Short Stories

Eternal Love (Romance Writers of Australia Sweet Treats anthology, 2024)

The Five Circles of Love (Romance Writers of Australia Diversions anthology, 2025)

Author's note

Hello!

Thank you for choosing to read my novel. I am an Australian author publishing in Australia; therefore, this novel is written in Australian English and uses our spelling and publishing standards. This means spelling with an 's' instead of 'z' or an '-our' instead of '-or' and single quotes for dialogue instead of double.

When I was a young adult living in London many years ago, I discovered drag kings through reading a magazine article. I think that same article might have also introduced me to gender diversity, although that phrase wasn't common then. That didn't exactly set me on a course of following drag kings or understanding gender diversity, but it's a memory that's always stayed with me. So when I started writing fiction more seriously, I added kings to my 'to write' list.

I found the opportunity when I wrote *King Love* as a 4000-word short story for a competition in late 2023. It wasn't selected so I parked it while I wrote the draft of another novel, then spent the first half of 2024 re-publishing *Normal Functioning Adult* and publishing *Meet Me in Berlin*.

Once *Berlin* was released, I decided to extend *King Love* into a short novella to use as a newsletter magnet. However, my main characters had different ideas and the story evolved into the full-length novel you're about to read. Yes, this is a story that features kings, but it's also a story about love, self-expression, gender, performance, and being your authentic self. Having my characters express all of that through the art of drag seemed fitting.

The setting is my home city of Brisbane. The suburbs, street names and some places are real; however, City Books is fictional, and sadly, Club Sappho does not exist. At the time of writing, regular Thursday and Saturday night drag king shows are not a thing here (and probably not in many other cities either). Having my kings change after the shows so that they can be in the club as themselves is somewhat unrealistic, but hey, this is fiction, so you may need to suspend your disbelief.

Finally, it saddens me that I have to explicitly state this in my works now, but I support human creation, and every sentence in this book has come from my human brain. No GenAI was used by me or by the professionals I engaged to write, edit, format or design any part of this novel. Supporting human creation also means I do not permit any of my writing to be uploaded into AI platforms for any purpose. This work is protected under Australian copyright law.

With that out of the way, back to the fun stuff. Drag is an art form and kings are underrepresented. If you find some in your local area, support them!

Happy reading,

Sam x

For anyone who's ever felt that life is a performance.

Chapter 1
Callie

I peek through the side curtain, scanning the audience for the familiar figure. She's sitting two tables back from the stage, her fingertips poised on the stem of a wine glass, her dark eyes fixed straight ahead, eagerly awaiting the next performance. *My* performance. I exhale a long, calming breath. *I can do this –* Tom *can do this.*

A hush ripples through the audience as Krissy, acting as the evening's emcee, steps across the small stage, the soles of her sneakers scuffing the wood. She lifts the microphone to her mouth and booms an enthusiastic, 'Are you ready for your next act?'

The club is full tonight, the crowd lively, and they respond with a raucous cheer.

'You think you can handle it?' she teases, pacing the stage.

A chorus of whoops and whistles answers her question and an anticipatory shiver sweeps over my skin. I tip my head from side to side, stretching out my neck, and check that my suspenders are sitting tight on my shoulders. I listen for my introduction in *three, two, one...*

'Then give it up for one of Brisbane's hottest drag kings' – Krissy pauses for effect – 'Tom Cruisin'!' She hurries back down the steps to revert to her substantive position of club owner and bar manager.

The crowd erupts and an electronic beat pulses from the speakers. I dance across the stage, lip-syncing to 'One Margarita', deliberately showcasing my rhythm and flexibility. I make eye contact with random audience members – my ritual at the start of every performance to build rapport – before my gaze lands on the familiar face. The woman who's been here every Saturday night for the past month. The woman I've also seen at the bar after every show but haven't had the courage to approach out of drag.

Our eyes meet, and the current that zaps between us almost makes me forget the lyrics. I regain composure and deftly move to the small drinks trolley that's part of my act. I toss a bottle of tequila in the air and catch it with the pourer facing down, as I've practised every day for the past two weeks. The crowd whoops in appreciation and I add the triple sec and lime juice to a salted tumbler. Jogging the three steps down from the stage, I hold the margarita high, raising a questioning brow.

Calls of 'Me!' and 'Over here!' pierce the air as I weave through the tables, exaggerating my masculine swagger. When I reach my destination, I place the glass down. The delighted smile I'm rewarded with makes my stomach flip. But a drag king always plays it cool, so I give her a wink, bow to the crowd and head backstage.

My body buzzes as I stride through the backstage corridor, a disbelieving grin on my face because I finally found the courage to do *something*. In the dressing room, I tug off my wig and give my head a good rub with a hand towel to mop up the sweat on my scalp. I remove the suspenders and bow tie, strip off my dress shirt and trousers, then squirt baby oil over the strips of kinesiology tape flattening each breast. While I wait for the oil to take effect, I soak a fresh cotton pad in coconut oil and swipe it along my jaw.

As I remove my make-up, my mind drifts, as it often does, to the beautiful stranger. This is the fifth Saturday night in a row she's been here. Yes, I've counted them, because every week I've turned into a red-faced, fumbling mess whenever there's been even a sniff of her being in my personal space. My cheeks warm, recalling the night she was at the bar waiting to be served. In my haste *not* to serve her, I'd busied myself collecting empty glasses, only to trip over my own feet and fall against the doorjamb leading to the prep area behind the bar. I managed to stay upright, but the tray of glasses plummeted to the floor, landing with a spectacular crash. As I cleaned up shattered glass, I noticed her buy a margarita and the idea of a cocktail act blossomed.

With my face mostly free of make-up, I strip off my trousers, underwear and soft silicone packer. The edges of the tape covering my breasts has started to curl from the baby oil, and I slowly peel it off. I gently mop at my chest with baby wipes and head for the shower, still grateful that Stevie and Krissy – owners of Club Sappho and married to each other – made a last-minute decision to install a bathroom between the dressing rooms during the renovation. A small owner-managed club means the kings' job descriptions extend beyond being the talent. After a show, we often revert to being bartenders, door staff, emcees, lighting techs, and even the occasional DJ. Stevie and Krissy also spend a considerable amount of time here, so a fully functioning bathroom is a necessity. They even have a sofa bed in the office for those nights they're too exhausted to drive home.

In the shower, I scrub away the residue of make-up and sweat, but nothing can wash away the high of executing my act with precision. I dry off, lather my chest with a creamy avocado body butter and pull on jeans and a plain black T-shirt. I've just finished blasting my hair with the dryer when a knock sounds at the door.

It opens a crack and Stevie calls, 'Are you decent?'

'Yep,' I call back.

She bursts into the room, fresh from the stage, dressed as her alter ego, The King Laroi. She yanks off her wig and gives her short blonde hair a vigorous rub with a towel. 'What a crowd tonight! Krissy is run off her feet at the bar; lucky we got extra staff in.'

'My marketing posts must be working,' I say, warming moulding clay between the pads of my fingers and smoothing it through my short strands, followed by a spritz of lacquer that adds a nice sheen to black hair.

'Uh-huh. Keep it up.' Stevie kicks off her boots and shoots my reflection a curious glance. 'What's with the cocktail act, Romeo?'

I twist to face her. 'Romeo?'

She steps out of her baggy jeans. 'Hand-delivering a margarita to your *very* attractive audience member? You kept that quiet.'

The warmth rising in my cheeks belies my nonchalant shrug. 'Just entertaining the crowd; they love that sort of thing.' I bend down to slip on a pair of socks, hoping Stevie hasn't caught my blush.

'Yeah, right. You've been lusting over her for weeks, and you've turned beetroot. Didn't think you'd have the courage to do something that bold, though.'

I sit up. 'Am I that obvious?'

Stevie laughs her low, dirty laugh. 'To me, yeah. And probably to everyone else, given the lyrics to "One Margarita".'

The heat in my face intensifies. 'I only picked that song because I was making a margarita.'

She snorts. 'Oh my god, Callie. Turn around. I want to get this off,' she says, gesturing to her crotch. 'And I don't want you watching me when you're all hot and bothered.'

'You wish,' I say, but I avert my gaze and tug on my Converse.

'So, does this mean you might actually talk to her tonight?' Stevie asks.

I tie my laces and stay silent.

'You can look now,' Stevie says. When I straighten, she's sitting at the other dressing table in her T-shirt, the lights framing the mirror casting a soft sheen across her face. 'Callie, you have to talk to her. She's into you and after that performance, the timing is hot.'

I frown. 'She's into Tom, not me.'

Stevie soaks a cotton pad in oil and wipes it under one eye. 'I reckon she knows someone else is under the Tom act she's keen to meet.'

'But I don't have the confidence of Tom Cruisin'.'

Stevie gives my reflection a sympathetic smile. 'I know, but you'll never find *the one* if you don't put yourself out there even a tiny bit.' She douses a second cleansing pad in oil and concentrates on the other eye. 'She's here every week and she watches your act more closely than anyone else's. It's obvious she's interested.'

I let out a shaky breath. 'Okay, so I'll just walk up to her and say...' My mind blanks. 'What do I say?'

'Just introduce yourself. She won't bite.' Stevie twists her head to look at me and waggles her eyebrows. 'Unless you want her to.'

'Ugh,' I say, holding my stomach as though it will quell the nerves. 'Don't.'

'Let's practise.' Stevie spins on her seat and flicks some imaginary long hair. 'I'm her and I'm sitting here looking all beautiful, having a quiet drink after that incredible show—'

'No, Stevie,' I say with a defiant shake of my head. 'I am not doing this.'

'Do you want to talk to her or not?' She picks up a water bottle. 'I've got my glass of white wine' – she gives me a sly smile – 'or margarita, and I'm casually glancing around the club, waiting for that hot drag king – who I really hope is now out of drag – to talk to me.' She crosses her legs, her dark blue eyes wandering the dressing room. When I don't react, she says in a singsong voice, 'I'm waiting.'

I huff out a resigned sigh and quickly say, 'Hi-I'm-Callie-do-you-want-a-drink.'

Stevie pulls her head back, brows creased. 'You're not a fucking robot, why do you sound so monotone?'

I slump against the back of the chair with an agonised groan. 'See, I can't do this. I'm not a "make the first move" type of person.'

Stevie holds up a hand. 'Sorry. That was insensitive. Let's try again. Just start with a hello.'

I nod. 'Okay. Erm ... "Hello."'

'There you go. Now, I'm her.' Stevie lifts her chin. '"*Hi*",' she says, adopting a high, breathy voice.

I make a face. 'Why are you talking like that? I doubt that's what she sounds like.'

Stevie widens her eyes at me. 'Work with me here. I'm role-playing. Then you say...'

'Oh, then I say, "I'm Callie."'

'And...' Stevie circles her hand in the air encouragingly.

'And "Can I buy you a drink?"'

Stevie blinks at me like I'm a lost cause. 'Well, yeah, but don't cower when you say it.' She jumps up, pulling her T-shirt down so it covers her underwear. 'Like this.' She saunters towards me, wearing a sultry half-smile, her eyes soft. 'Hi. I'm Callie. I've seen you around the past few weeks. Can I buy you a drink?' She loses the sexy. 'Not so hard, is it?'

I look at her, deadpan. 'Don't *ever* try and hit on me again. It's weird, cuz.'

She grins and ruffles my hair. 'We're only related by marriage; it's allowed.'

'Eww.' I push her hand away. 'It's not allowed; don't even joke about it, and now you've messed up my hair,' I say, turning back to the mirror.

'Anyway, good luck with this one.' Stevie grabs her pants off the back of a chair. 'Because I reckon your admirer's got straight girl energy.'

I spin to face her. 'You reckon? You think she's coming here every week to fulfil a lesbian fantasy?'

Stevie shrugs. 'She wouldn't be the first.'

'Nah,' I say, shaking my head. 'She's got femme lesbian energy.'

'Ooh.' Stevie grabs a leather whip from the clothes rack, throws it around the back of her neck and shimmies like she's working a feather boa in a cabaret act. 'Like dom femme energy.'

I laugh. 'Since when are dom femmes associated with whips?'

She grins. 'You tell me; you're the expert.'

I arch a brow.

'What? Too soon?' Stevie places the whip back on the rack. 'It's been a year.'

'Well, she didn't whip me, I can tell you that,' I reply.

Stevie slips on her shoes. 'You're a sucker for a femme alright.'

I give a defeated sigh. 'I know.' I watch her lace up her

sneakers, only now realising she's dressed to go back into the club. 'Why aren't you showering? You'll stink of BO and you haven't removed your make-up properly.'

'No time. I need to help in the bar. Besides' – she smirks – 'Krissy likes me all sweaty. She thinks it's sexy.'

'Ha, she so doesn't,' I say to Stevie's retreating back as she walks into the bathroom.

There's a knock at the door and I hop up to open it. It's Amber, another king and club colleague. Her auburn hair is piled on top of her head, and her sharp grey eyes drag over my body. *Very subtle, Amber.*

'Are we getting an after-show drink?' she asks, lifting her gaze.

'Not for me,' I say. 'I'm going to help out behind the bar.'

'No,' Stevie says, emerging from the bathroom and pointing a finger at me. 'You booked a week off and it starts now.'

'But you said Krissy is run off her feet—'

'I also said we have extra staff and that I'm helping her,' she says and ushers me out of the dressing room.

We pass through the prep area – a narrow, dimly lit space that houses sinks, dishwashers and extra stock, and doubles as a thoroughfare between backstage and behind the bar. I slip under the bar hatch into the club, closely followed by Amber. The drag show has finished, our regular Saturday night DJ has started, and people fill the dance floor.

My eyes sweep the room, an anxious flutter in my stomach, but I don't see the margarita recipient. My heart dips a little, but I'm also relieved that I won't need to approach her after all. The tension in my shoulders eases and I absorb the atmosphere instead. I love Club Sappho – the queerness, the euphoric vibe, the sense of community – it's an indelible part of me.

Stevie and Krissy bought the building a couple of years ago – a small, rundown theatre in a prime location in Fortitude Valley. They spent twelve months transforming it while holding down day jobs. A year of managing tradies, dealing with councils, shopping for furniture and stock, and renovating on evenings and weekends. Dated, worn furnishings were ripped out and replaced with modern tables and chairs made with reclaimed wood and copper legs, cushioned bench seats and bar stools in vintage leather, a small dance floor, and a mahogany bar that runs half the length of one side of the club. The only original features are the dark wooden flooring, the exposed brick walls that were hidden behind plasterboard, and the small stage, which was sanded, polished and reinforced. Backstage, existing rooms were knocked down and replaced with two dressing rooms, a bathroom and a spacious office. At the time, the strain on their relationship made me question if they were making the right move. But they had a vision, determined to create their industrial-chic-design sapphic club, and now I can't imagine our lives without this place.

I swivel on the stool and face the bar. Stevie is behind the counter kissing Krissy deeply as though they've been separated for months rather than the past hour.

'Stop, you two,' I say loudly so they hear me over the music. 'It's sickening.' I make the same comment every time I witness one of their PDAs, but the truth is, I love their relationship; it gives me hope. They've been together eight years, meeting in their mid-twenties, and marrying six months ago. It was the most romantic event I've ever been to. Held on acreage in the hinterland, a cold winter evening, enclosed marquees decorated with hanging fairy lights, heat lamps aglow, long tables topped with floral centrepieces bursting with colour, guests in black tie, wait staff circulating with champagne, and a love so pure and deep flowing between them that it was impossible not to get swept away and fantasise about my own soulmate that I hoped was out there somewhere.

Krissy halts the kiss, wrinkling her nose and putting distance between them. 'You smell sweaty.'

'Told you,' I say to Stevie with a laugh.

She pulls Krissy close again and whispers in her ear. Krissy's mouth twitches, her dark eyes smouldering as she gives Stevie a heated look.

'Ahem,' I say. 'Wouldn't mind a drink over here.'

Krissy grins at me and takes two bottles of lager from the fridge, flips off the lids and places them on the counter for Amber and me.

'Ta,' I say, taking a swig.

Amber leans in, her shoulder brushing mine. 'You were great tonight.'

'Thanks. You too.' I turn on my stool, lean back against the bar and resume club watch.

'I messed up the second act,' she says. 'But I don't think anyone noticed.'

'Nah. You nailed it.'

'You think so?'

'Mm-hmm.'

There's a pause, then Amber says, 'What's with the new act?'

That catches my attention and I look at her.

'Making audience members cocktails?' she clarifies.

'Nothing. I just like to mix it up and try different things.'

She sips her beer, eyeing me suspiciously. 'I thought you were going to drop to one knee and propose.'

I laugh. 'You think she'd say yes?'

Amber's jaw twitches, but she doesn't banter back. Instead,

she shifts her attention to the person sitting on the other side of her and I skim the crowd once more, my stomach somersaulting when I spot *her* at a table on the opposite side of the club.

She's with someone I've seen her with before and I'm curious about their relationship. They're sitting side by side at the end of a bench seat, but their body language is giving good friends rather than partners or people on a date. Maybe even relatives, given their similar facial features and wavy brown hair.

I turn away, rest my elbows on the bar and run my fingertips back and forth along the shaved sides of my head, as though the action will stimulate my brain's ability to converse with an attractive stranger. *Just walk up and say hello – one simple word. Then introduce myself – two simple words. Then ask to buy her a drink – five simple, no, six ... oh, god, too many words.*

'You've seen her, I take it?' Stevie's voice cuts through the chatter in my head.

I nod.

'What's the worst that can happen?' she asks, pouring two glasses of white wine for a customer. 'She says no?'

'Um, yeah!' I reply, my eyes wide. 'That would be mortifying.'

Stevie tilts her head sympathetically. 'I don't reckon she will, given she watches your performances like a hawk.' She screws the lid back on the wine bottle and places the drinks on the bar for the person to my left. 'And if she does say no, well, she's missing out on getting to know an amazing person. There're plenty of other people here who'd love to have a drink with you.'

'Yeah,' the person beside me purrs. 'Like me.'

I turn my head slowly, raising a brow. One corner of their mouth curves up in a sultry smile and they turn back to their friend.

Stevie laughs, her eyes bright. 'There you go. Never short of admirers.'

I appreciate what Stevie is doing, but the hollowness in my chest tells me I want so much more than a hookup. What she said earlier is true, though; I'll never meet anyone if I don't at least try.

I slip off the stool and start across the club, my throat suddenly scratchy. *Breathe. She's just a person.* As I near her, she stops talking and turns to me with an alarmed expression. Her eyes are a warm cinnamon brown and I'm momentarily lost in them, then I remember I'm supposed to speak.

My lips part and an agonising few seconds pass before I blurt, 'You're pretty.'

I gasp as the reality of what I've said registers and my face burns. My fight-or-flight response kicks in and I dart into the side corridor, dodging people as they emerge from the bathrooms. I rush to the end of the walkway, punch in the staff access code and escape backstage.

In the dressing room, I pace the floor, my breaths coming short and sharp. 'You're pretty?' I say to myself, my voice strangled. 'You're pretty!' *No, no, no.* I grab my bag, exit the club via the back door, jump into my car and head north to the safety of home.

Chapter 2
Maya

'Why are you so reluctant to go to your parents' place today, Maya?' Dr Garcia asks thirty minutes into our fifty-minute session.

I look up from picking at some chipped polish on my thumbnail. The strip lighting in the ceiling emphasises the silver strands in her black hair and the soft lines marking her face. 'Because it's exhausting sometimes,' I say. 'Mum's comments about me being single are wearing thin. It's like she's panicked that I'm twenty-eight and don't have a partner.'

Dr Garcia remains silent, allowing me the space to continue. When I don't, she says, 'So your parents not knowing about your sexuality is starting to impact you? Making you feel like you don't want to spend time with them?'

This is my third session with Dr Garcia. The connection between my sexuality and how I relate to my parents is a topic she keeps returning to. 'It's not that I don't want to spend time with them,' I say. 'I love them, and I know I've made things harder by not telling them sooner. But it never feels like the right time, like I've left it too long.' I release a tired sigh. 'It would just be so much easier if I had someone to tell them about.'

Dr Garcia tilts her head. 'As though you need evidence?'

I shrug. 'I suppose.'

'You can be single and gay, Maya. Your relationship status doesn't determine your sexuality.'

'I know that. It's just' – I shake my head – 'I don't know, saying, "I am seeing someone actually and *her* name is..." is a whole lot easier than saying, "Hey, Mum and Dad, even though I'm twenty-eight and have known I'm a lesbian since high school, I haven't quite got round to telling you, because, you know, life ... sorry about that."'

She offers a kind smile.

'Anyway,' I continue, 'that isn't the only reason I don't want to go over there today. I wanted to do something else. Not this afternoon, but I wanted to go out tonight.'

'Okay, so if you've only committed to this afternoon, why can't you still do your own thing tonight?'

I slip my feet out of my sandals and cross my legs on the sofa. 'Because Mum and Dad are having friends over for a barbecue to celebrate this building award Dad's company has been nominated for. It will continue into the evening and they'll expect me to stay.'

She nods. 'I see. You could enjoy the barbecue, then let them know you have plans; that's an option.'

'I could, but if I say I'm leaving to go to a club, they'll ask questions.' I frown. 'Although I'm not sure why I'm worrying about it because my sister has changed her mind about going with me.'

'You don't want to ask someone else?' Dr Garcia asks. 'A friend?'

I haven't talked about my friendship circle, or lack thereof, in any of our sessions. I've drifted apart from the few friends I had from high school and university. I had a nice group when I was with my ex, but they were Arianne's friends and stuck with her after the breakup. Ash, my work colleague, has become close though. 'I've been out a few times with my work colleague,' I say. 'But they're busy tonight with their partner and I don't want to ask anyone else. I don't want people's opinions.' I press my lips together, uncertain why I added that last statement.

Dr Garcia's brows rise quizzically. 'Opinions? Why would someone have an opinion about being in a club with you?'

I shake my head. 'I don't know why I said that.'

'Okay,' she says softly, 'but you did, so there might be something in it.'

I reach for my glass of water, thinking about how to answer. 'I don't hide my sexuality,' I say, 'except from my parents. But I don't really talk about it either. I've distanced myself from my friend group. They're all so ... heteronormative. There's probably one or two I could call and ask out, but I feel like they'd be watching my every move if they were with me in a lesbian club, so I guess that's what I meant. I wouldn't want their opinions if they were out with me.'

'Like they'd be judging you?'

I nod.

'But a club is a club, isn't it?' Dr Garcia asks. 'You'd drink, dance, meet people. Why would you be concerned if someone was watching your every move?'

I tap my fingernail against the side of the glass. I'm hesitant to be honest, but I've quickly learned that she has a knack for drawing information from me, so it will come out eventually. 'There's someone I'd like to meet,' I say, 'and I really don't want an audience for that.'

Dr Garcia crosses her legs and places her notepad in her lap – a signal that what I've said is worthy of exploration.

I take a sip of water and return the glass to the ceramic coaster, manoeuvring it so it's perfectly centred. 'Every Saturday night, this club has a drag king show. There's one drag king in particular who I thought might be interested in…' I trail off, because now the words are outside of my head, it sounds ludicrous.

'In you?' Dr Garcia gently prompts.

I nod. 'Last week, she did this new act and made a drink onstage, then ran into the audience to give it to someone and that someone was me. It was a margarita – the only other drink I've bought there apart from wine. She must have known that? That couldn't be a coincidence?' I look at Dr Garcia, seeking reassurance, but her face is impassive.

'Go on,' she says.

'A while after the show finished, she turned up in the bar, which isn't unusual; the drag kings normally change and come out afterwards. Sometimes they work behind the bar, sometimes they just have a drink. I was with one of my sisters and the drag king who gave me the margarita approached me. I was shocked at first because it was so unexpected. She said something but then ran off and I don't know what I did to scare her away.'

Dr Garcia scribbles on her notepad for a few seconds, then asks, 'Why do you assume you scared her off?'

A million reasons have circled in my head all week, the loudest being *maybe I'm not gay enough*, but that's not something I want to delve into right now. 'Maybe up close I wasn't what she expected? Maybe I came across as too eager? Maybe my breath smelled?'

Surprise registers on Dr Garcia's face. 'Your breath? Do you have bad oral hygiene?'

'No,' I say emphatically. 'The opposite, in fact. I floss twice a day and use the two-minute timer on my toothbrush, plus I get a dental check-up every six months.'

Dr Garcia smiles, the creases around her eyes deepening. 'Then I think it's safe to assume she didn't run off because you have bad breath.' She pauses, her smile fading. 'You said she made a comment?'

'Oh, er, yes. The music was loud, but it sounded like' – my cheeks flush because I can't be a hundred per cent certain, and it's embarrassing to think I might have it wrong – 'you're pretty.'

'And then she left?' Dr Garcia asks.

I nod.

'Maybe speaking to you was overwhelming for her and running off was the only way she could cope with that.'

I scrunch my nose at the suggestion. 'But she performs every week in front of a crowded club, and she's definitely not shy up there, so it must be me.'

'A person's behaviour is usually driven by their own beliefs and insecurities, Maya, so it's probable that her actions were about her and not you. I assume if you're interested in meeting her, and she approached you, last week wasn't the first time you've noticed each other?'

'No. I've been there every weekend since the beginning of the year, and she caught my attention straight away.' A memory surfaces of my first night at the club, Tom Cruisin' walking onstage and looking out into the crowd. Their heated gaze stopping on me, making my heart stutter and sending a shiver through my body. 'I wanted to know more about her,' I say. 'So I found the club's Instagram account and saw a "meet the kings" post. I know her name is Callie, that she uses "she/her" pronouns, she likes dance and theatre, and that she lives for drag.'

'Okay,' Dr Garcia says. 'So you know enough to establish

that you're attracted to her and would like to meet her. If going to this club to watch the drag kings perform is something you enjoy doing, and there's someone you'd like to meet, why not go on your own?'

I pull my head back. 'On my own? To a club?'

She shrugs. 'You'd be going to watch a show, slightly different to going to a club on your own. There's no reason you can't do that and approach Callie afterwards, instead of waiting for her to approach you.'

I entertain the idea, but my head conjures up different scenarios of everything that could go wrong. 'I have thought about talking to her,' I admit, 'but I'm not sure how to go about it. I mean, other than some looks between us, last week was the first time we've come face-to-face. If she's not working, it's hard to find the right moment. The drag kings are popular and they're not short of admirers, on and off the stage. Besides, what if I'm wrong and she's not interested?'

'Let's look at the facts,' Dr Garcia says. 'She made your favourite cocktail as part of her act. Out of everyone in the club, she delivered it to you, and afterwards she approached you. What she did or didn't say is irrelevant. I think that means there's a very good chance she's interested in meeting you, Maya, and is trying to find a way to do that.'

'Oh,' I say, a flicker of hope igniting in me. 'When you put it like that.'

She smiles. 'Have you seen her with anyone else, as in a partner?'

'No,' I say, with almost-certainty because it is something I've paid close attention to. She either works or talks to the other kings or bar staff. Although there is that one person I've wondered about ... the friend with the auburn hair, who also works behind the bar and has an entertaining drag act. I haven't seen hard evidence they're together, but there's a familiarity between them, a closeness. 'At least, not that I've noticed.'

'Okay, and is this club a space where you feel safe enough to be on your own?'

'Yes, I think so. The staff are welcoming and friendly, and I've never felt unsafe. Plus, the shows are amazing,' I say with a rush of enthusiasm. 'I love theatre and live performances, and I'd never seen a drag king show before I went there. How they express themselves is fascinating to watch. It's a whole hour of pure joy.' My skin bumps talking about it. There's something else that excites me about these performances, and that's how they've reignited my own desire to perform, a desire that I'd buried after chalking up a few failures. But I'd prefer to keep this to myself for now.

'Well, that sounds very positive,' Dr Garcia says. 'So what's stopping you going alone?'

I shrug. 'People might think a woman sitting on her own is cringe or something.'

'Wouldn't people be watching the show instead of you?' she asks softly.

'Maybe.' I hesitate to state my real fear but remind myself I'm here for help, so I spit it out. 'What if she doesn't come out after the show? What if she's hooking up with someone? Or I introduce myself and she's not interested, and I'm left standing there on my own, humiliated?'

Dr Garcia considers me thoughtfully. 'So, what you're asking is, what if it doesn't go perfectly?'

I drop my gaze and pick at my nail polish again.

'This is where you treat yourself with compassion, Maya,' she says. 'You shift your mindset to understanding that if something doesn't go exactly how you want it to, it doesn't mean you're a failure.'

'But I don't know how to do that,' I say. 'I don't know how

to stop overthinking this stuff or how not to give myself a hard time if things don't go right. It's hard-wired into me and I can't unwire it.'

She gives me a kind smile. 'You're already unwiring it by being here. You're open to becoming more self-aware by bringing aspects of your personality and behaviours to your conscious mind. You're learning that when something doesn't go as planned, instead of beating yourself up and telling yourself you've failed, you can take a step back and look at it from a loving place.' She pauses as her eyes flick to the clock on the wall behind me. 'I'd like you to try a new exercise to help with overthinking.'

'Okay,' I say, grabbing my phone and opening the Notes app.

'Let's say, hypothetically, you've decided to go out this evening. When you return from your parents', grab a notebook or open a document, and create two columns. In one column, write down all of your worries about going out alone and about meeting this person. Then in the other column, write the facts – the ones I mentioned earlier and anything else you can think of.'

I tap the instructions into Notes.

'This gives you rumination time,' she continues, 'so you don't need to keep going over it because it's out of your head. It will give you some distance and help you to see things objectively. Then, while you get ready, stay present. Focus on the sensation of warm water on your skin while you shower, the heat of the hair dryer, music playing while you decide what to wear. If your mind wanders, remind yourself of the facts. When you arrive at the club, buy yourself a drink and enjoy your show. If you're uncomfortable, or the night doesn't work out how you hoped, you go home knowing that you've taken a risk; you've learnt something about yourself and what you're capable of.' She pauses, letting the words sink in.

I repeat the main points, 'Write it down so it's out of my head. Focus on the facts. Stay present. Take a risk. I'm going to try and do that.'

Her face brightens with a wide smile. 'Good. I look forward to hearing if it helps. And remember, you don't wait for the confidence to do the thing; you do the thing to gain the confidence.'

I nod, repeating the comment in my head. *Don't wait for the confidence to do the thing; do the thing to gain the confidence.*

'You've made some excellent progress since you've started these sessions,' she continues. 'To get to the point where you're willing to consider doing something that's just for you and to embrace your sexuality more is wonderful. You should be very proud of yourself.'

I return the smile. One of many things I like about Dr Garcia is how she always takes the time to find the positives at the end of every session. 'Thank you.'

'You're welcome. I'll see you soon.'

I lift myself from the couch and leave the consulting room, pass through reception and exit the heavy glass doors of The Psychology Centre onto Adelaide Street. Grey rain clouds hang low in the sky and the air is thick with February humidity. The number 196 bus approaches, and I jump on board and slip into a free seat.

Dr Garcia's comments spin in my mind as I watch the city buildings pass by. It never occurred to me to go to Club Sappho alone and introduce myself to Tom Cruisin', but the idea of it, and the possibilities of what that could lead to, sends a thrilling jolt right through my core.

Chapter 3
Callie

'Callie...' A hand shaking my foot wakes me.

'It's too early,' I mumble, pulling the pillow over my head.

'It's three p.m., love,' Mum says. 'You've been asleep for hours.' I hear the zip of the blinds being hoisted up. 'And Stevie's here.'

I remove the pillow, squinting against the daylight. 'I don't want to see anyone today.'

Mum stands to the side of my bed, arms folded, her dark hair blowing under the ceiling fan. She's dressed in her teal ambulance services uniform, ready for work. 'Not even your cousin? And your boss. She might need to talk to you about work since you've been off and she's been away all week.'

'Stevie's not the boss of me,' I say. 'I take orders from Krissy only.'

Mum grins and pats my shin. 'Come on.'

I heave myself from the bed and follow Mum along the hallway, the tiles cool beneath my bare feet. The rich, smoky aroma of coffee floats through the house, making my mouth water.

'Ah, here she is,' Stevie says with a smile that's far too luminous for my darkened mood and this miserable weather. She splashes milk into a mug of coffee and passes it to me.

'Why are you so happy?' I ask, taking it from her and sitting at the kitchen table.

'It's a beautiful day,' she says, placing another mug under the spout of the coffee machine and slipping in a pod. 'There's a lot to be happy about.'

I glance out at the grey sky and drizzle. The scent of wet earth and the distant call of a storm bird drifts through the open window. 'It's raining and a storm's on the way.'

'You know how much I love this weather,' Stevie says, joining me at the table.

'I hope you can cheer her up, Stevie,' Mum says, rinsing her cup. 'She's been sulking all week and won't tell me what's wrong.'

Stevie raises a brow at me. 'Has she?'

'I haven't been sulking,' I say sulkily, then hop up to add more milk to my coffee. Stevie never gets my milk-to-coffee ratio right.

'And she's been hinting about not wanting to perform tonight,' Mum continues. 'So something is definitely wrong.'

'Hmm, I've got that feeling too, Aunty Donna.' Stevie's eyes stay fixed on me. 'She's been very quiet since last Saturday night.'

I sit back down and slide an open packet of Kingston biscuits into the middle of the table. 'That's because you were away all week. Bit hard to talk when I haven't seen you.'

'Nuh,' Stevie says, shaking her head. 'You always send at least one message when I'm away, and Krissy said you've been avoiding her, too.' She looks at Mum. 'I guess she's lost her phone because she doesn't seem to have received any of our messages either.'

Mum shoots me a look. 'I hope you're not keeping things bottled up? We talk about things in this family.'

I sigh, exasperated. 'I'm not bottling things up. Nothing's happened and nothing's wrong.' It's not a lie; nothing *did* happen.

'Well, since you didn't reply to any of my messages,' Stevie says, rustling in the packet for a biscuit, 'I've had to revert to a good old-fashioned house visit.' She takes a bite, watching me while she chews.

I grab myself a biscuit and bite into it. 'I responded,' I mumble around my mouthful. Crumbs fall onto the tablecloth and I scoop them up and dump them on a napkin.

'Okay, you responded, but you didn't answer my questions about where you disappeared to last week,' Stevie says. 'One minute you were there, next you were gone, and I assume you were alone because *she* was still sitting in the same spot.'

Mum whips around, brows raised, the fridge door still open. 'Oh. *She.* Girl problems. Now we're getting somewhere.' She grabs a container with last night's leftovers and slips it into a chiller bag.

'A woman, Mum,' I say. 'I'm twenty-seven, not fifteen, which means I'm interested in women, not girls.' I frown. 'Anyway, I hope I never see her again.'

Stevie sips her coffee, then says, 'I suppose there's a chance she won't return, but she hasn't missed a Saturday night for weeks, so—'

'Five,' I mutter, grabbing another biscuit, pulling it apart and popping one half in my mouth.

'What was that?' Stevie says.

'Five weeks,' I say. 'She hasn't missed a Saturday night in five weeks.'

Mum and Stevie exchange a look.

'Oh, you crushing haaard,' Stevie says.

Blood rushes to my face. 'I'm not. I'm just … observant.'

'Five weeks and you haven't found out anything about her?' Mum says.

'Krissy has tried,' Stevie says. 'All we know is that one of the two people she goes to the club with is a friend, that she uses "she" pronouns, and that she drinks white wine and margaritas.'

Mum's brows crinkle in confusion. 'And how do we know all this but not her name?'

'The friend was at the bar,' Stevie says, 'and Krissy asked, "What will your partner have?" The reply was, "She's not my partner and she'll have a white wine."'

'And I saw her buy a margarita,' I chip in, just in case they've forgotten I'm here.

Stevie jerks her thumb in my direction and says to Mum, 'She's come up with a new act making cocktails onstage. No prizes for guessing who received the margarita.'

Mum gapes at me. 'You're womanising with a cocktail act?'

'Just engaging with the crowd,' I say, then widen my eyes at Stevie. 'Like you with your final-act thrusting, encouraging people to shove fake money in your pants.'

Stevie laughs. 'Fair enough. You do you. I thought it was excellent, and the crowd loved it. You're definitely bringing out Cocktail Tom on a regular basis.'

The humiliation from a week ago rises, thick and fresh. 'I'm sure my offstage performance made more of a lasting impression.' I bury my face in my hands with a groan. 'I'm sooo embarrassed.'

'It can't have been that bad,' Mum says, giving my shoulder a pat as she walks past.

I drop my hands. 'Believe me, it was.'

'All I know,' Stevie says to Mum, 'is that Callie planned to introduce herself to Mystery Woman but disappeared instead and won't tell Krissy or me what happened.'

I let out a defeated huff. They'll harp on until I tell them. 'Fine. This is what happened. I walked up to her, planning to say hello, like we talked about. But her eyes were all twinkly and this gorgeous shade of cinnamon, and her eyebrows were all dark and you know how much brown eyes and dark eyebrows do it for me. It was the first time I'd properly looked at her, and I got this weird feeling and' – I take a breath – 'my mind went fuzzy and I couldn't think.'

Mum gives Stevie a bemused look. 'Twinkly and cinnamon? Fuzzy mind? Oh, she has it bad alright.'

'She sure does,' Stevie says. 'So, you just stood there? You didn't speak?'

I close my eyes briefly, a pained groan escaping. 'Oh, I spoke. I said, "You're pretty" and when I realised what had come out of my mouth, I took off.'

Stevie puts a hand over her mouth, but her eyes are creased with laughter.

I give a small laugh myself, because with hindsight... 'So you can see why I can never face her again.'

'Oh, love.' Mum grabs her car keys from the basket on the island bench and tosses them in her handbag. 'I'm sure she didn't think anything of it.'

'Yeah,' Stevie agrees. 'She probably thought it was cute.'

I scrunch my face. 'Cute? I don't want to be *cute*. I want to be someone's hot, sexy girlfriend.'

'Don't you mean *woman*friend if you're not into girls?' Mum says.

'Oh, you're funny, Mum.'

Mum chuckles and kisses the top of my head. 'And you will

be someone's hot, sexy girlfriend one day. I have to go to work. I'll see you tomorrow.'

'No,' I reply. 'I'll see you when you get home because I'm not performing tonight. I'm sick.' I look at Stevie and fake a cough.

Mum slips her work lanyard around her neck and lifts her bag onto her shoulder. 'I'll leave you to talk to her, Stevie. I'm going to be late.'

Mum leaves and Stevie says, 'You can't not perform because of one person. Besides, she might not have even realised who you were.'

'That's bullshit and you know it, given my stage make-up is minimal sometimes and I often wear jeans and a T-shirt both in and out of drag. Plus you did that "get to know our kings" Insta post the other week. If she saw that then she'll know who I am.' I pick up my mug with a self-pitying sigh and gaze out the window at the darkening sky. 'Nah. It wasn't meant to be. Besides, love doesn't last anyway. Being single and living with Mum for the rest of my days won't be so bad.'

Stevie snorts. 'Talk about an overreaction. You know Saturdays are our most popular night and they all come to see the kings. There will be an uprising if their favourite doesn't perform.'

'You're their favourite,' I say, with a sulky pout.

Stevie flashes me a cheeky grin. 'Well, yeah, I am, but I was trying to make you feel better.'

I laugh, despite myself. 'Piss off.'

Stevie laughs, too. 'Good to see you smile.' She drains her coffee, then watches me for a moment. 'I know you don't like me to say anything in front of your mum, but I also came over because I wanted to make sure nothing else happened last week. Like, the anxiety didn't get to you?'

I stare into my mug, swirling the remnants of my coffee. I'm not sure I understand what happened, so I definitely can't explain it to Stevie. 'I was just nervous, I think. You know I'm not the greatest small-talker.'

Stevie considers me, her lips pursed. It's the look she gives me when she doubts what I'm saying is true but knows not to push. 'You can talk to me or Krissy if something's up.'

I give her a quick smile. 'I'm fine, Stevie. I haven't been curious about someone in a while and I couldn't find the words.'

'Okay. As long as you're alright.' She hops up and washes her mug, turning it upside down on the drying rack. 'I need to get some groceries, then get to work.' She ruffles my hair as she walks past. 'See you tonight, Romeo. I'll let myself out.'

'Bye.'

I stay seated at the table, watching the raindrops roll down the windowpane. *Am* I alright? I don't know that I am. My social anxiety hasn't been a problem for a while now and I don't understand why talking to an attractive woman would trigger it. I've spent my week off dissecting what happened, being disappointed in myself that I'm incapable of getting past a simple hello when I'm interested in someone. I have the tools to help – *make eye contact, focus on the person, relax and be myself* – but who can remember that when your heart is racing and your limbs feel like jelly?

My stomach grumbles, reminding me that all I've eaten today is two biscuits. I reheat the leftover chicken stir-fry and retreat to the lounge room, sinking onto the couch just as a loud crack of thunder booms overhead. My late grandmother looks on from the photograph on the shelf. What would she say if she were here now? *Any young lady would be privileged to be your girlfriend.* I twirl noodles onto my fork, smiling at her memory. I can hear her voice so clearly, like she's here with me.

'Thanks, Grandma,' I say to the photo. 'But I'm not sure it's ever going to happen for me.' The statement hangs stale in the air, causing the loneliness to unfurl in my chest. I'm truly starting to believe that there isn't a match for someone like me. The awkward, shy, anxious person who no one can work out or wants to spend the time to get to know. The one who has a carefully curated comfort bubble around her, whose best friends are her cousins and who loves hanging out at home with her mum and aunties. The one who can only find her confidence when she's dressed up as someone else.

My phone pings: a message from Krissy checking what costumes I need for tonight. It's the distraction I need and my mind shifts to this evening's performances. There's no time for melancholy when I have a show to prepare for. I'm a professional, after all.

While I eat, I run over the acts in my head – the music, my costumes and routines – and reply to Krissy. Once my bowl is empty, I wash the dishes and head to my room to change for work, lifting my chin and adding some swagger to my walk, getting into my masculine energy because Tom doesn't feel shame and loneliness; he's all confidence and bravado.

Chapter 4
Maya

By the time I reach my parents' place, the storm has passed. I slip my sandals off in the foyer to save treading rainwater through the house, knowing that Mum would've spent the morning cleaning while my sisters shopped and Dad prepared the food. Inside, the tiles in the open-plan lounge and kitchen have a freshly washed gleam. The dining table and counters are clutter-free. A bouquet of native flowers sits in the middle of the coffee table, and the fruit bowl is loaded with bananas, red apples and nectarines that my sisters would've bought at the market this morning. I follow the hum of voices and the sweet smell of barbecuing sauces to the back patio. The outdoor ceiling fans whirr on high and the passing storm has delivered a short reprieve from the oppressive humidity.

Dad glances up from turning a piece of steak. 'Here she is. Thought we'd have to send out a search party.' Even at home on a Saturday afternoon, he's smartly dressed in a branded polo shirt and long shorts. His greying hair is neatly styled and his beard manscaped. An aged, well-worn apron printed with the slogan 'World's Best Dad' is tied tightly around his waist. It's at odds with his look, but he refuses to cook without it. I bought it for Father's Day when I was sixteen, and twelve years later it's still his favourite.

'Hi, Dad.' I peck his cheek. 'Sorry I'm late. I had something to do in the city after work.'

'Working on a Saturday?' he says with mock surprise. 'No weekend work if you take a management job at my—'

'Dad!'

He holds up the tongs in peace with one hand and pretends to zip his lips with the other. Then he grins, deep lines framing his eyes. 'I know, I know, I'm not allowed to give job offers.' He transfers the steaks from the hot plate to a serving platter. 'And you're not late; you're just in time because we're eating shortly.'

'I'd never miss your barbecued steaks, Dad.' I walk across the patio to the outdoor kitchen where Mum and my two younger sisters are unwrapping salads and placing bread rolls in baskets. All three are dressed in shorts and T-shirts. Mum's shoulder-length hair is loose and wavy – her weekend vibe – the opposite of the styled and sprayed corporate look she goes for during the working week.

'Hi, Mum,' I say, shifting straight into help mode and taking cutlery from the drawer.

'Hi, sweetheart. We'll need more cutlery than that. The new neighbours will be here shortly.'

'You have new neighbours?' I ask. 'When did that happen?'

Before Mum has a chance to answer, Bella, my youngest sister, says, 'You should see their son.' She fans herself with her hand, her blue eyes wide. 'His name's Mason.'

'He *is* very handsome,' Mum says, giving me a pointed look. 'I think he's around your age, Maya. You might want to position yourself strategically at the table.'

My hand tightens around the cutlery. 'Position myself strategically for what? The best steaks in North Brisbane?'

'I was just trying to help,' she sniffs. 'Lord knows you don't seem inclined to find a boyfriend yourself.'

I roll my eyes and behind Mum's back, Liv, my middle sister, gives me a sympathetic wince.

'If you don't want him, I'll have him,' Bella says, which I assume is for Mum's benefit, since she is well aware that I won't want *him*.

'He's not leftovers I don't feel like eating, Bella,' I say, keeping up the charade. 'Why do you all assume he'd be interested anyway?' I hesitate for a beat, then blurt, 'Maybe he's gay!'

'Hmm,' Mum says, pushing her glasses up the bridge of her nose. 'I don't think so; he doesn't look gay.'

My jaw tenses. If there's one comment I despise, it's that. I've lost count of the number of times I've been told *you don't look like a lesbian*, even by people my own age and among my former friends – another reason I've distanced myself from them. I might not be ready to out myself, but I can defend others. 'What does that mean, Mum? What does *gay* look like?'

'Oh,' she says, surprised by the question. 'Well, you know, he's not' – she pauses, brows furrowed as she searches for a description.

'Camp?' I finish for her.

'Yes, I suppose.'

'People don't need to look or act a certain way to be gay,' I say, hyper-aware of the defensiveness that's crept into my voice.

Mum clicks her tongue. 'Okay, Miss Woke.' She steps over to the sink and fills a glass pitcher with cold water.

I give an exasperated huff. 'Not making assumptions about people because of the way they look isn't being woke; it's just being a non-judgemental pers—'

'Anyway, if you let me finish,' she says, oblivious to the

irony of not letting me finish, 'I was also going to say that his dad mentioned something about a recent split with a girlfriend.'

My shoulders drop. 'Oh, well, that's a better indication of his preferences and what you should've started with.'

Mum shakes her head at me while she fills a second jug, then walks over to the table, placing the pitchers at either end.

'Bit harsh, Maya,' Bella says, tucking a strand of loose hair back into her topknot. 'Mum didn't mean anything by it.'

'Harsh?' I hiss. 'I'm tired of stupid comments like that. I've literally just walked in the door.'

Liv, always the mediator, places a hand on my back and says in a gentle voice, 'Then maybe you should tell Mum and Dad the truth.'

I throw her a look. 'Yes, because they really give me confidence they'd be okay with it.'

'They would be once they had time to process it,' Liv says, her brown eyes wide and sincere.

'I shouldn't have to tell them,' I say stubbornly. 'You'd think they would've worked it out by now.'

'Nope,' Bella says. 'Not their perfect, beautiful daughter.' She tears off a piece of bread roll and pops it in her mouth. 'You know Mum still talks about you wearing her wedding dress one day, right?'

'Maya can still wear the dress, Bella,' Liv says, wrapping the cloth napkin over the rolls.

'Shh. You know how voices carry out here,' I whisper. 'Can we drop it, please?'

'You can't live like this forever,' Bella whispers back. 'And it's hard for us too, you know, having to be careful about what we say, worried we'll put our foot in it. You're going to have to tell them at some point.' She picks up a stack of plates and walks away.

'She's right,' Liv says.

I sigh. 'I know. But today is not that day.'

The afternoon passes quickly with Mum and Dad's friends busy with work talk, gushing over Dad's new sticky glazed rib recipe, and hyped about the building award Dad's company has been nominated for. I enjoy the company of my sisters and chatting to the neighbour's son, who is friendly and engaging. Mum refrains from matchmaking, but her eagle eyes dart between us from time to time, assessing our compatibility. Even if I was into men, I'd have stiff competition from Bella, who *did* position herself strategically at the table.

Despite my reluctance to come over today, it's been surprisingly pleasant, and a relief to get out of my own head after a week of overanalysing why someone would run away from me. But now evening has fallen, I'm eager to go home so that I can properly process the session with Dr Garcia and do the exercise she recommended. I collect some dirty plates and carry them inside, with a plan to fill the dishwasher and quietly leave.

I've only rinsed a few dishes when Liv walks in. 'Poor Mason is not getting away from Bella.' She places some glasses on the side to be washed.

I glance out through the bifold doors. Bella is giggling at something he's saying, her face dipped coyly. 'Could she make it any more obvious?'

Liv smiles. 'No. He is cute, though. If I wasn't with the one, I might be flirting, too.'

'The one?' I say, stunned. 'I knew you were into him, but, seriously, Livvy, *the one*? It hasn't been that long.'

Her eyes turn dreamy. 'It doesn't need to be that long when you meet the right person. It just feels right, and besides, Dylan and I have been together six months. That's long enough to know.'

'How does it feel right?' I ask curiously.

'Hmm...' She leans back against the island bench as she ponders my question. 'I think about him constantly. I want to be with him all the time. The butterflies in the stomach thing is real.'

I frown, unable to relate. 'I don't think I've ever felt like that. I mean, I've had strong feelings for people, but looking back, I don't think I was in love – more that I cared deeply for them.'

Liv nods. 'I know what you mean.' She takes over stacking the dishwasher. 'But be grateful for those other relationships because it's good to know what love *isn't*. You don't want to spend your life with the wrong person.' She straightens and gives me an earnest look. 'You'll meet someone, May. The right person hasn't come along yet, that's all.'

'You think so?' I ask, an all-too-familiar yearning filling my chest.

'I do.'

She has no way of knowing that, but I appreciate the sentiment and give her a grateful smile. I glance at the wall clock in the dining area – seven p.m. The brief thrill I felt earlier about going out alone has dissipated. 'Since Dylan's away,' I say, 'have you changed your mind about tonight?'

Liv's eyebrows pull together. 'What's happening tonight?'

'You said you might change your mind about going to Club Sappho with me?'

'Oh,' Liv says, clicking shut the dishwasher door and switching it on. 'But we went last week.'

'We can go again.'

She wrinkles her nose. 'I don't really feel like it. I've had a hectic week at work and I got my period this morning so I feel a bit rubbish.' She eyes me curiously. 'Why are you so keen to go? Haven't you been there every weekend lately?'

I give a nonchalant shrug. 'It's fun, and you know how much I love live shows.'

'Yeah, but it's the same show every Saturday night, isn't it?'

'Not always. They perform different acts sometimes.'

'Uh-huh. And this has nothing to do with that drag king you have a thing for?'

'No,' I say unconvincingly.

'Mmm, if you say so. I'm sorry. I don't have the energy tonight. Why don't you stay here? I promise I'll go with you next weekend. Mum and Dad will get the games out soon and you know how much they love a family giant Jenga team.'

Normally, I'd relent, but Dr Garcia has planted a seed. 'I'm not in the mood for games. Actually, I'm kind of tired myself. I'm going to go home.'

Liv frowns. 'You're going to spend the night at home alone instead of with us?'

'I feel like some me time,' I say. 'Can I borrow your bike?'

'I guess,' Liv says.

I hug her goodbye. 'I'll drop it back tomorrow.' As I pull away, Mum walks in and I silently berate myself for not leaving two minutes earlier.

'Is everything okay?' Mum asks.

'Yep. I was just saying goodbye to Liv,' I say, keeping my tone upbeat.

Liv retreats outside and Mum's brows shoot up. 'Goodbye? Where are you going?'

'Um ... home.'

Mum tsks and walks over to the fridge, removing a bottle of white wine. 'Don't be silly. The night is just starting.'

'I've got plans,' I say.

'Oh. A date?' she asks, her words loaded with hope and intrigue.

I could lie; she'd leave me alone if she believed there was a potential partner on the horizon, but then she'd want details about *him*. 'Not a date, no. Just going out. To a thing. A show.'

'The theatre? You didn't mention it.'

I wave a hand. 'Slipped my mind.'

She stares at me expectantly. When I don't elaborate, she says, 'That sounds fun. I know how much you love the theatre. What show?'

'Oh…' I think fast. 'A local show. Near my apartment. A small theatre.' It's technically true. Club Sappho was a theatre once. I recall going there with my grandparents when I was six years old, gazing up at the stage, spellbound by my first experience of a live production. Sparkly tulle and chiffon costumes shimmering under stage lights, music that filled my young heart with joy, a sense of magic sweeping through the theatre and carrying me away. I rush forward and hug Mum before she can fire more questions at me. 'Sorry I can't stay. Thanks for dinner.'

'Okay, we'll miss you, but have a nice time,' Mum says.

'I will.' I collect my bag and shoes from inside the front door, grab Liv's bike from the garage and set off on the short ride to my place. I cycle through New Farm, a mist of soft rain coating my face, a freedom pulsing through my body, and the scent of optimism in the late summer air.

Inside my apartment, I slide open the balcony doors to release the hot, stuffy air that's been trapped all day and switch on the ceiling fan. I pour myself a glass of cold water and settle on the couch with my laptop. On my newly created document, I insert a table with two columns and type the heading 'Thoughts' at the top of the left column. With my fingertips poised on the keyboard, I let said thoughts spill onto the screen. *What will people think of me being in a club alone? What if she doesn't come out? What if she's with someone else? What if she laughs at me? What if I don't blend in?* My fingers fly across the keyboard trying to match the speed of my self-doubt. Once my mind is depleted of worst-case scenarios, I shake out my hands and begin column two. Facts.

1. I'm going to a club to have a drink and watch a show.

2. There are no rules about that.

3. I was the recipient of the stage-made margarita.

4. Tom Cruisin' approached me last week.

5. I've caught her watching me more than once, both in and out of drag.

6. I desperately want to meet her.

I read through what I've typed. Manic me versus measured me. Something is tugging at me to go out. To see what can come of it. To give myself a chance to be the person that's trapped inside. I think back over the past few weeks, how alive I felt watching the drag kings, how much I resonated with them. Maybe Dr Garcia is right and Tom Cruisin' has been trying to find a way to meet me.

With my decision made, I put on some music and turn it up loud. In the shower, I stay present, focusing on the warm water pummelling my skin and the fresh citrus scent of lemongrass soap filling the shower recess. I dry myself with a fluffy towel and pad into my bedroom to search for something to wear.

After going back and forth between options, I opt for a black denim skirt that sits just above my knees, a red vest top and sneakers – a blending-in outfit – then pull out my favourite matching bra and underpants in a fuchsia lace. No one is going to see it, but nice lingerie never fails to make me feel good.

I go for minimalist make-up with a light foundation, a slick of mascara and some cherry lip gloss, then blast my hair with the dryer, letting it fall in natural waves around my shoulders. I fix my chipped nail polish and hook in my favourite earrings – a pair of white gold diamond drops that my parents bought me years ago to celebrate graduating a master's degree in business.

As I walk back into the lounge, my mouth turns dry and doubt begins to creep in. I let out a slow breath. *Facts – I'm going out for a drink and to watch a show. If I'm uncomfortable, I'll leave.* It's already 8.45 p.m., which means I'll miss half the show, but at least people will be watching the stage and not looking at who's walking through the door.

Outside, the rain has eased but I still walk slower than usual. Wet footpaths and my sneakers don't mix. At the entrance of Club Sappho, the regular Saturday night bouncer gives me a smile and opens the heavy wooden door for me. There's a couple in front chatting with the person behind the counter. The door staff vary from week to week; sometimes it's one of the kings already dressed for the stage, or someone who later appears behind the bar, but I've never seen Tom Cruisin' out here.

'Hi,' I say as I step up to the counter, my confident demeanour incongruous with my racing pulse.

The drag king lifts their head. It's The King Laroi, popular with the crowd, very entertaining, and often behind the bar, in and out of drag, kissing someone I assume is their partner. Recognition registers in their bright eyes.

'Hi, yourself,' they say, their enthusiastic tone and kind smile alleviating my nerves slightly. 'You're becoming a Saturday night regular.'

'Oh.' A blush creeps over my cheeks. 'Yes, I live in that apartment block on the corner,' I gesture in the general direction of my place. 'So it's easy to stop in. And I love the show.'

'Great! We love it when people return for the show.' They hold the EFTPOS machine out for me to pay and raise a fake, bushy eyebrow. 'You got quite the treatment last week with that margarita. There were a lot of envious audience members.'

I feel the blush deepen. 'Just sitting in the right spot, I guess.'

'Mmm, I guess.' They press the entry stamp to my wrist. 'You'd better get in there. Tom's saved that act until last. You might find yourself sitting in the right spot again.'

My heart rate spikes at the prospect but I fight the urge to overanalyse the comment.

The second I step into the main club, I'm swept away by the atmosphere. The crowd are engrossed in the show and the tightness in my shoulders loosens. The music pulses through me and it's liberating to be here alone, to have this night just for me. The drag king performing makes the audience laugh with their robotic moves and contorted facial expressions. I smile too, the vibe catching.

I skim the space for a free seat, spotting a stool at the bar. I cut across the club, order a white wine and wait for Tom Cruisin' to grace the stage.

Chapter 5
Callie

When I stepped onstage for my first act earlier, I'd scanned the audience, my heart dropping over not spotting that familiar face watching me. But deep down, I wasn't surprised. I didn't match up to what she thought I might be and she had no interest in coming back, so I had no choice but to chalk it up to experience and get on with the show.

Now, ready for my final act of the night, I stride along the backstage corridor, my drag confidence high, the rush from my earlier performances spurring me on.

Waiting in the wings, I watch Amber bow to the crowd and rush off as Krissy bounds up the wooden steps. 'Let's hear it for Hairy Styles!' she booms into the microphone.

There's a raucous cheer and Krissy holds her free hand up for calm. 'Are you ready for your next king?'

I roll my shoulders and do some quick arm stretches, then peer through the curtain to select a close-by audience member to give the cocktail to, mentally calculating the timing from the stage to their seat.

'I hope you're thirsty,' Krissy continues. 'Please put your hands together for Tom Cruisin'!'

I burst onto the stage to ear-piercing applause, lip-syncing to 'One Margarita'. As I scan the crowd, my gaze is drawn to a figure perched on a bar stool and my stomach cartwheels. Under the pretence of a dance move, I spin, my back to the crowd, and take a split second to compose myself. *Get it together, Tom.* I shift back into top performance mode, with fast footwork and seductive pelvic rolls, earning me some wolf whistles.

Delivering the margarita to the bar will throw my timing, but this act only exists because of her, and I feel oddly disloyal giving it to someone else. Swiftly, I mix the cocktail, jog down from the stage and weave through tables. Her heated gaze is on me the entire time, drawing me towards her, sucking me in. Our eyes lock as I place the glass down. I'm frozen to the spot, but my heart warms from the small smile that plays on her lips. Krissy catches my attention by pointing to the stage and I snap back to reality with a jolt. I race back, just in time for the final beat of the track. I give the crowd a wave and slip backstage, whoops and whistles in my wake.

'Nice work, Tom,' I say, entering the dressing room. I play some music and work through my make-up and breast tape removal routine, followed by a brief shower, then dress in my own clothes. As I sit at the dressing table, there's a rap at the door before it cracks open.

'I'm coming in,' Stevie calls, not waiting for a reply before she enters. She eyes my reflection curiously. 'For someone who didn't want to work tonight, you certainly turned it on, particularly that last performance.'

I manoeuvre short strands of my hair into place with the moulding clay. 'I needed to redeem myself.'

'Oh, I think you did that.' Stevie shrugs off her jacket. 'Are you heading to the bar now?'

'Nah. Reckon I might go home.'

Stevie's brows pull together. 'If you were going home you wouldn't have changed or be making sure your hair is perfect.'

With all traces of Tom gone, so has my courage. I swivel on my chair. 'I don't think I can face her.'

'Callie, you can't avoid her forever if she's becoming a regular, and you just gave her a drink – she knows you're in the building.'

'But walking up to someone, blurting "You're pretty" and racing off is really fucking embarrassing,' I say with a wince.

'Maybe she didn't hear you over the music.' Stevie reaches into a drawer and pulls out a large strap-on that's part of her final act. 'Look at it this way. You made it obvious last week that you wanted to talk to her,' she says, waving the strap to match the cadence of her words. 'And she's returned, so you haven't scared her off. She arrived alone, too.'

My eyes widen. 'She's out there on her own?'

Stevie shrugs. 'Unless she met up with a friend inside, but she was by herself when I served her on the door, and word from Krissy is that she sat at the bar alone to watch the end of the show.' She tips her head towards the door. 'Go on, get out there. She's interested and I need to get changed for my finale.'

I let out a shuddery breath and head into the club, grabbing myself a beer as I pass through the bar.

Before I have a chance to scan the club, Amber says, 'What took you so long?'

I shrug. 'Chatting to Stevie.'

'Your performances were good tonight,' she says, leaning in. I catch the scent of musky perfume, recognising it as one I'd once told her I liked.

'Everyone was good,' I say, but she's distracted by someone

sidling up beside her and introducing themselves. Her grey eyes flash with interest and I let out a quiet, relieved sigh that her attention has shifted from me. But she gives me a sideways glance, as though she's checking if I've noticed someone might be interested in her. I respond by turning away and facing the bar, and Amber saunters off with the interested party.

I sip my beer and run over my performances in my head, analysing whether I need to tweak the routines, but I can't move past the cocktail act, how my breath felt like it was being siphoned from my body, the electricity that crackled around us...

There's a tap on my shoulder. I twist around and my heart leaps. There she is, all glistening dark eyes and glossy red lips and thick caramel-coloured waves.

'Hello again. You're Tom Cruisin', aren't you?'

I blink, the reply stuck in my throat.

'I'll be pretty embarrassed if you're not,' she says.

'Um...' I shake my head to regain my senses. *Speak, Callie.* 'I am. I mean, Tom is me, yes.'

Her shoulders drop and her face brightens. 'I thought so. I'm Maya.'

'Maya,' I repeat, a sense of gratification from finally discovering what her name is. 'That's a nice name.'

'Thank you.' She pauses, then says, 'A lot of people pronounce it *Myer*, like the department store, but it's *May-ya.*' Panic skates across her face and she averts her gaze, shaking her head a little.

The awkward slip both surprises and comforts me. 'Pronunciation is important,' I say quickly, hoping she doesn't do my trick and disappear.

She gives me a grateful smile. 'I take it your real name isn't Tom Cruisin'?'

'Oh, no. It's not,' I say and swig my beer.

Another pause. 'Can I ask what it is?'

My cheeks warm. 'Sorry. Callie. I'm Callie.'

Her smile widens. It's bright and beautiful, and I can't believe what's happening right now. 'Hi, Callie. You work here, too? Other than performing, I mean.'

'I do.' I take another mouthful.

'Right.' Maya tucks a strand of hair behind her ear, revealing a glittery earring.

My gaze drops to her shoulder; the edge of a lace bra strap peeks out from under her vest top. Her hand reaches up to adjust it, her nails painted a marshmallow pink. My body stirs. Stevie's right: I'm a sucker for a femme.

'It doesn't look like you're working now,' Maya says, forcing my gaze upward. Maybe I could get you another drink?' She gestures to my bottle. 'You're halfway through that one, and, well ... I didn't get a chance to ask you last week.'

I close my eyes briefly, letting out a remorseful sigh. 'Sorry about that.'

She gives me a small smile. 'That's okay. I hope I didn't scare you off?'

'God, no!' The volume of my reply causes her to flinch, and if there was ever a time I'd want to be above a sinkhole, it's now. In my normal voice, I say, 'No, just me being ... me.'

Something that looks a lot like relief flitters across her face. 'In that case, I owe you a drink after you made me a cocktail onstage. Twice. Same again?'

I nod, a little too stunned to speak, then throw in a random 'thank you' when she's in the middle of ordering. I inwardly groan. *I'm so bad at this.*

Krissy places our drinks on the bar top. Her eyes flick to me, a ghost of a savvy smile on her lips. I offer Maya my stool, grabbing another for myself, and glance around for evidence of a friend. 'Are you on your own?'

'Oh, um, yes,' she says, fidgeting with the stem of her wine glass. 'I live close by and like the show, so...'

I want to kick myself because the question came out the wrong way. 'That's awesome that the show brings you to the club,' I say. 'Loads of people come on their own to see it.' *Loads* isn't exactly accurate, but I want her to feel welcome.

She meets my gaze. 'I especially love your act.'

'Oh,' I say, genuinely surprised by the compliment. 'Thank you.'

She lifts the glass to her mouth and my eyes drifts to her soft lips pressed to the rim as she sips. 'I like your *Risky Business* act the most, though.'

I break into a smile. 'That's my favourite to perform but I don't do it every weekend. I like changing it up for the regulars.'

'The new cocktail act is great, too. That was a good margarita you made me,' she says, her tone teasing.

I dip my head shyly. 'Glad you liked it.'

'Are you a fan of old movies?' Maya asks. '*Risky Business* and *Cocktail* are old-school.'

I nod, my shyness starting to dissolve from discussing my favourite topic. 'Kind of. I like mixing old with new for my performances and I love eighties pop culture – my mum and aunty's influence. They gave me the idea for the drag act, actually.'

Maya's brows rise. 'Your mum and aunty? That's very cool. My parents wouldn't know drag kings existed.'

I shrug. 'Loads of people don't know they exist. We're doing our bit to change that, one Saturday night at a time.'

Our conversation is interrupted by Krissy's voice echoing around the club. 'It's time for everyone's favourite final act – The King Laroi!' She jumps offstage, frantically handing out fake cash on her way back to the bar.

The intro to Lola Young's 'One Thing' begins and Stevie's

alter ego bursts onto the stage, lip-syncing, 'Oh, hi.' All Stevie's performances are brilliant, but this one catapults her into a different frequency. My skin goosebumps with the elated mood surging from the crowd as they sing along.

A fake note flutters to the ground and I swoop to pick it up. 'You've seen this act?' I ask Maya loudly over the music.

She nods.

'You know what to do with this then?' I say, passing her the note.

She grins and takes it from me. 'I do.'

Stevie works the crowd, thrusting to the chorus, deliberately drawing attention to the stiff bulge in her pants. People slip notes into her waistband, singing the lyrics to her as she dances past them. She stops in front of us, eyes darting between Maya and me. She gives a suggestive waggle of her brows, then playfully thrusts her pelvis at Maya, who tucks the note into Stevie's waistband.

The touch of pink that stains Maya's cheeks causes an unfamiliar ache beneath my ribs. I swallow hard and focus on the performance.

Stevie hoists herself onto the bar and drinking glasses are cleared as she strides the length of the mahogany. She climbs down the other side and pulls Krissy close, kissing her on the mouth. It's the pinnacle of the act and the audience laps it up. Stevie races back to the stage for the end of the track, dropping onto her back and thrusting in time with the music. She leaps to a standing position and rips off her tearaway trousers, revealing a pair of white jocks taut over the strap-on, her pastel blue dress shirt hanging open to show off the six-pack she's created on her stomach with bronzing powder.

I grin to myself. She's so going to complain of a sore back tomorrow throwing herself around like that, pretending it's in the name of art, rather than the truth: she loves showing off.

The applause eventually dies down and the DJ resumes their set.

Maya and I sip our drinks, eyeing each other awkwardly. I'm not sure how to follow up a performance like that with conversation, so I blurt, 'I've noticed you,' then begin to pick at the label on my beer bottle.

Maya is quiet for a beat. 'I figured, considering you made me part of your act and approached me last week.'

I meet her eyes. 'Hard not to notice someone so lovely watching me.' I press my lips together, uncertain where that comment came from, but it's rewarded with a slow smile that heats my insides. I swig my beer, a futile attempt to cool myself down.

'I think you said something too?' she says.

I nod. 'I did and it's true; you are pretty.'

She drops her gaze, a smile emerging. After a beat, she asks, 'Have you been a drag king long?'

'I've been performing for about a year but dabbled in it a bit before that. Playing around with costumes and make-up, making up routines, that sort of thing. When it finally came time to get onstage, though, I was so nervous. But as soon as I stuck on a wig, taped down my boobs and shoved a silicone packer between my legs, I felt like I could do anything.'

Her eyes widen. 'That sounds so liberating.'

She's right; it is liberating. But being a king is so much more than the act of dressing up. It's been my saviour, helped me to understand who I am and find my voice. It's filled a void and enabled me to explore aspects of myself I couldn't access out of drag. It's given me a sense of community and belonging. It allows me to blur the gender binaries in a way that feels safe. But all of that is probably a little intense for a first meeting, so I simply say, 'It is, and I love playing with gender like that.'

Maya shifts on the stool so that she's facing me. 'What you do is so inspiring. I don't think I could do it.'

'Would you want to?' I ask, surprised by the statement.

'Oh' – she shakes her head – 'no. I've always had a fascination with the theatre, but I wasn't cut out to be on the stage.'

I disagree, I think, but I've probably reached the compliment quota for someone I've just met, so I keep the response to myself and stick with drag talk. 'We have amateur night every Thursday if you ever want to give it a go.'

Maya's brows rise. 'Amateur night?'

'Yep. It's how lots of our kings get started.'

We talk more about drag over another round of drinks that I insist on buying despite Maya trying to pay me back for the second margarita, then we move on to other topics. I discover that she works at City Books in Queen Street, that she grew up ten minutes away in New Farm, has two younger sisters who still live at home, and that she loves theatre, music and all kinds of dance, which began when she saw a show in this very theatre at the age of six. She discovers that I live at home with my mum, that my all-rounder job at Club Sappho is full-time, that we went to university at the same time, but at different institutions, and that I also love theatre, music and all kinds of dance.

The natural flow of our conversation fills me with an optimism I haven't felt in a long time, and I don't want this night to end.

But Maya says, 'I'd love to stay, but I have an early start for work and if I don't get enough sleep, I'm no good to anyone.'

'Oh,' I say, silently cringing at the desperation dripping from that one simple exclamation. 'How will you get home?'

She slips off the stool. 'I'll walk. It's not far.'

'Walk?' I stand. 'You can't walk on your own.'

She breaks into that smile, the one that makes her entire face glow. 'It's just down the road and the area is well-lit. Plus,

I'm pretty sure your security guard out there watches to make sure the customers are safe around the club.'

'That's Kai and yes, she does, but I'll still walk you home,' I say.

'But then you'll have to walk back on your own.'

I shrug. 'That's okay.'

She shakes her head. 'No, that's not fair.'

'Okay,' I say, shifting into problem-solving mode, or self-interest mode, depending on how you look at it. 'How about I walk you home and if I don't feel safe, I'll call Kai to come and meet me?'

Maya tips her head, considering me. 'Only if you're sure?'

I gesture for her to walk ahead of me. 'I'm sure.'

Outside, the footpaths are slick with residual rainwater and the evening air is warm and sticky. As we walk side by side, I only now notice that Maya is a good ten centimetres shorter than me. An image of me pulling her into an embrace, her head nestled in the crook of my neck, forms in my mind.

'You and The King Laroi are good friends?' Maya asks, yanking me from my fantasy.

'Yep, that's Stevie. We're more than good friends, actually. We're cousins by marriage. She's my aunty's wife's niece.'

Maya's brows furrow as she processes that. 'Aunty's wife's niece...' she repeats slowly. 'Oh, so your non-blood aunty's niece?'

'Uh-huh. My Aunty Gina – Mum's younger sister – is married to Lisa, who's Stevie's aunt.'

'Right,' Maya says as we continue walking along Wickham Street. 'That's so cool you get to do this together. She's quite the performer.'

Out here, Maya's voice is clearer. Soft and smooth, vowels and consonants clearly enunciated, different to my drawn-out vowels and flat T's. Although we grew up only thirty kilometres apart, I imagine her upbringing worlds away from mine, but it only makes me more curious about her. 'Yep. Stevie's one of the best. She's got big king energy, for sure.'

Maya gives me some side-eye, the corner of her mouth lifting. 'Big dick energy, too. That bulge in her pants is huge.'

The unexpected comment makes me laugh out loud. 'Yeah, she packs it big and hard for the final act of the night. People love it and she loves that they love it.'

Maya cocks a brow. 'Big and hard?'

'Mm-hmm. She uses a strap-on for the final performance as opposed to a soft silicone packer.'

Maya's lips twitch. 'I see. And the person behind the bar she kisses all the time is her partner, I take it? And the manager?'

'Yep, that's Krissy, her wife. They both own and manage the club, but Krissy is definitely the boss – at home and at work.'

'Their chemistry is off the charts,' Maya says. 'When Stevie kisses her like that, I can't help but think' – she pauses, her cheeks flushing – 'nothing.'

'That they go home and have hot sex?' I finish for her.

Maya grins and tucks a strand of hair behind her ear. 'Yeah. Something like that.'

'I don't want to know what those two get up to, but I don't doubt it.' I clear my throat, keen to move on from talk of sex and strap-ons while being this close to Maya. 'Do you normally start work so early on a Sunday?'

'Not every week. We alternate shifts, but it's my Sunday on and we have a heap of new stock to put out before we open.

Plus I'm one of the assistant managers, so I need to open up.' She stops, pointing to a set of glass doors. 'This is me.'

I glance up at a high-rise. 'I didn't realise close by meant almost next door.' I face Maya. She looks radiant under the buttery glow of the streetlight.

'Maybe we could swap numbers and catch up again?' she says. 'Only if you'd like to, that is.'

My stomach swoops. 'I'd like that.'

That flicker of relief again as she holds my gaze, then she pulls out her phone and I quickly reach for mine. We exchange numbers and slip our phones away, looking at each other uncertainly.

'Erm, well, it was nice to finally meet you,' I say.

Maya's eyes drift to my lips. 'It was.'

She inches closer and I fumble back, caught off guard by her closeness and the scent of delicate, floral perfume making me heady. 'Goodnight then,' I say, my voice thick.

She steps back and the moment is gone. 'Goodnight.' She points in the direction of the club. 'Will you be okay walking back on your own?'

I look over my shoulder. A well-lit footpath stretches back to the club, Kai's silhouette in the distance, and the road busy with traffic. 'I'll be fine.'

'I can watch to make sure you're safe before I go upstairs?' Maya offers.

I smile at her thoughtfulness. 'No, you're good.' I hold my phone up. 'I'll keep this out, just in case.'

'Okay.' Her warm cinnamon eyes scan my face. 'We'll speak soon.' She gives me one last smile and disappears into the foyer of her building.

I drift back to the club, high on the evening's memory, unable to wipe the ecstatic grin from my face.

Chapter 6
Maya

It's been two days since I followed Dr Garcia's advice and went to Club Sappho alone. Being chosen twice as the drink recipient couldn't be a coincidence and it gave me the courage to introduce myself. Callie was surprisingly subdued for someone who's so lively onstage, but the contrast just made her more intriguing. She was also interesting, attentive and thoughtful – all traits that are important to me. She made me feel welcome too, giving up her stool for me, including me in Stevie's act, then insisting on walking me home. No one has ever insisted on walking me home.

And I finally had the opportunity to properly look at her, to appreciate how lovely she is make-up-free, with her soulful green eyes and inky black hair, high cheekbones and the sprinkling of freckles dusted across her face. When that genuine smile emerged, the one that made her spark and glow, I had to remember to breathe. Revealing that I knew her name from the Instagram post felt too stalkerish, but I'll tell her when we meet again – *if* we meet again. I shouldn't make assumptions.

'What planet are you on?'

My head snaps up at the sound of Ash's voice. 'Sorry?' I glance at the sticky labels I've been preparing for our damaged books. 'Have I done something wrong?'

They lean against the counter, wearing a bemused expression. 'No. I mean the dreamy face and faraway eyes.'

'Oh' – I shake my head – 'nothing, just thinking.'

'Uh-huh. Only thinking about a specific person causes a look like that.'

I bite my lip to suppress my smile, but it breaks through.

'Wait – you've met someone?' Ash says, then gasps, their hazel eyes wide. 'The drag king?'

I nod. Ash knows all too well my keen interest in the drag king. 'On Saturday night.'

Ash glances at their watch. 'I was just about to have my break. Have you had yours yet?'

'Not yet.'

They glance around the shop floor. 'It's not busy. We won't be missed for ten minutes. I'll let someone know we're on break.'

'Okay,' I say, placing a pile of books onto a trolley. 'I'll put these out and meet you in the staffroom.'

Ash hurries towards a colleague, their small body taking short, quick steps across the shop floor, and I take the damaged books to the discount bin at the front of the store.

Ash and I became firm friends when they moved to the city branch three months ago – the first person I've gelled with in a long time and my only non-binary friend. I love how open we can be with each other and the discussions we have about gender. I didn't realise how deep my own gender biases ran until I met Ash, not from anything they've directly highlighted to me, but through our conversations and watching them live how they want to live. It's made me question how I show up in the world and revealed how so much of my life has been about conditioning and presenting as a female in a certain way, rather than in my own brand of femininity that's comfortable to me.

Ash is also the person who introduced me to Club Sappho and invited me to watch the drag kings, knowing how much I love live shows. I had promised myself that this was going to be my year; the year I live in my authenticity, so it felt apt to spend the first weekend of a new year doing something completely different. I had enjoyed the show, but when Tom Cruisin' stepped onto the stage, I was mesmerised. And when our eyes connected, something clicked in me, a profound, inexplicable knowing that the trajectory of my life was about to change, and I felt a sudden need to know more about this person.

By the time I walk into the staffroom, Ash is pouring milk into two steaming mugs of tea. The harsh strip lighting directly above highlights the fresh copper tones in their cropped hair.

'Want one of these with your tea?' Ash asks, gesturing to a clear plastic container filled with jam and cream lamingtons.

'Ooh, yes please.' I remove two cakes and we settle at the small, round table that sits in the middle of the room.

'Tell me everything,' Ash says, reaching for a cake.

I've already bitten into my lamington and lick the desiccated coconut and cream from my lips. I dab my mouth with a napkin, take a sip of tea and give Ash the short version: Dr Garcia suggested that I could go out alone and introduce myself; I arrived in time to watch Callie's final act and received the margarita again; and I finally took the plunge and said hello.

Ash stares at me wide-eyed, fully engrossed in my story, cream clinging to their upper lip as they chew. They swallow their bite. 'So, what's she like?'

'A bit different to what I expected. I was kind of intimidated to approach her. She's so bold onstage and I thought there was no way someone like that would be interested in someone like me. But she was down-to-earth. Kind. A good listener. Shy, but really opened up when we talked about drag. Thoughtful, too. She insisted on walking me home so I didn't have to walk alone.'

Ash holds a hand to their chest. 'Aww. I think I might have a little crush, too.'

I chuckle. 'We exchanged numbers, she went back to the club and I went to sleep.'

'Oh,' Ash says, their disappointment palpable. 'Not even a kiss?'

I shake my head. 'I wanted to and I thought it might happen, but when I leant in, she kind of stepped back,' I say with a wince. 'Maybe she wasn't as keen as I thought? Or maybe it was too soon?'

Ash purses their lips thoughtfully. 'Mmm, maybe too soon. So, what's next? Did you arrange to meet up?'

I wince again. 'No, and I'm annoyed at myself, because now I don't know what to do. Do I contact her? Wait for her to contact me? Like, I want to message now, but is that too keen?'

Ash shrugs. 'It's been two days since you met. That sounds like a reasonable waiting time when you like someone.'

'You're right. Why do we put these stupid dating rules on ourselves? I want to ask her out, so I should just do that.'

Ash places the last of the lamington into their mouth and mumbles, 'You definitely should. I bet she's wondering the same thing.'

'You think so? Or maybe she's not that keen after all?' I say. 'Maybe I wasn't quite what she expected?'

Ash's brows rise. 'Maya, she talked to you all night and walked you home. She didn't want a kiss, so what? You said yourself she's shy. You might need to take the lead on this one.'

I nod. 'Yeah, you're right. Overthinking again. I've got those moonlight cinema tickets that I need to use by the end of the month. You think that's a good date?'

'The best! I'd be stoked if someone took me to the moonlight cinema.'

I smile, the idea of asking Callie out making my stomach flutter. 'Thanks, Ash.'

'You're welcome.' Their phone buzzes and they tap the screen. 'I'm needed on the shop floor.'

Ash heads back into the shop and I pull my phone from my pocket, rehearsing some message content out loud. 'Hi. It's Maya. From Saturday night.' I shake my head. 'Hi, Callie. Remember me?' I tsk at myself. 'Just send the message.'

> Hi Callie. It's Maya. How are you? Did you get back to the club okay?

I hit send, then groan. Why did I ask that? What's she going to say if she didn't get back okay? *No, I didn't, but thanks for asking two days later.* My phone dings and my heart jumps.

> Hi. Got back safely ☺

I smile at the smiley face. I'm about to reply when my phone pings again.

> I'm good. How are you? How was your Sunday shift?

She remembered I had to work *and* asked me about it? Green flag alert.

> It was fine and I'm fine. I'm at work again today.

Same

The club is open on Mondays?

No. But I do admin stuff too – socials, marketing, accounts. I'm the everything staff member.

Employers love versatile employees!

They do! Especially mine

Nerves fire in my gut and the voice in my head urges me to stop procrastinating. I type a message and hit send before I can talk myself out of it.

Are you working Friday night?

I chew my thumbnail, staring at the three dots pulsing on the screen.

Not this week. Working Sunday night instead.

Excitement surges and I let out a little squeal.

Would you like to do something? I have tickets to the moonlight cinema.

The reply doesn't come immediately, so I wash my mug and pack the cakes away. By the time I head back out onto the shop floor, my message remains on read and I blow out a puff of nervous energy. I pick up the pile of staff recommendation cards from under the counter and head across the store to the Australian fiction section.

Ash finishes with a customer and catches up to me. 'Well?'

'We exchanged a few messages, then I asked her out Friday night and silence.'

'How long since you sent the message?' Ash asks, taking half the cards from me.

I shrug. 'Five minutes.'

'Five minutes?' Ash says with a laugh. 'Give her a chance.'

I slip a card under the face-out of the corresponding book. 'I wouldn't normally be so impatient, but her replies were instant and when I asked her out, she read it but didn't respond.'

'She probably got sidetracked. She likes you, Maya. She'll reply.'

My pocket vibrates. I scramble for my phone, my heart lurching.

> The moonlight cinema? Yes. Sounds good.
> Thanks.

Okay, a slightly awkward message, but a yes nonetheless. I beam at Ash.

'She's keen then?'

I nod and tap out a reply.

> Great! Meet me in the foyer of my building around 6? Press the buzzer for 805 and I'll let you in. Do you remember where I live?

Send. 'Shit,' I say. 'I shouldn't have said "great" with an exclamation mark. That's too desperate, isn't it?'

Ash chuckles and shakes their head. 'Chill, Maya, chill.'

My phone buzzes.

> I look forward to it and yes I remember. See you Friday 😊

'She remembers where I live,' I say to Ash, slipping my

phone away. 'And she looks forward to it.' I pause to catch my breath. 'God, I haven't been out on a date in forever. Not sure I know what to do.'

'Just go with it,' Ash says, slotting cards under the books. 'Talk, get to know each other, enjoy the movie. I don't think it's that hard.'

'You're right,' I say with a nod. 'Just go with it.'

Chapter 7
Callie

Sitting in my car at the back of the club, I flip down the sun visor and check my hair in the tiny mirror. I manoeuvre a wayward strand back into an upright position and run my fingertips along the freshly shaved sides of my head to smooth out any strays. 'Get out of the car,' I mutter. 'It's just a date. With a person. A very attractive person that I'd like to get to know.' I exhale a shaky breath, lock up and head inside via the back door.

It's 5.30 p.m. on a Friday and the bar is busy with after-work drinkers. The air is filled with the soft lull of conversation and mellow music playing through the speakers.

A customer is waiting to be served, and Krissy and Amber are both busy tending to orders, so I step up to the counter. 'What can I get you?'

'A large Sauv Blanc and a pot of pale ale.'

As I pour the drinks, Stevie walks towards the bar carrying a tray of dirty glasses, watching me with a perplexed expression.

The customer pays and I pick up Stevie's tray, take it to the prep area and begin stacking the dishwasher.

'What are you doing?' Stevie asks, following me.

I glance at her briefly. 'Customers were waiting and these need to be washed.'

'I meant, *why* are you working?'

'It's busy,' I say, walking back out to the bar.

'Thought you were going on a date,' she says, rushing after me.

'Ooh, that's right,' Krissy chimes in while she vigorously shakes a cocktail mixer. 'Your hot date.'

The tips of my ears warm. 'We're just going to an outdoor cinema. Hardly a hot date.'

'Aww,' Krissy coos. 'So romantic. And today of all days.'

I open my mouth to respond, but Amber walks towards us. 'You're going on a date?' she asks, with no attempt whatsoever to hide the astonishment in her voice. 'Who with?'

I give her a stony look. She's been fishing all week to find out more about the person I spent a good chunk of last Saturday night with.

Stevie juts her chin towards the end of the bar. 'Customer waiting, Amber.' When she walks off, Stevie says, 'So, back to my original question, why are you trying to work when you should be meeting Maya?'

I grab a cloth and begin wiping the bar top.

'Callie, just be yourself,' Krissy says, gently taking the cloth from me. 'She can't not like you.'

Stevie gives my back a supportive rub. 'Pretty obvious she already does.'

My mouth turns dry. I fill a glass with water and down it. Being myself is what I'm worried about. 'It's Valentine's Day,' I say. 'It didn't register when she asked me out. Do you think she realises? I've never been out with anyone on Valentine's Day. Am I supposed to turn up with a rose or some—'

Krissy grabs my hand, her warm brown eyes filled with concern. 'Breathe.'

My hand tightens around hers as I inhale, hold and release.

'Maybe Maya didn't realise either,' Krissy says. 'If you're worried about that, just tell her.' She hugs me. 'Go and have a great time. And you look hot, by the way.'

That makes me smile. 'Hot is good.'

'And remember,' Stevie says. 'She asked you out.'

This is true but so have others. It's not a precursor to things going smoothly. But I nod and say, 'Yes. Okay. I'm leaving now.'

Outside, the edges of the day are starting to fade, and the sinking sun casts scorched orange hues across the sky. There's a steady flow of traffic along Wickham Street; people whizz past on e-scooters and stroll by with dogs, and relaxed laughter floats from a pub's beer garden as I pass. My mind shifts to Tom and how he'd act on a date. He's the person who won Maya over, after all. I'd like to think he wouldn't be awkward or tongue-tied or afraid of what a future with love in it might look like, but he's made for the stage, manufactured for the comfortable confines of a club, so I'm not sure he'd know how to act out here either.

I arrive at Maya's building one minute early and press the buzzer for Apartment 805.

She answers with an upbeat, 'Hi, Callie, come in and wait by the lifts. On my way down.'

'Sure,' I say. There's a click and I open the door to a spacious foyer. The last of the sunlight filters through a floor-to-ceiling window, spotlighting rows of metallic grey post boxes embedded into the wall and framed by two giant fiddle-leaf figs in copper pots. The display over one of the three elevator doors glows with the number eight. My pulse quickens as I watch the numbers descend. Four, three, two, one, ground.

The doors slide open to reveal a fresh-faced Maya. She's wearing a dandelion-yellow dress that complements her summery glow. I blink at the lovely vision in front of me, words caught in my throat. She is, quite simply, breathtaking.

'Jump in,' she says, pressing her finger down on the console. 'We're taking my car and it's in the basement.'

'Hi,' I say as I step into the lift. My gaze drops to a large bag stuffed with cushions and a wicker picnic basket by her feet. 'I didn't know we needed to take stuff. I could've brought something.'

She waves a hand. 'It's just a blanket to sit on, a cushion each and some snacks. I have soft drink because we're both driving tonight, but we can stop and grab wine if you'd like it?'

I shake my head, taken aback. 'No, soft drink is great.'

When we reach the basement, I grab the picnic basket and follow Maya a few metres to a small, silver hatchback. She loads up the boot, then holds the passenger door open for me, giving me a dazzling smile as she gestures for me to hop in. A date opening a car door for me is definitely a first.

She reverses out of the parking bay, moves slowly through the car park and edges up an incline, pressing a remote in her console for the gate to slide open.

'I've never been to the moonlight cinema,' I say, as she merges onto the main road.

Maya glances at me briefly then re-focuses on the road. 'Well, I'm glad to be the one to introduce you to it. You never asked what movie was on. Hope you like romcoms.'

Valentine's Day. Of course. 'Yeah. I do.'

She gives me another quick glance. 'Should we talk about the elephant in the car?'

'Erm,' I say, uncertain where this is going. 'Sure.'

'Valentine's Day,' she says. 'It didn't click when I asked if you wanted to meet up.' She pauses. 'Not that I mind seeing you on Valentine's Day,' she adds quickly. 'I hope you didn't cancel other plans.'

I have to stop myself from laughing. If only she knew the unlikelihood of that. 'I forgot, too. And I had no plans. I would've hung out at home with Mum or worked on my night off.'

She smiles. 'I'm glad I gave you another option, then.'

By the time we arrive at the Parklands, the twilight sky is a tarpaulin of vibrant pink, gold and indigo, and the paths are lined with solar lights. On a whim, I pluck a yellow flower from a shrub and hand it to Maya. 'It matches your dress.'

She stops walking and faces me, her mouth slightly open in stunned silence. I have to admit the action surprised me, too. The type of thing Tom would do. Our fingers brush as she takes it, making a shiver run through me.

'Happy Valentine's Day,' I say as an afterthought.

She gazes at the flower, then at me. 'This is the first flower I've ever received on Valentine's Day.'

My brows rise. 'I find that hard to believe.'

She laughs a little. 'Believe it.' She tucks the stem behind her ear, the vibrant petals sitting flush against her hair. 'How's that?'

I swallow. *Beautiful.* 'Yellow's your colour.'

She starts walking again, sneaking glances at me, then points to a patch of grass a few metres away. 'That looks like a good spot.'

We navigate around couples on picnic blankets, groups in deckchairs and sleeping cavoodles. Maya spreads the blanket out and tosses down two plump cushions covered in a dusty pink velvet that look far too luxurious for an evening outdoors. She takes the hamper from me, placing it in the middle. The image is so surreal that I want to snap a photo so I have evidence that this moment actually happened. But that would be odd on a first date, so I shove my hands into the pockets of my cargo pants and wait.

She gestures to the ground. 'After you.'

Opening my door, inviting me to sit before her ... the reversal of masc/femme stereotypes is throwing me, but it's also refreshing.

'Is this comfy for you?' she asks as I sit.

'Yes. It's' – I shake my head, amazed at the trouble she's gone to – 'It's incredible.'

She treats me to a smile as sparkly as the fairy lights woven through the trees, and my insides melt.

'I have lemonade or passionfruit,' Maya says, opening the hamper and removing two bottles. 'You choose.'

'Oh ... lemonade is good.'

Maya hands me the bottle. 'I knew you'd go for lemonade.' She twists the lid on the passionfruit, releasing a soft hiss. 'At the club, you always drink a beer or a large glass of something clear and fizzy. I figured it was soda water or lemonade.'

'You watched me that closely you knew what I drank?' I ask, surprised.

She arches a brow, a wry half-smile tugging at her lips. 'You also watched me that closely you knew what I drank.'

I nod, a grin emerging, and the comment helps me loosen up. 'That's fair.'

She plucks the flower from her hair and twirls it in her fingers. 'Can I tell you something?'

'Sure,' I say, screwing the lid back on my bottle and placing it beside me.

'I saw that "meet the kings" post on the club's Instagram, so I knew your name was Callie, but it felt weird saying, "You're Callie, aren't you?" I didn't want you to think I'd been monitoring you outside the club or stalking your socials.' She pauses, concern creeping into her brown eyes. 'Does that make you feel uncomfortable?'

I shake my head, giving her a reassuring smile, because I have my own confession. 'No. I'm flattered you wanted to meet me after you saw it.' I pause. 'Can I tell you something?'

Her brows knit. 'Yes.'

'Krissy tried to find out some info about you one night for me, but all she discovered was that the person you were with was a friend and that you use "she" pronouns.'

Maya laughs. It's bewitching and the sound of it causes a delicious warmth to unfurl in me, spreading through me like honey. 'I remember that night,' she says. 'Ash – that's my work colleague – returned from the bar and said, "That person who just served me asked the strangest question."'

I groan. 'Sorry about that. Krissy and Stevie don't do subtle well.'

'It didn't click that was for you.' She looks at me coyly. 'If I had've known that, I would've walked straight up to the bar and introduced myself.'

I dip my head shyly. 'I'm not great at talking to new people. Especially ones I'd like to meet.'

'Well, we're talking now, so we got there eventually.' She places her drink down and pulls out some containers. 'I don't know what you like to eat, but I have vegetarian quiche, cheese, crackers, and if you don't like any of that, then I have' – she reaches into her hamper and holds up a recognisable packet – 'Twisties.'

She did all of this for me? 'Um, I like all of this.'

'Good, and I hope you're hungry because there's plenty

here.' She places a slice of quiche on a napkin and hands it to me.

I take a bite, not expecting such a flavoursome, velvety texture, and a small moan escapes.

'I love food – both eating it and cooking it,' she says, squashing some blue cheese onto a water cracker. 'Homemade chocolate cake is my favourite. I'd live off it if I could. But I worked today and didn't have a chance to make one for tonight.'

I file away the cake fact then say, 'Looks to me like you've outdone yourself.'

She shrugs. 'Just threw some things together and cooked the quiche while I was getting ready.'

I swallow another delicious bite. 'You made this?'

She nods.

'Wow, that's impressive.'

She smiles. 'Not sure it's impressive, but thanks.'

We're both silent as we continuing eating, then Maya asks suddenly, 'Do you do other performances besides drag?'

I shake my head. 'No. When I was at school, I did a few plays and musicals, though.'

'You studied drama at school?'

'Uh-huh. Outside of school, too. I was such a timid kid that Mum took me to an after-school drama club. I loved music and TV, so she thought I might want to act or dance or play an instrument. Drama club was free at the time, music lessons weren't, and she was a single mum, so she took the free option.'

Maya shifts the picnic basket to the side, removing the boundary between us.

'I'd just turned seven when I took my first class,' I continue. I was curious and petrified at the same time, but the teacher was so kind and encouraging, I started to look forward to it. Then I took it as a subject in high school.' A swell of nostalgia rises in me. 'It's where I was happiest and felt the most accepted. Loved the costumes and wigs and make-up, and the feeling of being someone else. I guess I found my voice, in a way.' I pause and sip my drink. 'How about you? You seem to have a passion for the theatre.'

Maya nods. 'I do. It's not something we did much as a family when I was growing up, though. My grandparents took me sometimes and I'd always ask for theatre tickets for birthdays or Christmas. Drama wasn't an option for me in primary school, but I did it for a couple of semesters in year ten.' She frowns. 'My parents were so focused on us doing subjects they thought were worthwhile for future careers, so I didn't feel encouraged to continue. I don't think they were aware they were doing that,' she says, almost defensively. 'It's just the way they are. But it meant my love for the arts wasn't nurtured, and I never got to explore that aspect of myself when I was growing up.'

She pauses and takes a sip of her soft drink. 'At uni I felt pressured to do the degree they wanted,' she says, 'since they paid for it. I mean, a business degree is always helpful but before you know it, you're a twenty-eight-year-old still carrying around the unfulfilled performing dreams you had as a kid and slightly resentful towards your parents that it never happened for you.' She gives a rueful smile and turns her focus to cutting a piece of brie. 'Sorry, that was bit heavy for a first date.'

'It's not too late,' I say. 'There are heaps of adult theatre classes around.'

She wrinkles her nose. 'Mmm, there's one in the Valley actually, near my place. I went for a little while but it kind of didn't work out. I can't sing and I'm not particularly good at acting. Then there's the whole getting up in front of an audience thing.' She shakes her head, like the very idea of it makes her brain hurt. 'How do you do it? Because, I hope you don't mind me saying, but you seem shy and onstage you're so confident.'

I give a small laugh. 'Yep. Everyone says that. I'm not sure I understand it myself. All I know is that as soon as I'm in drag, it brings out this inner confidence I can't find otherwise. That's what I loved about drama when I was a kid, too. It was like' – I pause, searching for the words to embody what I felt – 'whatever costume I put on was a protective shield between me and the world, and I was safe to express myself. I guess now it's helping me discover myself in my adult life.' I shake my head. 'That probably makes no sense.'

'It makes sense. Almost like the costume gives you permission to be something else?'

'Yes. Exactly that.' An idea pops into my head. 'Hey, if you're free on Thursday night, you could come to our amateur night. It's loads of fun and it might inspire you to give that theatre club another go.'

The corners of her mouth lift. 'Another date?'

My heart expands. Who knew dates were like buses – you wait forever for one and then two come along at once?

'I'd love to,' she says.

The cinema screen lights up and sound travels across the park. Maya lays back against the cushion, making herself comfortable, and my stomach knots. I hadn't thought about how we'd position ourselves at an outdoor theatre, but I follow her lead.

'Let me know if you get cool or if you're getting bitten by mozzies,' she says in a hushed voice.

'Okay,' I reply, but I'm distracted by Maya's closeness, the delicate sweetness of her perfume, the sheen of her hair, how soft she looks in the moonlight.

I manage to shift my attention to the movie and stay focused for a good forty-five minutes. It couldn't be more hetero, but it's cute and funny in parts, and there's a tangible romantic air rippling on the breeze.

Maya sits up and grabs the extra blanket, flicking it open. 'Are you cold?' she whispers.

'A little,' I admit.

She shuffles closer and spreads the blanket over us, her eyes lingering on mine for a beat. When she lies back down, she reaches under the cover and takes my hand, making my pulse race. 'Is this okay?' she asks.

More than okay is what I want to say, it's what Tom would say, but all that comes out is a hoarse, 'Good. Yeah.'

She rests her head on my shoulder and as if sensing my thoughts, she looks up at me, her lips centimetres from mine. 'Can – can I kiss you?' she says.

I nod, my brain losing the ability to form words.

The charged space between us dissolves as our mouths meet. Her lips are soft and syrupy-sweet and I try not to whimper. Her body presses against me as her tongue finds mine, tentative at first, then more probing, making my insides heat. My hand slips around to the back of her neck, her skin silky against my palm. The caress of a late summer breeze on my skin and her gentle lips on mine makes my head swim and my heart sing.

We eventually break apart, our breaths shallow as we stare at each other.

'Damn,' Maya breathes.

I swallow, too stunned to speak. *Damn, indeed.*

Chapter 8
Maya

Anticipatory jitters fill my stomach as I walk into Club Sappho. It's been almost a week since my first date with Callie and *that* kiss. A kiss that was followed by another mind-altering kiss when we said goodnight. I couldn't come to the show on Saturday because I'd committed to Ash's birthday dinner, but I'd thought about Callie. Maybe too much, considering we'd just met. I also thought about whether someone else would experience Tom's simmering look as he handed them a margarita.

I scan the club, spotting Callie at the bar talking to her auburn-haired friend. She hasn't noticed me yet, and I take the opportunity to appreciate her. She's a presence with her physical attractiveness. But it's what she exudes that's most captivating – a tangible humility, a decency, the sense she'd be loyal to the core. There's something else about her in this space, too, that I've only now recognised since I've seen her outside the club. She carries herself differently here – stands taller, moves easier, is less guarded.

As though Callie senses me watching her, she turns, her

expression changing from solemn and serious to beaming and bright. Within seconds she's across the club, drawn towards me like a magnet.

'Hi,' she says. 'You came.'

'Of course. I'm intrigued about what happens at a drag king amateur night, and we had a date, right?'

Her smile widens. 'We did.' She guides me towards the bar, stopping in front of her friend. 'Amber,' she says. 'This is Maya.'

Amber blinks at me, her smile tight. 'Hello.'

My spidey-sense prickles, but I say a friendly, 'Hi, Amber. Nice to meet you.'

'You too,' she says, a cool edge to her voice.

If I wasn't so adept at reading people, I'd have missed the fleeting narrowing of her eyes as she assessed me. I resist the urge to look at Callie to check her reading of the situation.

'Catch you later, Callie,' Amber says, and without acknowledging me, she slips under the bar hatch and disappears into a room that presumably leads backstage.

I glance at Callie. 'I hope I didn't interrupt you and your friend?'

'Oh,' Callie says with a shake of her head, seemingly oblivious to the one-sided coolness of our exchange. 'Not at all. She's emceeing tonight so she was about to get ready for that anyway.'

I don't have time to process what's just happened because Callie introduces me to Stevie.

'Hello, again,' Stevie says with a broad smile. 'It's nice to properly meet you. And this is Krissy, my wife.' She gestures to the tall, attractive brunette behind the bar who's been serving me for the past month.

'It's really nice to meet you, Maya,' Krissy says warmly.

Callie touches a gentle hand to my waist. 'Would you like a drink?'

The gesture is so tender that all thoughts of Amber's attitude towards me evaporate. 'Sure, let me get them—'

'No,' she says, quick to cut me off. 'You covered all the food and drink last week.' She points to a free table a few rows back from the stage. 'If you grab that, I'll be over in a minute.'

I leave her to order and make my way to the free space. There's about a third of the usual crowd here tonight, but still enough people to perform for. I take a seat, glancing at the small sign on the table that states recording of amateur acts is not permitted and anyone caught doing so will be asked to leave.

Callie places a flute of fizzing prosecco and a small glass of beer on the table and takes the seat beside me.

'I've been looking forward to tonight,' I say. 'Not just the show, but to seeing you.'

She gives me a shy smile. 'I've been looking forward to it too. Saturday night felt different without you in the audience.'

I smile, relieved she noticed I wasn't there. 'And I missed watching you. I hope I didn't miss any new acts?'

She shakes her head. 'No, just pulled out some old routines that are popular.'

I want to ask if she performed the cocktail act, ask whether anyone else received a stage-made margarita, but there's no way to do that without sounding possessive, so I brush it aside and focus on now. 'So, what happens in tonight's show?'

She swallows her mouthful of beer. 'It's just about having fun. Giving people a chance to try drag.'

The club darkens, cutting our conversation short, and Amber walks onto the stage, a confidence to her gait. I shift my chair so that I'm closer to Callie. One hand is sitting on her thigh and I place my own hand over it. She glances at me and smiles, twisting her hand around so that our fingers are linked.

Amber beams at the audience, the sunny disposition softening her. I'm surprised to feel envy slither through me over how natural she is onstage, both as herself and as her alter ego.

She announces the first act and they burst into view, lip-syncing to an old Australian rock song. They're dressed in shorts, thongs and a singlet stretched across a fake beer belly. Their make-up is artfully applied to give a weathered look, as though they've spent a lifetime in the sun. I watch how they move, the precision of their lip-syncing and routine. The crowd lap it up. *This* is amateur?

When they finish, I say to Callie, 'What was amateur about that? That was as good as every other king I've seen.'

She nods. 'They've been doing Thursday nights every week for a couple of months, so lots of exposure and time to get used to the stage. Stevie's just given them a Saturday slot, so this is their last amateur night.'

We watch the next couple of acts, who are both at the beginner level I expected, but still great. Callie talks me through the performances – their make-up, clothing, choice of music, what they do well, areas they can improve, how they express masculinity or blend the binaries. Some minor lip-syncing mishaps occur, along with the occasional out-of-time dance move, but the audience are encouraging, and the kings laugh it off and get on with their acts.

I admire their courage for putting themselves in a vulnerable position, for exposing themselves. I particularly admire their ability to recover from mistakes, like they're nothing. Seeing everyday people do this makes the cogs whirr in my brain, unlocking the possibilities. I think back to high school, the short time I spent in drama class, and the longing to be chosen for the lead in the school play. I put weeks into preparing for the part, only to fail at the audition from nerves and to be offered a minor part instead. I took the rejection personally; evidence I wasn't good enough, that my audition wasn't perfect enough. I withdrew from drama class altogether, too embarrassed to face people after a failed audition. Then there was the local drama club I tried more recently. I couldn't quite grasp the exercises and was too self-conscious to throw myself into it, which made me feel like an outsider.

'What did you think?' Callie asks, pulling me from my thoughts. The loud stage music has been replaced with something softer.

'Fantastic!' I say. 'Even the kings who messed up were good, if you could call it messing up.'

Callie nods her agreement. 'It's a great opportunity for people to try out what works and what doesn't,' she says. 'Dancing around your lounge solo doesn't always translate well to the stage, so it's a good way to learn. And if doesn't go right, they can return the following week and try again.'

Her pragmatic approach to performing amazes me. 'They didn't all have flat chests and' – I gesture to my crotch – 'stuff going on down there.'

Callie shakes her head. 'No, it's about playing with masculinity in a way that suits the individual, whatever that means for them. Lots of kings like to mix their masculine and feminine.' She watches me with inquisitive eyes as she sips her beer. 'It's very cool that you're into this.'

My brows rise. 'Is it?'

'Yep. Pretty sure I bore most people with my constant drag king talk.'

I smile. 'It is *so* not boring, and I admire anyone who has the courage to do that. Did you start by dancing around your lounge?'

'Yeah,' Callie says, her eyes softening, as though she's reminiscing over fond memories. 'I'd dress up at home, put on shows for my gran.'

I laugh. 'Your gran?'

Callie laughs too, but there's a sadness there, and the use of the past tense tells me that her gran is no longer here. 'She loved it. I'd go easy on anything in the pelvic area for her shows, but she'd hoot with laughter when I pulled out a packer or strap and tell her it was part of the costume. It was a great way to get my lip-syncing right and work out some acts. Then Stevie was doing gigs around the city, so I thought why not?'

'And now you're one of the best up there,' I say.

She lowers her gaze. 'Ah, I'm okay.'

'You are better than okay, and I really admire you for doing what you love.'

She shrugs. 'I feel like it wasn't a choice, you know? More like a calling.'

I gaze at her, mesmerised. She is by far the most interesting person I've ever met, and even more endearing is her apparent unawareness about that.

She tilts her head at me, eyes scanning my face.

'What?' I ask, touching a hand to my lips, paranoid I've spent the last hour with dinner crumbs on my mouth. 'Something on my face?'

'No. I was just thinking that you look really pretty tonight. I mean, you always do, but extra pretty.' She gives a small laugh. 'I don't know why I said that. I have no idea what "extra pretty" means.'

My heart billows and I lean in, mindful that we haven't shared a kiss the entire night. She presses warm lips to mine in a tender, lingering kiss.

When we part, my eyes are drawn to the bar and an icy stare directed my way. Amber's sunny stage presence is gone and I shrink in my chair, feeling a sudden urge to keep myself small. But then I remind myself that Callie invited me, that she wants me here, so I kiss her again and say, 'Extra pretty is an extra-sweet compliment.'

Chapter 9
Callie

I dump my gym bag on the kitchen tiles, switch the air conditioner on high and stand directly under the vent, breathing out a relieved sigh as the icy air cools my sweaty skin. Once my body temperature drops, I walk across to the fridge, drumming my fingers on the edge of the open door as I gaze at the contents. After a one-hour dance class and no food beforehand, my stomach is grumbling. I grab ingredients for a cheese and salad sandwich, dumping them on the countertop, then peel the lid off a container of salted macadamia nuts and shove a handful in my mouth, moaning as the salty, creamy flavour dissolves on my tongue. I make the sandwich, pour a glass of orange juice and sit at the table.

As I eat, I read Maya's last message, sent at ten p.m. last night.

Goodnight, sleep well

The mouthful of food can't stop my smile emerging. The kiss emoji is everything. Our date at amateur night ended with a goodnight kiss on the footpath outside of her apartment block and a promise to meet soon. We've messaged all week, and even spoke one night, but we haven't made any concrete plans. I'm not sure what to do from here. Do I send a casual 'Do you want to meet up?' Do I ask her out on a proper date? Do I wait to see if she shows up on Saturday night?

I recall the last time I asked someone out on a date. The thought causes me to put my sandwich down, a sudden bad taste in my mouth. But Maya isn't Lacey, I remind myself, plus it's been three weeks since we met and no red flags as yet. In fact, this back-and-forth between us seems to be working, and it feels good, healthy, what I expected the start of a relationship to be. I push aside the comparisons and tap my phone screen to message Maya.

Hi

I start on the second half of my sandwich and send another message.

It's me. Callie

😈 I know it's you. I have your number saved in my phone.

I chuckle.

Oh 😅 Would you like to do something soon?

With me, I mean.

I groan at myself. Of course she knows I meant *with me*.

> I would love to do something. With you. I finish an hour earlier than normal tomorrow if that works?

I'm scheduled to work tomorrow night, but I don't want to miss an opportunity to see her. I switch to the planner app to check the work roster. Amber might be keen to swap shifts since she prefers Sunday nights off. I shoot off a message to check with her, and she replies agreeing. She asks why, but I avoid specifics, simply telling her I have something on, then message Maya.

> Tomorrow is good. Do you want to meet after you finish work or in the evening?

> Either. I need to get back on the shop floor but let me know and I'll be there. Can't wait to see you x

I smile, a warm glow flourishing in my chest like a glorious sunrise. *She* can't wait to see *me*.

'What are you smiling at?'

My head snaps up to see Mum and Aunty Gina dumping grocery bags on the bench.

'Nothing.' I flip my phone over. 'What's with sneaking up on me?' I ask, getting up to help them.

'We didn't sneak up; you were somewhere else,' Mum says, then looks at Gina. 'It'll be the new girlfriend. She's had this look on her face for weeks.'

Aunty Gina looks at me, her dark eyebrows rising over the rim of her clear-framed glasses. 'You've got a girlfriend? When did this happen and why am I only hearing about it now?'

'Because we only met a few weeks ago,' I say. 'And she's not my girlfriend.'

'You've been on two dates,' Mum says, passing me items for the freezer. 'Three if you count the night you met, and you message each other constantly.'

Gina throws Mum a bemused look, then gives me a wry smile. 'Your mum is part of the relationship, I see.'

I laugh. 'Seems that way.'

'What?' Mum says, folding up the shopping bags and placing them in the pantry. 'I'm just happy you've met someone you like so much.'

'I know, Mum, I know.' I fill the jug with water and set it to boil. 'Want a coffee, Gina?' I'm keen to change topics in case one of them inadvertently brings up the last person I 'liked so much'.

'If you're offering,' Gina says, sitting on the stool at the island bench.

'I'm going for a shower,' Mum says.

Gina watches Mum disappear into the hallway, then says, 'Okay, now she's out of the way, am I allowed to know anything about this new non-girlfriend? Her name? How you met? What she does?'

I unscrew the lid from the jar of instant coffee we keep solely for Gina and spoon a heaped teaspoon into a large mug. 'Her name's Maya. We met at the club and she works at City Books in the mall. And' – I shrug – 'I like her, I guess.' I top up the mug with boiling water, add milk and a teaspoon of sugar, give it a vigorous stir and slide it across the bench to Gina.

'Your mum's happy about it,' she says, grabbing the handle and lifting the mug to her lips.

I walk over to the window and tilt the blinds up slightly to shade us from the mid-afternoon sun, then sit on the stool next to Gina. 'Yeah, it just feels a bit premature, you know?'

She gives an understanding nod, lips pursed thoughtfully.

We're similar in a lot of ways, Gina and me. She also struggled to find romantic partners in her twenties, finally meeting Lisa just before she turned thirty and, as the saying goes, lived happily ever after. They've been together for twenty-four years now, and they're still happy, in love and have been the best relationship role models for our family. 'Anyway, enough about me. How are you? How's Aunty Lisa?'

Gina takes another sip of coffee and nods as she places her cup down. 'Good. Not much to tell – same, same.' She tugs an envelope out from under her car keys and slides it towards me. 'I stopped by to give you these, if you want them.'

I peek inside the envelope. 'A theatre ticket?' Gina is the Director for Marketing and Communications at a global PR company – regular theatre tickets are a perk of the job. I pull out the cardboard strip and skim the text. 'For the ballet? Aunty Lisa likes ballet. Why don't you want them?'

'They're for tomorrow arvo and she's got something on at work she can't miss. You can probably fit it in before you start. Plus, you like ballet a whole lot more than we do.'

'Tomorrow arvo?' I check the session time – three p.m. 'I'm off tomorrow night, but I've already planned to meet Maya.'

'Is she free in the afternoon? There's two tickets there.'

I unfold the strip to reveal the second ticket. 'She is finishing early, but I'm not sure it's early enough to make a three o'clock show. I did want to do something nice for her.' I scrunch my nose. 'You think that's a good date for someone you've just met?'

'Are you kidding?' Gina says, her eyes wide. 'It's a great date! How do you think I won over your Aunty Lisa?'

I smile. 'Your *rizz*?'

She laughs. 'Yes. That, too.'

I glance at the tickets again, working out the travel time from Maya's shop to the theatre. 'She does love theatre and dance, so I guess that includes ballet.'

'Then you'd better check if she's free.'

'Thanks, Gina. I will.'

It's warm the following afternoon, but a good five degrees cooler than yesterday with plenty of cloud cover – not too hot for walking across the bridge to the theatre. After Gina left, I messaged Maya to check her finish time and arrange to meet her afterwards. I didn't tell her what I had planned because I like the idea of surprising her, but also because I need to gauge her reaction. Figuring out the nuance of a message overwhelms me sometimes, and I'd drive myself mad trying to work out if she was genuinely excited or was obliging me.

As I stroll through the Queen Street Mall and approach City Books, the knot that's been in my stomach all morning tightens. I'm half an hour early so I sit on a bench to wait. But after a few minutes my leg starts to bounce and my heart rate begins to spike. I'll be a complete mess if I sit here and let this escalate for another thirty minutes.

I vacate the bench and head into the shop. Maya is nowhere in sight and I dart behind a shelf, second-guessing my decision to come in, now that I'm actually in here.

'Can I help you?' a voice behind me says.

Startled, I spin and knock a book off the shelf. 'Oh, erm' – I bend down to retrieve it and wave it in the air – 'found what I'm looking for. Thanks.' I flip over the paperback and pretend to read the blurb until the staff member walks away.

Once they do, I wander deeper into the store, my heart lifting when I spot Maya at the counter. She's talking to some-one, then she steps closer and wraps her arms around them. I slip behind a shelving unit and peer around the end. Unless they go above and beyond on customer service, I assume this is not a customer. A relative? But there are no similarities. I've seen her sister at the club and the person in Maya's arms is not her. This person is tall and blonde, not small and brunette like Maya and her sister. A friend? But they look closer than friends. They release each other, but Maya keeps hold of the other person's hands, then draws them back into her arms, kissing their cheek and running a hand over their hair.

There's a sour twist in my gut and my legs wobble, a dizzying sense of déjà vu washing over me. The person leaves, blonde hair swishing as they walk, long legs extending from a short summer dress. My breathing turns shallow and the books start to close in on me. I check the coast is clear and make a beeline for the exit. I'll message Maya with an excuse about why I can't make it. It's self-preservation.

Chapter 10
Maya

Bella leaves and I notice a customer speed-walking towards the exit. It takes my brain a second to register the cropped black hair and familiar, lean figure. 'Callie?' I call, rushing towards her.

She spins, her eyes wide and watery, her freckled cheeks stained pink. 'Oh. You. Hi.'

My brows draw together. 'Yes, me. What are you doing?'

'Just, erm, looking at books, and I' – she shakes her head – 'nothing. I should go.'

I grab her arm as she turns. 'Wait. I thought we were meeting after I finished work.'

'Yeah. I um ... I was early.' She hesitates a beat, then blurts, 'I didn't realise you had a partner.'

I draw back in shock. 'I *don't* have a partner.'

Her jaw tightens and she gestures to the counter. 'I saw you with ... you looked close.'

I glance over my shoulder, expecting to see someone, then realisation dawns. 'Oh, that's because we are close. That's my little sister. She's upset because she thinks she failed an exam today so I was giving her some support.'

The colour in Callie's cheeks deepens. 'But I've seen your sister at the club; that's not her.' She points to the counter again, her finger trembling. 'You and that person look nothing alike.'

What's happening right now is unsettling, something we should talk about, but she's visibly upset and I don't want to accuse her of overreacting. Dr Garcia's comment about why Callie fled after she first approached me materialises in my mind – *it's probable that her actions were about her and not you.* 'No, you've seen Liv,' I say gently. 'That was Bella. Liv and I take after Mum, and Bella looks like Dad.' I laugh a little, hoping it will ease the tension, and say, 'No one ever believes we're related.'

Callie closes her eyes briefly and releases a remorseful groan. 'I'm so sorry.' There's a weighty silence and she shoves her hands into the pockets of her jeans. 'I was early. I should've waited for you outside like we planned.'

I give her a reassuring smile. 'There's nothing wrong with early. And I'm nearly finished anyway. Let me go and grab my stuff.'

She gives me a sheepish look. 'Okay. I-I'm sorry,' she repeats.

'It's fine.' I head for the back of the shop, slightly unnerved by Callie's reaction, particularly the fact that she chose to walk away rather than talk to me. I shake my head, clearing the thought. *She's here. We resolved it and I want to enjoy my afternoon with her.* I punch in the staff access code and head into the staffroom.

'Oh my god,' I say to Ash, who's sitting at the table drinking a cup of tea. 'Callie's here, in the shop.'

'Ooh.' Ash jumps up and starts for the door.

I pull them back. 'What are you doing?'

'I want to get a proper look at her out of drag. It's hard to see in that dim club lighting.'

'You can't do that. She might recognise you and it will look too obvious.'

'She's not going to recognise me.'

I raise my brows.

They sigh and sit back down.

'We were supposed to meet outside after I finished,' I say, grabbing my handbag and tossing in my phone. 'I mean, I like that she's early, but now I don't have any time to sort myself out.'

Ash gives me a once-over. 'What's to sort out?'

I throw my hands up. 'Hair, face, clothes. She just turned up and surprised me.'

'Surprise and spontaneity. I like it.'

'I like that too, but I'm not' – I look down at myself – 'dressed for a date.'

'Maya, I'm sure Callie doesn't care what you're wearing. You were meeting after work anyway, so she probably expected to see you in work clothes.' Ash hops up and carries their mug to the sink. '

'Yes, but I was going to change my shirt at least.' I lift my arm and sniff. 'I smell okay, I suppose.' I smooth a hand over my hair. 'Do I look okay?'

Ash smiles at me. 'You always look great and you don't smell. Don't stress.'

I run my tongue over my teeth. 'Maybe I should clean my teeth quickly?' I hold a hand to my face and breathe into my cupped palm, then groan. 'Why did I have pasta for lunch? My breath smells like garlic.' I retrieve my cosmetic bag from the small locker where I stash my personal belongings, unroll my clean shirt and give it a shake, then head to the bathroom to change and get myself date-worthy.

By the time I return to the staffroom, Ash is gone. I curse them under my breath and head back out to the shop floor. Ash is straightening books in a display unit close to where Callie is standing.

'Could you be any more obvious?' I hiss-whisper as I pass.

They smirk at me and mouth, *She's hot*, then scurry off into the maze of the store.

Callie is reading the back of a novel when I approach, her brow dented with concentration.

'Are you a reader?' I ask.

She looks up, her brow smoothing. 'When I'm in the mood.'

'Ah, a mood reader. Do you have a favourite author or genre?'

She takes care to put the novel back where it belongs. I want to kiss her right there; returning books to their rightful place on a shelf says a lot about a person. 'No favourite authors,' she says. 'But I love a good crime novel, even better if it's lesbians solving the crimes.'

I nod in agreement. 'That's two things we have in common now – eighties pop culture and lesbian crime novels.' Callie's delighted smile makes her green eyes glimmer, and I melt a little over how utterly gorgeous she is. Excited to start our afternoon together, I say, 'Ready to go if you are.'

We step out into the mall and Callie navigates around people, heading in the direction of the river. I hurry beside her, trying to keep up with her long strides.

'So, what would you like to do?' I ask.

She gives me a sideways glance. 'I've got something in mind, but I'm not sure it's your thing,' she says, her tone hesitant.

'I'm intrigued.'

'I thought we could go to the ballet?' she says.

I stop walking and face her. 'Seriously? You want to take me to the ballet?'

Panic skates across her face. 'It's fine if you don't. It's just that my aunty gave me tickets and I thought you might be into it but—'

I grip her forearm, hoping to quell her doubt, plus I need a moment to find my voice because no one has ever taken me on a date to the ballet. Any unease I felt about her racing away earlier dissolves, washed away by the thrill that someone would do this for me. 'I would love that.'

Relief replaces her panicked expression. 'Don't you want to know what it is?'

I shake my head. 'I don't care what it is. I'm blown away. I love ballet.'

Callie gives me a shy smile. 'That's three things in common now.'

I grin. 'So it is!'

'It's not too hot today,' Callie says. 'Are you okay to walk over to QPAC? Or we can get the bus?'

'Walking's good.' We cross Victoria Bridge and I look out over the Brisbane River, astonished by the turn of events the afternoon has taken. A CityCat passes underneath, slicing through the water, and I make a mental note to catch the ferry home. 'I haven't ever been on a date to the theatre,' I say, then feel the need to justify my comment in case I've inadvertently moved us to 'we're dating' status. Our messages were just about meeting up, after all. 'Oh, this is a date, right?'

Callie side-eyes me. 'Erm, yeah. If you want it to be.'

'I want it to be,' I say. 'You didn't want to take someone else? A friend? Family?'

She arches a brow. 'On a date? No.'

I laugh. 'I mean you didn't want to take them to the ballet instead?'

Callie shakes her head. 'Nah. My Aunty Gina gets tickets through her job and she couldn't go, and my friends aren't into ballet. Besides, even if they were, I'd still want to take you. You said how much you like dance and theatre, so' – she shrugs – 'I thought you might like it.'

My stomach flips. *A listener; I've found a listener.* 'That's so thoughtful, Callie. Thank you.'

She gives me a pleased smile and points to the left. 'This way.'

At the performing arts centre, I order two proseccos, which are served in plastic stemless wine glasses, and Callie leads the way into the theatre and up a short, curved stairway to the balcony.

She stops at row C and gestures for me to walk ahead of her. 'Twenty-two and twenty-three in the middle.'

People already seated twist their legs to the side as we pass. I fold down seat twenty-two, glancing around as I sink into the cushioned surface. The theatre is magnificent. High beamed ceilings, rows of chairs in soft mulberry velvet, gold handrails lining carpeted stairs, and a blood-red curtain hiding the stage. The orchestra practises in the pit, a cacophony of instruments reverberating around the space.

'I love the Playhouse,' I say in a low voice. 'I haven't been here in forever, though. I forgot how quaint and intimate it is.'

'It's really beautiful,' Callie says, gazing into my eyes, and for a moment I think the comment is meant for me, but then she looks around. 'My aunties brought me here a lot when I was young.'

I shift so I'm angled towards her, my prosecco cradled in my palm. 'Sounds like you're really close with your family.'

She nods as she sips her drink, then nestles the cup between her thighs. 'Yeah, we're pretty tight. How about you? You're obviously close with your sisters.'

'Oh, I'm close with my parents, too. I'm just not' – I pause to think about how to phrase my reality – 'open about everything with them, which can be a little frustrating.' Callie's eyebrows draw together, like she's trying to figure out what that means, but it's not a topic for the ballet, so I divert the discussion. 'Thank you for this. It's really special.'

Her smile is pure elation. 'You're welcome. You still haven't asked what we're about to watch, and you didn't seem to notice it on the screen out there,' she says, nodding towards the foyer.

'I intentionally didn't look,' I reply, 'because I love the surprise element of this date, but I can't hold out any longer. Tell me.'

'Hope you like Shakespeare,' Callie says. 'It's *A Midsummer Night's Dream*. Hope you understand it too because I won't be much help.'

I clutch my chest. 'Ugh, I work in a bookshop – of *course* I like Shakespeare, and midsummer night's dream is one of my favourites.'

I don't get time to fully appreciate her overjoyed expression because the lights dim. A rich, deep voice amplifies through the theatre, delivering the Acknowledgment of Country, paying respect to the Yuggera and Turrbal people. Then we're plunged into darkness as the orchestra strikes their first note. Goosebumps sweep my skin and I lean closer to Callie, our forearms brushing on the armrest.

I lose myself in the fluidity of the dancers' movements, the exquisite costumes, the narrative being told through motion and music, the upbeat soundtrack from the orchestra embodying the spirited theme of the play, and the scuff of ballet slippers against wood between music beats.

Further into the show, I rub my arms, the air conditioning cool on my exposed skin.

Callie's shoulder presses against mine. 'Are you cold?' she whispers, her breath warm against my ear.

'A little bit,' I whisper back, drawing closer to her.

She takes my empty cup from me and places it by her feet, then quietly rustles in her bag. A second later, she spreads a jacket over me. Who *is* this woman? I reposition the coat so that it partially covers both of us and take her cool hand into the warmth of my lap. In my peripheral vision, I catch a hint of a smile as she focuses on the stage, and my insides turn to mush.

'That was incredible,' I say as we leave the theatre. 'I'm always so inspired after a live show.'

'It really was fantastic,' Callie says. 'What they can do with their bodies...' She gives a disbelieving shake of her head.

We follow the crowd down the stairwell and step outside. The clouds have parted, allowing the silky golden hues of the late afternoon sun to shine through.

'You know,' I say as we follow the path towards the river, 'I wanted to be a ballet dancer when I was a kid.'

Callie's brows rise. 'Yeah?'

'Mmm. It didn't progress much further than a childhood dream. I had lessons but I'd get frustrated because I could never perfect a pirouette, so I stopped.' A vision surfaces of a young me, spending hours and hours in my bedroom, twirling until I was dizzy, followed by throwing myself on my bed in exasperation because I couldn't do it to the professional standard I expected of myself.

'How old were you?' Callie asks.

I shrug. 'Around eight, I think.'

Her face splits into a grin. 'Eight? You put that much pressure on yourself to perfect a pirouette at that age? I reckon that's something that takes years.'

I grin, too. 'Yep. I'm sure I was the only kid in dance class who thought they should be a professional after three lessons.' I tuck a strand of hair behind my ear. It's been the nicest afternoon and I'm not ready for it to end. 'Would you like to get something to eat? Or I have some food at home I can heat up for dinner? There's plenty for two.'

Callie glances at me. There's something unreadable in her eyes but she looks away before I catch it. I hold my breath, ready for the sting of rejection, but she nods. 'I'd like that. We can grab something if it's easier. I don't want to eat all your food.'

I breathe out. 'I'm sure you won't eat all my food.' I point to the South Bank terminal. 'We can take the ferry and walk to my place from Howard Wharf.'

Her face lights up. 'I never catch the ferry,' she says excitedly.

We pick up our pace, approaching the pier as a CityCat docks.

As we take seats on the open back deck and the ferry sets off, Callie twists her head from side to side, taking in the city buildings and South Bank views. 'Brisbane is so beautiful this time of day.'

I'm too taken by how beautiful she is to notice the setting and only realise she's spoken when she looks at me expectantly. 'Oh, yes, it is. I get the ferry as much as possible. It's relaxing, especially after a day on my feet at work.'

Her gaze lingers on mine, then drops to my lips, causing a shiver to shimmy down my spine. I skim the deck – only a couple of people a few rows ahead with their backs to us, the other passengers all inside. I brush a wind-blown strand of hair from my face and say, 'I didn't kiss you hello earlier.'

Callie responds by pressing her mouth hard against mine, like she's waited an eternity to kiss me. As the ferry meanders along the curves of the Brisbane River, we melt into each other. My body heats and my heart warms, and already, I never want to let her go.

Chapter 11
Callie

On the eighth level of Maya's building, she unlocks the door to Apartment 805 and stands aside to let me pass. When I walk into a stylish open-plan lounge and diner, my first thought is *holy shit*, but what comes out of my mouth, thankfully, is a polite, 'This is nice.'

It looks like a new build, with walls painted in a satiny stone shade and soft beige carpets. Cushions in vibrant pinks and yellows are scattered across a large couch that looks comfortable enough to sleep on. A tall, wide shelving unit stuffed with books organised by spine colour decorates one wall. The kitchen is modern with crisp white benches and walnut cabinetry. Trays of fresh herbs line the bench, and a few pot plants, with leaves so lush and green I can't tell if they're real or fake, are dotted around the room. The décor fits with the Maya I've come to know – both colourful and earthy.

'You afford this on a bookseller's salary?' Not so polite, but I ask from a place of interest. Maybe there's a government rental scheme I don't know about where I can live on my own like an adult, all within walking distance of work.

'Yes and no.' Maya places her handbag on the coffee table and tosses in her keys. 'My dad's company owns this chain of buildings, but the deal for cheaper rent was taking one of the smallest apartments with a view of the next apartment block, and I have to serve on the building committee for at least a year. I'm halfway through my term.'

I wonder what it would've been like growing up with a dad who owns his own building company, or even just growing up with a dad. 'Sounds like a pretty good deal to get your own place.'

She nods. 'I'm grateful to Dad for helping me out. Some of the committee members are a nightmare, but I love it here.'

'You even have a balcony,' I say, peering through the glass at a small, round table with two chairs, an array of potted plants and a folded clothes airer propped up against the wall.

She unlocks the balcony door and slides it open, letting in the early evening air.

'It's tiny,' Maya says, 'but I get the morning sun and have room for plants. The balconies on the other side of the building are double the size with a view of the city. Maybe I'll end up in one of those one day.' She moves over to the kitchen, opening the fridge and removing a water jug. 'Do you like living at home?'

'I do,' I say, following her. 'I lived in a share house for a while, but I was working for a theatre at the time, mainly in the box office, and no shows during the pandemic meant no work, so I moved home. Plus my gran was living there and Mum had to work a lot, so I wanted to be there for Gran.'

Maya listens quietly as she slices a lime and drops a couple of wedges into two glasses, the fresh citrus scent making my mouth water.

'Five years later I'm still there,' I continue, taking a seat at the table where she's placed a glass of fizzy water for me. 'The house is a good size, we have a bathroom each and a couple of spare rooms, so I've got one for all my drag stuff. And we get on well.'

'Also sounds like a good deal.' Maya slides a glass container into the microwave and sets it to heat. 'I hope you like lasagna. It's homemade.'

'*Your* homemade lasagna?' I ask, impressed.

Maya smiles. 'Yes. Lasagna is my thing. Do you cook?'

I take a sip of water and nod. 'A bit. Kind of had to learn young with Mum working a lot.'

'It was just you and your mum growing up?'

'Uh-huh. Mum and Dad split when I was four. He visited for a few years afterwards. He was supposed to take me out for my seventh birthday – bowling and pizza.' I give a dry laugh. 'I was so excited because Mum didn't have money to spend on luxuries like takeaway food or days out. But he never showed and he never came back.'

Maya stops chopping and looks up, her eyes wide. 'Did something happen to him?'

'Oh.' I wave a hand. 'No. Nothing bad. He just couldn't deal with parental responsibilities, apparently. Mum said it was after that I became more withdrawn. He contacted me when I was in my mid-teens and I met up with him.' I pause to take a sip of water. 'He was nice enough, told me about his other kids and said sorry for what had happened, explained it was him, not me. I guess it gave me a bit of closure.' A familiar dull ache expands in my chest. I give a quick smile and mask with a jokey comment, 'Pretty pissed I never got my bowling and pizza party, though.'

Maya watches me intently as she whisks olive oil and vinegar with a fork, and it's as though she sees right through the mask. 'Did you see him again after that?'

'Nah. Didn't feel like much point, you know? I didn't want

a relationship with him. I had my family unit – Mum, Aunty Gina and Lisa, my grandparents, and Stevie and her family – I didn't want him disrupting that.'

'It sounds like you grew up in a really loving and supportive environment, though,' Maya says, pulling two plates from an overhead cupboard.

The ache in my chest eases, remembering noisy weekends filled with music and games, putting on performances in the lounge room after I came home from drama classes, chaotic Christmases with stuffed turkey and jumbo prawns, and being surrounded by strong, independent, non-judgemental women. Plus my granddad, a gentle, kind soul who passed too young. 'I did, and I can't imagine my upbringing any other way. I didn't have many friends, though. My gran was my bestie.'

'Your gran?' Maya asks, bringing our meals over to the table.

'Yep. We did everything together,' I say.

'She's not with you anymore?' Maya asks.

I shake my head, the grief not as sharp as it once was, but still present. 'No, she passed away a couple of years ago.' I pause, suddenly conscious that I'm oversharing, and pick up my cutlery. 'I'm impressed you've just rustled this up.'

She chuckles. 'It's leftovers and a salad of lettuce, tomato and cucumber, but thanks.'

We fall into easy conversation as I eat one of the nicest lasagnas I've ever tasted, the combination of different flavours hitting just right. Maya talks fondly about her sisters, then tells me about her parents' companies. Although she's close with them, there's a tightness to her tone, suggestive of friction with her mum and dad. I'm tempted to ask questions, but she changes topic, back to how enjoyable she found the ballet.

Afterwards, I clean up, refusing to let Maya help, then join her on the couch. She stretches her legs out, her toes brushing my thigh. My finger itches to trace a line along her delicate foot.

'You know,' Maya says, yanking me from my foot fantasy, 'I couldn't believe my luck that you were single.'

The sudden comment surprises me and I meet her gaze. 'That's exactly what I thought about you.'

'Really?'

I nod. 'Yep.'

'I've been single for a while,' she says. 'Split with my ex eighteen months ago. She, um' – Maya reaches for her glass and takes a sip of water – 'dumped me for someone else. Her best friend, in fact.'

My mouth drops open. 'Shit, Maya.'

She shrugs, but her expression has hardened. 'How about you? You must have a story about an ex. Or lots of exes.'

I consider playing it cool or giving an evasive answer, but it's probably obvious that I don't have much experience at this relationship stuff. 'I've, erm, pretty much always been single.'

Her eyes widen and she places her glass on the coffee table. 'Always? What do you mean?'

I scratch the back of my neck, averting my gaze. 'I've never had a girlfriend. Not really.'

'Oh, a boyfriend?' she asks, without conviction.

That makes me laugh out loud. 'Do I look like I'd be into blokes?'

Maya laughs, too. 'Well, no, but I try not to make assumptions or stereotype people.'

'I've been out with people casually,' I say, crossing my ankle over my knee. 'I've just never been with someone long enough to call them a partner or girlfriend. I've had sexual partners, if that's what you're wondering,' I add, then inwardly grimace. *What a thing to say.*

She cocks her head. 'So, has it been a case of wanting to have relationships but not meeting the right person?'

I shrug. 'Something like that. I've had what I'd call a ... situationship is probably the best description. It was around this time last year. At the time, I thought it was a relationship, but...' I shake my head, my pulse beating that little bit faster. 'She wasn't a good person.'

Maya watches me, her eyes narrowing slightly, trying to figure me out. 'Do you mean she didn't treat you well?'

I've worked hard the past year to rid myself of my time with Lacey, and I generally don't talk about it, but there's something about Maya that's trustworthy and I want to be open with her. 'No, she didn't. But it's hard to see that when you're in a situation sometimes, isn't it?' When I look at Maya, her eyes are misty. 'Have I said something to upset you?'

She clears her throat. 'No. I just can't believe someone wouldn't treat you well. You're so lovely and kind and thoughtful.'

The compliment causes an unexpected lump to form in my throat. No one I've ever been interested in has described me like that.

'Does this former situationship have anything to do with why you jumped to conclusions seeing me hug Bella in the shop?' Maya asks in a cautious voice, as though I might crack if not handled with care.

I give a tentative nod.

'She wasn't physically harmful?' Maya says.

'No.' What I don't say is that sometimes sex was rough, rougher than I liked, but it was Lacey's kink and I wanted to please her, keep her interested. I wasn't completely against it; I'm just not a kink kind of person. It also wasn't the sexual relationship I longed for or imagined for myself. I yearned for emotional connection and loving caresses and passionate kisses, not bruises on my wrists and bite marks on my chest and an emptiness in my soul.

'I'm sorry she treated you like that,' Maya says.

I shrug like it's nothing, like it didn't destroy me at the time. 'I'm glad I discovered what she was really like before it was too late, and since then, well, I haven't found the right person. And probably haven't tried that hard to either.'

'Do you want to find the right person?' Maya asks.

The tinge of hope in her voice makes my heart warm. 'Yeah. Figure I should've had some sort of meaningful relationship by now. I don't know too many twenty-seven-year-olds who haven't had at least one person they could call a partner.'

Maya lifts a shoulder. 'I've only had two what I'd call meaningful relationships myself and I'm a year older than you. One when I was in my second year at uni – that lasted six months – and the one I just told you about, and that lasted two years.'

My fingertips run over the edge of her jeans. 'Two years and she left you for her friend? That must've been hard.'

She's silent for a beat, a darkness descending over her face. 'It was. I was a mess.' She takes a deep breath, the shadow lifting. 'We weren't right for each other, and it had been unravelling for a while. I'd just ignored the signs. We were housemates first but it turned into more. Living together from the start was too much too soon. I lost friends over it, too, so it wasn't a nice time.'

My fingertip slips under the cuff of her jeans and makes small circles against the soft skin of her ankle. When I realise what I'm doing, I jerk my hand away. 'Sorry, I didn't mean to' – my face burns – 'God. Sorry.'

'It's okay. It was nice.' She watches me a moment, then says, 'I've thought a lot about you this week. About us.' She draws her legs in and shuffles closer. 'Haven't you?'

'I've thought about little else,' I say truthfully.

'Your kisses,' she says. 'No one's made me feel that way with a kiss before.'

My head reels, that sense of déjà vu again. *Did Lacey say that to me?* But Maya isn't Lacey and I need to stop comparing. My gaze drops to her lips. 'No one?'

She shakes her head slowly before our mouths crash together in an urgent kiss. A fire races through my body, an immediate throb between my legs. But as quickly as my arousal peaks, my stomach knots and my chest tightens. I pull away, my breathing rapid. 'I, um, I should go.'

Maya blinks at me. 'Oh.'

I stare at her, trying to make sense of the conflicting physical sensations and racing thoughts. 'Yes. I should definitely go.' I stand. 'Thanks for dinner and coming to the ballet.'

'We don't have to' – Maya stands and gestures to the couch – 'if you're uncomfortable. We can talk or watch a movie.'

I scramble for an excuse. 'I, ah, I promised Mum I'd make dinner for her tonight since she's been on a double shift today.' I feel heat creep up my neck, but the words keep spilling. 'She works for the ambulance service as an emergency medical dispatcher, so she's always exhausted when she gets home.'

Maya's brows pull together. 'I see. That's a tough job.'

'It is. I-I don't want to let her down by not having some food for her. Not dinner for me because I've eaten.' The heat travels from my neck to my face. 'You gave me dinner. But dinner for Mum.' *God, shut up, stop talking,* my head screams at me, but the link between my brain and my voice box is evidently faulty.

Maya gives a single nod. 'How will you get home?'

'My car's at the back of the club.'

'Right.' She smiles like we're having a normal conversation, albeit a little tightly. 'Well, thanks again for this afternoon. I had an amazing time.' She steps forward and pecks the edge of my mouth. 'I'll call or message, or I'll hear from you?'

Her doubtful tone makes my heart crack, but this apartment suddenly feels too small, the air eight floors up too thin, and I can't get enough oxygen into my lungs. 'Yep,' is all I can manage before I rush to the door. 'Bye,' I call over my shoulder as I head for the lift, her devastated expression in my wake.

Chapter 12
Callie

My breathing begins to regulate once I'm in the open air, but my head is foggy with confusion about why being around Maya is making me anxious. This is what I've longed for, to meet someone I like as much as I like her, to embark on a relationship with someone who appears to also like me. A functioning relationship is supposed to fill the emptiness in my heart, not force me to run from a heated kiss or overreact in public or blurt out-of-context comments.

I burst into the club, duck under the hatch and serve a waiting customer.

Krissy watches me, perplexed, and Amber says, 'What the fuck, Callie? You swapped shifts with me! I could've done something else if you were going to work.'

I shrug. 'Go then. I'm here now.'

She rolls her eyes and walks away.

I clear a stack of dirty glasses and set them to wash. When I move back behind the bar Stevie is there, arms folded.

'What are you doing?' she asks.

'These need to be cleaned,' I say, pulling a rubber mat from the bar top and rinsing it. 'There's spillage everywhere. Why hasn't someone cleared it up?'

'No, no, no,' Stevie says, taking the mat from me, flicking off the water and putting it back. 'What's going on?'

I step away from her, grabbing a second mat to rinse. 'Nothing. I was passing and thought you might need some help. And lucky I did.'

'You were passing?' Krissy says, stepping over to us. 'From your place?'

'No,' Stevie says. 'She was out with Maya today. Something's happened.'

My jaw tenses. 'Nothing's happened. Just let me work.'

Stevie coaxes me out from behind the bar and leads me to a table in the back corner. 'You were taking Maya to the ballet this arvo,' she says, sitting opposite me in the booth seat. 'Didn't it go well?'

My shoulders slump, the adrenaline of the last twenty minutes whooshing out of me. 'It was amazing.'

Stevie's brows knit. 'Okay, so why are you here buzzing around like you've skulled ten energy drinks?'

Krissy appears and places a couple of soft drinks down for us.

'Thanks, babe,' Stevie says. After she takes a gulp, she asks, 'Maya liked the surprise date?'

I nod. 'Loved it.'

'Okay, then what's happened?'

'She invited me back to her place for dinner. We took the ferry and kissed the whole way.' I let out a soft moan. 'Have you ever kissed someone on the back of the ferry at dusk?'

Stevie shakes her head slowly, with a bemused half-smile. 'I don't believe I have, no.'

'Then we had dinner. In her gorgeous apartment. Where she lives alone.' I lean forward. 'Homemade lasagna. It was delicious. You know how sometimes leftover lasagna is dry?' I shake my head. 'Not this one. It was sublime.'

Stevie arches a brow. 'Sublime, hey?'

'Uh-huh. And she made that quiche when we went to the moonlight cinema. She cooks and lives alone and blows my mind when she kisses me, and is lovely and kind and thoughtful, and she thinks *I'm* lovely and kind and thoughtful.'

'Oh-kaay,' Stevie says, with a bewildered expression. 'It sounds like you're made for each other, so why are you here trying to work on your night off and not with Maya? Not to mention pissing Amber off, since she swapped shifts with you.'

I fiddle with the straw sticking out of my lemon, lime and bitters. 'Things heated up after dinner, and I got nervous, I guess. Then I said' – I let out a mortified groan – 'I had to get home to make Mum dinner because she's an emergency medical dispatcher and was on a double shift today, so she'll be tired.'

Stevie presses her lips together, but her eyes sparkle with laughter. 'Sorry, I don't mean to laugh, but why were you even thinking of Aunty Donna at a time like that?'

I throw my hands up. 'I don't know. It all happened so fast. I felt like clothes were about to come off and it's what came out of my mouth.'

She tips her head sympathetically. 'You could've just told her you're not ready.'

'But I *am* ready. Really fucking ready. I haven't slept with anyone since' – I look up at the stage as Amber walks across it to open the amateur show – 'that thing with Amber, so there's a lot of tension going on.'

'Okay, so if you're ready and it sounds like Maya is too, what's the problem?'

I chew my bottom lip.

Stevie narrows her eyes. 'Wait, back up a bit. When things

got heated, you said you were nervous. By nervous, do you mean anxious? Panicked?'

I sip my drink.

'What were you talking about before that?' she asks, leaning forward and raising her voice over the music that's started playing for the first act.

I shrug. 'Family stuff. Exes.'

Her brows shoot up. 'Exes? *Your* ex?'

'Maya's exes, and well, mine isn't really an ex—'

'She's an ex of sorts,' Stevie says.

I take another sip and shift my focus to the stage, watching the amateur king fumble with the microphone.

Stevie lets out a bitter scoff. 'Fucking Lacey, still messing with your head and giving you anxiety—'

'No,' I say, cutting her off before she works herself up. 'It wasn't just that. I think it was ... performance anxiety?'

'Performance anxiety?'

I nod. 'Things never work out after I sleep with someone I like, do they? They lose interest or I lose interest, and it's not like I have heaps of experience. Maybe I'm a dud in bed and she'll be like "bye" or keep seeing me out of pity. Maybe she's only being nice now to sleep with me and then she'll turn mean or something—'

'Callie,' Stevie says, placing a supportive hand on mine. 'Firstly, you were triggered by what happened with Lacey, and secondly, Maya isn't her and you don't need to rush into a sexual relationship.'

Lacey coercing me into her bed on our second date is fresh in my mind, the way she showered me with compliments, telling me no one made her feel the way I did. *No one had made her feel like that from a kiss before.* 'But Lacey was nice at the beginning and she changed as soon as she got what she wanted.'

Stevie recoils. 'Lacey was a toxic moll from the start; you

were just too fucking gaga over her to realise it. Maya does not have that vibe. Have you seen any red flags yet?'

I think about the few dates we've been on, our messages and phone calls. 'No, none.'

'There you go,' Stevie says. 'Besides, sex isn't about experience or how good you are. Maybe she doesn't have a lot of experience either. Did you think of that?'

'She's had two decent-length relationships; that's two more than me.'

'That doesn't mean she's any good at them, and it doesn't matter anyway because every relationship is different.'

I huff out a weighty sigh, an attempt to rid my nervous system of the overwhelm of new emotions. 'I really like her, Stevie. I want this to work, but I'm scared she'll figure out that she can do better, that I've got zero to offer, or that I'm not this kind, thoughtful person she thinks I am. I'm really punching with her.'

'*Excuse* me?' Stevie says, her eyes wide. 'You are absolutely good enough for her and anyone would be lucky to be with you. Besides, Maya doesn't strike me as the sort of person who puts herself above people.' She pauses. 'She likes you, Callie. It's obvious to anyone with seeing eyes. She came here week after week to watch *you*. She introduced herself to *you*, even after you were too shy to speak to her. She's taken you out. She's come to amateur night with you. She went out with you today. She's invited you back to her place for dinner. She wants to be intimate with you. That means she likes you and wants to find out where this can go.'

'Oh. When you put it like that.'

Stevie watches me for a beat, then says, 'I don't think this is the case, but I'm going to ask anyway. She didn't pressure you to take things further?'

'No,' I say with a firm shake of my head. 'Nothing like that.

She was considerate and acted normal when I was anything but. I feel stupid for running off like that now.'

Stevie gives me a kind smile. 'You're not stupid. You're trying to figure this out because it's new for you.'

I could go back there. Get up right now and walk to Maya's, press the buzzer for Apartment 805 and say sorry, explain everything I've just explained to Stevie. But what makes sense in here doesn't always make sense out there. And Tom is nudging me, itching to come out. I skim the club. 'Pretty busy tonight. Since I'm here and you don't need bar staff, want me to do the end performance?'

'Yeah? You up for that? It'll save me doing it. My back's killing me at the moment.'

I laugh. 'You're getting way too old to be jumping on bars and throwing yourself on the stage.'

She grins. 'Hey, I'm only five years older than you.'

'I'll do it. Need to get rid of this frustration somehow.' I grab my drink and slip out of the booth. 'I'll let you know when I'm ready.'

In the dressing room, I flick through costumes on the rack and pull out a black suit with tearaway pants. An old act blooms in my mind and I smile – it's ideal for getting rid of pent-up sexual tension. I switch on some music, strip off my T-shirt and rifle through a drawer for a role of K tape. Apart from not wanting to waste tape or stick it to large areas of my skin for only one performance, this is an act where I love to blur the binaries, so I cover my nipples only. I cleanse and moisturise my face, then apply primer and foundation before filling out my brows with a black kohl pencil and creating a quick and dirty five o'clock shadow with a dark bronzer.

I don't have any of my own packers or straps here, but I do have plenty of socks, so I shove a few pairs into my underpants and adjust them as best I can. Next are the suit trousers, then double-sided clothes tape on each breast to keep my dress shirt in place. I fit a tie, keeping the knot loose, and don my usual brown, floppy-haired wig.

I check my reflection. My humiliation from earlier is gone, replaced by Tom's self-assuredness. I roll my neck, shake out my limbs, and do a few high knee jumps to warm myself up and test out the outfit. I search through my music app for the track I want, then run through the routine. It'll be rusty, but I'll figure it out better onstage. I message Stevie to let her know I'm ready and give her my song choice. She replies with an exclamation mark and three fire emojis, making me laugh.

As I wait in the wings, Stevie bounds onto the stage as the last amateur act finishes. 'Let's hear a round of applause for tonight's acts. What a great line up!'

The crowd cheers and I high-five the king who passes me on their way backstage.

'Keep that applause going,' Stevie continues, 'because one of Brissy's hottest kings just happened to stop by and offered to do a performance for you.' A lone whoop comes from the back of the club. Stevie laughs. 'That's the spirit. I hope you've all got a drink to cool yourselves down because this act is smokin'! Give it up for Tom Cruisin'!'

The haunting drum and bass intro of Billie Eilish's 'Bad Guy' thumps through the speakers, and I dance seductively across the stage. As the lyrics start, I slowly undo my tie, earning me a few appreciative whistles, and take my time unbuttoning my shirt while I lip-sync, throwing seductive looks to the crowd. I ignore the twinge of guilt flickering in my chest over Maya not being here to watch me, and turn on the performance charm.

I dance through the rest of the track, with impromptu moves that coordinate with the music, letting my shirt stay open but taped in place to cover my breasts. The song draws to a close and I grip the bottom of my trousers, waggling my brows suggestively. The audience cheers as I rip one trouser leg open from ankle to thigh, followed by the other side. I slip my thumbs into the waistband and raise my brows. They whoop and I hold my hand to my ear to encourage them to yell louder. The crowd obliges and on the final note of the song, I rip off the trousers, giving them a split second to ogle me in my jocks and open shirt before I dash off. I'd normally spend longer in my underpants, proudly strapped and packed, but the socks are loose and out of place.

I peer back through the curtain as Stevie takes to the stage, grinning and holding her hand up for calm. My body is thrumming. My head has cleared. I feel like me again. I button my shirt, slip on the trousers and head straight for the bar. A minute later Krissy places a large glass of iced water in front of me and I gulp it down, then wipe the sweat from my forehead with the back of my hand.

'I don't know what you're on tonight,' Krissy says as I tug off my wig and give my hair a ruffle. 'But we'll have some of that sass and sexiness on Saturday night, please. I've already had people asking if you're here this weekend.'

I grin. 'I forgot how much I like that one.'

Stevie jumps off the stage and comes over to me. 'Feel better?'

I nod. 'Loads.'

'You're going to call Maya?' she asks.

'I will. Just need to think about how to explain things.'

'You'll figure it out,' she says. 'And invite her to Krissy's party this weekend. We've got club cover, so it's definitely going ahead.'

She walks away and Amber approaches, eyeing me suspiciously. 'Didn't know you were performing tonight.'

I shrug. 'Neither did I. Just felt like it when I got here.'

'Right. Thought you were catching up with that woman you've been seeing,' she says. 'So where is she?'

I shoot her a look. I didn't tell her I was meeting Maya today, so she's been fishing. 'We did meet and now she's at home.'

Amber arches a sardonic brow. 'She's at home when you're here doing performances like *that*?'

'We have just met, Amber.'

'So it's nothing serious then?'

My brows pull together, puzzled as to how she's come to that conclusion.

She glances at her watch. 'I finish in fifteen, if you want to grab a drink, or' – she gives a casual shrug – 'come back to my place.'

I almost choke on my water. 'Seriously? You're propositioning me?'

She smiles coyly, as though she's mistaken my questioning tone for interest. 'I'm sure I'm not the only person in here who wants to take you home after watching that. It's what we do, isn't it?'

I give an incredulous scoff. 'No, Amber, it's not what we do. It's what we did – twice. And you weren't interested. What was it that you said after you'd slept with me the second time?' I glance up at the ceiling like I can't recall her cutting comment. 'That's right: "It's been fun, but I'm not looking for anything serious and you're kind of giving clingy right now. I can't deal."' I drop my gaze and glare at her.

Her cocky expression vanishes. 'I don't want to be serious with anyone, don't take it personally. That's how I felt at the time. I'm allowed to change my mind.'

'Ugh.' I shake my head. 'Why have you changed your mind? Because I've met someone I like?'

She stiffens. 'No.'

I take another gulp of water and stand, ready to walk away, but the opportunity to have the final, spiteful word is dangling in front of me, so I grab it. 'Well, you know what, Amber? I was only "giving clingy" because you were a rebound after Lacey destroyed me. I used you and I was trying to be kind because I'm not an arsehole.'

Her mouth drops open, a shocked scoff escaping.

I head backstage, a ripple of shame passing through me for being so harsh and saying something that wasn't entirely true. Amber was a rebound, yes, but I also kind of liked her, and pushing me away like that, especially after I'd just been so badly hurt, stung. Still, it doesn't give her the right to worm her way back in now and undermine what I have with someone else.

I lift my chin defiantly, grab my bag from the dressing room and jump in my car to drive home.

Chapter 13
Callie

The following morning, I pad into the kitchen at ten a.m., yawning. The house is quiet, Mum already having left for work. I make a coffee and take it out to our small patio that looks out onto the backyard. It's a warm, sunny day and the neighbour's dog peers at me through a gap in the fence, wagging his tail. 'Morning, Kobi,' I say, my voice still husky from sleep. I stretch my legs out, letting the sun warm my skin. He runs off, the doggy door swooshing a few seconds later as he goes back inside. I sip my coffee and gaze into the bottlebrush tree blooming in our garden. A lorikeet ducks its head, pecking at a flowering brush.

I need to call Maya, but I'm struggling to figure out how to explain myself without sounding like an emotionally immature adult who can't deal with social interactions or intimacy.

I lay awake for a good hour last night, thinking about yesterday's events. It was a shock to be reminded so vividly of my time with Lacey. But it was one incident in particular that swirled in my head – the day I saw her with someone else.

After two weeks of doting on me, love-bombing me with messages and compliments, I'd quickly come to trust Lacey and believed I'd potentially met the one. We had arranged to meet outside the theatre where we both worked, after she finished her shift. Except I was early and decided to go for a walk. As I rounded a corner into the street that ran parallel to the theatre, I spotted her. She was outside the side entrance, her arms wrapped around someone's waist, their lips locked. I ducked into a café, taking a seat to relieve my shaky legs, catching glimpses of them through the window. Was I imagining things? Someone who looked like her? How could that be the same person who'd lavished attention on me, who'd told me I was the one they'd been waiting for?

I still went to meet her, believing I'd find evidence that I was wrong. I raised it; she denied it. Asked me what she had supposedly been wearing. *A red T-shirt,* I had said. She smiled convincingly and said, 'Well, this shirt is black, isn't it? So it wasn't me.' I had nodded, despite knowing she would've likely changed her red work shirt before meeting me. We spent the night together, but she didn't speak to me for days afterwards, ignoring calls and messages. When she finally answered my call, her tone was cold, and I felt myself clutching for her, desperate for her attention again. I apologised for my oversight, pleaded with her to give me another chance. She came to me then, rewarded me with the attention I craved and I stupidly kept seeing her. But that day turned out to be just the start of the bad behaviour that I put up with for another six weeks, before I finally cut ties because I was losing my mind and all sense of self.

A couple of months after we finished, she had the audacity to come to the club, bringing someone with her who looked a lot like the person she was kissing that day. I had nothing to say to her and retreated backstage. Stevie was more than happy to deal with it and Lacey never returned. At least I had confirmation that I didn't imagine it.

I pull my phone from my pocket and stare at the screen. I can't let my bad experience with Lacey ruin what could be something amazing with Maya. I take a deep breath, scroll to Maya's number and hit the call icon.

After a few rings, she picks up. 'Hi, Callie.' Her tone is cool, not her usual jovial greeting.

My mouth turns dry. 'Hey. How are you?'

'Fine. Did you get home okay? I was worried with you rushing off like that.'

I close my eyes, the guilt thickening. 'I, erm, yeah, all good. I stopped in at the club for a little while first.'

The line falls silent, then, 'Right. Your mum must have been starving by the time you arrived home.'

I release a heavy sigh. I deserve that. 'I'm sorry, Maya, for running off like that. I was' – I pause, searching for a word that sums up the enormity of what I was experiencing – 'a bit overcome with, um, just overwhelmed, I guess.'

That dense silence again. 'Okay. Well, I'm sorry if I made you feel pressured.'

'You didn't,' I say quickly. 'It was nothing to do with you. It was me. I just, I don't know, something came over me and I had to go. I was pressuring myself.'

Now she sighs and I sense her defences lower. 'You could've talked to me, Callie, tried to explain,' she says, her voice softer. 'I wouldn't have been upset.'

'I get that now,' I say. 'But at the time, I couldn't think.'

'I didn't invite you here planning for anything to happen,' she says. 'It wasn't a ploy to get you into bed. We had a nice time and I wanted to spend more time with you, and after dinner, well, it happened and it felt right, so I went with it. But if you're not ready to take things further, that's alright.'

'It felt right to me, too,' I say. 'But then it didn't, and I should've tried to just breathe and talk to you. At your shop yesterday afternoon, too. I totally overreacted.'

She falls quiet again and I feel her drift away, second-guessing her interest, another person who can't cope with the reality of me. I hunt for something to fix this, for something I can offer her, and an idea pops into my head. 'Hey, are you free on Saturday night?'

She doesn't respond immediately and my pulse quickens, but then she says, 'I am.'

I let out a relieved breath. 'Why don't you come to the club early and hang out in the dressing room while I get ready?'

'The dressing room? I'm allowed to do that?' The vibrancy has returned to her voice and I feel like punching the air. 'I wouldn't be in your way?'

'Not at all.'

'What about the others? Don't they get ready in there, too?'

'We have two dressing rooms,' I say. 'Stevie and I share one and we stagger our dress times fairly well, so we don't have too much crossover. She might be in there briefly, but mostly I'm on my own.'

'I'd love that,' Maya says, then adds softly, 'I'd also really like to see you.'

I smile, the tightness in my gut easing. 'I'd like to see you too. Oh, and Krissy and Stevie are having a party at their place after the show for Krissy's birthday. They give themselves Saturday nights off for special occasions if they can get club cover. I'd love you to come, but if you're not keen, we could do something else?'

'That sounds like the best Saturday night I could ask for,' she says, and I can hear the smile in her voice.

Chapter 14
Maya

Callie met me at the front of the club as promised, with an enthusiastic smile and a tentative kiss.

I felt better after her phone call, but up until that point I had spent too much time overanalysing how things had gone so wrong so quickly after our date. And simmering underneath was an irritation that she'd run off rather than talk to me, once again. I had to seriously ask myself whether I wanted to embark on a relationship with someone who did that, who had done that for the third time in the very short space I'd known them. But my heart overruled my head, because the truth is I like her; I *really* like her. I like the way I feel a little bit breathless when I'm around her, the way my heart bounces around my chest when she kisses me, the way my skin bumps when her fingers brush mine, and the way she's renewed my faith in romance. Besides, none of us are perfect, despite my desire to be so. She gets overwhelmed – so what? We can deal with that. It's one con in an otherwise long list of pros.

Now I'm in the dressing room while Callie prepares for the

show. I didn't expect to walk into bona fide theatre dressing rooms, with racks of costumes, and dressing tables, and mirrors framed with radiant bulbs, and an array of different wigs. It's pure escapism, and I get why Callie loves it in here, why it's her sanctuary.

I watch curiously as she feathers the tip of a black kohl pencil through her eyebrows with artful strokes, giving the illusion of thickness. Next, she applies contouring cream from her ear along the hollow of her cheek, stopping mid-way, and repeats it on the other side. Then she draws a line from her inner eye down along her nose on both sides. The warm, earthy make-up tones, combined with the glow from the mirror lights, turn her eyes a deep green.

Callie side-eyes me as she continues contouring. 'Why are you staring at me?'

'Your eyes are such a pretty colour,' I say.

The corners of her mouth lift, and if she wasn't wearing thick foundation, I'd guarantee her cheeks would be pink.

I gesture to her face. 'Why do you contour like that?'

'To create a more masculine look.' She blends the cream, then turns to me. 'See how it makes my face look broader? And more angular?'

I lean back on my chair for a wider view. 'Huh, so it does.'

She picks up a small, textured sponge that resembles a mini kitchen scourer.

'What's that?' I ask as she clicks open a compact to reveal a dark creamy blush.

'It's a stipple sponge. They're great for creating stubble without sticking on fake hair and quicker than using a pencil. Cream blush washes off easier too, which is good for when I want to change here. Plus I hate the smell of the glue when sticking on facial hair.'

She holds the sponge out for me to feel. I run a fingertip over the surface and give it a gentle squeeze. It's coarse to the touch and bounces back after being pressed. I'm amazed that something so simple can create the effect of facial hair.

Callie presses it to the blush and pats it along her jawline. 'If I'm going straight home or plan to stay in drag after the show, I'll go a bit heavier with the make-up – bolder eye shadows, glitters, that sort of thing.' She repeats the action on the other side of her face, then pats her upper lip. She turns to me with a flourish. 'Ta-da. Tom's arrived.'

I'm fascinated by both the process and the transformation.

'Just need some finishing touches,' she says, using a soft brush to add bronzer from her hairline to meet the stubble. 'Sideburns,' she explains.

'It's an art form,' I say.

'Uh-huh. I think it took me longer to learn how to do my make-up than it did to come up with some routines.' She picks up a roll of tape. 'Time to get dressed.'

'Is that sports tape?' I ask.

'Kinesiology tape – better for movement and sweat. Sports tape is an option, but it's more restrictive. I've known a couple of people who've used duct tape but it can damage your skin. If you ever get into drag, don't use that,' she says casually.

My brows shoot up. 'If *I* ever get into drag? Why would you think that?'

She grins, giving me a look that suggests she knows something I don't. 'Because the questions you're asking are exactly the questions I asked Stevie when I was curious about it. Plus, you mentioned your interest in performing.'

I blink at her, taken aback. I've hinted to friends and family over the years about my desire to perform, but their lack of interest or belief in me meant I stopped talking about it and didn't try very hard to accomplish it. A few conversations with

Callie and she takes me seriously. 'Were you just curious or did you have a strong urge to perform?'

'Mmm...' She glances up briefly from cutting small squares of tape. 'There was something urging me to try it. I loved the idea of dressing up as someone completely different, rather than having a pressing desire to be onstage. But because kings don't draw big crowds, I felt like I could handle it.' She places the tape and scissors back in a drawer and says, 'I reckon you'd make a great king.'

My eyes widen. 'Do you?'

'Absolutely.' She stands, tugging on my hand to join her. She twirls me under her arm and pulls me close. 'You can dance. You've got rhythm. You'd have a magnetic stage presence.'

I kiss her, careful not to mess up her make-up. 'You're an amazing listener.'

She cups my face and returns the kiss. 'That's because you're very easy to listen to,' she says and steps away, picking up the squares of tape, bronzing powder and a large brush. 'Better finish getting ready, otherwise I'll have Stevie on my tail.'

She goes into the bathroom, and I step over to the clothes rack and flick through the hangers. There are suits in various colours, different fabrics and styles, jeans, dress shirts, tees, leathers. I run my hand up the sleeve of a watermelon pink jacket, the sequins cool against my palm, imagining what it must feel like to wear onstage. I move back to the dressing table, inspecting Callie's make-up, careful not to put my fingers on any brushes or sponges. My gaze lifts to my reflection and I pull my hair up, holding it in place as I examine my face, picturing myself made up as a king. My eyes move lower, over my fuller breasts, the curve of my waist and hips, my bronze sequined dress. Too feminine?

The bathroom door clicks open and I drop my hair and spin around.

Callie's changed into a pastel pink dress shirt, just long enough to cover her underwear. It's the first time I've seen her exposed skin in such close quarters. My eyes drop to the subtle curve of her thigh muscle, slide along the outline of her toned calf; the legs of someone who spends much of their time dancing. An unexpected image flashes in my mind: those legs wrapped around me ... slipping between mine ... casually slung over my shoulder. My body heats and when I lift my gaze, she's smiling. 'Your eyes are up there,' I say.

She laughs and opens a drawer, pulling out what I initially think is a strap but then realise it's too soft. 'I forgot this.'

I feel the colour rise in my cheeks. 'That's what you wear?'

'Yep, it's a silicone packer and it's soft.' She waves it to demonstrate. 'So it resembles the real thing.'

I clear my throat. 'Right. I haven't seen one before.'

She shrugs. 'Unless you're a drag king or wear them in your everyday life for whatever reason, or know someone who does, you'd have no reason to.' She disappears back into the bathroom.

I sit down before I collapse and take a gulp of water.

She's out in a few minutes, still trouser-less, but she's added white socks to her look.

I grin. '*Risky Business?*'

'You said it's your favourite.' She appraises herself in the mirror, her stance wider, her chin slightly raised, a sureness in her eyes. I like this version of her, the self-assuredness she carries in here. 'I'm ready.'

I stand, ready to leave, but Callie steps forward and wraps an arm around my waist, tugging me close and making me gasp.

'You in this dress...' She kisses me, then murmurs against my lips, 'I like you so much, Maya. I can't wait until later.'

It's a kiss loaded with promise and words I've been waiting to hear. But it also makes my head spin because I don't understand how she can go from the shy, anxious person who ran from a heated kiss to this assertive, assured performer who knows exactly what they want.

She releases me and touches up the make-up around her mouth. 'Are you okay if I include you in my final act? It's a new one.'

'Ooh, a new act. How do you want to include me?' I ask excitedly. She opens her mouth to answer but I hold a finger up. 'Actually, surprise me. I trust you.'

She grins. 'Okay, but I need to check that you're alright with me touching you while you're sitting in the audience.'

My brows rise, my body already tingling at the prospect. 'Touching me?'

'I don't mean' – she waves a hand over my torso – 'anything intimate. Just sitting on your lap and maybe a kiss? Only if you're comfortable with that. The audience loves the interactive stuff but I don't want to do that with anyone but you. We can ditch the kiss.'

She doesn't want to do that with anyone but me. She has no idea what a statement like that means. 'I'm fine with that, and don't you dare ditch the kiss.'

'Okay,' she says. 'But for the new act, I wear a strap, not a packer, so' – she points to her crotch – 'I'll be straddling you with a lot going on down there.'

I swallow. Hard. *Straddling?* 'That's all good.'

She beams at me. 'Awesome. But if it feels weird at any point, give me a signal.'

'Like what?'

'Erm...' She drums her fingers on the dressing table as she thinks. 'I don't know. I haven't done this before. Maybe tug on your ear?'

I do the action. 'Like that?'

'Yeah, and I'll stop straight away, okay? I don't want you to feel awkward or uncomfortable. I want it to be fun, and' – she scrunches her nose, the Callie-ness leaking out – 'I'm kind of going for sexy?'

My pulse quickens. 'I can handle sexy.'

Chapter 15
Maya

With my glass of wine in hand, I scan the club for a free seat, spotting one close to the stage. I weave my way through, soaking up the anticipation of the audience. As I sit, the stage lights come on, revealing a basic set furnished with a small coffee table and floor rug. Excitement bubbles in my belly; Tom Cruisin' doing the iconic scene from *Risky Business*.

Krissy opens the show, her infectious enthusiasm and natural warmth winning everyone over. She dashes off and the piano introduction to 'Old Time Rock and Roll' begins. Callie slides onto stage in white socks and the pink dress shirt, now fastened only at her navel. She's used bronzing powder to give the illusion of a six-pack, and her white Y-fronts are filled with the silicone packer. She skims the crowd, her eyes not landing on anyone until she finds me. She winks and starts to lip-sync, all cockiness and charisma, doing what she was born to do. The audience whoop when she drops to her knees, mimicking the action in the film, and I cheer along with them as fireworks explode in my stomach and oxytocin floods my brain.

Stevie is next, performing a duet with the not-so-amateur

king I watched a couple of weeks ago. They're both dressed as fresh-faced twentysomethings in baggy jeans, designer T-shirts and trainers, jumping around the stage in a coordinated fashion, lip-syncing to The Kid Laroi and Justin Bieber's 'Stay'. The energy extends to the crowd and everyone sings along.

The following act is Hairy Styles and it's hard to ignore the barb of jealousy that slices through me. Amber is good the way she commands the stage, making the crowd laugh with her improvised lyrics. I watch her closely, trying to push away the brittleness prickling inside me, but it's difficult to reconcile that person with the frosty version I was introduced to. But I suppose it's difficult to reconcile Callie's on and offstage personas too.

I grab myself another glass of wine and settle back for the rest of the show, including another two acts from Callie.

Almost an hour and a half after the show started, the club plunges into darkness and a spotlight tracks Krissy stepping across the stage. In the background, Callie's silhouette moves behind her. My skin prickles. She hasn't included me in any acts yet, so this must be it.

'Are you ready for your final act?' Krissy booms into the microphone.

The crowd, jubilant from alcohol, music and the earlier performances, responds with a rowdy cheer.

'I hope you've got some ice in those drinks to cool you down,' Krissy calls. 'You're going to need it! Welcome back to the stage, doing one of their hottest acts, Tom Cruisin'!'

The audience erupts as the distinctive introductory drum and bass to Billie Eilish's 'Bad Guy' pulses through the speakers. The spotlight shifts to reveal Callie dressed in a black suit straddling a chair, a sultry smile on her lips, a cocky lift of her brow. My flesh erupts in goosebumps, my simmering arousal peaking. The person to my right wolf-whistles and my head inflates a little, knowing I'll be the one leaving with Callie tonight.

Callie lifts herself from the chair and dances provocatively across the stage. My gaze drops to her crotch – definitely larger and stiffer than what she wears for her other acts. When my eyes return to her face, she's watching me as she slowly threads off the tie, then her penetrating green eyes move on to destroy other audience members. I let out a puff of air; it is suddenly far too warm in here. She unfastens the top button of her shirt, jogs down the three steps from the stage and runs the tie seductively across shoulders and faces. Then she's beside me, twirling her finger in the air for me to turn and face her.

Transfixed, I do as instructed. True to her word, she straddles me and guides my hand to the second button on her shirt, encouraging me to unfasten it with a waggle of her brows. She slings the tie behind my neck, using it to very gently nudge my head closer. Her mouth hovers over mine, the stiffness of the strap pressing against me in the most delicious way. A fire lights inside me, flames licking every cell. Tom's sultry look dissolves and Callie's kind eyes linger on mine.

'*Okay?*' she mouths.

I respond by pressing my lips to hers. Her tongue is sweet and hot, and the vibration of her groan moves through me. All sense of time disappears. I have no idea if it's seconds or hours that pass. All I know is that I've never felt this close to another human. My heart balloons, filling me with an ache I haven't experienced before.

Callie breaks the kiss and I'm sucked back to reality, head spinning, gasping for air. She's already gone, back to her performance. The crowd is delirious and I blink up at the stage as she rips her trouser leg open from ankle to thigh, then repeats it on the other side. She hooks her thumbs into the waistband and raises her brows questioningly, which is rewarded with a raucous cheer. The trousers are ripped off in perfect timing with the final 'huh' of the track, leaving her standing proud in an open shirt and tight white jocks straining over a stiff bulge. She bows, blows me a kiss and races off.

I cross my legs, snatch up my glass and gulp my wine.

'Oh my god, are you seeing Callie?' the person next to me asks.

'Oh, erm...' I'm not sure how to label a person who I only met three weeks ago, haven't yet slept with, but now can't imagine my life without.

Before I can elaborate, they say, 'I've been watching her since the club opened and I've *never* seen her kiss an audience member. I reckon everyone in here wishes that had been them.' They flash me a smile and leave the table with their friend.

I head to the bar to wait for Callie to change. The staff are frantic, tending to the after-show rush, darting around each other as they pour wine, mix cocktails and pull beers.

'Same again?' Krissy asks loudly over the music.

'Yes, please.'

'How're you feeling after *that?*' she asks as she pours me a glass of white wine.

'Like I need an ice bath.'

Krissy grins. 'That girl has got it bad for you.'

She's swift to move on to another customer, but before I can enjoy the swell of delight the statement brings, there's a brusque 'hello' behind me. I turn. It's Amber, already out of drag, her thick, auburn hair loose and brushing her shoulders.

I bristle but paste on a smile. 'Oh, hello. Amber, isn't it?' I say, going for friendly.

'That's right.' Her tone is cool. 'Did you enjoy that final act?'

'I did,' I say warily.

'Mmm. It's new, so it's good that Callie got some practice in Thursday night to iron out any issues.'

My stomach roils.

'She should be out soon,' she barrels on. 'She was caught up backstage.'

'Doing what?' I ask, my tone sharp. 'Getting changed?'

Amber smirks and wipes the corner of her mouth with a fingertip. 'Sometimes she needs help with that.'

A wave of nausea rolls through me, but she robs me of the chance to respond by walking away. *Thursday night.* Callie said she came in here before collecting her car, but she didn't say she performed, that she'd practised this act. My mind goes into overdrive, thinking about the shared dressing rooms with an adjoining bathroom. How easy it would be to do whatever they wanted in there. And just like that, my euphoria from this incredible night bursts.

I shrink a little, an overwhelming sense of not being worthy enough to be here, of not fitting in. I want to go home, leave Callie to her life, to whatever it is she has going on with Amber. But then Callie's face swims into my vision. The way she looks at me. The way she kisses me. Her comment that she didn't want to include anyone else in that act. Krissy's comment that Callie has it bad for me. All of that has to mean something. Dr Garcia's advice cuts through my thoughts – *focus on the facts.* The facts are that I have evidence Callie is interested and that Amber has an issue with me, so I need to give Callie the benefit of the doubt. Besides, when I arrived, she gave me the staff entrance code and told me to go backstage whenever I wanted to. She wouldn't have done that if she had anything to hide.

Almost half an hour passes before Callie appears, and she didn't respond to my message telling her I was at the bar and to let me know when she was on her way so I could buy her a drink.

'Sorry. Problem backstage,' Callie says. She leans in to kiss me but catches my cheek as I turn my head.

'I know,' I say, more stiffly than I anticipated. 'Your friend Amber told me.'

Callie's brows furrow. 'Amber?'

I look at her properly now, searching for clues that Amber might have been telling the truth, but all I see is genuine confusion. The tightness in my chest eases, and I soften my tone, but three wines in, my tongue is loose. 'She said you needed help getting changed. Then she wiped her mouth?' I phrase it as a question so that it doesn't sound like an accusation. I decide not to mention the comment about Thursday night right now. I don't want Callie to feel like I'm monitoring her or have an issue with where she goes or what she does, particularly not this soon, but I need to raise part of what Amber said because I don't want to get in deep with someone only to discover, once again, they have feelings for a friend.

Callie shoots Amber a dark look. 'I passed her in the corridor but that was it. I was helping Stevie with a sound tech issue. Didn't you hear that the music was off?' She considers me for a beat, eyes skimming my face as though she's trying to figure out what I need from her. 'Sorry I didn't reply to your message. I only checked my phone as I was walking out here.'

I shake my head, embarrassed for raising it. It's obvious Callie is telling the truth. 'No, I'm sorry. But why would she say that?'

Callie throws Amber another look. 'Ignore her. She says stupid shit all the time.' She reaches for my hand, her expression brightening. 'What did you think of the show?'

I'm shaken that Amber would lie like that, but I want to trust Callie and I want to enjoy this night together, so I smile and say, 'Fantastic.'

'Did I go too far with including you in that last act?'

'I didn't want to tug on my ear, put it that way,' I say.

She laughs. 'Good.'

My eyes drift to Amber. I'm not a game player when it comes to relationships, but she's triggered me and a petty urge rises. I step closer to Callie, wrapping my arms around her waist. 'Apparently you never kiss audience members during your performances.'

Callie shakes her head slowly. 'No. I do not.'

'Well, I think that makes me the luckiest person in here.'

She dips her head shyly, an adorably modest smile on her lips.

'You're incredible up there,' I say. 'You know that?'

'I'm not sure about that, but I try my best. Have I inspired you to give it a go?'

My brows shoot up. 'It? You mean drag?'

'Yeah.'

'Oh.' I look at the stage, my heart urging me to say yes, but my head telling me to stay in my lane. 'I'm not sure...'

'I could give you private lessons,' Callie says, her arms tightening around me.

I shift my gaze back to her. 'Private lessons?'

'Uh-huh. The perks of dating a drag king.'

I nod slowly, liking the sound of that. 'The perks of dating a drag king,' I repeat.

'Yep. Can I kiss you now?'

I tilt my face up and let her lovely mouth fall onto mine.

Chapter 16
Maya

When we arrive at Krissy and Stevie's, the party has already started. Guests are gathered in the open-plan living space and others fill the back patio that leads to a spacious yard and a sizeable pool enclosed in a glass fence. There are hugs and *happy birthdays*, and Stevie introduces me to those within earshot, including Krissy's older sister and younger brother who organised the party.

Callie points to a large L-shaped couch across the room. 'If you grab that seat for us, I'll get some drinks.'

'Sure,' I say and move over to the lounge.

As I sink into the couch, my dress rides up my thighs and I self-consciously tug it down. Only now as I pause among the flurry of activity do I notice how stunning this house is. Outside, it looks like every other low-set brick home on a suburban street, but in here it's bold industrial design, the same style as the club. Sharp, metallic surfaces, muted stone tiles, natural fibre rugs and furnishings, steel-framed light fittings, and industrial-size ceiling fans whirring on low speed. On the wall to my right is a large canvas. I immediately recognise the people in the photo as Stevie and Callie's alter egos. They're onstage together, Stevie's head tilted back slightly, mouth open wide mid-song. Callie's feet are off the ground, her arms in the air, her skin glistening with sweat.

I'm distracted by a couple asking if the other end of the couch is free.

'All yours,' I say as Callie approaches with our drinks.

She breaks into a smile when she sees the couple. 'Hey, you two. Didn't know you'd be here.' Callie hands me a glass of wine and takes the spot beside me. Placing a hand on my thigh, she says, 'This is Maya. Maya, this is Amy and Caz.'

'Hi, Maya,' they both say.

The one with the short, blunt bob called Caz glances at Callie's hand on my leg. 'Stevie didn't mention you were off the market, Callie. There'll be some broken hearts at Club Sappho.' A fond smile accompanies the comment.

Callie chuckles but a blush blooms on her cheeks. I know she'll feel awkward about people assuming the status of our relationship this soon, and the wine I've already drunk at the club is muting my inhibitions, so I jump in. 'This is very new, but we're' – I look at Callie – 'seeing each other.'

Callie gazes at me, her eyes soft, a small smile on her lips. She turns back to Amy and Caz. 'Yeah, we're seeing each other.'

'Aww,' the other half of the couple, Amy, says. 'New love. So romantic.'

Callie and I exchange a glance, that tiny little L word now dancing between us.

'Old love is romantic, too,' Caz says, running a strand of Amy's long, chestnut-coloured hair through loving fingers.

Amy responds by kissing Caz on the mouth. It's intimate and familiar, the kiss of two people who are connected on a soul level. An ache expands in my chest, a yearning for what they have, a longing to be kissing the woman I love, the person I've spent years building a life with.

'Is that wine okay?' Callie asks, drawing my attention back to her. 'It's not very cold. I can put some ice in it, if you like?'

'It's good, thanks,' I say, watching Amy and Caz as they move from the couch to the kitchen. 'Your friends look like they've been together a while, plus the "old love" comment.'

Callie nods. 'Yeah, a couple of years now, I think. They've known each other for forever, though.'

There's activity at the front door and my grip tightens around the stem of my glass when Amber walks in. I slug my wine, my inhibitions unmuting and making me feel unsettled by her presence and out of place among a group of people who all appear to be the best of friends.

'Are you okay?' Callie asks.

I force a smile. 'Yes. Why do you ask?'

She tips her head, eyes searching my face. 'You seem a bit anxious or something?'

'Oh, sorry,' I say, with a small shake of my head. 'All of this is just new for me.'

'Parties?'

'Well, no, not parties, although it's been a while since I've been to a house party. More being around so many new people.'

She nods. 'I get that. It can be a bit much sometimes. We can leave, if you like?'

'No,' I say. 'I want to be here and I want to spend time with you.'

'I want that, too.' She stands and pulls me to my feet. 'Come on. You've already met Amy and Caz. There's only one way for the others not to be strangers and that's to talk to them.'

Callie leads me over to the kitchen, not releasing my hand for a second. She introduces me to her friends and colleagues and to Stevie's siblings, who have just arrived. Everyone is welcoming and the tension in my body starts to ease.

As we move around the party over the course of the night, Callie's hand is always linked with mine or pressed to the small of my back, making it clear we're together, making me part of her world. She includes me in conversations, tops up my glass and fetches me finger food. She only leaves my side to use the bathroom and only if I have someone to talk to while she's gone. We dance, we drink, we kiss. The one person we don't spend time with is Amber, and Callie is quick to whisk me away whenever she's close. I like to think it's because of the lie Amber told me earlier, but the unease in the pit of my stomach tells me otherwise.

Eventually, I drop back onto the couch, kicking off my shoes and sinking my bare feet into the soft rug.

Callie hands me a tall tumbler. 'I got you some water.'

'Water?' I make a face. 'Thanks, but I'm good with wine.' I take a sip to prove my point and my eyes drift to Amber. She's leaning against the kitchen bench, her arm draped over the attractive brunette she arrived with. 'I don't think your friend likes me.'

Confusion crosses Callie's face, then she follows my gaze. 'Amber? She doesn't know you.'

'No, but the two times we've briefly spoken she hasn't been friendly, and that comment tonight when I was waiting for you was strange.'

Callie frowns and gives a nod of assent. 'Yeah, it was.'

I keep my voice low. 'I get the sense she's jealous or something?'

'I doubt that's it,' she says.

But the pink flush on her face makes my gut twist. I've had enough alcohol now that I can't stop the words spilling. 'Have you two had a thing? I mean, I know you said you hadn't had a girlfriend but I'm not sure what that means.'

Callie makes an odd sound, a kind of short, dismissive laugh. 'Why are we talking about her?'

I shrug. 'I'm interested.'

She huffs a little and for the first time since we've met, I sense a sliver of annoyance directed towards me. It's different to the irritation she displayed in the club earlier – that was at Amber. But this, the dip in her mood, the darkening of her eyes as she looks at me – it's aimed at me. 'It means what it means,' she says crisply. 'I *haven't* had a girlfriend.'

I should let this go, not paint myself as irrational and possessive, because I'm not irrational and possessive. But I am drunk, and I've been burned before by a partner and their close friend, been told it's nothing, and I won't ever put myself in that position again. 'Okay, but you had that toxicship,' I say. 'And you've dated and slept with people.'

She sighs. 'We went out a couple of times, that's all.'

I sip my drink, trying to wash away the jealously. 'So on a few dates or something?'

'Or something,' she says, with a shrug.

I don't know why, but the shrug irks me. Like this thing that feels so huge to me is nothing to her, and it makes me push harder. I swirl the wine around my glass. 'So you just went out, nothing else...'

Her mouth presses into a tight line and her eyes search mine. 'Are you asking if we've slept together? Do you really want to know that?'

The question causes my defences to crumble and I deflate a little. 'It might explain why she's cold towards me,' I say, my tone less accusatory. 'It's important to me that we're honest with each other.'

Callie's expression softens. She takes my glass, places it on the coffee table and grasps my hands. 'What I told you the other night is the truth. I've never been with anyone long enough to call it a relationship. But I've been out with people and I've hooked up with people, and since you asked, and you want us to be honest, then yes, Amber is one of those people.'

My heart shrivels. I can't understand how Callie was able to randomly sleep with Amber but couldn't be in the same room as me after a heated kiss.

'That was a while ago,' she continues. 'I'm not interested in her. It's just something that happened. She was there. I was lonely and struggling after what happened with Lacey.'

Questions crowd my head. *How did it happen? Does 'a while ago' mean one month or one year? Was it a quick, one-off drunken fumble or passionate, intimate sex many times?* And the most pressing question – *did Callie want more?* But even through my inebriation, I sense I've gone too far, pushed too hard, and it's not the time to throw in a casual, *She also said you practised the strip tease on Thursday night. You know, the night you couldn't kiss me but apparently could take your clothes off for an audience.* I inwardly sigh, exhausted by my own brain. Of course Callie had a sex life before meeting me, just like I had a sex life before meeting her.

'I think she's interested in you, though,' I say, offering an apologetic smile, hoping it will cut through the tension that's thickened between us.

She tucks a strand of hair behind my ear and runs her fingertips along the length of my dangly earring. 'What she said to you was just Amber being Amber. She's intense and pushes people's buttons. That doesn't make it okay and I'll be calling her out on it.' She hooks her finger under my chin, gently tilting my face upward to kiss me. 'I want to be here with you.' She gestures across the room. 'And we told Amy and Caz we're seeing each other, so how about we focus on that? On us?'

My shoulders slump. 'I'm sorry. I have no right to question you on any of that. It's none of my business.'

She gives me a genuine smile, all traces of her earlier irritation gone. 'It's nice that you care so much, and I'd be the same if it was the other way around or if I had to meet your exes. Especially that one who left you,' she says with a dramatic roll of her eyes.

I grin, grateful for her attempt to make me feel better about my unreasonable interrogation. 'Well, you'll never meet either of them. We didn't stay friends.' I retrieve my wine glass and take a gulp, then blurt, 'I've drifted apart from all my friends. I had nothing in common with them, and I'm always on edge when I'm with my family.' The sentence is disjointed, two unrelated matters squished together, but the room is starting to spin, and less and less is making sense. Still, I continue, 'My parents expect so much from me. I have to be the perfect daughter, be a role model for my younger sisters, do the right thing, say the right thing, be what society expects me to be.' I'm vaguely aware that I'm exaggerating.

Callie shifts on the couch, listening intently.

'Mum hassles me about finding someone, settling down, having a family, a career. It gets worse as I get older.'

Callie's brows crease. 'Having a family? Does she mean with a man?'

I nod.

Surprise flickers across her face. 'They don't know you're gay? Or however you label yourself.'

'No,' I say. 'My sisters know but I've never spoken to my parents about it. They didn't meet my exes. That was part of the problem. Arianne, the one I lived with, didn't like that I wasn't open with Mum and Dad. She always whinged about it to her best friend. The best friend she left me for.'

'I'm sorry that's your experience,' Callie says with a frown.

I shrug. 'That's life, hey? I was going to tell my parents. I had my speech all worked out. But I didn't do it and Arianne never forgave me for that. Next thing, she's sleeping with someone else.'

'She never *forgave* you?' Callie says. 'That's harsh. It's not easy for some people to tell their parents.'

'No, and I've struggled with it. You'd think Mum and Dad would've worked it out by now, though, since I've never had a boyfriend.'

'People make assumptions when it comes to sexuality,' Callie says. 'They believe what they want, judge by looks, how people behave.'

I nod. 'Yep. I get the "but you don't look like a lesbian" line all the time. What does that even mean? Because I wear dresses and make-up and have long hair and fit a stereotypical gender type? Because I *look* like a woman I can't be a lesbian?' I frown. 'But maybe they're right. Maybe I'm not gay enough. I never feel like I'm gay enough for people, you know?'

Callie shakes her head. 'There's no such thing as not being gay enough, Maya. You can dress how you want, look how you want, label yourself however you like. It's not up to other people; it's up to you. Knowing you're a lesbian makes you gay enough. It's not something you have to justify or prove to the world. You don't even need to tell anyone if you don't want to.'

I give her a grateful smile. 'My parents are right about one thing, though. I do want to find someone and build a life. It's just that my vision doesn't match theirs, and I feel like I'll let them down when they eventually find out.' My words have started to slur. I put a hand to my head, my vision becoming unfocused, and attempt to stand. 'I'm dizzy.'

Callie jumps up and slips an arm around my waist. 'Come on. I'll get you some water and some space.'

She leads me away to a quiet, dark room and switches on a

lamp beside the bed. I fall back onto a soft mattress. Through my drunken haze, I watch her open a window and roll down a blind. She switches on the ceiling fan and the warm air in the room circulates.

'I'll be back in a sec,' she says.

''Kay,' I say, squinting against the lamplight. My eyes close. Voices and laughter from the backyard float through the window. My head spins, so I open my eyes and place a foot on the floor to ground myself.

Callie returns and sits on the edge of the bed.

'I've had too much to drink and I've said too much,' I slur.

'You haven't said too much, but you probably have had too much to drink.' She hands me a large glass of water. 'Here. Drink this. All of it.'

I sit up and drain the glass, then lunge at her, catching her mouth. We share a brief, messy kiss before she pulls away.

I stare at her confused. 'You don't want to ... with me?'

'I do want to, so bad,' she says, brushing the hair from my face. 'But we've both had a lot to drink, and I want our first time to be special, and for us to be alone. Don't you?'

I frown, but even in this state, I know she's right. 'Can we cuddle at least?'

She smiles. 'We can do that. Let me get you something to sleep in. You can't sleep in that dress.' She hops up and opens a drawer, then hands me a folded T-shirt.

'Can't move,' I say.

'You just need to take your dress off and put this on. I'll turn away.'

'Callie, I can't. You'll have to help me. I've got a bra and undies on. It's no different to a bikini.'

'Alright, but I'll turn the light out.'

'Callie!'

'Okay, okay.'

I swing my legs off the bed and she helps me stand. I stick my arms up to let her remove my dress, which she does, then carefully lays it over the back of a chair. She faces me, fully dressed while I'm in my underwear, respectfully keeping her eyes on mine.

I give her a drunken smile. 'Sorry I ruined our night.'

She kisses me softly. 'You didn't. I had a great time.' She slips the T-shirt over my head and I manage to get my arms into the sleeves. Then she helps me back into bed.

My eyelids start to droop as she removes her shoes and jeans and crawls in beside me.

'Can you hold me?' I ask.

She slips her arm around me and I nestle into her side, breathing her in. 'You smell so good,' I say. But I'm asleep before she can reply.

Chapter 17
Callie

As I wake, a faint stench of stale alcohol fills my nostrils, and I blink at a wardrobe door that's not part of my bedroom. Beyond the door, there are muffled voices, the clatter of dishes and the whirr of a coffee machine. It slowly dawns on me where I am and I roll over, my heart swelling. Maya's still asleep, her thick waves of hair splayed across the pillow, her breaths slow and steady.

As much as I want to lie here reliving the sensation of her body pressed against mine, my bladder and primal need for morning caffeine urge me to rise. I slip out of bed, pull my jeans on and close the door behind me with a soft click.

After the bathroom, I head for the kitchen. 'Morning,' I say to Krissy and Stevie, making a beeline for the coffee machine. They're sitting at the table nursing mugs, with messy bed hair, eyelids heavy with tiredness and both still in pyjamas. 'You two are up early.'

'I've been up for at least an hour,' Krissy groans. 'I can never sleep in after I've had too much to drink.'

'And I feel guilty for staying in bed without her.' Stevie lays her head on Krissy's shoulder. 'So I'm up in solidarity.'

'The best wife,' Krissy says, kissing the top of Stevie's head.

I down a glass of water, then gaze out the open window as my cup fills, listening to the sounds of Sunday morning – the lazy caw of a crow, the buzz of a lawnmower, the hum of the ceiling fan, kids splashing in the pool next door, distant traffic moving along the Gateway.

'Did you sleep okay?' Krissy asks, pulling me back to the conversation. 'That mattress is a bit lumpy.'

'I had that much to drink, I could've slept anywhere,' I say, splashing milk in my coffee and joining them at the table. 'Maya was asleep in seconds and I wasn't far behind her.' I take a sip, glancing outside at the sun shimmering across the surface of the pool water, reliving those moments after she fell asleep. *Not far behind* was probably a good ten minutes of listening to her slow, deep breaths, inhaling the scent of her perfume, relishing the feel of her soft skin against mine. When I look back at them, they're both grinning at me. 'What?' I touch a hand to my head. 'My hair a mess?'

'You've got it bad,' Stevie says.

'Got what bad?' I ask, genuinely confused.

'Maya,' Krissy says.

I make a face. 'I don't think I've got it *bad*.'

'Oh, you do,' Krissy says, brushing a strand of dark hair out of her eyes.

I bite my bottom lip to suppress my smile. I'm not sure what having it bad feels like, at least not in a healthy, functional way. All I know is that while it's scary, it also feels right.

'She looked like she enjoyed herself,' Stevie says.

'Yeah, I think so.' I lower my voice. 'But she asked about Amber and I didn't want to lie.'

Stevie winces. 'How did you get on to that topic?'

I shake my head with an exasperated sigh. 'Apparently when Maya was waiting for me after the show, Amber said something to her about helping me get changed?'

'What?' Krissy says. 'Why does she do shit like that?'

I shrug. 'Who knows, but it was enough for Maya to ask questions.'

'Hmm,' Stevie muses. 'Amber's clearly jealous.'

I swallow my mouthful of coffee. 'Jealous? She wasn't interested when we hooked up and now she's jealous? Make it make sense.'

'I think she was interested,' Krissy says. 'She just played it cool like she always does, and now it's too late.'

Stevie nods. 'Yep. Agreed.'

I roll my eyes. 'Well, whatever it is, she needs to back off.'

The toilet flushes at the other end of the house and a minute later, Maya appears in the doorway.

'Hi,' she says in a hoarse voice. She's still in Krissy's T-shirt, which falls to her mid-thigh. Her hair is tousled and her face is crumpled with sleep. She looks beautiful and a yearning to see her wake up every morning rises in me.

'Hey,' I say, walking over to her. 'How do you feel?'

She blinks at me, black mascara smudged under her eyes. 'I've felt better.'

I'm unaccustomed to situations like this but she looks like she could use a hug, so I edge closer and open my arms.

She steps forward, pressing her face into my neck, just like I imagined the first time I walked her home. A contented sigh travels through my body. Who would've thought a morning hug from someone I'm dating would be so comforting?

'Would you like something to eat, Maya?' Krissy asks from across the kitchen. 'I'm about to cook brunch.'

Maya loosens her grip on me. 'That sounds good. I don't think I ate much last night.'

I take her hand and lead her to the table, pulling out a chair for her. The bottles and dirty glasses from last night have already been cleared away, replaced by mugs, phones and headache pills.

'Here you go, Maya. Reckon you might need this.' Stevie places a coffee, a large glass of water and two paracetamols on the table, then takes away a couple of dirty dishes.

'Thank you.' Maya pops the tablets in her mouth and drains the entire glass of water. She glances between the three of us, her forehead crinkled with worry. 'I don't know why I drank so much. I usually stop after a few, but I drank at the club and then here. I probably should've eaten something more substantial, too.'

'I was pretty drunk myself,' I say.

'I was completely smashed,' Stevie says.

'Everyone was,' Krissy says. 'You should've seen how messy everyone got after you two went to bed.'

Messy is probably an exaggeration, but I appreciate them trying to make Maya feel better. 'See?' I say to Maya. 'You weren't the only one.'

She nods, but the worry crease doesn't smooth out. I sense she'll beat herself up about this for days. I give her hand a reassuring squeeze and hop up to help Krissy make brunch.

We make soft poached eggs, crispy bacon and fried halloumi served with buttered toast made from grain sourdough. As we eat, we chat about the party and the show beforehand. Maya is quiet, slowly eating and sipping her coffee, but she brightens when we ask her opinion of the show and her cheeks turn rosy when she enthuses about my final performance. Almost an hour passes before Stevie and Krissy go to shower and change, and Maya and I tidy up.

'I'm working this arvo,' I say to Maya as I rinse dishes. 'You can come and hang out with me at the club, if you like. Have some of those lessons.'

'Lessons?' She looks over at me from the table, confused. 'Oh,' she says, waving a finger at me, the comment landing. 'The perks of dating a drag king.'

I smile. 'It's a good perk.'

'It is,' she says, hopping up and bringing the remaining dishes to the sink. 'You still want to spend time with me after last night?'

'Erm ... yes. Why wouldn't I?'

She shrugs. 'Rambling about my parents and hiding my sexuality, and' – she closes her eyes briefly, releasing a remorseful sigh – 'quizzing you about Amber. I am *so* sorry. I had no right to do that.'

'You weren't rambling,' I say. 'You were telling me about your life and I was interested. And I don't mind you asking questions about my past. It's not like I didn't jump to conclusions when I saw you with Bella in the shop. Plus, Amber saying that to you wasn't cool; of course it made you ask questions, especially after, well, what you told me happened with your ex.'

She lets out a relieved breath. 'Thank you for being so understanding. And for being honest with me.'

'Honesty is important to me, too, and people talk about their lives when they're' – I pause, hoping that the label she gave us last night wasn't the alcohol talking – 'seeing each other, don't they?'

Her face brightens. 'They do. You're being very reasonable and kind about this.'

'And you're being too hard on yourself.'

'Yep,' she says with a slow nod. 'And to answer your question, I would love to spend the afternoon with you, only if I wouldn't be in your way?'

My heart lifts. 'You won't be in my way. But you will be in a dark club with no windows instead of out in that,' I say, pointing out the window at the brilliant blue sky.

She glances outside, squinting against the daylight. 'Darkness sounds good today. My eyeballs hurt. I'll go home first, though. I need more sleep, and' – she looks down at herself – 'my own clothes.' She reaches for my hand. 'Thank you for looking after me last night.' A blush spreads over her cheeks. 'And having the sense not to take things further.'

I give a small smile. 'I don't think either of us were in a state to enjoy it.'

'Agreed, and I probably would've thrown up or passed out.'

My eyes widen. 'Oh, thanks.'

She giggles. 'Nooo. I didn't mean that. I meant from movement.'

I grin. 'I know what you meant. I just wanted to make you smile.'

She gazes at me, her eyes softening. 'You always make me smile.'

It's the simplest statement, but emotion edges up my throat, causing my eyes to sting.

Maya gestures to the bedroom. 'I should get changed and get home, let the three of you get on with your day.'

I nod and clear my throat. 'We can get a lift back to my place and I can drive you home?'

Maya opens her mouth to respond, but Krissy walks in and says, 'I'm heading into the Valley in about ten if you want a lift home, Maya?'

'Oh, are you sure?' Maya says. 'You can drop me at a train if it's easier.'

'It's no problem. You live near the club, right?'

'I do. Thanks, Krissy. I'll just get changed.'

She heads off to the bedroom, and I finish wiping down the

benches, then go to grab my shoes, socks and phone from the spare room while Maya is in the bathroom. I'm back in the kitchen when she reappears, wearing her shimmery bronze dress and sandals, huffing at her phone.

'Everything okay?' I ask.

She looks up. 'Oh, it's Mum, hassling me about Dad's building awards dinner. It's not until the end of the month, but they need numbers and I kind of have to go.'

'Don't you want to?' I ask.

'It's not that I don't want to. I want to support Dad, but it's just the expectation that I'll be there. They don't ever ask if I have anything else on or whether I even want to go.' She shakes her head. 'They're trying to make it more enticing by saying it's free alcohol and we can each bring someone.' She taps her screen, then pauses and looks up at me. 'I-I don't suppose you'd like to come?'

My brows shoot up. 'Me? To a building awards dinner? With your family?'

Her face falls, red blotches blooming on her cheeks, and her gaze drops back to her phone. 'Sorry. I … it doesn't matter.'

I cringe. *Very mature.* 'I'll go,' I say, ignoring the clench in my gut. 'Sorry, that wasn't the right way to respond. If you'd like me there, then of course I'll go. I was just surprised because last night you mentioned that your parents don't know about your sexuality, and you hadn't introduced them to your previous girlfriends.' My face warms. 'Not that I'm assuming I'm your girlfriend,' I add quickly. 'I meant that you hadn't introduced—'

'It's okay,' Maya says. 'You're right, that is confusing.' She tilts her head, contemplative. 'And since you said the word, I like the idea of *girlfriend*.'

My stomach swoops. 'You do?'

She nods. 'Yeah, I do.'

'So ... I'm your girlfriend?' I ask tentatively. 'And you're mine?' I groan and bury my face in my hands. 'Oh my god. Of course you're mine if I'm yours, otherwise a one-sided girlfriend arrangement would be a very unhealthy situation.'

She removes my hands from my face, chuckling. 'Yes, and I'm yours.' Her nose wrinkles. 'It's not too soon for the G word, is it? We've been dating for almost a month and I'm not interested in anyone else.'

She's not interested in anyone else. The idea makes me swoon. 'I don't think it's too soon, not that I'm across girlfriend protocol.' I pause. 'I've never had a girlfriend before. Not a nice one anyway.'

She kisses me. 'I'm honoured to be your first *nice* girlfriend.'

Honoured. She is honoured to be *my* girlfriend.

She steps back and takes a deep breath, lifting her chin with a determined air. 'And maybe it's time I told my parents. I'm an adult. I can be with whomever I choose.'

'Are you sure?' I ask. 'That's big and sometimes it's easier said than done.'

She frowns, her shoulders slumping. 'I know, but I've wanted to tell them for so long and this is a good opportunity. Anyway...' She shakes her head as though she's dislodging the thought. 'That's too heavy for a Sunday morning when I'm feeling ordinary. What time do you need to be at work?'

'Around two for a delivery.'

'Sorry, Maya,' Krissy says as she walks in. 'Ready now.'

Maya picks up her bag from the kitchen counter and says to me, 'See you around three?'

'Three's good,' I say.

She kisses me goodbye and leaves with Krissy.

I'm about to call out to Stevie when she appears. 'Want a lift home, Romeo? I need to duck down to the shops.'

'Please.'

As we jump into her SUV, she says, 'Things seem to be going very smoothly with Maya. She's really into you.'

It scares me how much I like Maya, and I can't quite get my head around this beautiful, intelligent woman being into me. 'I hope she keeps being into me.'

Stevie glances at me. 'Why wouldn't she? You're a catch.'

I shrug. 'I don't exactly have a great track record of things working out with people I like. I don't have *any* record.'

'That's because you haven't met the right one,' Stevie says. 'Maya's different.'

'You think so?'

Stevie nods. 'Yep. No question.'

'She asked me to go to her Dad's building awards dinner at the end of the month.'

'Wow. I hope you said yes.'

I nod. 'I did. The idea petrifies me but I didn't want to let her down. One little problem, though, her parents don't know.'

'About you?'

'About her sexuality.'

Stevie stops at a red light and looks at me, brows raised. 'Shit. Is she planning to tell them before the awards dinner? 'Cause that might be a little awkward.'

'She mentioned it, but I think it's hard for her. She said some other stuff last night, about not feeling gay enough and people always assuming she's straight because of how she looks.'

Stevie grimaces as she accelerates. 'Oops. I did that too, didn't I?'

'Yes, Stevie, you did, didn't you?' I twist in my seat, giving her a pointed look. 'You did,' I repeat emphatically.

'Sorry. That's only because we get heaps of straight people in the club, and plenty of these' – she takes her hands off the wheel for a split second to do air quotes – '"straight" people hook up with queer people. But I shouldn't have made that assumption, especially given her interest in you was obvious.'

'Mmm, I suppose I'll forgive you.' After a beat, I say, 'She called me her girlfriend earlier. I mean, it was after I accidentally called her mine.'

Stevie grins. 'Aww, you're finally someone's hot, sexy girlfriend.'

I laugh. 'Well, she didn't use any adjectives to describe what type of girlfriend I am.'

'I'm happy for you, Cal. If anyone deserves a beautiful, loving relationship, it's you.' She nods sagely. 'I've got a feeling about this one.'

I gaze out the window. I've got a feeling about this one, too.

Chapter 18
Maya

Callie opens the heavy wooden door of Club Sappho and greets me with a warm smile. The mid-afternoon sun falls across her face in a golden shadow, highlighting the tiny hazel flecks in her green eyes, the dusting of freckles across her sharp cheekbones, and the soft pout of her mouth. Her hair isn't styled in its usual moulded, upright fashion. Instead, it's straight, glossy black and swept across her forehead.

'Hello,' she says. 'Why are you looking at me like that?'

'Because you're so lovely to look at,' I reply.

She drops her gaze with an adorably humble smile, and steps aside to let me pass. 'Come on.'

I follow her through the entrance and into the club. The lights are dimmed throughout, apart from over the bar where a row of pendants shine brightly. 'Do you often hang out at the club on your own?'

'I do. There's something about the solitude I like.' She slips behind the bar, scoops ice into two pint glasses and fills them with soda water and lemon slices. She passes one to me. 'Did you sleep?'

I nod as I take a gulp, my body still craving fluids. 'Mm-hmm. For a couple of hours.'

'Feel better?'

'Physically, yes. Mentally' – I shake my head – 'ugh. I hope I didn't embarrass you.'

Callie's brows pull together and she comes around to the other side of the bar, taking the stool next to me. 'You didn't embarrass me or yourself. We had a great time. I don't know what happens at parties with your friends, but with mine, as long as you're not an arsehole, they don't care. And you certainly weren't an arsehole.'

'Well, not being an arsehole is good,' I say. 'I'll take solace in that.'

'You're an overthinker, hey?' she says.

'Ha, an understatement. I've been seeing a psychologist and we talk about it a lot. She's given me some exercises and coping strategies. I'm not great at remembering to do them, though.'

Callie cocks her head quizzically. 'You go to therapy?'

'Uh-huh. Not for anything traumatic, just ... stuff. Over-thinking, perfectionism, sexuality, nothing major.' Guilt rises in me that my privilege gives me access to a therapist to talk about overthinking. 'It's through my dad's work so it costs me next to nothing,' I justify, but then regret it because now I sound like a spoilt brat who can't stand on her own two feet.

'But those things *are* major,' Callie says. 'If they affect you and the way you live your life, then they're major, especially feelings around your sexuality. That's huge.'

I stare at her. *God, this woman.* 'Thank you. You probably think I can't do anything without my parents' financial assistance.'

She shrugs. 'Milk it, I say. The cost of living in this country is extortionate so if we can get financial help from our parents then why not? My mum means the world to me but it's not the reason I live at home. I get cheaper living expenses and she gets help with the bills.' Callie sips her drink and says matter-of-factly, 'I've also had mental health help through Mum's work, so we're not that different.'

'You've seen a therapist?'

She nods.

'Can I ask what for?' I say tentatively. 'Also okay if you don't want to talk about it.'

'I'm okay talking about it. It was for anxiety and messed-up head stuff after the situationship.'

'Shit, Callie,' I say. 'It was that bad you needed a professional afterwards?'

Callie's face clouds. 'For me it was. For her, I would've just been another puppet on a string. I've always been a slightly anxious person, but that situation made it worse, so it helped to talk to someone.'

My heart cracks knowing she went through that. 'I can't believe anyone would treat you badly. You're such a beautiful person.'

She gives me a sad smile. 'Well, one thing I learnt is that the way she treated me was about her and not about me.' She stirs the straw through her soda water, the ice cubes clinking as they hit the glass. 'Hard not to take the way people treat you personally, though, isn't it?'

'Yes, that is hard,' I say. I want to ask more questions about this person, what she did, how they met, but mostly I want to bundle Callie up and treat her like she deserves to be treated. I slip off the stool, slide my arms around her neck and kiss her. She sighs softly, wrapping her arms around my waist.

When we part, I cup her cheeks, looking directly into her eyes. '*That* is how you deserve to be treated.'

She blinks at me, her swallow audible.

I give her a quick smile and sit back on the stool. 'I'm distracting you from work.'

She shakes her head. 'You're not. I got here earlier than planned, so I've managed to get a heap done. I can have a break for a while.' She gestures behind me. 'Want to see what it's like up there?'

I look over my shoulder briefly at the stage. I know she mentioned drag king lessons but I didn't think she was serious, not today anyway. 'The stage? And do what? Just stand there?'

'I can play some music.' She stands, tugs me off the stool and adopts the waltz pose, shuffling a few steps to the left. 'Show you some moves.'

I press myself against her tall, lean body, my own body warming at the thought of being this close all afternoon. 'Oh, some *moves*.'

'Uh-huh.'

I peer at the stage again. There's a rumbling deep in my belly, a part of me that's desperate to let go, to dance and dress up and sing badly. But there's also something heavy and suffo-cating swirling, keeping the desire hidden. I turn to Callie, a *no* on the tip of my tongue. She smiles at me, brimming with enthusiasm. She sees something in me and she wants to do this for me, so I take a fortifying breath and say, 'You promise we're alone?'

'Promise. Nobody comes in this early on a Sunday, and I always keep the doors bolted when I'm in here by myself, so no one can get in without contacting me anyway.'

I give a tentative nod. 'Okay.'

Callie beams and takes my hand as we weave through the tables and up the steps to the darkened stage. She positions me in the centre and my insides thrum with nervous excitement.

'Stand right here,' she says. 'Back in a sec.' She jogs back down the stairs and disappears behind the bar and out of sight. A second later, harsh lights come to life and I shield my eyes.

'Sorry,' Callie says as she emerges from the bar. 'Your eyes will adjust.'

I lower my hand, squinting into the empty club. Sunbeams shoot through the narrow panes of glass that line the upper walls, highlighting floating dust particles, and the seating slowly comes into focus.

A chill dance track begins to play as Callie walks back onstage. 'We have a low-tech lighting system, so the settings are bright or brighter, and we have a spotlight we can operate from the back of the club, but that's about it.'

I stand rigid, looking straight ahead.

'Relax. Feel the music,' Callie says, moving behind me.

I drop my shoulders. 'Come closer,' I say, peeking over my shoulder.

She steps forward and wraps her arms around my waist, her body pressed against me. I lay my head back against her shoulder and her fingertip trails down my jaw. 'You're so beautiful,' she whispers.

I tilt my face up and our lips meet in a slow, deep kiss that almost makes me buckle. It's the type of kiss that I'm quickly learning Callie saves for when she's in her comfort zone. Unhesitating. Passionate. Even a little bit forceful. By the time we break apart, there's a burning heat between my legs.

'That is not why I brought you up here,' she murmurs.

I twist around to face her. 'Do all drag lessons lead to that?' I mean it as a joke, but my words have a territorial edge and I desperately want to take them back.

'You're the only person I've ever offered lessons to,' she says softly.

I nod, trusting her. I reach up and brush the pad of my thumb over the two freckles under her eyebrow, then trace a fingertip from freckle to freckle across her cheek. 'Your freckles are like the Milky Way, did you know that?'

She smiles, a nostalgic look in her eyes. 'Mmm. My gran told me that when I was a kid. We'd sit outside when Mum was on a late shift, and Gran would tell me about the Milky Way in the sky, and on my face.'

'It sounds like you had a special friendship.'

'We did,' she says. I think she's going to tell me more, but she takes a deep breath and says, 'I have a surprise for you.'

'Oh.' I release my grip and step back. 'A surprise?'

'Yep. This way.' She takes me backstage along the short, narrow corridor and into a room different to the one we were in last night. It's a similar setup to Callie and Stevie's except it's bigger, with three dressing tables instead of two and an additional rack stuffed with costumes. She stands in the middle of the room and spreads her arms. 'Try out some drag outfits.'

I blink at her. 'Seriously? I can actually try on these clothes?'

Callie nods, a gratified smile emerging. 'Go for it.'

I squeal and rush over to the costumes. The suits are tempting, but I pull out men's jeans with designer rips and a white vest top. 'I'll start simple.'

Callie turns away while I change and gathers up accessories for me, then helps me fit a short-haired wig, the caramel colour similar to my own.

I stare at my reflection. 'Wow. I'm me, but not me.'

'Very handsome,' Callie says, standing behind me, arms folded. 'Like a young George Michael.'

'Yeah, kind of, and I'm a huge George fan.' From nowhere, an idea lands in my head and I spin to face Callie. 'That could be my drag name, except I could be *Georgie* Michael.'

Callie's brows shoot up, but she grins and says, 'It could.'

'Oh, wait, Geor*gie*? Shouldn't it be more masculine? Being a king is about expressing masculinity, right?'

'It is, but masculinity can be anything you want it to be. It's not just about being a man. If you want your masculine to be feminine, or you want to blur the binaries, that's up to you. And you can always spell Georgie with a Y if you want to differentiate from the female name. But George Michael is a great act, a gay icon for a gay club, and no one is doing his music here.'

I shake my head, coming to my senses. 'I'm not sure why I even suggested that. It was like I was possessed.'

Callie chuckles. 'It's a bit like that. You're allowed to have a name that's just for you. It doesn't mean you need to perform anytime soon, or ever for that matter.'

I nod slowly. 'A name just for me. Georgy with a Y. I like it.'

Callie picks up a pair of black ankle boots and hands them to me. 'Try these.'

I slip them on. They're too big, but I like the feel of them with the outfit. I look in the mirror again, running a hand over my chest and assessing my crotch. I grab some socks and shove them down the front of my jeans, making Callie laugh. 'Can we get back to those lessons?'

She grabs my hand and we run back to the stage. She positions me in the middle once again and says with a shy smile, 'I'll keep my hands to myself this time.'

I grin. 'I don't mind your hands on me, but I'm not sure I'll learn much about being a drag king if we keep getting distracted.'

'True,' she says and sets a microphone stand in front of me. 'Here's your mic.'

I stare at it and then at her. 'What do I do with that exactly?'

'It depends on the act. Stevie often carries it around with her. I'll use it sometimes, but when I do *Risky Business*, I'm too active so I don't use a mic at all. For a beginner, I'd recommend using it. It can help ground you and give you something to grip to help with the nerves, and to stop your arms flying around aimlessly.'

I hold the microphone. 'Okay, so I just stand here and lip-sync?'

'You can sing if you like. Some kings do, but I don't have a good singing voice, so I'm all about the lip-syncing.'

'I'm definitely not a singer,' I say.

'Okay, that's good, one less thing to think about. You just need to learn the lyrics to a song or two and away you go.'

'You make it sound so easy.'

She lifts a shoulder. 'It kind of becomes second nature after a while.'

I face the empty club, grasping the microphone stand. I imagine music playing, an audience, me performing, and the fun of dressing up is washed away by a wave of nausea rolling through my stomach. 'Oof. I don't know how you do this.'

'It takes time to get used to it,' Callie says. 'When I started out, I'd get a rush when my performance was over, this high that I'd done something I'd never do out of drag. I could be someone else for a few minutes, an escape from reality. That's how I got over the initial nerves – just kept reliving the after-buzz.'

I face the crowd-less club once again and think about what an after-buzz must feel like. 'I love the idea of doing this,' I say. 'And I love what I'm wearing right now. I'm just not sure I have the courage or can get over my insecurities to perform.'

'Maya,' Callie says pointedly. 'Like I said in the dressing room, having fun with this doesn't mean you need to perform. You can dress up in costumes because it feels good, or be a king in your house, or muck around on the stage when I'm here on my own. You can still be Georgy Michael. No one needs to know.'

Her words hit home, and it occurs to me that I just did what I always do – jumped to the end result, expecting the perfect outcome, leaving no room for the experience. 'I can be a secret drag king?'

'Sure. You can be any type of king you want.' She pauses, considering me, as though she's in tune with the chatter in my head. 'How about this: instead of worrying about performing or not performing, I'll put some music on and we can have fun working the stage with you looking very hot in half-drag.'

I smile. 'So what you're saying is, "Stop bloody over-thinking everything, Maya, and let yourself go."'

She grins. 'Yeah.'

'You're right. I need to just go with it. Let's do this.'

'I'll change the music.' Callie disappears into the room off the bar and a new track spills from the speakers. It's early Wham! and it immediately fills me with joy.

She walks back onto the stage and grabs a second micro-phone, singing into it, rhythmically swaying her hips. Her enthusiasm is infectious, and I do the same with my own mic. Before long, we're singing loudly, dancing, completely absorbed in each other's company. And I get it. I get what Callie is talking about – being dressed as someone else on a stage is liber-ating and I never want this moment to end.

Hours later and back in my own clothes, I sit at the bar while Callie works. It's my first Sunday night at the club and there's a nice, relaxed atmosphere – more pub than club. No DJ. No kings. And thankfully, no Amber. Just downtempo music playing through the speakers, half the tables occupied and a few customers perched at the bar. When Callie isn't serving, she busies herself stocking fridges, ensuring the bar top is clean and replenishing the water canisters that sit at either end of the bar. She chats to me whenever she can, sneaking chaste kisses when she passes, and Stevie and Krissy keep me company too, learning more about my life and telling me about theirs.

While they're all busy, I gaze at the stage, still on a high from the afternoon of expressing myself in a way I never have before. It's the most fun I've had in a long time and I felt part of an exclusive club. I can see how it helps Callie find her place in the world and builds her confidence. I know she said not to think about performing right now, but ever since I stepped off the stage all I can think about is whether it's something I could do. I wouldn't have to learn more than one song – that's all some of the amateur kings do.

'Another drink, Maya? A glass of wine?'

I twist on my stool, startled by Krissy's voice. 'Oh, no, I'm good with soda water, thanks. Can't face alcohol after last night.'

'Mmm, I'm starting to wane, too,' she says, her eyelids drooping. She glances at her watch. 'Only an hour to go.'

Callie emerges from the prep area carrying a tray of clean wine glasses and begins to hang them by the stem in the overhead racks.

'You can head off if you like, Callie,' Krissy says. 'It's not going to get any busier. Stevie and I can handle it.'

'You sure?' Callie says, sliding in the last wine glass.

'Yep, see you Wednesday night.'

Krissy walks off and Callie disappears again, emerging a minute later slipping her phone into the bag that's slung across her chest. 'Well, that's a bonus, finishing early,' she says to me, flipping up the hatch and stepping through.

'It is, and I'm not working tomorrow,' I say, willing her to pick up on my inviting tone.

'Me either,' she says.

My pulse quickens. *Please let tonight be the night.* 'My place is very close.'

The corner of her mouth lifts in a sultry half-smile. 'And I don't like you walking home alone,' she says.

'And I don't like walking home without you.' I slip off the stool, take her hand and head for the exit.

Chapter 19
Callie

After Maya makes us a simple dinner of leftover chicken pie and vegetables, we leave our dishes in the sink and slump on the couch. She flicks on the TV and nestles into me, her head resting against my shoulder, and I press a kiss to the top of her head.

'You don't have to rush off tonight, do you?' she asks, looking up at me.

I shake my head and lower my mouth to hers. She makes a low guttural sound and our kiss quickly turns urgent, gasping breaths and probing tongues. A fire lights low in my belly, stoked from the kiss we shared on the stage, and every kiss since. A sudden, conflicting tightness grips my chest and my head fills with thoughts of nakedness. I force them away. I want this. I want to be here with Maya, and I want to be the type of girlfriend I've never had the chance to be.

Maya breaks the kiss and clutches my face. 'You're not running away.'

'No. I don't want to run from you.'

We stare at each other, the question of what happens next

wedged between us, but I sense that she doesn't want to make this decision for me. 'I-I'd like to stay,' I say. 'If you want me to, and, if you're ready to—'

'Yes, please,' she says, 'and I am very, very ready.'

She leads me the short distance to her bedroom, partially closing the door. The low light from the lounge room seeps through the narrow gap. Maya doesn't switch on a light or lamp, and I'm grateful.

I make out her silhouette pulling back the covers. 'Come here,' she says softly.

I move towards her, my stomach jittery, and stretch out beside her.

Her kiss is tentative, and I know she'll be conscious of moving too quickly, being too forceful. So I yield to the kiss and slip my hand under her T-shirt, stroking her back, signalling I'm okay with this.

She gently tugs on my shirt. 'Can we take some clothes off?'

'Yes,' I breathe.

She pulls off her own top first, followed by her bra, then unbuttons my shirt, my skin tingling as her fingertips brush against me. She drapes herself over me and the sensation of her bare torso on mine forces me to let out a deep, gratifying moan. Her palm skims my breast, making me shiver, while her mouth trails my jaw, nips at my neck, kisses my collarbone and my chest.

'Is this okay?' she asks.

'Yes.'

Her tongue moves over my nipple and I suck back a breath, the ache between my legs becoming too urgent. I guide her mouth back to mine, kissing her hard, groping for the buttons on her skirt. 'Can we take more clothes off?' I ask.

She hurriedly removes the rest of her clothing and touches the waistband of my jeans. 'How about these?' she asks.

'Take them off,' I say.

She does, followed by my underwear, and my head spins from the intoxicating feeling of hot skin against hot skin. We hold each other tight, fingers sinking into flesh. But being this close, my body glued to hers, our mouths joined, doesn't feel like enough. I need more of her. I need all of her.

She guides my hand lower and murmurs, 'Only if you want to.'

'I want to.' My fingers slip between her thighs and she moans a long, satisfied moan.

Our breathing becomes more ragged as my hand moves in a firm, fast rhythm. Sweat builds between us and the burn between my own legs intensifies.

Maya rolls onto her side, causing me to whimper at the interruption. 'I need to touch you,' she says.

I shift to give her access, groaning when her fingers find my clit. I push against her hand, my body taking over. My hand moves back between her thighs. The pressure in my pelvis peaks and I can't contain it a second longer. My legs shake, my arms tense, and my mind goes blank as Maya gasps and jerks through her own orgasm.

When the moans and tremors have left our bodies, we lie there, stunned, shallow breaths, sticky skin, entwined limbs. It was fast, desperate, urgent sex, and it was perfect.

I wake with a start, the unfamiliar surroundings not registering, then I feel the warm, naked body spooning me, an arm draped across my waist. I smile, still heady from last night. Afterwards, we lay in bed, talking softly, exchanging gentle kisses that led to deeper kisses, wandering hands, stirred arousal, warm tongues. I can still taste her, smell her on my skin, hear her moans, feel her body moving underneath me. Already, I'm desperate for this to happen again. One night with her isn't enough, and something deep in my soul tells me a lifetime with her won't be either.

Maya stirs and rolls over, facing away from me. I need the bathroom and some fluids, but my brain shifts into dilemma mode. If I dress just to go to the bathroom, and she's awake when I return, being fully clothed will look odd. But if I walk around naked, I risk giving her a full frontal when I walk back in and I'm not ready for that. I glance at my pile of clothes on the floor and reach for my shirt, quietly slipping it on and leaving the room.

After I use the bathroom, I examine my reflection as I wash my hands, half expecting to see a different person given my life has taken a significant turn. I'm now someone with a girlfriend. I'm in a relationship. We spent our first night together. I've met someone who doesn't want to leave or go straight to sleep after sex. She wants to talk and have more sex and fall asleep in my arms murmuring, 'Don't you dare run off in the morning without waking me.' It feels good. It feels right. It feels exactly like the missing link I've been searching for.

I head for the kitchen, the carpet spongy underfoot, or maybe I'm walking on air. I fill the jug with water and flick it on to boil. My phone is on the coffee table where I left it last night and I walk over to retrieve it. There's a message from Mum asking if I'm okay. I wince. The one rule she insists on is telling her I won't be home.

> Sorry. I'm okay. Stayed at Maya's.

Within seconds, my phone beeps.

I send her a grimace face emoji followed by a kissing one and get back to making two cups of tea, adding one sugar to mine and milk to both.

In the bedroom, I place Maya's mug on her bedside table and take mine to the other side. I glance down at my shirt. Seeing each other naked is part of being in a relationship. If I want this to work, I need to be comfortable with her. I strip it off and slide back into bed, pulling the covers over my breasts.

Maya rolls over, blinking at me.

'Hi,' I say, propping my head in my palm. 'Sorry if I woke you.'

She smiles sleepily. 'You didn't run off to make your Mum brekkie.'

I chuckle. 'No, I think she's old enough to look after herself. Made you a cup of tea, though,' I say, with an upward nod towards the mug.

'You made me tea?' She glances behind her. 'Aww, thank you.' She reaches for it and takes a sip, the sheet dropping to her waist. 'Mmm, nice.' She turns back to face me, her breasts exposed.

My gaze drops, my face warming, but before I can continue ogling her as though I've never seen boobs before, she cuddles into me, her soft lips brushing mine.

'Morning,' she murmurs.

I sigh. I could wake up like this every morning for the rest of my life. 'Morning.'

'Last night was so nice,' she says, stroking my back with featherlight fingertips. 'I'd like more nights like that with you.'

The relief that whooshes through me is unexpected and my throat thickens. 'I'd like that, too,' I say, my voice cracking.

She scans my face, evidently picking up on my emotion, but she presses a kiss to my shoulder and says, 'Would you like something to eat with that tea?'

'I would, but I didn't want to help myself to your food.'

She grins. 'You don't ever need permission to eat my food. I'll get us something. Any allergies I need to know about?'

'Mushrooms. Not an allergy; they're just disgusting.'

She laughs and hops out of bed. I try not to gawp at her, but she's so exquisite I can't stop myself. My eyes move down her smooth back, along the dip of her waist, over the curve of her hip and arse. She slips on a long T-shirt, smiling at me as she leaves the room. I let out a breath and reach for my own shirt. As much as I love the idea of sitting up in bed naked and walking around her flat the same way, I'm not there yet, and maybe she isn't either.

I prop up the pillows behind me, sip my tea and scroll through socials on my phone. Soon the warming scent of toasting bread wafts through the apartment and my stomach rumbles.

When Maya returns, she hands me a plate with a thick slice of toast loaded with lush, green avocado and creamy feta. 'Here you go.'

'Ooh, you're spoiling me with your food.'

She hops back into bed, balancing her plate on her lap. 'I've given you picnic food, lasagna, pie and now toast. I think you're easily pleased when it comes to meals.'

I nod as I chew. 'Mm-hmm.'

She takes a bite, watching me while she eats, then asks, 'Do you have any plans today?'

I shake my head, hoping she also has none and isn't about to ask me to leave.

'Did you want to spend the day with me? A lazy day here? Or we could go out?'

I smile. Things just get better. 'I'd love to spend the day here. I like lazy days, especially on a Monday when I've usually worked four or five nights in a row.'

'Same,' she says.

'Do you want me to make you another tea?' I ask.

She grins and holds out her mug, which is still half-full, but has turned tepid. 'I could get used to this, you know.'

I take her mug and hop out of bed. *So could I.*

Chapter 20
Maya

I pick up my pace as I close in on the club. It's only been three days since I've seen Callie, but the gap feels too long. Hiding away in my apartment, taking our relationship to the next level, and not talking about exes or past hookups, was the antidote we needed. She's working tonight, both behind the bar and doing the final performance to end the show: a duet with another king. But she was as desperate to see me as I was to see her, and I was eager to watch the amateur kings again, now that I have my secret alter ego's perspective.

Inside the club, soft music plays overhead, the air is heavy with the smell of wine and beer, and the space hums with customer chatter.

Callie is serving when I approach the bar. Her eyes flick to me as she pulls a beer, tilting the glass under the spout, and her face brightens. The way she lights up when she sees me melts my heart.

She finishes with the customer and comes out from behind the bar. 'Hey,' she says, kissing me hello.

I breathe in her fresh, spicy scent. 'Hi.'

She pulls out a stool for me. 'Would you like a drink?'

'Yes, please, and I think I'm ready to face alcohol after Krissy's party, so a wine sounds good.'

Stevie emerges from the prep area as Callie pours me a small glass. 'Hey, Maya,' she says as she passes.

Amber trails behind her, side-eyeing us as she walks by, and my stomach clenches.

Callie pays zero attention to her and says, 'Show's about to start. Only three acts tonight and my duet partner hasn't turned up yet, so Georgy Michael might need to help me out.'

'Ha,' I say. 'That's not going to happen.'

She grins. 'I can dream.'

I gesture to the tables. 'Do you mind if I sit closer and watch, since you're working?'

She shakes her head. 'Go for it. I have to head backstage and change soon anyway.'

'Okay, I'll see you afterwards.'

I find a seat as Stevie walks onstage to open the show. I watch the first performer closely – how they move, lip-sync, engage with the audience. They're good, not fazed by an unco-ordinated step or getting some lyrics wrong, and the audience either don't notice or don't care. I cast my gaze around the club. It's not busy – thirty people maybe? I could do that, couldn't I? Lip-sync and dance for a few minutes in front of thirty people?

The show is over in half an hour, and I scroll on my phone while I wait for Callie's duet. Stevie lets the audience know there's a short delay, so I grab myself another glass of wine and wait patiently, trying to ignore the fact that both Amber and Callie are no longer behind the bar.

My phone vibrates in my jeans pocket and I reach for it, finding a message from Callie.

Sorry this just happened x

I frown in confusion and reply with a question mark as Stevie jogs up the stage steps.

'Let's hear another round of applause for our amateur kings,' she calls into the mic. The comment gets a few claps and a lone whistle. 'Hopefully, we can get a few more whistles from you for this next performance,' Stevie says. 'Welcome to the stage your two fave regulars, Tom Cruisin' and Hairy Styles!'

I stiffen. Hairy Styles is Amber's drag name.

They saunter onto the stage and Callie throws me an apologetic glance, but her head snaps away when Amber grabs her hips and yanks her close. Callie looks momentarily stunned before she adopts a sultry expression and palms Amber's fake hairy chest. The audience hoot and clap, except for me. All I can do is swallow back the sourness edging up my throat over watching Amber grind against my girlfriend, and visions of them being that close offstage fill my head. Amber's eyes skim the club, stopping when they land on me. She smirks, then dips Callie, going in for a kiss.

The hurt from my previous relationship surges, fresh and raw. Arianne's betrayal. I trusted her and her friend because I wasn't the jealous type. I ignored the looks between them and the tactile nature of their friendship because I never thought they'd do that to me. My face turns hot and a red mist coats my vision. I'm not going to ignore behaviour like that again when someone is important to me, and I'm not going to be drawn into whatever game Amber is playing.

Rashly, I leave the table, disappearing into the bathroom corridor, then walk determinedly to the backstage door and punch in the code Callie gave me on the weekend. She told me to use it whenever I wanted to. Well, now I want to.

I hear whistles from the audience and it pushes my head into overdrive about what's happening onstage. The track finishes and my heart rate speeds up. I generally shy away from conflict but Amber is like a schoolyard bully, the type who will continue to push if you don't stand up to her.

Callie bursts through the curtain, a hardness to her expression, Amber trailing behind wearing a delirious smile.

Callie freezes. 'Maya. I—'

I step around her. 'Callie is with me,' I say to Amber.

Amber rolls her eyes. 'It was a performance, Maya. You don't own her.'

Adrenaline rushes through my body, but I won't back down. Callie and I sleeping together meant something to me; what we've developed over the past month means something to me. 'You don't own her either,' I say, my voice shaky. 'And you need to back off.'

Callie steps behind me, placing a supportive hand on my lower back. 'You crossed a line with that performance, Amber.'

Amber shoots her a look and gives an incredulous scoff. 'It's the same act we always do and now it's crossing a line?'

'It is not the same act!' Callie says. 'And we haven't done *that* act for ages, and you know it.'

Amber glares at her, nostrils flaring.

'And there's something else I want to know,' Callie says to her. 'What was that bullshit comment you made to Maya on the weekend about helping me get changed?'

I didn't expect Callie to say that but relief passes through me, because it means she believes me.

Amber's jaw twitches as she glares at us. 'Ugh. You're welcome to each other,' she hisses and strides off.

I glance at Callie, unnerved by what's just happened, but we need to air this. I head for her dressing room and she follows, locking the door behind us.

She removes her jacket and wig, rubbing her hair with a hand towel.

'Don't change,' I say. 'You might need to do another simulated sex act with Hairy Styles – run your hands over his hairy chest.' My words are sarcastic, but my tone is light. I have no doubt Amber orchestrated this.

Callie sighs. 'That wasn't supposed to be the act.'

I lean against the edge of the dressing table, arms folded. 'It just happened when you got onstage? You didn't tell me the duet was with Amber.'

Callie perches beside me. 'That's because it wasn't supposed to be with her. It was supposed to be a fun, innocent duet with our regular Thursday night king. But turns out the delay I mentioned when you got here was more serious and they couldn't make it. I told Stevie I'd do a solo act but the audience like the Thursday night duets, so she wanted to keep it going and asked Amber, since she was performing anyway and was almost ready. I texted you the minute I found out.'

'But *that* act?' I say. 'When you have others to choose from?'

She shifts her focus to the ground. 'That's an act we did ages ago, before we...'

Had sex, I want to say, but I press my lips together because it is *so* wrong to make Callie feel bad for having a past. Besides, this isn't about who she's been with; it's about Amber's behaviour towards me.

'Went out a few times,' Callie finishes. 'I insisted we do another routine and she agreed, but when we got onstage, she went straight into that one. I had to go with it. I can't look like I don't know what I'm doing up there.'

I release a heavy sigh. 'I know you can't, and I'm not surprised to hear she'd do something like that.' I pause, another question pressing on my tongue. 'I understand it's a performance, and you're a professional, but did you have to kiss her in front of me?'

Callie's brows crease. 'What? I didn't. I pulled away and put a heap of distance between us.'

'Oh.' The knot in my stomach loosens.

Callie lifts herself off the dressing table and stands in front of me, hands resting on my thighs. 'I wouldn't do that to you. Well, I wouldn't do that to anyone, but especially not to you.'

My instincts tell me to trust her, and I didn't actually witness a kiss, but I need to fully resolve this so Amber can't come between us anymore. 'She's trying to be with you, or get me out of the way, or, I don't know, something, but I'm not imagining it.'

Callie frowns. 'She's definitely been acting differently around me lately.' She breaks eye contact. 'I didn't mention this at the time, but that night after the ballet when I left your place and came here ... I performed. It wasn't planned. I needed to deal with what happened and performing helps me do that. I didn't intentionally keep it from you, it just didn't come up, that's all.'

'I know.'

She looks puzzled. 'You know?'

I nod. 'Yes, because Amber told me that, too.'

A flash of anger sparks in her eyes. 'What?'

'When she made that other comment, she also asked if I liked the act and said that it was lucky you got some practice in on Thursday night.'

Callie's mouth drops open and she heads for the door. I hurry after her, grabbing her arm. 'Wait, where are you going?'

'To fucking say something to her.'

I shake my head. 'Please don't. I think we've had enough confrontation for one night, and maybe she'll back off now.'

Callie's lips press together, but she says, 'Okay, if that's what you want.' She takes a seat at the dressing table and gestures for me to take the other chair. 'I might as well tell you this, too. After I performed that night, she propositioned me.'

My jaw tenses. 'After the striptease act?'

She nods. 'Obviously it was a hard pass and I went home thinking about you.'

'It's good to know my instincts aren't off about her.'

'I'm sorry,' Callie says. 'She knows how much I like you and for some reason she has an issue with it.'

I fiddle with the top button of her shirt. 'Why does she know how much you like me, but I don't?'

She pulls her head back. 'Maya. You *must* know that. I've told you and it's so obvious that I—'

I meet her eyes. 'No, Callie. *Tom's* told me and made it obvious. With you, things aren't as clear.'

Her cheeks redden and she shakes her head. 'Last weekend in the dressing room, making you drinks onstage, the kiss in the audience—'

'You were in drag every time,' I say. 'I adore Tom, but it's *you* that I want to be with, Callie; it's you I like. And I want to know that you like me. As much as I like you,' I add softly.

'But we spent the night together, and the next day – that was all me.'

'Yes, it was, but you're nowhere near as forthcoming with your feelings as when you're here and in costume. It's confusing for me.' I drop my gaze. 'I guess it's nice to hear how much someone likes you sometimes. Plus, if I'm going to tell my parents about my girlfriend, then I want to be certain about us.'

Her eyes widen. 'You're going to tell your parents about us?'

I nod. 'I think it's time. And you're coming to Dad's event, so I want you to be there as my partner.'

Something indiscernible flickers across her face, and for a moment I think it's because she doesn't see a future for us or want me to include her in my family life, but then she says, 'Okay. No more duets with Amber since they make us both feel uncomfortable. This' – she places her hand flat against her chest – 'is all an onstage persona. When I'm offstage, I'm a different person and I like you, Maya. I *really* like you.'

'But you're still in drag—'

Callie shakes her head. 'Only half – no wig, no jacket, no stage, no lights, no Tom charm. And tomorrow, I'll be dressed as me and I'll tell you again how much I like you, and the day after that, and the day after that, for as long as you'll have me.'

My defences dissolve and a rush of affection floods my body. 'And I want to hear it for as long as you'll have me.'

Chapter 21
Callie

The doorbell rings as I spread the last of the icing on the cake.

'Oh, here she is,' Aunty Gina says. 'The new girlfriend.'

'Womanfriend,' Mum says. 'Callie isn't a girl, and neither is Maya, she keeps reminding me.'

'Mum,' I say, shuffling past her, 'please don't embarrass me.'

She stops me and pinches my cheeks. 'I wouldn't do that to my little girl.'

'Stop,' I say with a laugh, brushing her hand away. On my way to the door, I glance around, a last-minute check that I haven't missed any specks of dirt with the mop. In addition to attempting to bake, I spent the morning cleaning, although I doubt this house measures up to what I imagine Maya's family home looks like. Not that there's anything wrong with ours. It's not the designer's dream that is Krissy and Stevie's house or the stylish inner-city apartment that is Maya's, but it's modern, clean and homely. Mum followed me around, helping but also lecturing about cleaning for show. 'Maya's coming to see you, not the house,' she constantly reminded me.

I open the door and there she is, a bright beacon against the backdrop of a gloomy day. My insides liquefy, the way they always do when I see her. 'Hi.'

'Hi,' Maya says, lifting her face to mine.

I kiss her, a small moan escaping, and my hands grip her face, keeping her close.

'Mmm,' Maya hums against my mouth. 'I've been looking forward to that.'

'Me t—'

'Oops, sorry.'

I jump back. 'Jesus, Mum.'

'I didn't mean to interrupt,' Mum says, holding her hands up. 'I was just passing through.'

Maya giggles and steps inside, holding out her hand. 'Nice to meet you, erm—'

'Call me Donna, love,' Mum says, rushing forward. She sandwiches Maya's hand between both of hers and holds on for longer than necessary.

My aunty appears behind her. 'And I'm Gina.'

'My mum and my aunty,' I say to Maya. 'Mum, Gina, this is Maya.'

'Hi,' Maya says, treating them to one of her sparkly smiles.

'Well, come through,' Mum says, gesturing her inside. 'Don't stand on the doorstep.'

Maya looks around as she follows Mum into the kitchen. 'I love this house. It's so cosy.'

Mum raises her brows at me as if to say, 'I told you so.'

'Do you want a coffee?' I ask. 'Something to eat?' I point to the sad-looking cake on the bench. It's uneven and a little flat, with patches of visible sponge where I missed with the icing. 'That chocolate cake is freshly baked.'

Maya's face lights up. 'Someone baked? I thought I smelled something delicious in here.'

I hold my hand up. 'Me.'

Her eyes widen. 'You made me a chocolate cake?'

I nod.

'You didn't tell me you baked.'

I laugh. 'That's because I don't. And it looks a little worse for wear, so I have no idea what it will taste like.'

Her eyes turn soft, and she gives me a doe-like smile. I love the way she looks at me when I remember a little detail about her, like I'm the most considerate person on the planet.

'It's perfect,' she says.

'I offered,' Mum says, 'so I could get birthday cake practice in, but she insisted.'

'Mum, you don't need to bake me birthday cakes.'

Maya's smile fades. 'It's your birthday?'

I shake my head. 'Not until the eighteenth.'

'But that's only a week and a half away,' Maya says. 'You didn't mention it.'

I shrug. 'It's just a day.'

'Birthdays are special,' she says.

'I agree, Maya,' Mum says. 'And she won't admit it, but she still loves my birthday cakes.'

'There's nothing better than a homemade cake,' Maya says, then turns to me. 'We are definitely celebrating your birthday.'

Mum and Gina exchange a look, one that says, *This one's a keeper*.

I give Maya a small smile. 'Okay, we can do that.'

Gina makes herself an instant coffee, then pours boiling water into a plunger for the three of us. 'So, Callie said you'd like to try drag?' she says to Maya.

My cheeks flush. It was a conversation I had with Gina yesterday, but I didn't think she'd blurt it out. 'I didn't exactly say that, Gina. I said she's *curious* about it.'

Gina waves away my comment. 'Same thing.'

'Well, it's just some fun at the moment,' Maya says, looking between us and tucking her hands into the pockets of her shorts. 'Callie thought that if I came up with some acts and practised, it might encourage me to take it further.'

'She knows her stuff,' Gina says, pointing in my direction. 'She's one of the best kings I've seen.'

I open my mouth to protest, but Maya responds first.

'She's amazing,' Maya gushes. 'I don't know how she does it.'

'Loads of practice,' I say. 'Which is what we're doing very soon.'

'Ooh,' Mum says. 'Can we join in?'

'Oh' – I glance at Maya – 'I'm not sure.'

Maya shrugs. 'I don't mind. Callie said you both gave her the idea for her act, and I could use all the help I can get. Besides' – she takes a deep breath and lifts her chin – 'I should probably get used to having people around if I ever do want to perform.'

Mum and Gina's faces light up like toddlers who've been given ice-cream for breakfast.

'Alright,' I say, 'but only because Maya's okay with it.'

As we settle in the lounge with our coffee and cake, Mum says to Maya, 'Gina knows the history of drag kings like nobody's business.'

'That's right,' Gina says. 'Ask me anything.'

'Don't,' I counter. 'You'll be stuck on that couch for hours.'

Maya chuckles, then asks Gina, 'You didn't do drag yourself?'

Gina shakes her head as she swallows her mouthful. 'It wasn't something that was available to me when I was younger. If I was in London or New York, maybe, even Sydney, but not

Brisbane. So I had to enjoy it from afar and now I live vicariously through Callie and Stevie.'

'It's never too late,' Maya says.

My heart warms that she's picked up on Gina's wistful tone and wants to be encouraging.

'Ha,' Gina says. 'That's kind, but at my age with plenty of aches and pains, not to mention the hot flushes, I'll leave it to the young ones.'

'You're only fifty-five, Gina,' I say. 'You're not dead.'

'I know, I know,' she says, waving her fork, then points it at Maya. 'But you, you're young and have years in front of you, so why not?'

Maya gives a tentative nod. 'Yes. That's what I'm trying to convince myself of – why not?'

'What kind of acts are you interested in?' Mum asks. 'Modern? Older?'

Maya has just put a forkful of cake in her mouth, and she touches her fingers to her lips as she chews. There's a tiny dab of icing on her top lip, and I wish Mum and Gina weren't in the room so I could lick it off. She pats a napkin to her mouth, then says, 'I like Callie's old-with-new thing, and she said that I looked a bit like a young George Michael when I tried on some outfits and wigs.'

'Maya was thinking *Georgy* Michael,' I say. 'And that's Georgy with a Y. It's a great act to start with.'

'I like it,' Gina says with a nod and scrolls through her phone. 'How early? Are we going back to Wham! days?'

Maya shakes her head. 'No, that's too bouncy for me to start out with. Maybe late eighties? His "Faith" era? I know the songs well.'

'Great choice.' Gina switches on the TV and screen mirrors her phone.

We watch a few music videos, commenting on George's brand – fitted clothing, fast footwork, a camp masculinity, oozing sex appeal.

Maya gazes at the TV, mesmerised by his music, by him, and I instinctively know that this is the right act for her.

She comes out of her trance, takes her last bite of cake and groans her appreciation. 'That has to be one of the best cakes I've ever tasted.'

I grin. 'It was average, but thanks.'

Maya stands to take everyone's plates but Mum jumps up. 'I'll take that. You concentrate on becoming a drag king.'

Maya chuckles. 'I think drag kings need to wash dishes too, but thank you.'

Mum collects plates and mugs, and Gina stands in the middle of the lounge room floor and claps her hands together. 'Okay, let's do this.'

Maya shifts her weight from one foot to the other. 'I'm-I don't really know—'

'Wait,' I say and rush to the laundry, returning with a broom and a mop. I thrust the broom at Maya. 'This is your microphone.'

Gina resets her phone and the opening notes of 'Faith' flow from the TV. 'See how he starts with a foot tap, then his hips?' she says.

Maya nods.

'That's all you need to do. It's easy.' Gina moves her hips from side to side, readjusting her glasses as they slip down her nose. 'Like this.'

Mum returns and sits on the couch, like she's ready for a show, but Maya stands rigid, staring at Gina.

'This is about having fun,' I say. 'There's no pressure to perform. It's just us here, listening to music. But if these two are making you nervous, they'll be happy to leave.' I glance between them. 'Won't you?'

'Oh, sorry. Yes, of course,' Mum says, getting ready to stand back up again.

'No,' Maya says. 'You're not making me nervous. I'm making myself nervous. Please stay. Aunty Gina's got good advice.'

My eyes widen. Did she just say *Aunty* Gina?

The knowing smile Mum gives me suggests she picked up on it, too, and Gina looks delighted.

Maya, oblivious to what she's just said, positions the broomstick in front of her. 'No pressure. I can do this just for me. Do you mind playing it again?'

Gina obliges and Maya taps her foot, her hips stiffly jerking from side to side.

'That's it,' Gina says encouragingly.

I grab the mop. 'When you lip-sync, you want it to look as realistic as possible,' I say. 'Singers breathe when they sing; they open their mouths and connect emotionally with the lyrics, so you want to do that, too.' I start lip-syncing the chorus to 'Faith' to demonstrate.

She watches me, then tentatively follows along.

'Don't overthink it,' I say. 'You know this music, you love his songs, they're already part of you, so be yourself. Push all the worry about what others might think out of your head.'

She starts to relax, her body becoming more fluid, then starts singing along, losing herself. She knows every word, every nuance of the song, like she's lived and breathed this music her entire life, and I can already see audiences lapping it up.

Gina turns up the volume, playing another track.

For the next hour, the four of us play music from the eighties and nineties, sing, dance and choose songs we think would be good to perform. I have a string of tracks listed in my

Notes app and my head is crammed with ideas for new performances.

Maya drops onto the couch, her cheeks flushed, wearing an ecstatic smile.

'You're a natural,' I say, sitting beside her, and forgetting where I am, lean in for a kiss.

'I think that's our cue to leave, Gina,' Mum says.

Blood rushes to my face. 'Oh, god. I almost forgot you two were here.'

'Obviously,' Gina says. 'But, good timing, because we're due to leave anyway. I'm taking your mother for a sleepover.'

'So the house is all yours,' Mum says, looking between Maya and me with an innocent expression.

I groan. 'Mum. Stop. You don't need to stay at Gina and Lisa's. We're adults. We can control ourselves, and if we can't, we'll go to Maya's, okay? Just come home.'

Mum shakes her head. 'Nope. It's all arranged now. We're having fun sister time, and your Aunty Lisa already has dinner planned and some expensive wine that it would be rude not to drink when I have the next two days off.' She hugs me, followed by a quick one for Maya. 'Lovely to meet you, Maya. Keep going with this; there's a drag king in there ready to burst out.'

Surprise flickers across Maya's face. 'Thank you.'

Mum walks off to her bedroom, reappearing a minute later with an overnight bag.

I walk them to the front door, more to check they leave the house than anything else. 'Bye, you two,' I say, holding the door open.

'Well, she's very beautiful,' Mum says in a hushed voice that's far too loud. 'And genuine, too.'

'Yeah. I got lucky there.'

Gina tweaks my chin. 'She got lucky too, you remember that.'

'Okay, Aunty Gina. I'll try.'

They run through the drizzle to Gina's car. I wave as they drive off and head back to the lounge room.

Maya is grinning at me. 'They like embarrassing you, hey?'

I roll my eyes but I can't help smiling. 'Yep.'

'You're lucky to have such an accepting and loving family.'

'I am,' I say, slipping into the space beside her.

'What your mum said about me having an inner drag king ready to burst out, that was really nice to hear. My parents would never hang out with me while doing this. They've never taken my interest in performing seriously. You, your mum and Gina, you take me seriously and that means so much.'

I rub her thigh. 'I'm glad we make you feel like that.'

'It's encouraged me to want to do more. Like, maybe I could try?' she says, her tone uncertain.

My brows rise and I point to the empty space in the room where we've just spent the past hour. 'You mean Georgy? Onstage?'

'I-I think so? I mean in the future, not anytime soon.' She places a hand on her stomach. 'Something in here is urging me to do it. I felt good in those clothes last week, felt alive on that stage, like I was tingling all over, and I had so much fun today. That has to mean something, right?'

I nod. 'For sure. If that's how it makes you feel, then go for it. Does that mean you want to keep going?'

She shakes her head. 'I'm ready for a rest and we do have the house to ourselves,' she says, manoeuvring herself to straddle me. 'So maybe we could do something else?'

I run my hands up her bare thighs, my fingertips slipping under the hem of her shorts. 'Something else is good.'

She kisses me and murmurs, 'You haven't showed me the whole house yet.'

There's a nervous flutter in my stomach. It's only been a

week since we slept together, and that was in her dark bedroom, not in the harsh daylight that floods my room. But I'm in a relationship now, and I want to be in the type of relationship where we have loving, spontaneous sex, so I ignore the vice around my chest and say, 'Well, that was very rude of me.'

Chapter 22
Callie

I open the door to my room. It's not the type of room you bring your beautiful girlfriend to for sexy times; it's the room of a twenty-seven-year-old who still lives at home. No stylish design, just a basic queen-sized bed, a built-in wardrobe, two bedside tables and a chest of drawers in the corner. I hadn't bothered to tidy in here since I didn't expect we'd have the house to ourselves and thought we'd go to Maya's.

'Welcome to my messy room.' I start clearing the drag outfits off my bed that I dumped there this morning from my work bag. 'It took me all morning to clean the rest of the house and make the cake, so I didn't get time to do in here,' I say. At least it smells nice with the clean sheets I put on yesterday and fresh air drifting through the open windows.

Maya closes the blinds and steps over to me. 'Callie, I don't care how messy or clean your house is.' She kisses me, softly at first, but it quickly deepens. 'I missed you last night. I thought about you when I went to bed.'

'Yeah?' I breathe between kisses.

'Mm-hmm.' She reaches down to unbutton my shorts.

'About what I'd like to do to you. And what I'd like you to do to me.'

We collapse onto my bed, atop a pile of clothing. Her words are barely registering because all I can think about is that we're about to have day sex. Not something I've had a lot of experience in. My sex life to date has mostly taken place in dark bedrooms after a drunken night out, an occasional morning handjob under covers. Even spending the day with Maya last week, I was guarded and covered myself as best I could. And then there was Lacey.

Maya halts the kiss and reaches underneath her hip, pulling out my packer. Her brows rise. 'This could be handy.'

I prop my head in my palm. 'You like that sort of thing?'

'Mmm, sometimes. Do you?'

I give a tentative nod because I do like straps, at least I think I'd enjoy it a whole lot more with Maya. Lacey and I used one a few times, but when we did, she wielded a power over me that made me uneasy. I point to the packer. 'That's too soft,' I say, then hesitate for a beat, reluctant to voice what I want. But I trust Maya and my arousal is more heightened than my vulnerability. I reach behind me and open the bottom drawer of my bedside table, pulling out my strap. 'This isn't.'

Maya looks at it, then at me, her dark eyes turning smoky. 'Is that what you wore for your sexy striptease?'

'Uh-huh.'

She whips off her T-shirt and kisses me. 'What you pressed against me when you straddled me?'

'Yes,' I say, kissing her back, trying to shake the intruding *it's not dark enough* thought.

Maya pulls back a little, searching my face. 'Are you okay?'

'I-I'm' – I swallow – 'can I tell you something?'

'Of course.'

'I, um, I haven't had a lot of day sex before.'

She tilts her head, brows furrowing. 'But Monday at my place...'

'Yes, but your room is so dark, even during the day. And I covered myself. But being naked with someone in daylight, having sex ... you're my first real relationship, so there hasn't been a lot of opportunities, and I don't know how to do all of this. How to be okay with it.' I hold up the strap. 'This is for performances. It's not something I use with people.'

She brushes a thumb across my cheekbone and kisses me. 'Okay. I want you to feel comfortable and special, so we don't need to use it and we don't need to have sex right now. I just assumed since we already had, you'd want—'

'I do want,' I say quickly. 'Sooo bad. I just need you to lower your expectations.'

Maya's eyes widen. 'My expectations? I'm not some superstar lesbian lover, Callie. I can count on one hand the women I've slept with and I've never slept with a man.'

'Oh.' I haven't slept with a man either, but I have slept with more than five women.

'And I hardly have the perfect naked form,' she says. 'I have cellulite on my arse and one boob bigger than the other, a bruise on my thigh from walking into the cupboard door handle, midgie bites on my ankles, scars on my elbows from falling off my bike when I was a kid—'

'Okay,' I say with a small laugh, my tension easing. 'I get your point. Although all I see when I look at you is perfection.'

'And that's all I see when I look at you,' she says. 'We can go slow. And we can stop whenever you want.'

'I don't want to stop,' I say. *I don't ever want to stop with you.* But there's a niggling thought, a voice at the back of my head questioning whether she'll still like me after we've done whatever it is that we're about to do, whether she'll still like me when I'm stripped bare.

'Then let's not stop,' she says. 'Do you trust me?'

'Yes.'

She reaches for the top button of my shirt. 'Can I start here?'

I nod and lie back, my skin goosebumping as she undoes each button and dips her head to press soft kisses along my stomach. She slowly pushes my shirt open, exposing my breasts. I squirm a little under her gaze but fight the urge to cover myself.

Maya unfastens her bra and drops it to the floor. The upside of day sex is seeing her. I reach out, enjoying the sensation of her nipple hardening under my touch. She closes her eyes, sighing when my mouth makes contact.

'We need more clothes off,' she murmurs, pushing me back and hooking her thumbs into the waistband of my shorts. 'Is this okay?'

I lift my hips in response and she gently tugs my shorts down. Her eyes flick from my underwear to my face. 'Keep going,' I say.

She peels them off and my face warms as her eyes travel slowly up my body. 'You're so beautiful, Callie,' she whispers.

A lump forms in my throat. No one has ever spoken those words to me while in this position, or looked at me the way she is looking at me now, like I'm a goddess she's ready to worship. And I'm ready to worship her, too. I flip her over so that I can even up the naked playing field, and remove her shorts.

'And the rest,' Maya says, gazing down at me.

I strip off her underwear, letting out a soft sigh as my eyes take in every inch of her. I don't see cellulite or bruises or insect bites, only smooth skin, the swell of her hips and the dip of her waist, dark hair between her legs and erect nipples. I want to capture this image of her. Remember us like this next week, in a year's time, in thirty years' time.

'Callie,' she says, her voice husky and pleading. 'Please touch me.'

'Sorry,' I say. 'Sidetracked.' I kiss her hipbone, her stomach, slide my tongue and teeth over her nipple, drape myself over her and kiss her. 'I am so turned on right now,' I murmur against her mouth.

Her eyes drift to the strap. 'Would you like that?'

'God, yes,' I say, reaching for it, but Maya grabs it first.

'No,' she says. 'I meant would *you* like that?'

A shiver sweeps over my skin and I give a tentative nod. 'Yes. I don't want to kill the mood, but it probably needs to have lint washed off after being in that bag.'

'I'll take care of that,' Maya says, slipping off the bed, her gorgeous hips swaying as she walks out of the room.

'Fuck, fuck, fuck,' I mutter. *This is happening. This is real.* I glance down at myself, exposed and vulnerable. My hand reaches for the sheet but I take a deep breath and fight the urge to cover myself.

When Maya returns, she stands at the end of the bed, her brown eyes locked on mine as she steps into the harness and adjusts it to fit. I whimper at how hot the vision is and she gives me a coy half-smile. She's enjoying me watching her, but it's different to Lacey. This feels equal and safe, and Maya's doing this to please me, not just for her own gain.

She kneels on the end of the mattress, bending to brush her lips over my thigh. 'Let me see you,' she says gently, and I tentatively part my legs. 'Gorgeous,' she breathes and slides her tongue between my thighs, making me gasp.

I push against her mouth, threading my fingers through her hair, already starting to come undone, but she crawls up and settles on top of me, the strap pressing against my wetness.

'What do you like?' Maya asks, trailing kisses along my jaw.

'I-I don't really know.'

'What do you think about? Fantasise about?'

'You,' I say. 'I fantasise about you.'

'Have you thought about me wearing this for you?'

'I have,' I say honestly, my voice hoarse. 'I want you on top of me like this, so I can kiss you and see you.'

'Oh,' she coos. 'Then I don't want to disappoint you.' She kisses me slow and deep, her pelvis rocking gently, the strap edging inside me.

I suck back a breath as she pushes in further.

'Are you alright?' she asks, worry creeping into her voice.

'Yes.' I wrap my legs around her. 'Keep going.'

She begins to thrust, murmuring, 'God, Callie, you feel so good.'

I start to relax as we get into a rhythm. She kisses me lovingly and moves inside me slowly. A warmth flows through my body and my heart fills. *This is how it's supposed to be.*

It doesn't take long before our pace quickens, our breathing becomes more rapid and I start to lose control.

'Okay?' she asks.

I can't respond; my brain is already mush. She's hitting all the right spots and I'm desperate for this to last, but the burn in my pelvis is too intense. I slide my hands over her arse and push her in deeper.

She brushes a hand over my hair. 'Tell me if I'm hurting you or you want to stop.'

'Do. Not. Stop.' A quiver snakes up my legs. 'Don't shift from that position,' I pant. My groans begin to grow louder, my legs tighten around her, sparks and fireworks erupt behind my eyes. Soon, I'm gasping her name, reaching an explosive peak, every molecule fizzing, unravelling bit by bit.

The intensity eventually eases but my body continues to spasm as the last of the orgasm dissolves and my breaths come short and fast.

Maya slows her pace. 'Do you want me to keep going?'

I give a tiny shake of my head.

She withdraws slowly and slips off me, a lazy smile on her face. 'Well, that was seriously hot. Are all of our drag lessons going to lead to very satisfying sex?'

I whimper in response.

Maya's smile drops. 'Are you alright?' When I don't answer, she says, 'Blink once for yes, twice for no.'

I close my eyelids slowly, then open them again.

She waits, then grins. 'That's a yes.'

I groan.

Maya chuckles and removes the strap, placing it on my bedside table, and cuddles into me.

I wrap my arms around her, her skin warm and sticky, and hold her close. 'Sweet Jesus.'

'I think you enjoyed that,' she says.

'Uh-huh.' My heart rate has started to ease and oxygen is flowing to my brain again. 'Thank you.'

'Oh, I think I should be thanking you,' she says.

I skim my hand over her hip. 'We haven't finished yet.'

Her brows lift. 'You've still got energy after that?'

'You've seen me onstage,' I say. 'You know how much energy I have.'

She laughs a little. 'That is true.' She traces a fingertip down my chest, over my nipple, and says, 'What do you want to do to me?'

I slip my leg between her thighs and kiss her. 'I want to taste you. I always want to taste you.'

She releases a long sigh and rolls onto her back. 'Please.'

I shimmy down her body, relishing the sensation of her satiny skin on my lips, then settle between her legs, her breath hitching when my tongue brushes against her clit. I take my time, licking her slowly, savouring her musky smell and taste, savouring this moment of daytime intimacy that I've never let myself enjoy before.

But Maya pushes against my face, moaning, fingers gripping my hair, making my body throb all over again. Suddenly, taking my time doesn't matter; I just want to please her. She rocks faster against my tongue, her groans and gasps loud and urgent. Her back arches as her thighs squeeze my shoulders and a heel digs into my side. My fingertips sink into her hips as her body convulses and I groan at the feel of her orgasm on my tongue. I can't get enough of her and grip her tight as she shudders against my mouth.

After a minute, she gently nudges my head away with trembling fingers. 'Come back up here.'

I crawl up the bed and gather her into my arms. Our bodies are melded together from our feet to our chests, hot skin on hot skin. The breeze from the ceiling fan dries the sweat along my hairline and neck. Closing my eyes, I soak up this moment. Her breasts pressed against mine, the smell of sex, the taste of her in my mouth, her fingertips stroking my back, and the churn of emotions in my heart.

'That was very hot for someone who hasn't had much day sex,' Maya says, breaking the silence.

I pull my head back to look at her. Her hair is tousled and she has a sleepy, contented smile. 'And you're very experienced for someone who hasn't slept with many people,' I say.

She laughs. 'Well, I was motivated to please you.'

'Oh, you definitely achieved that. My bones feel like rubber.'

'Mmm. Same.'

This sensation in my chest is intensifying by the second. So different to anything I've felt before. 'I like you so much, Maya; you mean a lot to me.' The words don't come close to whatever this ache is deep in my soul, but it's all I have, and I know she wants to hear it.

Her eyes narrow slightly, trying to read me. 'You mean a lot to me, too.' After a beat, she props herself up, head in palm. 'If you're home alone tonight, does that mean I can stay?'

'Yes, and you could stay even if I wasn't home alone. But it's nice we've got the place to ourselves. Would you like something to eat?'

Maya nods. 'Mmm, food sounds good.'

Chapter 23
Callie

We pad out to the kitchen, messy hair, bruised lips, blissful smiles.

'What do you feel like eating?' I ask. 'Eggs?'

'Eggs are great,' Maya says.

I crack four into a bowl, add a dash of milk and a pinch of salt and whisk.

Maya reaches for the loaf of bread. 'I'll do the toast.'

I turn on the gas and pour the egg mix into a frying pan. As I wade the wooden spoon through for maximum fluff, my mind drifts, thinking about how incredible this moment is. Then, unexpectedly, Lacey's face swims into view, her dark eyes cold and her lips fixed in a mocking smile, and the moment is soured. Memories surface of her leaving here straight after sex or urging me to leave her place because she had 'things to do'. It always left me feeling empty, confused and unworthy.

'Hey.' Maya's hand smooths across my back. 'Everything okay?'

I blink at her and shake my head, clearing the image. 'Yeah, sorry. Just a little dazed.'

She considers me with an uncertain air. 'You'll tell me if something's up?'

'I am feeling very, very good,' I say with a smile, then pick up the frying pan. 'This is ready.'

She slides two plates along the bench. I scoop the scrambled eggs onto buttered toast and carry them to the table. Maya has already poured us a glass of orange juice each.

She sits across from me and takes a large bite. 'Mmm, delicious.'

I grin. 'You have to say that after all the food I've complimented you on.'

She shakes her head. 'No, I mean it. I never get scrambled eggs right. These are perfect.'

'It was my go-to dinner when I was a teenager and Mum was on late shift.'

'You spent lots of your childhood on your own?' Maya asks, a surprised note to her voice.

I swallow my mouthful. 'Not when I was a kid but as an older teenager. Sixteen and up. Before that, Mum wouldn't let me be on my own. Gina and Lisa were always here, or I'd go to Stevie's house. I also spent a lot of time with my grandparents.'

'You and your Mum spent a lot of time together otherwise?'

'Yeah. Whenever we could. I think she always felt guilty about me being an only child and her being a single mum and a shift worker, so she poured everything into making us a strong family unit.'

'It's nice you were close,' Maya says. 'I barely saw my parents during the week because they worked so much. That meant our weekends were crammed with family time, like they were trying to make up for everything they didn't do with us through the week.' She picks up a triangle of toast. 'They're still like that now, although Dad's more relaxed the closer he gets to retirement.'

'That sounds like it would've been tough on you,' I say.

She shrugs, swallows her bite of food and says, 'I guess it was, being the eldest. I had to look after my sisters a lot, be responsible at a young age.' She frowns. 'I was resentful about that at times because all I wanted to do was be a kid – dance, dress up, read, watch movies. But Mum and Dad were so driven, and I felt pressure to be like that too, like my own interests weren't really important, or not as important, at least.' She sips her drink, then continues. 'They didn't say anything when I got the job at the bookshop, but I sensed their disappointment that I wasn't following in either of their career footsteps, especially since I'd worked at Mum's accounting firm for a while and didn't take a job that was on offer at Dad's company. They'd just paid for me to do an MBA at university and I chose a job in a bookshop because I wanted to be surrounded by stories all day.'

'But your degree would've helped you get the job at City Books and you love it. They must know that?'

Maya nods. 'They do. Although, to be fair to them, they don't give me a hard time about it. It's more a case of what they don't say, and my own guilt, I think.'

'A job in a bookshop is very cool,' I say.

'A job in a lesbian club and being a drag king is much cooler.'

I grin. 'It is an amazing job.' I collect our plates and carry them to the sink. 'Do you want some dessert? We've got ice-cream.'

'Ooh, yes, please,' Maya says, hopping up and rinsing the dishes.

I open the freezer, bending down to check what we have. 'We've got butterscotch or chocolate.'

'Butterscotch? Oh my god. My favourite.'

'Mine, too.' I dish up two bowls and tip my head towards the lounge room. 'Let's go in there.'

We relax on the couch and Maya moans as she spoons some ice-cream into her mouth. 'So good.'

'It is delicious, and it's Mum's fave too, so I'll get her more tomorrow.'

Maya pauses, spoon halfway to her mouth. 'You didn't say it was your mum's. I'll buy her more.'

'It's fine. She won't care, and she really likes you.'

'You think so?'

'Definitely.'

Maya stirs the ice-cream until it starts to resemble a thick shake. 'You haven't introduced her to anyone before?'

'There hasn't been anyone to introduce her to,' I say.

'What about the not-nice situationship?'

'Ha, not a chance. Mum would've hated her. I thought about it, but Stevie always talked me out of it, and for good reason.'

Maya opens her mouth like she's about to speak, but closes it again.

I narrow my eyes at her. 'You want to ask me something.'

She gives a small smile. 'I'm curious about what happened with her? If you're okay to talk about it.'

I place my empty bowl on the coffee table and pull my legs up onto the couch. 'It went on for about, hmm, two months maybe, from the time we met until the time I had to cut ties for my own sanity. I thought I loved her. But it wasn't love; it was an unhealthy obsession.'

Maya pulls her legs up too, wrapping her arms around her knees.

'I couldn't see that at the time,' I say. 'Lacey had been the only person who'd paid me attention for more than one night, at least that's what it felt like, and I latched onto that in a dysfunctional way. It wasn't until I told Stevie and Krissy a few things about how she treated me that they sat me down and gave me a "good talking-to", to quote my gran. They were wary of her from the start. Said she had a vibe.'

Maya stays silent, giving me the space to continue.

'She'd do this thing,' I say, 'where she'd make me feel guilty if I paid any kind of attention to someone, or made a comment about someone being attractive, even though it was always innocent on my part. A really ugly jealous streak. But I'm fairly certain she was sleeping with other people the whole time. She'd leave me on read for days when I messaged her, then tell me it was because she was busy. But then I'd see on her socials that she was out, so she was just too busy for me. If I took too long to reply to her, though, I'd get the silent treatment.' I take a breath. 'And she'd say things about my body after we'd slept together and then' – I pause, deciding not to mention that Lacey would leave here because I don't want Maya ever thinking about another woman in my bed – 'she'd tell me to leave her place because she had things to do, and I never questioned that.'

Maya's mouth drops open. 'She said things about your body and kicked you out?'

I nod. 'Stuff like, "You're skin and bones. I can't lay on you because your hips are too sharp." Then she'd scroll through her phone or watch something on TV and comment on women's bodies, on their curves and how much she liked that. But then we'd go out and she'd comment on mascs and how hot they were.' I let out a heavy sigh. 'It was confusing and really messed with my head.'

Maya blinks, her eyes misty. 'You've got a beautiful body, Callie. Everything about you is beautiful. I don't understand how anyone could treat you like that.' She takes my hands. 'No wonder you panic about being intimate and want to cover yourself up.'

'It's not entirely because of what happened with her. I've never been overly confident. But that situation certainly brought my insecurities to the surface. This is why I love being Tom so much. He was just an act at first, but he's become a vehicle for me to be this completely different person. Someone who takes charge, who isn't afraid to show off their body, who wouldn't stand for anything like that or let anyone treat him badly. And he's become the brand of masculinity I want to see more of in the world – strong but vulnerable, confident but respectful, assertive but gentle.'

Maya smiles. 'You do realise you've just described yourself.'

'Oh.' I shake my head. 'I'm not strong, confident or assertive.'

'I think you are, Callie,' she says softly. 'It's there, under the surface, seeping out slowly. Tom just makes you feel less exposed so that you can express it. He's helped you find yourself.'

I nod, a fondness rising in me for this persona I've created. 'He has.'

She cups my cheek. 'I'm glad you trusted me earlier because I think you're beautiful and I could look at you all day, every day.' She pauses. 'I'm so lucky I found you.'

My eyes prickle and I drop my gaze, blinking rapidly. I give myself a second for the emotion to pass before I speak. 'That's exactly what I think about you, and I'm lucky I found you because you make me feel like I'm someone worth lov—' I bite my lip, my cheeks warming over the slip. 'Worth caring about.'

She kisses me, her mouth cool and sweet from the ice-cream. 'And you make it very easy because you *are* someone worth loving.'

Chapter 24
Maya

I hop off the bus and take my time walking to Mum and Dad's, going over the conversation with Dr Garcia about coming out to my parents from my earlier session. I visualise a scenario where they're completely accepting, happy for me even, but the image quickly fades because I know deep in my heart it won't be as smooth as that. But it needs to be today. Callie's birthday is next week so we're having an early celebration later, and I want to tell her that my parents know.

When I walk in, Bella is on the couch, her laptop balancing on her thighs and an open textbook beside her.

'Hey, Belly. You studying?'

She tilts her head back to look at me. 'Assignment due first thing Monday.'

Dad steps out of the butler's pantry, carrying a bottle of red wine. He grins at me, the late afternoon sun shining through the patio doors turning his grey hair a shimmery silver. 'Hello, sweetheart.'

'Hi, Dad.'

'Would you like a glass of wine?' He holds up the bottle.

'Your aunty and uncle sent this shiraz over from the Adelaide Hills.'

'Hmm...' A wine would calm my nerves, and I love a South Australian shiraz, but I need to stay composed. 'Tempting, but no thanks. Water's fine.' I take the water jug from the fridge as Mum and Liv descend the stairs.

'You're saying no to a shiraz?' Liv asks, taking a seat at the dining table and lifting a half-drunk glass of wine to her mouth.

I sit beside her. 'I might have one later.' *To celebrate. Or commiserate.*

'Hello, darling,' Mum says, squeezing my shoulder as she passes. She takes the glass of wine that Dad's poured for her and sits across from Liv and me. She sips, eyes narrowing as she assesses me. 'Something is different about you.'

My stomach tightens and heat crawls across my face, millimetre by agonising millimetre. 'Is it?'

'Yes.' She tilts her head. 'Have you changed your hair colour?'

'Um, no,' I say, touching a hand to my head, 'same as always.'

'What are we talking about?' Bella asks from the couch.

'Maya looks different,' Mum says, still scrutinising me. 'It's your skin. You're glowing.'

Liv twists to face me and Bella hops up and walks over, peering at me.

'I don't think I'm glowing,' I say with a nervous laugh, my eyes darting between them.

'Are you using new skin products?' Mum asks, determined to get to the bottom of my glow.

'No, although I did use a serum mask last night,' I say honestly.

'Ah.' She waggles a finger at me. 'That's it. I swear by those masks. You'll need to tell me which one.'

'Erm, sure,' I say, nudging Liv under the table as she struggles to keep a straight face. *Now*, a voice in my head says. *Tell them now.* I take a deep breath. 'There's something—'

'Is that a phone ringing?' Dad asks, looking around for the source.

Mum turns her head, listening. 'I think it's mine.' She hops up and walks out to the patio, and I watch her, exasperated.

'Hungry?' Dad asks, glancing between the three of us.

'Starving,' Bella says, sweeping her hair up into a messy bun and securing it with the band around her wrist.

'I'll get started on dinner,' Dad says and heads out to light the barbecue.

Once the room is parent-free, Liv barks out a laugh. 'A face mask? That is *so* not why you're glowing.'

'Oh my god, Maya,' Bella says, grinning. 'If they only knew what you were really putting on your face. I don't think Mum will want the brand when she finds out.'

Liv snorts.

'I was about to tell them when she started talking about that,' I say in a quiet voice.

Liv's smile falters. 'Tell them? About your sexuality?'

Bella's smile fades, too.

I nod. 'I don't want to keep it from them anymore, and I don't want to keep Callie a secret from anybody.'

Liv winces. 'Sorry, we were just teasing you.'

'Yeah, sorry, May,' Bella says, squeezing my hand.

'Why right now, though?' Liv asks. 'Has Callie said something to you about—'

'No,' I say, cutting her off, remembering how upset she became over Arianne having an issue with me not telling Mum and Dad about her. 'Of course not. She'd never pressure me to do that. I'm just tired of hiding my life from them. And Callie is part of my life now and I want everyone to know that.'

Bella hugs me. 'I'm happy you've found someone you like so much.'

'Me, too,' Liv says. 'It would be nice to meet her properly.'

'I asked her to Dad's dinner and she said yes, so you'll meet her then.'

Liv's eyes widen. 'Wow, way to come out with a bang.'

I grimace. 'Too much too soon?'

Liv shakes her head. 'No. It's still a couple of weeks away. Mum and Dad will just need to get used to it.'

'You're overthinking this, May,' Bella says matter-of-factly. 'They won't care.'

'How can you be so sure?' I challenge her. 'You've heard Mum go on about me finding a boyfriend.'

Bella rolls her eyes. 'Because you're single and you're the eldest and she thinks you like men. If she knew the truth, I guarantee she would've been trying to set you up with a woman this whole time. They're not homophobic. My queer friends come over all the time; they don't care.'

'Your queer friends aren't their children.' I give a frustrated sigh – at what, I don't know. At myself? At them for not working it out? At the world, because I live in a society where I have to justify who I'm attracted to with a label? 'I suppose I have no idea how they'll react,' I say. 'I'm not glowing, though.'

'Oh, you definitely are,' Liv says. 'You've been like walking sunshine since you met Callie.'

My stomach flips and I bite my bottom lip to suppress a smile, but it breaks through.

'See, right there,' Liv says, pointing at me. 'Whenever she's mentioned, you go all gooey.'

Mum walks back in, her face heavy with worry, Dad in tow.

'Is something wrong, Mum?' Liv asks.

'It's your grandmother. She's been taken to Emergency.'

She puts a hand up at our gasps. 'It's okay. Your uncle is with her. She had a fall and landed hard on her hip.'

'But she's alright?' Bella asks.

Mum nods. 'Apparently so. The paramedics don't believe she's broken anything, but they wanted her to go to hospital, and of course, she's in a lot of pain.'

'Poor Grandma,' I say. 'She must be in shock, too.'

'Yes. I should probably go to the hospital,' Mum says, looking to Dad.

He nods. 'That's a good idea.'

All four turn to me. I look between them, unclear why the focus has shifted to me. 'Oh, yes, if that's what you want to do.'

'I can't drive,' Mum says. 'I've been drinking.'

Dad lifts his glass of wine. 'So have I.'

'And this is my second,' Liv says, 'so I'll be over the limit.'

I turn to Bella, who shakes her head. 'I can't drive a manual and Dad won't let me drive his BMW.'

'He'd let you drive it in an emergency.' I give him a pointed look. 'Wouldn't you, Dad?'

'Well, yes,' he says hesitantly, 'in an emergency. But she's not on the insurance and you are, and you're here and you haven't been drinking.'

'Plus I've got this assignment due,' Bella adds with an apologetic wince.

'But I had plans,' I say in a small voice. *Plans to spend the night with my gorgeous girlfriend, celebrating her birthday and making her feel valued and seen because I finally came out to my parents and told them about her, and she's the one who gave me the courage to do that.*

'Well, you can drop me off and I'll get a taxi home if you don't want to see your grandmother,' Mum says stiffly.

I stare at her, my mouth pressed into a tight line. 'Mum, that's not fair. I had plans with ... I was going out. Of course I want to see Grandma, but she's in Emergency and she'll be either waiting for X-rays or getting transferred to a ward, so we might not be able to see her anyway. Plus you said that Uncle Grant is with her.'

'She still needs our support,' Mum says incredulously.

I sigh heavily. It's not worth the grief. 'Fine. I'll drive.'

'I'll come too,' Liv says.

'Sorry, Mum,' Bella says. 'But I've got to finish this assignment. I'm literally so close to having it done. Tell Grandma I love her and I'll visit tomorrow.'

Mum reaches across the table and pats Bella's hand. 'That's fine, darling. Your studies are important; she'll understand.'

I shoot Bella a look, but she returns to the couch and picks up her laptop.

'I'll stay here and deal with all of this,' Dad says, gesturing to the food and dishes spread across the kitchen counters. 'I'll visit tomorrow with Bella.'

I lift myself from the table, my body heavy, the weighty words I didn't get to voice stuck inside me with nowhere to go. I retrieve Mum's car keys from the hook inside the pantry. Mum grabs her bag, Liv slips her phone into the pocket of her skirt and they follow me to the garage.

'Which hospital?' I ask, touching my finger to the car door to unlock.

'Royal Brisbane,' Mum replies.

We're silent for the ten-minute drive to the hospital. The only sounds are the purr of the engine and the click, click, click of Mum tapping at her phone screen, presumably exchanging messages with my uncle. Liv keeps glancing at me, trying to break the tension with sympathetic smiles, but my emotions are up and down – my jaw clenched with frustration over not getting a chance to tell my parents, my chest tight with guilt for even thinking about myself when my grandmother is in hospital, and my heart heavy from having to let Callie down tonight of all nights.

I turn left into Butterfield Street and take another left up the incline into the hospital, pulling over to let Mum and Liv out at Emergency. 'I'll park and come find you.'

'Thank you, Maya, you're a good girl,' Mum says. She jumps out and strides towards the entrance.

I close my eyes, my hands tightening on the steering wheel. I want to scream after her, *Would you say that if I were a man? Would you call your twenty-eight-year-old son 'a good boy' for giving up their night out to drive you to the hospital?* My grip loosens. She probably would.

'I'll come with you to park,' Liv says.

I shake my head. 'No. Go with Mum. I need to call Callie and tell her I can't make it tonight.'

Liv frowns, her dark eyes growing wide with concern. 'I'm sorry, May. I would've driven if I hadn't been drinking.'

I shrug. 'Mum would've made me feel bad for not coming anyway.'

She nods. 'Yeah. See you in a minute.'

She closes the passenger door and I accelerate, driving straight ahead for the car park, and call Callie.

She answers after two rings. 'Hey, are you on your way? I was getting worried something happened with your parents.'

My chest squeezes. 'I'm sorry. I can't make it. I'm at the hospital.'

'The hospital? Oh my god. Are you hurt? I'll come to you.'

'No. Not me. My grandmother. She had a fall. I was at Mum and Dad's when they found out and I was the only one who hadn't been drinking, so I drove Mum and Liv here. I felt guilty just dropping them and not going in.'

'Of course,' Callie says. 'You need to be with your family.'

If she's disappointed, there's no hint of it; she's just her usual considerate self.

'I, um, I didn't get a chance to tell them about me, about us. I was about to when my uncle called to tell Mum what had happened. I'm sorry, Callie. I wanted—'

'Maya,' she says softly. 'It's okay. You don't need to do that for me. You do that for you, when you're ready.'

'I am ready. It just didn't go to plan.'

'You'll find the right time,' she says.

'I so badly wanted to see you tonight,' I say. 'To celebrate your birthday and celebrate coming out to them.'

'I wanted that, too, but stuff happens. Besides, it's not my birthday yet, and I'm sure your grandma will appreciate you being there.'

My heart expands with affection for her. 'You're so sweet.'

A soft chuckle fills the car. 'So you've said.'

'I hate missing your show.'

'I hate you missing it, too, but I'll just have to imagine you watching me.'

'Please don't include any other audience members in your striptease or margarita routines.' My tone is light, and I meant for the comment to be playful, but there's an envious edge to my voice and I wince, praying Callie hasn't picked up on it, particularly given what she told me about Lacey's ugly jealous streak.

She's silent for a moment, then says, 'Those acts are for you only. You know that, don't you?'

I let out weary sigh. 'I do. I'm sorry. That came out wrong. You don't owe me anything on that stage.'

'I'm not doing either act tonight anyway. Trying some new stuff, so it's probably good you're not there to watch me mess up.'

'You'll be amazing and I should let you go. I'd like to say I'll come and meet you afterwards, but I have no idea how long I'm going to be here, and I'm working tomorrow.'

'It's all good.'

'Okay, but we're celebrating your birthday next week, no matter what, since we couldn't do it tonight.'

'I can't wait,' she says.

'Night, Callie. I...' I what? I'm sorry that I didn't come out to my parents? I care about her? I *love* her? 'I'll see you soon.'

Chapter 25
Callie

I ignore the doorbell and open the birthday cards from Mum and my aunties. It stops for a second, then chimes again. Huffing at the interruption, I walk over to the window and peek through the blinds. A silver hatchback is parked in the driveway and my heart leaps.

I rush to the front door and swing it open. 'I thought you were working today,' I say to Maya, un-snibbing the lock of the security screen and propping it open for her.

'Change of plan,' she says. 'Close your eyes.'

I do as she asks, my stomach fizzing with excitement.

'Keep them closed,' she says, her voice moving further away.

A few seconds pass before I hear the car door shut, then her sandals scuffing on the footpath.

'Okay, open,' she says.

I open my eyes and she thrusts something towards me.

'Happy birthday.'

I take hold of the ribbon and tilt my head back. Three silver helium balloons, each marked with a multicoloured '28' bob in the air. 'You brought me balloons?'

'Well, it's your birthday and people have balloons on their birthday.'

'Thank you,' I say, stepping aside to let her pass. I lock the security screen behind us and head back into the lounge room. A small weight is already attached to the end of the ribbon to stop the balloons floating away, and I place them on the floor. 'Why are you off work and bringing me balloons?'

She wraps her arms around my waist. 'Because I don't want you spending your birthday alone, and I wanted to surprise you.'

'I'm surprised,' I say. 'Does this mean I get a whole unexpected afternoon with you?'

'Mm-hmm.' She gives me a lingering kiss. The taste of my first girlfriend birthday kiss is as delicious as I always imagined it would be. She pulls away and says, 'So, birthday girl, what would you like to do?'

I kiss her again, deeper this time. 'This,' I murmur.

She smiles against my lips. 'This is nice, but I thought you might like to go out.' She tilts her head back marginally, eyes scanning my face, as though she's gauging my reaction. 'But it's your day, so it's your choice.'

'Out is good, too.'

She gives me a sheepish look.

I narrow my eyes at her. 'You totally have something planned.'

'Kind of...' she says.

'Okay. What are we doing?'

'I thought we could go to that nice pizza place at Chermside?'

I nod. 'Sure.'

'And do something fun. Like bowling.'

My brows shoot up. 'Bowling? Ten-pin or lawn?'

She grins. 'Ten-pin. I don't think we're at the lawn bowls stage of our lives yet.'

'Hey, loads of young people play lawn bowls. Barefoot bowls is a thing.'

'I'll put that on next year's birthday list.'

Next year's birthday list. The idea of us still being together in a year makes me want to squeal, but I control myself and say in an even voice, 'I didn't know you were a bowler.'

'I wouldn't say I'm a bowler, but I've been a few times.' She sits on the couch, encouraging me to join her. 'You said that you never went bowling again after your dad was going to take you, but that you always wanted to.'

I blink at her, a sudden lump in my throat.

Maya's expression changes. 'You're upset. Sorry. I should've talked to you first. I—'

'No,' I say, squeezing her hands. 'I'm not upset. I love the idea. I'm just ... I can't believe you remembered that.'

Surprise flickers across her face. 'Of course I did. Birthdays are important to kids and that would've been hard for you. I want you to have nice birthday memories.' She releases my hands and cups my cheeks. 'But if it's going to bring up stuff that's difficult for you, we don't need to do it.'

My eyes sting but I give her a reassuring smile. 'It's a lovely idea. You know I can't bowl, right?'

'I'm not very good either,' she says. 'So this should be fun.'

'I'll get changed.' I take her hand and head for my room.

Maya sits on my bed cross-legged while I look for something to wear. I dig out shorts and a T-shirt and strip off my pyjamas, not as self-conscious about Maya seeing me naked during the day now that day sex is a regular thing. She gives me a slow, seductive smile as her eyes slide over my body. 'If you look at me like that,' I say, 'we won't leave the house.'

She crawls to the end of the bed and grabs my hips, pulling me toward her and pressing a kiss to my stomach that sends a wave of heat through me. 'When you stand in front of me like this, you are very hard to resist.'

I brush the hair from her face, my heart smashing against my rib cage, then bend forward to kiss her. 'You are also very hard to resist but I'm looking forward to my party now. Then we can come back here, eat my homemade birthday cake and spend the rest of the night in bed, because Mum's at work.'

'Cake and bed and the house to ourselves?' she says with a sigh. 'It does not get better than that.'

Forty-five minutes later, we stroll into the bowling alley. Although it's been revamped since I was a kid, this is where Dad would've taken me. A memory materialises of a young me waiting excitedly by the lounge room window for him to arrive, wearing the new shorts, T-shirt and sneakers Mum had bought me, my short, boy cut freshly washed and brushed. Then the anxiety, hurt and confusion when he didn't show. Emotions that were too big for my small body to process and my young brain to comprehend. An hour later, I was on Mum's lap, sobbing, asking what I'd done to keep Dad away and not get my birthday party.

'Hey,' Maya says, touching a hand to my back. 'We can leave.'

I shake my head and give her a quick smile, burying the memory. 'No. Just having a moment.'

She searches my face. 'Are you sure? You don't talk about

your dad much, and I thought ... well, I don't know, that you deserved to have the party you never got, I guess.'

I nod. 'I'm sure. Now, let's bowl – badly.'

We pay for two games, slip on the bowling shoes and choose our balls.

Maya bowls first, the ball hurtling down the left side of the lane to knock over four pins. She spins to face me, her smile wide.

'Erm, I thought you said you couldn't bowl,' I say, folding my arms.

'I can't!' She picks up the ball and lines up another shot. The ball rolls down the lane at speed, curving to the right and knocking over another four pins. She turns, laughing, her face radiant. 'That's just lucky.'

Her hair is pulled up in a loose top knot, revealing the soft contours of her face. Her dark eyes glisten, her mouth is stretched in a wide grin and a pink flush tints her cheeks. The vision makes my heart hurt, and I feel myself falling hard for her, like I'm hurtling through space, and it's terrifying and exhilarating all at once. I pull myself together and remember to speak. 'Mmm. I'm not sure I believe you.' I clumsily pick up my ball, gripping it with two hands.

'Put your fingers and thumb into those holes,' Maya says, her tone teasing.

I look at her with a deadpan expression. 'I know that much.' I fit the ball and walk up to the lane.

Maya steps up alongside me. 'Twist your arm so that your palm is facing upward and your wrist is flat. That way, when you release the ball, it should go straight.'

I follow her instructions. 'Like this?'

'Uh-huh. When you swing your arm, don't drop the ball. Crouch a little and release it, but with a bit of force so that it lands gently and goes straight down the centre.' She points to the markings on the lane. 'Aim for that middle arrow.'

'Don't drop. Use a bit of force. Middle arrow. Too easy.' I take a few steps back and hold the ball in front of my face, copying the person two lanes away, then do a little trot as I swing my arm and unleash the ball. It tracks smoothly down the centre of the lane and hits the pins with force, knocking down all ten. I spin, giving Maya a cheeky grin. 'Something like that?'

Her mouth drops open. 'No more lessons for you.'

I laugh, throw my arm around her and plant a kiss on her temple. 'That was a fluke, or you're a very good teacher.'

'Mmm. A fluke, I think.'

It takes an hour to play two games, Maya winning both and my first strike definitely being chance. We leave the bowling alley and wander through the outdoor eatery area of the shopping centre. There's a lightness to my step, like my inner seven-year-old is enjoying her party.

'I promised you pizza,' Maya says.

Five minutes later, we're seated at the back of the restaurant. We've ordered watermelon mojito mocktails and a large supreme to share. It's the late-afternoon lull, the lunch rush finished and dinner customers still a few hours away, so we almost have the place to ourselves.

'This has been the best birthday,' I say.

Maya gives me a delighted smile. 'I'm glad you've enjoyed it, but there's more. I have a gift for you.' She reaches into her bag and hands me a small, rectangular package wrapped in pink tissue paper decorated with cupcakes.

My eyes widen. 'A gift? You didn't need to do that.'

'I wanted to.'

My throat thickens, and I'm grateful for the server delivering our drinks, the interruption giving me a second to compose myself.

They walk away and Maya says impatiently, 'Open it.'

I unwrap the paper to reveal a black box. I flip the lid and gasp.

'I hope you like it,' she says softly.

I glance at her, stunned, then return my gaze to the silver link bracelet glistening from the cushioned felt. I carefully remove it, catching the inscription on the tiny plate that reads *Callie*.

'Look at the other side,' Maya says.

I twist it and see *Tom*.

Pressure builds behind my eyes. 'You bought me and Tom a bracelet?'

She nods. 'You said you'd like more of him in your everyday life and I thought, this way, you can carry him around with you without having to be in drag. I know he's always there inside of you, but this way, he's on the outside, too.'

I breathe through the rising emotion, blinking to stop the tears. I'm desperate to kiss her, though I'm not sure how comfortable she is with PDAs in a suburban shopping centre. But it's the first time a girlfriend has bought me a gift and spent my birthday with me, and that deserves a kiss at the very least.

'What are you thinking?' she asks.

'That I want to kiss you,' I say, my voice shaky.

Her eyes dart around the restaurant. 'Then kiss me.'

I lean across the table, our lips meeting tenderly. 'Thank you,' I say as I sit back. 'It's the most beautiful gift.'

'For the most beautiful person.'

The statement is so soft that I almost miss it, her words disappearing into the white noise of the restaurant. But I'm certain about what I heard and for the rest of my life, no matter what happens between us, those words will be burnt into my memory.

I thrust my arm towards her. 'Help me put it on?'

She clasps it around my wrist, running her thumb over the small, engraved plate. 'Who do you feel like today?'

'Since it's my birthday, I feel like Callie today,' I say, straightening the plate so that my name is facing outward.

'Good.' Maya leans forward conspiratorially. 'Because, don't tell Tom, but she's my favourite.'

I lower my gaze, my cheeks warming as I sip my drink, a delirious smile making my face ache.

She laughs. 'You're adorable.'

Our pizza arrives and we each take a slice. After she swallows a bite, she says, 'We haven't talked about the other thing.'

'The other thing?' I ask, tipping my head back to catch the stringy cheese.

'Me not telling my parents on the weekend and Dad's dinner next week.'

My gut twists at the mention of the awards dinner, particularly given her parents don't know who I am, but I don't want her to feel any worse than she already does. 'But your gran was in hospital. It wasn't the right time.'

She gives me a grateful smile. 'Mum's going to be busy this weekend helping get Grandma settled back in her house with the adjustments she needs, so I don't think I'll be able to tell them this—'

'Maya,' I say, putting the pizza down and reaching for her hand. 'It's fine. You don't need to come out to them for my sake.'

'But I wanted to introduce you as my partner. I want to be honest about our relationship.'

My pulse quickens thinking about how we'll manage this,

but I want to do this for her, for us. 'I can be your friend at the dinner, can't I? And your sisters know who I am.'

'Well, yes, you can and they do, but you're nervous about going and I don't want you to feel uncomfortable.'

My leg begins to bounce under the table. I feel more than uncomfortable; I'm petrified. But she'll be there beside me and she makes me want to lower the safety guards I've built around myself. 'I'll be okay,' I say, giving her what I hope is an assured smile. Eager to return to our joyous mood, I pick up my mocktail and clink it against hers, my bracelet shimmering under the spotlights. 'Now, let's enjoy my very special birthday party for two.'

Chapter 26
Maya

'This is one of the best shops for king clothes,' Callie says as we step into a men's clothing store. 'They have everything and it's affordable.'

I take in the rows of suits along one wall, the shelves of jeans and T-shirts lining another, and the racks of shirts, trousers and shorts filling the space between. 'I have no idea where to start.'

'You want simple, right?' Callie walks further into the store. 'George in the late eighties wore tight jeans, T-shirts and leather jackets. So if you want to imitate that, let's start with jeans.' She stops in front of a shelf. 'These clothes are for you to wear at home to get used to them, so don't think too hard about it.'

I nod. 'Okay. Maybe I'll try a dark blue denim?' I rummage through, sliding out a 28 and a pair in a size up, then move over to the folded tees.

Callie picks up a black shirt and holds it against me. 'This looks small enough for you, and black is good to hide anything underneath, like tape or a bra.' She points to the other side of the shop. 'Changing rooms are over there.'

A shop assistant approaches. 'Can I help you?'

'I'd like to try these on,' I say, then quickly add, 'It's for a performance.'

They give me a friendly smile, take the clothes from me and lead the way.

In the dressing room, I groan. 'Why did I say that? It's not exactly for a performance. Even if it was, what a wanky thing to say.'

Callie sits on a plastic chair in the corner. 'It's your first time trying on men's clothes in a men's shop, you're bound to feel strange. And the staff are friendly here; they couldn't care less who's trying on their clothes, as long as they get a sale.'

'It does feel strange,' I say. 'Not bad strange, just different. Though I don't know why when it's standard jeans and tees.' I kick off my sandals. 'Deeply ingrained gender conditioning that says I have to wear women's jeans and T-shirts, I suppose.'

Callie nods her agreement. 'Yep.'

I shimmy out of my skirt and Callie's eyes roam my bare legs, her cheeks flushing when her gaze lands on my lace G-string. Her eyes flick up to meet mine, the corner of her mouth lifting. 'Your eyes are up there.'

'They are,' I say with a chuckle and tug on the jeans, slip off my shirt and try on the tee. I turn from side to side, assessing myself in the mirror. 'Jeans not too tight?'

She shakes her head. 'I don't think so. If you wear a packer, it will make it obvious, but that's not a bad thing. If you're not comfortable with that, go for a bigger size or different cut.'

I stare at my crotch, trying to imagine a bulge and how it would feel to wear a packer. The concept sends a thrilling tingle through me, but when my eyes skim my reflection – my hair twisted up in a butterfly clip, a fine gold chain around my neck, small hoops in my ears, and the curve of my breasts – the thrill dies because even in men's clothing, I look feminine.

'What are you thinking?' Callie asks.

'That I'm too girly to be a drag king.'

She meets my eyes in the mirror. 'It's not about whether you're too girly or not. It's about how you want to express yourself in drag. Besides, drag blurs the boundaries between masculinity and femininity; it challenges the status quo and gender norms.' Her voice is confident and authoritative. 'Kings can be feminine,' she continues, 'and that can be part of your alter ego. Or you can go in the other direction and make yourself more traditionally masculine-looking with make-up and wigs and flattening your chest and your choice of clothing. Or you can land somewhere in the middle. Get creative with it. Express yourself in a way that feels good to you.'

I nod emphatically. 'You're right. I'm bringing in my own gender biases and conditioned thinking, aren't I?'

She shrugs. 'It's the world we live in. We've all been conditioned around gender. That's part of what makes being a king so fun and liberating.'

I change back into my own clothes and we head to the counter. While I pay, Callie's phone pings with a message. She reads it and gives a small grunt.

'Everything okay?' I ask.

'Yeah. It's Stevie asking me to do extra shifts over the next couple of weeks with all the public holidays, and Amber needs a week off apparently, so I have to do her amateur night emcee cover.'

My ears prick up. 'So you'll be covering next Thursday?' I ask casually.

'No, second week of April.'

I mentally tally up the days. That's nineteen days away. Could this be my chance to try this without Amber present? It's soon, but I have an act and a song, and now clothes, and Callie's showing me make-up later. If I practised for three weeks ... how hard could it be?

'Now for the fun part,' Callie says, drawing me back to the conversation as we leave the shop. 'Make-up.'

I give a little squeal because buying make-up is something I can resonate with. We enter a variety store and head for the make-up section.

'As much as I love make-up, I think I'll start simple,' I say.

'That's wise,' Callie says. 'Unless I've got a reason to go bold, I prefer tones that give me a natural look – kind of goes with my act, and that would suit a George look, too.'

'The first night I went to the club,' I say, 'you were serving behind the bar in drag, and your make-up was all glitter and bright colours.'

Callie nods. 'It was a big show, being the first of the year, so Stevie wanted glam. I was supposed to go straight home, but then I noticed you in the audience.'

My brows lift. 'You stayed because of me?'

'Mmm, there was something about you that had me captivated. My make-up was too heavy to wash off properly in the dressing room, so I kept it on and helped behind the bar.'

My mind rewinds to that night. Ash and I were out to celebrate the new year and finally getting a short break after the Christmas retail rush. 'You were incredible that night,' I say. 'I couldn't stop watching you. Then you looked directly at me, and your eyes...' A shiver passes through me. 'I can't tell you what that did to me.'

She dips her face shyly. 'You can tell me, if you like.'

'Let's just say the club became very hot, very fast,' I say with a grin. 'Why didn't you come and say hello to me that night since you were still in drag? Tom could've really turned it on.'

She shrugs. 'You were with Ash and I wasn't sure if they were your partner, although you were definitely giving friends. I was stoked when you came back the following Saturday.'

'How could I stay away?' I say. 'You were like a magnet.'

She reaches for my hand. 'Thank you.'

'For what?'

'For coming to the club every week. For introducing yourself. For not being turned off by me running away. For being in my life.'

'Oh, Callie.' I step closer. 'I love being in your life and I love having you in mine, but I should be thanking you. You've given me so much.' I resist the urge to glance around for unwelcome voyeurs before I kiss her. 'Let's get this make-up so we can get out of here.'

She clears her throat and averts her gaze. 'Yes. Let's do that.' She removes a tube from the shelf and hands it to me. 'Primer. This is the best, cheapest one,' she says, shifting back into teacher mode. She grabs a tester of liquid foundation and dabs it on the back of my hand. 'You want an oil-free matte foundation so it's not shiny under the lights,' she says, blending it with her fingertip. 'Hmm, a shade darker maybe.' She picks up another bottle and dabs again. 'That's good. Okay, facial hair – what do you want to try? Stubble? Goatee? Full beard?'

I shrug. 'I'm not sure, but George is well put together – designer facial hair.'

'Yeah, that's a very deliberate five o'clock.' She runs her fingertip along the plastic colour tabs of the cream blushes, stopping at a deep burgundy. 'You can use hair, but make-up is easier, especially when you're starting out.' She clicks open a tester compact, dips in her pinky and strokes it along my jaw, pursing her lips as she considers the colour. 'That will work nicely.' She replaces the tester and puts a new compact in my shopping basket. 'You'll need a contour stick, again in a shade darker than what you'd normally wear.' She slides one out of the holder. 'This is a good brand and the colour will work. Do you have bronzer and a kohl pencil in black or dark brown?'

'I do, but I only brought brushes with me. I'll get more, they won't go to waste.'

'Okay,' Callie says, examining the bronzers. 'We need a warm, yellow tone – makes you look more awake onstage.' She tosses another compact into the basket, followed by a kohl, then says, 'Let's get your king on.'

Chapter 27
Maya

As we step through Callie's front door, a warm, sugary scent greets us and we follow the smell into the kitchen.

Donna's face brightens when she sees me. 'Hi, Maya. Callie didn't mention you were coming over today.'

'Hi, Donna.' I hold up shopping bags. 'I've bought make-up and men's clothes and Callie's going to teach me drag make-up.'

'Good for you,' she says. 'I told you there was an inner king in there.'

I smile. 'You did.'

'Would you like a cuppa?' she asks me. 'I've just boiled the jug.'

'Ooh, yes please. Exactly what I need after hours of shopping.'

'And for my darling daughter?' Donna asks, turning to Callie.

'You noticed me then?' Callie says with a jokey tone.

Donna raises a brow at me and shakes her head.

Callie chuckles. 'Tea's great, thanks, Mum. What are you cooking? It smells so good in here.'

'Anzac bickies for our late shift at work tomorrow,' Donna says, slipping her hands into a double oven mitt and removing a tray from the oven.

'Your late shift?' Callie throws Donna a sceptical look. 'You sure they're not for your new boyfriend?'

'He's not my—'

'John and Donna sitting in a tree,' Callie sings, 'K.I.S.S.I.N.G.'

Donna tuts, but she's grinning, colour rising in her cheeks. It's very cute, but I give Callie a playful swat on the arm. 'Leave her alone. The biscuits look and smell amazing, Donna.'

'Thank you, Maya,' she says. 'Give them a few minutes to cool down and I'll bring you some.'

Callie gives her a bear hug. 'Thanks, Mum. You're the best.'

When we reach the spare room, I say, 'She really is the best. I can't imagine my mum welcoming my girlfriend into the family home and making them tea while they were experimenting with drag make-up.'

Callie pulls out a dressing table chair for me. 'Yeah, reckon I hit the mum jackpot.' She digs into one of my shopping bags and lays the make-up out on the dressing table, her expression turning pensive. 'You don't think your parents would be welcoming of your partner?'

'Oh,' I say, surprised by the question. 'Well, I suppose I don't know for sure. Bella and Liv think they'd be fine after they got used to the idea, but' – I shrug – 'they've never given me reason to think they'd be fine with it. Especially as Mum constantly talks about me finding a boyfriend.'

Callie wheels over a low stool and sits close to me. 'That must be hard for you.'

I nod. 'It's unsettling. But I'm the one who keeps putting off telling them.' I reach into my bag and pull out the cosmetic brushes I brought from home. 'Kind of wish they'd figured it out, rather than me having to tell them. I bet Donna figured it out?'

'Yep. Probably wasn't hard to work out, though,' Callie says. 'I only ever had girl crushes, and having Stevie, Gina and Lisa around me all the time, I understood what being gay was and that it was just part of life. I never needed to come out. Everyone in my family just knew.' She pauses. 'You'll know when it's the right time to tell your parents.'

'I guess.' I fix my hair so that my face is free of loose strands.

Callie douses a cotton pad with a cleansing toner and gently smooths it over my skin. I close my eyes, trusting her to take control. 'It's important to start with a clean face,' she says. 'I know you only had a shower a few hours ago, but it's good to remove any build-up.' Next, she rubs moisturiser over my face with gentle strokes. 'Primer and foundation sit better on freshly moisturised skin.'

The bedroom door creaks open. Donna walks in and sets down a tray with two mugs and a plate of biscuits. 'There you are, for your dress-ups tea party.'

'You're funny, Mum,' Callie deadpans.

Donna chuckles and says, 'Enjoy.'

Callie rolls her eyes as Donna leaves the room, but she's grinning. 'I think she's more in love with you than I—' her smile falters, her neck turns beetroot, and she rustles through the make-up bag. 'She, um, likes you more than I do.'

My heart hammers and I want to tell her that I love her too, but it's too soon; we're not ready for such declarations after only six weeks. I don't want to make that mistake again. But the comment hangs between us and I need to clear the air. I gently turn her face towards me and kiss her. 'You're adorable,' I say, cupping her cheeks and pressing my forehead against hers.

'Mmm, let's get back to doing make-up before I make things more awkward.'

I kiss her again and sit back down. 'Let me try this first,' I say, taking a sip of tea followed by a large bite of the Anzac. 'Oh my god,' I moan as the sweet, chewy oats melt in my mouth. 'I think she's going to win John over with these.'

Callie takes a napkin and picks up a biscuit, bites into it and mumbles, 'She is. They're good.'

I gesture to the napkin. 'I didn't realise you had such dainty tea-party etiquette.'

She laughs as she swallows her bite. 'I'm keeping my hands clean since they'll be on your face.' She pulls up an image of George Michael on her phone and props it up against the mirror, sipping her tea as she examines it. Primer is applied to my face first, followed by blobs of foundation, evened out with a blending brush. 'It looks dark,' Callie says, 'but under stage lights, it would work.' She picks up the contour stick and waggles her brows at me. 'This is where the fun begins.' She presses the dabber on the side of my face, close to my earlobe, and draws a thick horizontal line, stopping mid-cheek. She repeats the action on the other side, then draws some triangles on each temple and some lines at right angles on my forehead. 'This is to create squareness to your face, especially as yours is more heart-shaped.' She passes me her phone. 'See the shape of George's face? It's all about angles.'

'Huh, and you'll do that with contouring?'

'Yep. You can use different shades of foundation to create shadow, too, but we'll work up to that.' She blends the contouring cream with care, stopping every now and then to check her handiwork. Next, she pencils the kohl through my eyebrows with careful precision, slowly building them up.

She wheels back for a wider view, nodding. 'Good.' She picks up the bronzer. 'We can do a five o'clock shadow with a bronzer or with a blush and sponge. Or I can do half and half and see what you prefer?'

'Let's go half and half.' I turn away from the mirror. 'I don't want to watch; I want a surprise.'

She takes a large, soft-bristled brush and dips it in the powder, tapping the side to shake off the excess, then applies it in light circles along my jaw, over half my chin and upper lip. 'Now for the other side.' She opens a drawer, pulls out a packet of sponges that look like the stipple sponges she showed me in the dressing room and cuts one in half. She presses it in the cream blush and dabs it along the opposite jaw. It scours my skin.

'Ooh. I didn't expect it to feel rough,' I say.

Once she's done, she picks up the bronzer again. 'Just need to fix your sideburns.' She applies it, then stands back, eyes roaming my face. 'Incredible.'

'Really?'

'Oh, yeah. Are you ready to look?'

'Yes.' I close my eyes as she spins me on the chair.

'Okay, open,' Callie says.

I open my eyes slowly and gasp. I lean closer to the mirror, squinting at my reflection. 'That's really me?'

'It's really you and you're hot.'

'I am, aren't I?' I say with a slow nod.

Callie laughs. 'There you go, your confident masculine is coming out already.'

'I kind of look like George, don't you think?' I ask, still appraising myself.

'You do. I copied the shape of his eyebrows and tried to make your nose wider.'

'I love it.' I point to the side of my face where she used the stipple sponge. 'I like this the best.'

Callie steps behind me and assesses my reflection. She nods. 'Yep, it works. Let me fix it so you have that on both sides.' She takes a minute to even-up my facial hair with powders and creams and sponges. 'Done. Want to try your clothes on?'

'Yes!' I jump up and grab the jeans and T-shirt from the bag, then slip out of my own clothes and into my new ones.

Callie rifles around in the bottom of her cupboard and pulls out some boots. 'These will be too big for you, but it'll give you an idea of how the whole outfit looks.' She grabs some socks from a drawer. 'Here, shove these down your jeans.' She hands me a black jacket. 'Not leather, but try this.'

I slip my arms through the sleeves and shrug it on.

She looks me up and down. 'Suits you, sir.'

I take another look in the mirror and say tentatively, 'I feel like I've been waiting forever to dress like this.'

Callie's mouth stretches into a wide grin. 'Definitely an inner drag king who's been desperate to break free. You know your bestie Donna will be waiting to see the finished product, right?'

'Well, let's go. I don't want to let down my future mother—' I press my lips together and clear my throat. 'Your mum.'

Callie stares at me, a perplexed dent in her brow. She kisses me and says, 'You're adorable.'

I laugh. 'I'm glad I'm covered in thick foundation because my face is burning right now.'

She gives me a smile and walks out of the room.

I follow her along the hallway, conscious of how I'm walking. I've watched the kings closely as they've moved around the club and onstage. They have swagger, hold their bodies differently, adopt a different stance and facial expressions. I try to inject some swagger into my walk, but I end up dragging my foot like I have an injury, so I revert to my normal walk.

In the lounge, Donna pauses the TV and stands up, letting out a long whistle. 'Well, look at you, Georgy Michael with a Y.'

'She looks amazing,' Callie gushes.

Donna circles me, examining my outfit, then scrutinises my make-up. 'You really do, Maya. Feel good?'

'Incredible,' I say.

'I'll get myself out of here,' Donna says. 'Because you need a cool place to have a full dress rehearsal and the air conditioner is on.'

'Oh, you don't need to leave,' I say.

'It's fine,' she says. 'Air con is on in my room, too.'

'Mum's favourite pastime is lazing on her bed in the air con watching telly,' Callie says. 'She'll use any excuse to hide out in there.'

'Thanks for the bickies and tea, Donna,' I call after her.

'Anytime, love,' she calls back.

'You don't have to practise if you don't want to,' Callie says to me. 'We can just hang around the house so you get used to being in costume.'

'No, I want to. I think being fully dressed will help me get into character more. And maybe I can practise other stuff, like walking and getting into a masculine energy?'

'Thinking like a king. I like it.' Callie puts on some music and ducks to the laundry to grab our broom and mop microphones.

'We'll start with your act, then we'll cover some other stuff,' she says.

For the rest of the afternoon, we sing, dance and talk drag. We don't discuss coming out to my parents or how we'll act at the awards dinner. We don't talk about Amber or my jealous slip-ups. I get swept away in the present moment and absorb every second of this time with Callie. I throw myself into this lounge-room performance, letting myself embody this new alter ego.

And I think that maybe, just maybe, I can do this.

Chapter 28
Callie

I wasn't sure what to wear to a semi-formal building industry awards dinner, where my girlfriend's father's achievements in construction were being celebrated. Maya told me to dress how I felt comfortable, as long as it was semi-formal. I didn't think arriving as Tom would be wise, so I went with the next best option – a suit. But the only suits I own are designed for the stage, so Stevie lent me one of hers: a beautifully cut wool blend jacket and trousers in a slate blue.

I slip my arms into the jacket sleeves, questioning whether it works with the rust colour of my dress shirt. I slide my wardrobe door closed and catch my reflection – face pinched, shoulders hunched. 'Just a dinner,' I mutter, shaking my arms and rolling my shoulders. 'With my new girlfriend. Who, just for tonight and just for the sake of her parents, is my friend.' I huff out a breath and make my way to the kitchen, the soles of my leather shoes squeaking on the tiles.

When I walk in, Mum is emptying the contents of her lunch bag into the sink, having just arrived home from work.

'Oh, love, look at you,' she says, walking around the island bench to stand in front of me. She smooths her hand over the arm of the jacket. 'You look very, very handsome.'

I blink at her, my hands curling into fists.

Mum's eyes scan my face and she gently uncurls my hands. 'Listen to me. You mean a lot to Maya and she wants you there.'

'But she hasn't told her parents. How can we pretend we're only friends? What if her sisters don't like me? I can't make small talk with people. Who will I talk to if Maya's talking to other people? I've never been to anything like this bef—'

'Hey.' Mum grips my shoulders. 'Breathe.'

I inhale deeply, hold, and release a long exhale.

'And again.'

I repeat a slow in-and-out.

'There you go.' She pauses. 'Now, I'm sure that for one night you can act as friends. You're not going to be all over each other in a formal function, are you? Not even straight couples would do that.'

'No, I suppose not.'

She walks back to the sink. 'It's hard for some people to be open with their parents about their sexuality.'

'I'm not upset she hasn't told them. But how do I act if I meet them? What if the way Maya and I interact outs her or something? I don't want to do that to her. I mean' – I gesture to myself – 'I don't exactly give straight vibes.'

Mum dries her hands on a tea towel. 'Presenting in a way that means people assume you're a lesbian doesn't automatically make you their daughter's girlfriend. They're not going to jump to that conclusion if they're not aware of her sexuality. If you meet them, be yourself, be polite, and if things become too much, tell Maya how you're feeling so she understands.'

'I want to do this,' I say. 'For her and for us.'

She smiles. 'I'm proud of you, love. I know this isn't easy for you, but I think you've found yourself a good one and she's worth some discomfort every now and then, hey?'

My heart warms thinking about Maya. 'Yeah, she is. All going well, I'll stay at Maya's tonight.'

'It will go well. How are you getting into the city?'

'Taxi.'

'Cancel it. I'll drive you.'

I shake my head. 'I'll be fine, Mum.'

She picks up her car keys and purse. 'You need to stay calm and do some breathing exercises. That's easier in my car than in a cab.'

I give her a grateful smile. 'Thanks.' I fill a water bottle for the journey and follow her to the garage, cancelling the cab through the app on my phone.

'Plus, ninety dollars for a cab into the city?' she says. 'Ridiculous. That's ninety dollars you can give me for groceries.'

'Nice try, Donna. I bought a stack of food yesterday,' I say with a grin as I slip into the passenger seat.

Mum reverses out of the garage and I tap out a message to Maya to let her know I'm on my way. She replies in seconds saying she'll wait outside and I let out a relieved breath. Tonight is so far out of my comfort zone, I may as well be travelling to another planet. I close my eyes, breathe in for four, hold for four, and release for four. Repeat. After several rounds, the anxiety loosens its grip, just slightly. I gaze out the window, counting the streetlights as Mum drives along Sandgate Road.

'Hey.' Mum taps my thigh. 'Did that help?'

I nod. 'It did. You're right, it's more calming in here than a cab. Thanks.'

'Sometimes I know best,' she says.

'Mmm. Sometimes. Are you off work tomorrow?' I ask.

'I am.'

'You'll be glad I'm out then, to have the house to yourself.'

She pulls up to a red light and glances out her window. 'Uh-huh.'

I wait for her to say more, like she normally would, but she keeps gazing out the window. 'Light's green,' I say.

She plants her foot on the accelerator as the car behind gives her a beep.

'What's up with you?' I ask.

She glances at me briefly. 'Nothing. Yes, I'll have the house to myself. Good.'

'You're up to something.'

She scoffs and flicks on the indicator to turn right into the tunnel. 'Don't be silly.'

'Ah,' I say, waggling my finger at her. 'You're seeing that bloke from work.'

A blush creeps over her cheeks. 'We're just having dinner.'

'What?' I twist in my seat. 'I only said that to test you out! You're going on a date? Why didn't you tell me?'

She looks in the rearview mirror and merges into the right lane. 'Because it's none of your business.'

'Um ... it's totally my business. So dinner, hey? Where?'

'I'm, erm' – she clears her throat – 'I'm cooking.'

My eyes widen. 'I'm sorry, what? You're going to be alone in our house with him? How well do you know this guy?'

She rolls her eyes. 'We've worked together for years, Callie. I'll be fine alone with him.'

'I bet you will,' I say. 'Good thing I'm not planning on coming home tonight.'

She tsks. 'Don't be silly. Come home if you want to come home.'

'Nah, you're good. Don't want to cramp your style.' I unscrew the lid of my water bottle and take a swig. 'Do Gina and Lisa know?'

'Yes.'

'So I'm the last to know?'

She throws me a look. 'You've been a little busy with your own love life for me to update you on mine.'

I smile. 'Fair enough.'

We turn into the street of the hotel and the nerves start to jump in my belly again. But when Mum pulls into the drop-off area and I see Maya, my mouth falls open and my nerves are temporarily forgotten. She's wearing a slinky calf-length black dress and strappy gold heels, her hair falling in soft waves around her shoulders. Her skin looks like it's shimmering. 'Jesus,' I mutter.

'Wow,' Mum says at that same time. 'Maya looks even more beautiful than she normally does.'

I sigh. 'And we can only be friends.'

'You'll survive,' Mum says.

Maya's face brightens when she realises it's us. She steps up to the passenger door, smiles at me and says, 'Hi, Donna.'

'Hi, Maya, don't you look beautiful,' Mum says.

'Oh, thank you.'

'Don't keep her,' I say to Maya. 'Mum's got a hot date. Cooking John dinner. At home.'

'Ooh. That's exciting,' Maya says with genuine enthusiasm.

'Just a meal,' Mum says with a casual shrug.

But I see the hope in her eyes, and I feel a sudden rush of love for her, for everything she's done for me. She made me her priority, to protect me and keep me safe, sacrificing her own happiness for mine, choosing to stay single to avoid bringing more instability to my life after Dad disappeared. But a parent disappearing on your birthday does stuff to a child, and regardless of the love Mum poured into me, she still ended up with an awkward, shy kid who only felt confident when they were pretending to be someone else. The thought of her growing old alone, the idea that someone won't get to appreciate what a wonderful human she is, breaks my heart. So this John better be a good guy and I pray this works out for her.

I lean over and peck her cheek. 'Thanks for the lift, Mum, and the pep talk. I love you. Enjoy tonight. You deserve it.'

She smiles at me and a flicker of relief crosses her face. She'll want me to be okay with this. Even at my age, she still wants to protect me.

I hop out of the car and Maya's smile drops as she takes me in. 'Holy shit.'

I nervously run my hands over the body of the jacket. 'Too much? Too masc?'

Maya shakes her head. 'Too fucking hot.' She steps closer and touches the lapel of my jacket. 'This suit...'

'It's Stevie's. I only have stage suits.' I look her up and down. 'And you ... god, Maya.'

She twirls around, tottering on her heels. 'You said you like me in a dress, so...'

'And you said you like a masc in a suit.' I give her my own twirl, but less tottery.

She laughs, but it quickly fades. 'I want to kiss you so bad right now.'

I frown. 'Same, but getting caught kissing your girlfriend at your dad's event probably isn't the way you want to come out to them. Besides, it's his night.'

'Thank you for understanding,' she says, then links her arm through mine. 'Come on. Let's do this.'

We pass through the foyer of the hotel, navigating around people milling about, chatting and greeting each other with handshakes and bro hugs. We turn into a wide, carpeted corridor, the walls lined with digital displays advertising the event, and a queasiness rolls through my stomach. Maya pushes open a heavy door, revealing a ballroom filled with hundreds of people seated at round tables. The buzz of their voices fills the space and waitstaff dart from table to table offering drinks.

It didn't occur to me to ask about numbers or set up. It also didn't occur to me that this would be such a huge event. I follow Maya to the front of the room, feeling like every set of eyes is on me. On the table is a place card that reads *Callie*. I exist in Building Awards Land. My hands tremble as I remove my jacket and drape it over the back of the chair. I sit and Maya gives my thigh a supportive rub that does little to calm me. She introduces me to Bella, Liv and Liv's boyfriend, Dylan, and to two of her father's work colleagues.

Bella tilts her head at me with a cautious smile, but Dylan stretches across the table to shake my hand. It's a blokey gesture and my brain goes into overdrive about the assumptions he's making about my masc-presenting self. What would Tom do in this situation? He wouldn't overthink this. He'd think that someone would be honoured to shake his hand. I give Dylan a firm handshake and retract my judgement because his smile and 'nice to meet you' feels genuine.

Liv hops up and walks around the table, bending down to hug me.

I let out a surprised 'Oh' and return the gesture with my own awkward half-standing, half-sitting hug and a pat on the back, grandmother-style.

'Thank you for coming,' she says in my ear. 'It means every-thing to Maya.'

When she returns to her seat, Maya leans in and says, 'I forgot to tell you how tactile Liv is. Sorry about that.'

A waitperson appears offering drinks. I swipe a bottle of beer and take a good swig, then clench my fists under the table to stop myself picking the label off the bottle.

Maya catches my eye. 'You okay?'

I nod. 'Mm-hmm.'

Bella taps Maya's shoulder and she turns away. The work colleagues talk to each other with a comfortable familiarity, and Liv and Dylan are besotted with each other. Two, four, six, seven; an odd number at a table never works. An attractive older couple approaches our table. The similarities between Maya, Liv and the woman can only mean one thing. Maya shoots me a look, confirming I'm right.

She stands and pecks her mum on the cheek, followed by a quick hug for her dad.

'Darling, you look absolutely stunning,' her mum says, then turns to me with a bright smile. But before we have a chance to speak, someone from the next table whisks her away.

Maya's father looks at me expectantly, presumably waiting for an introduction. I stand, the chair wobbling behind me.

'Oops,' he says, his arm shooting out to grab it. 'Don't want you falling over.'

My face burns. 'Sorry. No.'

'Dad, this is...' Maya looks at me, her eyes pained. 'Callie. Callie, this is my dad, Gary.'

He proffers his hand and I shake it, praying mine isn't covered in a film of sweat. 'Hello, Callie. Nice to meet you. Thanks for coming along.'

I dig deep for my friendliest smile. 'Thanks for having me.' I pause, trying to think of something to say and go with, 'Congratulations. Maya said this is a big deal in your industry.'

He beams at me and behind him, Maya gives me a proud smile. 'Well, thank you very much. Yes, I guess it is a big deal.' He glances between Maya and me. 'I don't think I've heard Maya mention you before. Are you a work colleague?'

My brain freezes. 'Oh, no, erm ... friends from ... just friends.'

His eyes narrow slightly and he nods. 'Right, well, enjoy yourself, won't you?' he says and moves on.

I sit back down, undo the top button of my shirt, and gulp back my beer.

'You were great,' Maya says.

I nod, but my insides twist and turn, and I've never felt like such a fish out of water. A plate of food is placed in front of me, the other meals served in alternating plate fashion – chicken for me, steak for the person on my left. I pick up the cutlery, carving off a tiny piece of meat. My throat is tight and I have to force myself to swallow it. I try the mashed potato, assuming it will be more palatable, but it's claggy in my mouth.

Maya turns to me. 'Is your food okay?'

I open my mouth to reply, but Bella taps her shoulder again and Maya is gone. The man to my left makes eye contact and smiles politely, but my mind is devoid of small talk. The very little I could muster was used on Maya's dad. I stammer when he asks my name and don't correct him when he calls me 'Kelly'. My skin turns clammy, and despite the expanse of the room, the walls begin to close in on me. I drain a glass of water and pour another. I tell myself to stay calm, breathe, but my chest clenches and my throat starts to constrict. I tap Maya on the thigh.

She faces me with her beautiful smile and my heart cracks that we can't be us in this space, and that I can't do this after all. 'I'm going to go.'

Her smile falls. 'But it's only early and the awards are about to start.'

'I-I'm not feeling good.' It's not a lie.

'Was it the food?' She looks at my plate. 'You've barely eaten.'

'Maybe the food.' I push my chair out and whip the jacket off the back, then stride towards the exit, desperate to break free from this place.

I'm vaguely aware of Maya behind me and when I reach the corridor, she grabs my arm. 'Callie. Stop. What's wrong?'

I spin to face her. 'I can't be here, Maya. It's not me. I didn't think about how many people would be here, or the setup.' I shake my head. 'The noise. A room full of strangers. I can't make small talk with your dad's workmates, and you're busy with Bella.'

'I'm sorry,' she says. 'Her friend didn't end up coming and she's stressed about her exams—'

I hold up my hand. 'You don't have to explain. This is a family thing. I shouldn't have come.'

She stares at me, bewildered. Then her expression shifts and the air around us shifts too, becoming tense and heavy, and her normally soft edges harden, just slightly. At least, this is what I think is happening.

'I don't know what to say to you, Callie.'

I blink at her because I don't know what to say either, but there's a part of me that's very aware she isn't trying to change my mind.

'Are you going home?' she asks.

I shrug. But I can't go home because no matter how I feel right now, I don't want to ruin the first date Mum has had in forever. The tension between us is so thick and foreign that I need to extricate myself before it smothers me. I turn and walk away, feeling the heat of her gaze on my back.

Chapter 29
Callie

Geographically, it's a short journey in the cab from the city to the Valley. But emotionally, it's excruciatingly slow and the humiliation of the past hour taunts me.

When I walk into Club Sappho, Stevie lets out a long, low whistle from behind the bar. 'Well, well, look at you. That suit fits you better than me.'

The compliment does nothing to lift my mood, and I sit on a bar stool with a self-pitying sigh.

'Oh dear. I recognise that look.' Stevie pulls a beer from the fridge, flips off the lid, and places it in front of me. 'And you're alone.'

'I am not a corporate events person,' I say. 'There must've been at least four hundred people there. Maya was so comfortable and she talked to her sister more than me.' I lift the bottle, my hand pausing mid-air. 'I met her dad – her dad!' I swig the beer. 'I nearly fell fucking backwards over the chair when I stood up and rambled a *thanks for having me* or something.'

Stevie looks perplexed. 'Okay, slow down. One thing at a time. How was Dad?'

I shrug. 'Friendly. I was doing okay until he asked if Maya and I were work colleagues, then I turned into a spluttering mess.'

Krissy walks out of the prep area, giving me a double take as she passes.

'I'm sure you weren't a spluttering mess,' Stevie says, removing a couple of empty wine glasses from the bar top. 'Why are you here already? Don't these things run late?'

I pick at the label on the bottle. 'It was a bit too much.'

She's silent for a moment. 'And Maya was okay with you leaving for that reason?'

I chew my bottom lip.

Krissy sidles up beside Stevie and says, 'Hello, Callie. I don't think you're supposed to be here.'

'I don't think she is either,' Stevie says. 'You did tell Maya you were leaving?' she asks me. 'You didn't just walk out?'

'I told her I couldn't be there.'

Stevie comes out from behind the bar and sits beside me. 'What do you mean, you couldn't be there?'

'It was too overwhelming. I couldn't speak. I couldn't eat. I felt like I was drowning.'

A worried expression settles on her face. 'If you're having panic attacks again—'

'No,' I say quickly. 'It was just that room and I needed to get out before it became a panic attack.'

'And you didn't want to tell Maya that?' Stevie says. 'Or give yourself a bit more time to let it pass so you could go back in?'

I shake my head. 'I didn't want her to feel like she had to babysit me. And it was so ... hetero, and that really threw me for some reason. I felt like everyone was staring at me, making assumptions, not just about me, but about us. I didn't want people thinking that about Maya before she's had the chance to tell her parents.'

Krissy has been listening quietly on the other side of the bar. 'Well, firstly,' she says, 'you were at a tradie event. You reckon construction *isn't* full of gay blokes and lesbians? You won't have been the only queer person there. And secondly, Maya wouldn't have invited you if she was worried about what people thought.'

Being back in my safe space, talking to Stevie and Krissy, the brain fog shifts and my heart rate has returned to normal. Maya's face is clearer now and I don't think I imagined her annoyance. Guilt washes over me and suddenly I'm very aware of what I've just done and I'm desperate to fix this. 'Shit,' I say. 'What have I done? I need to go back there, don't I?'

Stevie shrugs. 'That's up to you. Do you like Maya or not? Are you serious about her?'

'You know I am, and I more than like her.'

'Then she's probably struggling to understand that right now,' Krissy says gently. 'Relationships are about compromise, Cal. Give and take, doing things that might be a little bit uncomfortable because your partner wants or needs you to. I think you owe it to yourself to do what it takes to make this work. Maya's good for you and I reckon she's a safe space for you.'

Stevie tips her head towards Krissy. 'The boss always knows best.'

Krissy smiles. 'I really do.'

'But what if she doesn't want me to go back?' I say. 'She seemed kind of pissed. She might be relieved that she doesn't need to be on edge around her parents.'

'Was she on edge when you met her dad?' Stevie asks.

'No. But she didn't try to stop me when I left either,' I say.

'She probably thought that's what you wanted,' Krissy says.

I nod and let out a shaky breath. 'Okay. I'm going back.'

Krissy walks away to serve and Stevie says, 'Remember to take yourself outside for air if you need it, and be honest with Maya about how you're feeling. And if it gets too much, call us.'

I give her a grateful smile. 'Thanks, cuz.'

Chapter 30
Maya

The four tables filled with Dad's colleagues clap and cheer as he finishes his humble speech and holds up the award, crediting the success to everyone in the company bar him. He leaves the podium, a broad grin on his face, and Bella, Liv and I hug him on his way back to the table and take the obligatory family selfie. He's worked tirelessly for this, and winning means taking the company to the next level.

As Dad walks off to celebrate with his colleagues, there's another buzz from inside my bag. Even without checking, I know it's Callie. I reach for my phone, my screen showing three missed calls from her.

I move out to the corridor and find a quiet space to think because I'm not certain I want to talk to her right now. I understand this environment was too much for her, but again she walked away instead of trusting me to help her. But as I sink into one of the soft armchairs, my defences lower. Am I being unfair? This isn't her scene and she did this purely for me. Maybe if I had've told my parents the truth, she would've felt more comfortable. I return the call and she answers after two rings.

'Maya, hi.'

'Hi,' I say.

'I'm outside.'

My heart lifts. 'Outside the hotel?'

'Yeah.'

'Give me a minute.' I hang up and walk out to the foyer, pass through the rotating doors and step out into the warm evening. Callie is standing to the side in the darkness. 'You came back,' I say, approaching her.

Her face is tight with worry. 'I'm sorry I left like that. I was overwhelmed and I didn't want to bother you with it. But I should've told you how I was feeling or taken myself outside for a few minutes.' She shakes her head. 'I don't know why I didn't. I guess I didn't plan ahead about what to do if that happened.'

The remaining frustration dissolves. How can I be annoyed at her for that? 'I didn't realise this would be so difficult for you.'

'I didn't either,' she says. 'I really thought I'd be alright.'

I nod. 'Okay, but I think this is something we need to work on together, because it's frustrating when you run off. I get that it comes over you suddenly, but if there's some way you can let me know, even if you can't voice it, maybe I can help?'

She nods, her face relaxing. 'Yes. I can do that.'

I step closer, the scent of her spicy perfume wafting around us. 'I should've made you feel more comfortable, and I shouldn't have put you in the position of meeting my parents when I hadn't told them about us. I'm sorry.' I slip my arms underneath her jacket and circle her waist. 'Thank you for being amazing with Dad.'

She rolls her eyes. 'More like awkward.'

'No. You were perfect.' I tilt my face up and kiss her. She

sighs, leaning into the kiss. 'Did you go to the club?' I ask. 'I know you wouldn't have wanted to go home and interrupt your Mum's date.'

'Yeah. Stevie and Krissy gave me a pep talk. My head cleared pretty fast and I wanted to be here with you. I'm happy to go back in, if you want me to.'

I step back and scan her face, looking for signs of distress, but she's calm. 'I would like that. The awards are over. Dad won and the' – I do air quotes – '"disco" is about to start. I could use a dance partner.'

She grins. 'We're going to dance with your parents watching on?'

I shrug. 'You've met Dad already and friends dance, don't they?'

'They do.'

'Besides, everyone's had that much free booze I don't think anyone will notice or remember.' I tip my head towards the hotel entrance. 'Come on.'

When we reach the double doors of the ballroom, Callie holds up a finger. 'Give me one sec.' She inhales deeply and releases a long, slow breath, then says, 'Okay, I'm good.'

'Are you sure?'

She gives a determined nod. 'Yes. Dancing is one thing I don't need to be self-conscious about.'

I push open the door and lead the way back to the table. Guests have shifted seats, tables are littered with wine glasses and beer bottles, jackets and ties are thrown over the backs of chairs, and the lights have dimmed. Liv and Dylan are dancing. Bella is sitting with some people around her own age, and Dad's two colleagues who were on our table have vanished. A DJ is on the stage, a well-known pop song blasting through the speakers.

I turn to Callie, my eyes subtly scanning her body. When

my gaze meets hers, it's smouldering, and my body heats. 'Would you like to dance?'

'I would.'

We walk side by side to the dance floor, our hands brushing, and it takes all my strength not to pull her to me and press my mouth to hers.

Liv and Dylan spot us, their faces brightening, and I love them for making Callie feel welcome.

For the rest of the evening Callie and I dance at a friendly distance. We take advantage of the free alcohol and sneak kisses in the bathroom. I focus solely on her and remind her to let me know if she feels overwhelmed. A few times she needs to catch her breath, but otherwise she's relaxed and happy, and popular on the dance floor, which makes her laugh. Mum and Dad occasionally glance our way, but they're having too much fun with Dad's colleagues to take much notice of us.

Just after midnight, I tug on Callie's hand and jut my chin towards the exit. 'Let's go.' It's a demand, not a question, and she rushes after me.

Outside, I whisper in her ear, 'I need to get you home so I can peel you out of this suit.'

She grabs my hand and jumps in the nearest cab, muttering, 'Compromise has its advantages.'

As soon as we step inside my apartment, we're engaged in a desperate kiss and I groan as my craving is satisfied.

Callie pushes me back against the wall, hands sliding up my thighs, my dress lifting. 'Fuck, Maya,' she murmurs against my mouth. 'It's been torture not being able to touch you.'

'I know,' I breathe, nudging her towards the lounge and

stripping off her jacket. I toss it over the armrest of the single sofa as she stumbles backward onto the couch.

She hurriedly removes her shirt, and her moan vibrates through me when my teeth graze her nipple. She tugs at my dress. 'Clothes off.'

I straddle her, lifting my arms to allow her to strip off my dress. She sucks at my neck as she unhooks my bra, tossing it across the room, then kicks off her shoes. I lift myself off her so that I can remove my own shoes, but she grips my wrist.

'Oh, no,' she says, her voice thick with want, 'they're staying on.'

I raise a brow, a smirk tugging at my lips. I like this side of her; assertive, trusting and willing to voice exactly what she wants. I stand, relishing her watchful eyes on me as she undoes her trousers and yanks them off.

'God, Maya,' she breathes. 'You're killing me.' She grabs my hips, pressing a kiss to my stomach. Her fingertips slip under the side straps of my underwear and she tugs them down a fraction, running the tip of her tongue along the delicate skin above my pubic line, making me gasp. She gazes up at me, green eyes smouldering. 'Take these off for me.'

Her tone is firm and it sends an electrifying shiver right through my core. I lower my underwear, not taking my eyes off her. The glow of the lamp casts a hazy shimmer across her face and shoulders. Seeing her like this, sitting on my couch in nothing but her birthday bracelet and jocks, long legs lazily parted, is the sexiest image I've ever seen.

She swallows as her eyes drag over me, enjoying me in nothing but a pair of heels. 'Come back here,' she says, her voice hoarse.

My eyes drop to her jocks. 'I want you naked.'

She quickly follows my orders, then pulls me back onto the couch, kissing me deeply as she settles on top of me. My flesh burns at the delicious sensation of skin on skin, and we melt into each other, hands in hair, limbs twisted, tongues mingling. The ache between my thighs is almost unbearable.

Callie kisses my neck, my chest, sucks my nipple, moves lower, her lips trailing my stomach, her mouth between my legs. I push myself against her, clutching her head. She edges my legs wider apart with her shoulders, forcing my calf to rest on the back of the sofa. She takes her time, her tongue teasing, driving me over the edge, making me break apart.

My pelvis begins to rock faster against her tongue, a tingle starting in my feet and sparking up my legs. Her finger inches inside me, forcing me to suck back a breath. I love that she's learned exactly what I want when I want it. Her finger curves upward, pulsing against the spot that makes me lose all sense of self. I grip a handful of her hair as I press even harder against her face. My moans become long and loud as my leg slips from the back of the couch and the heel of my shoe lands on Callie's back, causing her to release a pleasurable grunt.

My body fizzes on the inside and bucks on the outside as the pressure peaks. My back arches as my heel digs into her skin and her tongue laps at me, her finger still inside me. My eyes are squeezed shut as I gasp and moan for what feels like an eternity, my body shattering into tiny pieces, until my limbs finally slacken. I crash back to reality, my breaths shallow, my skin sweaty, my body weak.

Callie kisses my inner thigh and crawls up to slot in beside me. 'You're amazing,' she whispers in my ear.

'No. You.' I cup her cheek. 'I hope I didn't hurt you with this shoe. I was a little bit delirious.'

She kisses me. 'It was very, very hot.'

I roll onto my side and bury my face into her warm neck. My body purrs and my brain hums and, oh, my heart.

Chapter 31
Maya

Cool drops of water drip onto my bare stomach as Callie leans over and kisses me, her mouth wet and salty from the sea. She drops onto her towel, lying back and extending her legs out from under the beach umbrella.

'Water cold?' I ask.

'A bit, but in a refreshing way, not in an Antarctic way.'

It's the day after the building awards and we're an hour north of Brisbane. Both of us are feeling sluggish after too much alcohol, not much food, and a very late night enjoying each other. We were craving salty sea air and sunshine. The beach is deserted except for a few seagulls squawking overhead and a dog walker in the distance. The tide is high and the waves crash onto the shore, white foam gliding over the sand.

I roll onto my side and prop my head onto my palm, gazing at Callie. I'm still giddy from last night, and the situation that occurred after she first arrived at the dinner has been forgotten.

She shoves a rolled-up towel under her head as a pillow. 'Why are you looking at me like that?' she asks with a coy smile that suggests she knows exactly why I'm looking at her like that.

'I think you know why,' I say.

Her smile widens and she closes her eyes, letting out a soft hum, like she's lost in her own memories. 'I'm thinking about last night, too.'

This is my favourite version of her. Content, mask-free, at peace with her surroundings. Grains of sand cling to her cheeks, filling the space between her freckles, and beads of water glisten on her dark eyebrows.

'I can feel you watching me,' Callie says, one eyelid opening.

'Because you're so beautiful,' I say.

A flush creeps over her cheeks but she says, 'Thank you.'

My brows shoot up. 'What was that? Did you say *thank you*? You accepted a compliment?'

She grins. 'You must be good for me.'

I brush some sand from her face. 'You're becoming more confident around me. And last night...' I puff out my cheeks. 'Holy shit, Callie. I like you taking charge like that.'

She laughs. 'Free alcohol will do that.'

'I don't think it was just the alcohol,' I say.

'No,' she says, her voice soft. 'It's you. You make me feel safe.'

My heart swells. 'Safe? Really?'

She nods and closes her eyes again. 'Yeah.'

She makes me feel safe, too, like it's okay to explore who I am and who I want to be. Ever since she told me that Amber would be away for a week, I've wanted to bring up the possibility of performing. I've been reluctant, worried she'll tell me not to do it, or worse, laugh at me for even thinking I could. But I feel like we reached a new level in our relationship last night and my mask is dropping, too. 'I was thinking that I might give the amateur night thing a go.'

Her eyes open. 'Seriously?'

I nod. 'Maybe the week after next?'

Her brows rise. 'Wow. That's soon.'

Her reaction makes my gut twist, but I say, 'It's just one song, right? And I've got an outfit and an act.'

She sits up, bringing her legs under the umbrella and crossing them. 'Well, yeah, it is only one song, but I got the impression you weren't thinking about doing it anytime soon.' Her eyes search my face. 'You really feel ready?'

There's doubt in her voice, but I can't tell her that I have to do this without Amber present. I'm not sure I can even explain it to myself. The idea of standing onstage so soon makes me queasy, but I need to do this, and I need to do it on a night when the harshest critic in the club won't be watching me. 'I mean, I wouldn't be ready if it was tomorrow night,' I say. 'But in a couple of weeks, if I practise.'

Callie chews her bottom lip, brows furrowed. 'It's soon, Maya. It's not the kind of thing you want to rush.'

My heart sinks. Maybe she doesn't believe in my ability to do this after all. 'You're right. I'm rushing it.' I fall silent and look out to the ocean, watching a seagull scurry away from a wave.

A good minute passes before she shuffles closer. 'Hey. Talk to me.'

I look at her. 'Is it really not possible?'

'It's possible,' she says, 'of course it is, and like you say, you've got an act and it's only one song, which you know well. It's also a night to get up there and have a go, but I suppose I'm just surprised because it's not something you've thought about until recently.'

'Not drag, no, but I've thought about performing since I was young, and I have tried. It just hasn't worked out for me before. But this feels different and it's a different type of performance.'

She nods. 'Okay. We haven't talked about whether you want to tape your boobs or get a packer.'

'I have a strap,' I say, with a smirk, trying to lighten the mood.

She grins. 'I know you do, and if you have the confidence to wear a strap for your first performance, go for it.'

I laugh. 'I definitely don't have the confidence for that. Does it matter that I haven't worked out what I want to do with bulges and breasts?'

She shrugs. 'No, there're no rules, but it's stuff that adds to your character and can help you feel the part.'

Something deep in my core tells me to listen to Callie, not to push this, but my ego takes over. 'If I don't do it soon, I never will,' I say. 'And you said that sometimes it's easier to work things out on the stage.'

'It can be, if you've been up there before. Not sure that's sound advice for a beginner.'

I nod and shift my gaze back to the ocean, digging my toes into the sand. 'Okay. I'll leave it.'

She gives a small sigh. 'If it's what you want, then I'll help you.'

I look at her. 'You will?'

'Of course. I want this for you, but I want you to be certain and to be doing it for the right reasons.'

I ignore the twinge of guilt the 'right reasons' comment triggers and kiss her. 'Thank you.'

Chapter 32
Callie

'I don't know, Cal,' Stevie says, mixing a large bowl of salad with wooden servers. 'I know you said she's been dipping her toe in the water with clothes and make-up, but performing's a whole different ball game.'

We're at Stevie and Krissy's place having a small get-together with family and colleagues to celebrate the club being open for a year. I've been waiting for the right moment to raise the topic of Maya performing with Stevie.

'She's done more than dip her toe in,' I say, taking the salad dressing from the fridge and passing it to her. 'She's got an act, a drag name, she practises all the time.' Mum walks in, a beach towel wrapped around her waist, her hair damp from the pool. 'Even Mum thinks she's pretty good. Isn't that right, Mum?'

'What's that?' Mum says, grabbing a glass and filling it with tap water.

'Maya wants to perform at amateur night,' Stevie says.

'Oh, well, good for her,' Mum says enthusiastically.

'But next week?' Stevie says. 'Out of the blue?'

'I wouldn't say it's out of the blue,' Mum replies. 'She's

been at our place for weeks now, playing around with make-up and routines. She looks great in drag and she knows the music.'

'See?' I say as Mum walks back outside. 'And it is *amateur* night.'

'Yes, but the people who get up there have usually performed before in some capacity, or they've been preparing for months.' Stevie tosses some avocado skins in the bin. 'And they're a bit bold. Maya's kind of' – she shrugs – 'timid, I guess. Can't picture her tearing up the stage. Amateur or not, we've got a reputation to uphold. We want people to come back.'

Before I have a chance to respond, Amber strolls in. 'I've been sent in for more drinks,' she says.

Stevie takes a bottle of lemonade and a bottle of white wine from the fridge and passes them across the bench.

'I think she'll be fine,' I say to Stevie, continuing our conversation. 'She wants to do this. She says she's ready and it's one song. That's like, three minutes.'

'We have a new king starting?' Amber asks.

I'm about to tell Stevie to leave it and that we'll talk later, when she answers Amber's question. 'Maya wants to perform next Thursday and I'm not sure it's a good idea just yet.'

Amber's eyes widen. 'Wow. Didn't know she was into trying drag.'

I stiffen, my defences rising. 'She is, and I think she'll be good, if she's given a chance.'

'Huh,' Amber says, her scepticism palpable.

My jaw twitches. 'What does that mean?'

She shrugs. 'Nothing. Just seems sudden, that's all. Never been to a drag king show before, turns up out of nowhere and latches onto you, absorbs all your tips and tricks, and now she's performing?' She arches a brow. 'Lucky she met you for a leg up, hey.'

'Amber,' Stevie says, scrunching her face. 'Don't say shit

like that. Anyone can have a go. They don't need to embark on a relationship with one of our kings to do that. All I'm saying is that I like to vet people first, make sure they'll be okay up there.'

I'm still bristling at Amber's comment. 'You have a problem with more kings on the scene?' I ask her.

Amber rolls her eyes. 'No, the more the better as far as I'm concerned. Maya just doesn't strike me as the type of person who'd be into it, that's all.'

'Stop bickering, you two,' Stevie says. 'Or I'll send in HR for mediation sessions.' She gestures to the bottles of drink and says to Amber, 'Take those out. We'll be out in a sec.'

Once Amber's out of earshot, Stevie says, 'I hope you didn't believe a word of that?'

I shake my head, but it's hit a nerve because I'd be lying if I said the same thought hadn't crossed my mind.

'Hey,' Stevie says, leaning forward to meet my eyes. 'Seriously, Cal. Don't listen to her. Maya's mad about you.'

I nod.

She gives a resigned sigh. 'Look, if you think she's up for it, and it sounds like she's been doing more than I realised the past few weeks, then why not? You're right, it's a few minutes and it's a night to have a bit of fun.'

'Yeah? Thanks, Stevie. She'll be thrilled.'

We take the salads out to the patio where Mum, Gina and Lisa are seated around the table, chatting. Amber and a couple of other colleagues from the club are in the pool playing Marco Polo, and Krissy is cooking on the barbecue.

Stevie joins in the conversation, asking Mum a million questions about John and the date she has lined up for tomorrow night. I smile as though I'm listening, but Amber's comment has wormed its way under my skin. It's probably true that Maya only noticed me because I was onstage. Would she have been attracted to me otherwise? Noticed me without

Tom's charm? My thoughts shift to her performing in ten days' time. I agree with Stevie; I don't think she's ready, and because she's the type of person that she is, I'm worried about what will happen if it doesn't go well. But I want to give this to her, this special gift that no one else can give her. Because without it, I'm not sure I'm enough for her.

'Are you alright, Callie?'

'Hey?' I say, blinking at Mum. While I've been in my head, Gina and Lisa have moved over to the barbecue to help Krissy, and Stevie is in the pool, splashing around with her eyes closed trying to catch the others.

'You're okay with me seeing John, aren't you?' Mum says.

'What? Yes, why wouldn't I be?'

She tilts her head at me. 'You went very quiet just now when we were talking about it. I thought you might be upset.'

'Oh.' I shake my head. 'No. Sorry. I was thinking about something else. I'm fine with it. As long as he's a good person and you're happy, then I'm happy. Besides, it doesn't matter what I think. I'm not a kid anymore.'

She smiles. 'You'll always be my kid and you'll always be my priority.'

I slip my arm around her and kiss her temple. 'Then I give you permission to make yourself your priority and go on a hot date.'

'Thank you.' Her eyes examine my face, tuning into me as she's so good at doing. 'What's on your mind? Is it what you were talking to Stevie about inside?'

I nod. 'Yeah.'

'You're both worrying about nothing,' Mum says. 'Maya will be fine, but if you're concerned, tell Maya that and maybe encourage her to leave it for a while?'

'Nah, you're right, we're stressing about nothing.' I smile, but there's a niggling feeling in my stomach that I can't shake.

Chapter 33
Maya

Callie pauses the music. 'One more time.'

I throw my head back with a groan. 'Really? Again?'

She places her hands on her hips. 'There's only one way to get good at this, Maya, and that's to keep practising. I did it all day every day for ages before my first performance.'

I pull her down beside me. 'Can we have a break for a minute?'

Concern flitters across her face. 'Am I pushing you too hard? I was trying to help, but if you want me to drop it, tell me.'

It's been two weeks since my announcement that I'm going to perform, and every spare minute has been spent either practising or convincing myself that this is a good idea. 'I feel like I'll never get it.'

'But you are getting it,' she says, giving my thigh an encouraging pat. 'The idea is for the act to become part of you, so that the performance is second nature. That way, you don't need to think too hard about it and you'll have energy left to deal with stage fright, overwhelm, that sort of thing.'

'I'm all tense,' I say, shuffling closer and kissing her.

She murmurs against my lips, 'We spent hours getting rid of tension last night.'

I straddle her, clasping my hands around the back of her neck. 'Yes, but you getting your bossy on is hot.'

Callie laughs. 'Nice procrastination.'

'Nooo,' I say, bending forward to nip at her neck.

She manoeuvres me so that I'm lying back on the couch, then squishes in beside me. 'If you're having doubts about this, please don't force yourself to do it.'

I smooth my thumb over the silver links of her bracelet. 'What if I fuck it up so badly that someone records it and posts it online or something awful like that?'

'That won't happen,' Callie says. 'You've seen the signs up about no recording on amateur nights, and people are reminded on the door when they arrive. We take that seriously.' She slides her hand across my waist, fingers slipping under my shirt and stroking my stomach. 'I know you're worried. Everyone who gets up there for the first time is. But most don't regret it.'

I frown, unconvinced. 'Have you seen someone fail so badly they've never come back?'

'Hmm...' Callie purses her lips as she ponders my question. 'There's been a few who've decided it's not for them. But most come back and give it another go. They don't all go on to be professional kings, but they've had fun with the amateur stuff.' She pauses. 'What if you don't fuck it up? What if it goes really well? Have you thought about that?'

'Ha, now you sound like Dr Garcia,' I say, prodding her chest. 'At my last session she said, "All performers start some-where, Maya; how do you know you won't be good at it?"'

Callie grins. 'Maybe I missed my calling.' She considers me for a beat, then says, 'Do you think you could be overthinking this? Putting too much pressure on yourself?'

'Probably.'

'It's okay to be nervous,' she says. 'You wouldn't be human if you weren't. It's also okay to mess up; loads of kings do. It's how we learn and get better.'

I wrinkle my nose. 'I'm not very good at messing up.'

'Mmm,' she hums knowingly. 'Think about it like this – if it doesn't go exactly as planned, you refine it for next time. That's not failing; that's learning.'

'I'm wasting my money going to Dr Garcia when you can give me therapy,' I say with a wry smile.

She shrugs. 'Honestly, when you're up there, it doesn't feel so big.'

I nod, trying to be receptive to her good advice. 'You inspire me to try new things.'

She brushes a thumb across my cheekbone. 'You inspire me, too.'

'To do what? Read books?'

'Yes, I started a lesbian crime novel last week, actually.' Her smile fades and she turns pensive. 'You inspire me to be me.'

My heart swells. 'That means the world.' I kiss her, slipping my leg between hers. When the kiss becomes heated, I pull away and huff out a breath. 'Okay. I need to get back to it.'

Callie stretches over me, checking the time on her phone. 'I have to be at the club in an hour. Why don't you come? I'll be in the office and you can have the stage to yourself for a couple of hours before Krissy and Stevie get there.'

'Okay, sounds like a plan.'

I go to sit up, but Callie pulls me back, a teasing smile on her lips. 'Since we've postponed the practice session, didn't you have some tension you wanted me to take care of?'

～

Callie places a lemon, lime and bitters in front of me. 'The club is yours and I'm heading into the office.'

I glance across to the stage, my gut jittery. If I can't perform to an empty room, how will I manage in front of people? 'It doesn't need to be perfect,' I murmur.

'That's right,' Callie says. 'Why don't you see how you feel up there now, and if you don't want to do it tomorrow night, then don't. Even if you're about to go on, Stevie will just bring the next act forward.'

'Even if I'm about to go on?'

'Yep.'

I nod slowly, the possibility easing some tension. 'I like the sound of that.'

Callie walks through the open hatch and kisses me. 'You know where the office is if you need me. I'll turn on the lights for you.'

'Can I use the dressing room?'

'Sure.' She disappears into the prep area and seconds later, the stage is aglow with bright light.

I move closer, soaking up the solace of the club, and sit a row back from the stage, in the spot where I first saw Callie. I try to visualise myself performing tomorrow night but the image is nebulous. To have Callie and Stevie's stage presence and their ability to work the crowd is unfathomable to me. An off-kilter feeling simmers in the pit of my stomach, a nagging sensation that I'm being too hasty, that my reasons for performing this soon are driven by external factors. But I lift my chin stubbornly. If I don't do this tomorrow night, I never will.

I head backstage and change into my drag clothes. I'm wearing a well-fitting sports bra, which goes some way toward flattening my chest, and I shove thick socks down my jeans. I pull my hair up into a topknot but don't bother with the wig. I check my reflection, disappointed that I don't look anywhere near as masculine as the professional kings, so I adjust the socks, trying to make the bulge bigger.

When I walk past the office, Callie is at the desk, tapping at the keyboard. 'Have fun out there,' she says, her eyes fixed on the screen. 'Let yourself go while no one is here.'

'I'll try,' I call back as I continue down the corridor. I pass through the wings and step across the stage, the scuff of my soles on the wood echoing around the club. A George Michael song begins to play, making me smile. Of course Callie would time the music for me.

I grip the microphone, directing my gaze to the table in the back right, scan to the left, then to the tables at the front, making eye contact with imaginary audience members, the way Callie does. *It builds trust with the audience,* she'd told me. I swing my hips, self-consciously at first, paranoid someone will burst through the door. But the music starts to move through me, taking over. I stand taller, push my hips forward, pretend something more realistic-looking than rolled-up socks is in my jeans, and try to become Georgy Michael.

By the end of another two tracks, I'm warmed up and more enthused. The guitar intro of 'Faith' begins and I tap my foot, sway my hips and strum my air guitar. I sing loudly, letting myself go, not overthinking the performance, enjoying the moment. The track ends and I'm slightly out of breath, my face flushed. I text Callie to let her know she can come out, if she wants to.

I dance through another song before she strolls onto the stage. 'You've got a sweat on,' she says. 'That's a good sign.'

'I did it,' I say. 'I did the whole performance. It felt good – doing this for myself felt good.'

She slips her hands into the pockets of her jeans. 'One of the best feelings in the world, being up here.' Her gaze drops to my crotch and her eyes widen. 'What've you got going on down there?'

'Three pairs of hiking socks.' I place my hands on my hips and thrust my pelvis forward. 'I wanted Big. Dick. Energy.'

Callie laughs. 'You've certainly got that.' Her smile drops and her eyes search my face. 'You going to be okay tomorrow night?'

The truth is I have no idea, but standing up here right now, half-dressed as a drag king, I know that if I don't go through with it, it will be my biggest regret. *Five minutes of courage or five years of regret.* 'I need to try,' I say. 'It's important to me that I do that.'

She nods. 'I just want you to be alright.'

'I know you do. Can I stay up here a bit longer?'

'Sure. Stevie messaged a few minutes ago. They're on the way, which means you've got about half an hour.'

'Can you spare some time?' I ask.

She nods. 'Yep, other than stocking a fridge, I'm done until we open.'

'I was thinking that I should give the audience more? Like standing in the one spot lip-syncing isn't that entertaining?'

Callie shakes her head. 'Audience expectations are low on amateur night. They like to see new acts, enjoy the music. It's usually an older crowd, too, so they'll love a bit of "Faith" era George. How long's your track? Three minutes? Think of it like that – just three minutes, lip-syncing and moving your body.'

I nod, chewing at my thumbnail.

'You're mimicking him, right?' she continues. 'He doesn't do a lot in that song except this...' She faces the room and shakes her hips, singing the chorus to 'Faith'. 'If you really want to do more, in the instrumental, stride across the stage with your guitar and be back in front of the mic for the lyrics.'

'Stride across the stage,' I repeat. I sing the last lyric before the instrumental and start walking, adding a bit of swagger. I strum my air guitar and look into the pretend crowd, then work my way back to the microphone. 'Like that?'

'Exactly like that,' she says. 'As you get more experienced, you can explore different ways to express yourself up here. You don't need to have it all together the first time.' Callie steps over to me and kisses me softly. 'You're going to be an amazing drag king.'

I don't know why the compliment makes me feel like a fraud, but it does, and I can't even manage a thank you.

She gestures to the bar. 'Better get that fridge stocked before the bosses kick my arse.'

'Okay. I'll change and get out of the way.'

Callie jogs down the stage steps and slips behind the bar, and I return to the dressing room. Once I'm back in my own clothes, I hang Georgy's costume ready for tomorrow night, but a sudden wave of overwhelm hits me, forcing me to sit. I take a minute to breathe, waiting for the adrenaline rushing around my body to settle. I can't back out now. Callie believes in me and she's put so much into helping me. I let out a wobbly breath and head back to the bar.

'Hey, Maya,' Stevie says when I appear. 'Callie said you were getting some practice in.'

'I was. I hope that's okay?'

'Of course,' she replies.

'How do you feel?' Krissy asks.

I shrug. 'Nervous. Performing in front of no one is going to be a lot different to performing in front of people.'

'Just remember you can change your mind,' Stevie says. 'We've had plenty of people pull out before they're about to go on. You wouldn't be the first, so don't stress.'

'Thanks, Stevie.' I gesture to the main entrance. 'I'll go and let the three of you get to work.'

'I need to let you out,' Callie says. She walks me to the front of the club and pulls opens the door.

'I'm going to have a relaxing night and not overthink tomorrow,' I say.

'That sounds like a great idea,' she says.

I kiss her goodbye and walk off, giving her a wave over my shoulder and lying to myself that I'm ready to do this.

Chapter 34
Maya

The second I step into the club, my legs buckle and I lean against the wall to steady myself. Every table is taken and the customers at the bar are two deep. I frantically skim the crowd for Callie, spotting her at the end of the bar. When it registers who she's talking to, my hand flies to my mouth as the nausea rises.

Callie finally looks my way and cuts across the club. 'Hey, you're early,' she says, greeting me with a kiss. 'I was going to walk to your place and meet you.'

I lick my lips, my mouth dry, my eyes fixed on Amber. 'I thought you and Stevie were the only professional kings here tonight.'

Callie follows my gaze. 'Oh, Amber had to postpone her flight until the weekend, so Stevie called her in. We're down a staff member and overlooked how busy it would be with a holiday tomorrow.'

And you didn't think to tell me? the voice in my head screams at her. But why would she? She doesn't know the real reason why tonight has to be the night.

My gut is telling me to flee, to run back to the safety of my apartment, but Callie links her fingers with mine and gently squeezes. 'Come on. I'll help you get ready.'

She starts towards the bar, but I tug on her hand. 'Can we go the other way?' I ask. Amber is the type of person who'd smell my fear if I walked past her, and use it against me.

Callie's brow creases, but she nods. 'Of course.' She leads me to the staff door on the other side of the club and punches in the security code. 'You're worried,' she says as we head to the dressing room.

I nod.

She opens the door, lets me pass and clicks it shut behind us. 'Remember, it's *amateur* night. The audience are always supportive. Stevie and Krissy wouldn't run it otherwise.'

I nod again. With shaky hands, I slip out of my clothes and sit at the dressing table in my underwear, staring at my reflection. I'm pale, my eyes wide.

'Maya,' Callie says, wheeling over a chair to sit beside me. 'Look at me.'

I twist my head towards her.

'You don't need to do this if you don't want to.'

'I don't want to let you down,' I say.

Her brows shoot up. 'What? Of course you wouldn't let me down. I've encouraged you because I know how much you want it, but if you don't feel ready, please don't. I will never be disappointed in you for making that decision.'

I slump back against the chair with a defeated sigh. 'I'm sorry. It's myself I don't want to let down. I want to do this. I'm just petrified of messing up.'

'Of course you are. It's totally valid to feel like that,' she says. She stretches behind her, fills a glass of water from the canister and places it in front of me. 'Did I ever tell you that before my first performance, they had to shift my spot because I threw up?'

My brows rise as I take a gulp of water. 'Really? You?'

'Yep. And Stevie's first time, she slid onstage all cocky like she was the king of all kings, put too much into it and slid right off onto the floor.'

I give a small laugh. 'She didn't?'

'Uh-huh. And that new king who's started on Saturday nights, at their first amateur gig, they mixed up lyrics and dance moves and started doing this random uncoordinated stuff, mouth not matching the words, out-of-time steps. They laughed it off, came back the next week and nailed it.' She places a soft hand against my cheek. 'None of us have been perfect up there. We still mess up when we try new stuff. That's how we've got to the level that you see now. If you let yourself, you could be amazing at this. You've got the passion, the drive, the ability. But *you* have to want it. I don't care what your choice is. I just want you to be happy.'

I'm silent for a few seconds as I let all of that sink in. 'After you threw up, did you perform okay?'

'I did, and the buzz I got afterwards overrode the negative stuff. But I also felt ready. So if you have any doubts, it's okay to back out or try it another time.'

I turn back to the mirror, still mulling over Callie's words. I don't want to be the person who doesn't fulfil their dreams because of what one person will think, or the person who won't do something new unless it's perfect. But that's me. I'm risk-averse. An overthinker. A perfectionist. Someone who thinks she needs to live up to other people's expectations. I don't know how to be any other way. And maybe there will never be a way around that. Maybe I have to do this despite that. 'I won't be less nervous next week or the week after,' I say. 'You'll be there, won't you? Like to the side or in the audience – somewhere I can see you?'

'Of course.'

My thoughts about performing in front of Amber are on the tip of my tongue, ready to be voiced. But what's the point? She's here now and she'll probably be here next week, and the week after that and the week after that.

I let out a nervous breath. 'Okay. I'm going to do it.'

Callie applies my make-up, creating stubble with a blusher and stipple sponge, then thickens my brows with a kohl pencil. I fit my wig and hook in one earring – a dangly gold cross – and dress in faded blue jeans and a black T-shirt. To complete my outfit, I tug on a pair of ankle boots and a black leather jacket. Callie offers me some socks to put in my jeans, but I shake my head. All that will do is heighten my imposter syndrome.

I stand in the middle of the dressing room staring at myself, emotion burning my throat. I've worn this outfit so many times and played around with make-up at every opportunity. I've even had possession of the wig to get used to it. But being fully dressed and knowing I'm about to perform hits differently. Thoughts are racing through my head, like a six-lane highway with traffic driving at 120 kilometres an hour. *I haven't practised enough. I'm not a real drag king. Why did I think I could do this? My routine is boring. People will judge me. I don't fit in.*

Callie steps behind me and places her hands on my shoulders. 'The first time is emotional. But once that music starts, Georgy will possess you.'

I desperately want to believe that, but my pulse is thumping so hard I'm worried a vein will burst. I grab the mirrored sunglasses from the dressing table and hook them onto the front of my T-shirt.

Callie points to them. 'Use those if you're struggling and

want to conceal your eyes. It will take the pressure off looking at the audience, and it can help with the lights, too.'

I nod as though the information has sunk in, but there's no room in my head for more.

Callie picks up the prop guitar and we head to the wings and watch the first act.

'They're good,' I whisper to Callie.

'You're good, too.'

I blink at her.

She tips her head, considering me. 'Just say the word and Stevie will skip you and get the next act out.'

Cancel me is on the tip of my tongue, but something makes me shake my head. 'No. I'm here now.'

The performance finishes and Amber walks onto the stage. My body stiffens. Of course she's emceeing. She throws me a smirk, making my insides twist. *She knows I can't do this.* She lifts the microphone to her mouth, and it's like I'm watching in slow motion.

'Let's hear it for your first amateur king,' she says. She waits for the applause to ease then announces, 'Time for your next one. The act we've all been waiting for...'

My stomach drops and I look at Callie.

She rubs my back and says in a soothing voice, 'I'm here.'

'Please welcome Georgy Michael!'

The lights dim and I stumble onto the darkened stage, barely registering the claps, and stand stiffly in front of the microphone. The applause stops and the club is eerily quiet, the air dense with the cloying scent of anticipation. The music begins. My heart thumps. The stage is suddenly ablaze in harsh light. I instinctively look away, squinting. The lyrics start but I can't focus. The lights weren't this bright when I practised. *Callie will help me.* I turn my head to the side but she's not there. Instead, a couple of other amateur kings are nodding encouragingly at me, mouthing the lyrics. Panic surges and my eyes dart around the club, but I can't see Callie anywhere.

I open my mouth, but my lips fail to form words. Amber leans against the bar, watching me with laser-sharp eyes, her mouth stretched in a mocking grin. My brain freezes and sweat builds under the wig as I stare at the audience for an excruciating few seconds. My breaths come short and shallow. My legs begin to shake. I flee from the stage, pushing past the other kings who call after me. I pull off my wig as I hurry towards the dressing room, my head down as the tears fall, and bump straight into somebody.

'Hey,' Callie says. 'What are you—'

'Where were you?'

She points behind her. 'I went to fix—'

'I needed you,' I say, choking back a sob.

Her face reddens. 'But you were about to start. I was coming straight back.'

'You said you'd be there. You said to look at you if I got stuck. You knew I was terrified and you weren't there.'

'But I ... the lights. I-I'm here now.'

'Now? I needed you then! Ugh.' I push past her. 'Forget it. This was a stupid idea.'

'Maya, wait,' Callie says, racing after me. 'I'm sorry. I thought you were okay.'

'I said forget it. I just want to get out of here.'

'People choke up there all—'

I spin to face her. 'I don't choke, okay?'

Her face falls. 'Oh. Okay.'

'I'd appreciate some space so I can change,' I say.

She stares at me but then nods and steps back.

I slam the door of the dressing room, humiliation coursing

through my veins like blood flow, burning my skin. I sob as I roughly clean my face. The tears keep falling as I change back into my own clothes and shove the drag clothes and make-up into my bag. I can't face anyone, but I can't sit in here until the club closes either, mingling with the other kings who'll be on a high from their performances going well. I can't exit through the back door unless a staff member lets me out. That leaves the main entrance.

I stride from the dressing room, exiting through the backstage door that leads into the bathroom corridor. When I step into the club, my eyes are drawn to the bar. Callie is talking to Amber and everything inside me hardens. But what does it matter anyway? I don't belong in their circle. I don't belong with someone like Callie. I keep walking and just as I'm about to step into the entrance foyer, a hand clamps down on my shoulder.

'Maya, please don't go,' Callie says.

I shake myself free and escape outside, gulping back the fresh evening air, my tears starting again. But she's right behind me. 'I can't be here, Callie.'

'I'll come with you,' she says.

I spin to face her. 'Don't you want to spend the night with Amber?'

Callie scrunches her face, a flash of anger in her eyes. 'No. Why would I want to do that?'

I cross my arms. 'To have a good laugh at me. About how pathetic I am. Then you can go have sex.'

Callie lets out an irritated grunt. 'For fuck's sake! I don't want to sleep with Amber. How many times do I have to say it?'

I flinch at the outburst and turn to walk away.

Callie lets out a remorseful groan and grabs my arm. 'Maya, stop. I'm sorry. I wasn't laughing at you. I'm not even sure what happened up there, but we all mess up.'

'Have *you* messed up?' I say, facing her.

'Erm...' She pauses. 'Well, I was sick when—'

'No, Callie, not sick before you got onstage – choked when you were up there. Fucked up *so* badly you felt like you couldn't ever face anyone?'

Her brows knit.

'Of course you haven't. Because you're a natural. This is where you belong. It isn't where I belong. I was stupid to think I could do this, ever be part of this.'

'You weren't stupid to think that. You can try again.'

'I don't want to try again,' I say, my voice rising. 'Don't you see? I won't ever be able to look those people in the eye.'

'You will—'

I hold my hand up. 'I can't do this anymore, Callie. It's been fun.'

Her face contorts, a myriad of emotions playing out in her expressions. 'Fun? You mean the king stuff?'

I look down at the footpath. The anguish in her eyes is killing me.

'Y-you mean us? You're finishing with me? Because of *that*?'

I stay silent.

'Please don't,' she pleads. 'I don't care what happened up there. I care about you.'

I look up and my heart splits wide open at the torment on her beautiful face, but how can I possibly be around any of these people ever again?

'I-I was fixing the lights for you,' she says.

'The lights? I didn't need you to fix the lights, Callie. I needed you to be there when I drowned. But you weren't there. You ran away from me. Like you always do. At a time when I desperately needed you. I can't be with someone who keeps doing that to me.'

She opens her mouth but then snaps it shut.

I wait; for what, I'm unsure. For time to rewind? For us to be in a parallel universe where my performance went swimmingly and we're celebrating? For her to say something that will erase everything that's just happened? But she stays silent and I stay silent. Then I walk away, sobs racking my body, and I don't look back.

Chapter 35
Callie

Maya moves quickly along the footpath, her head down, her shoulders jerking. When she reaches her building several minutes later, she turns, looking back towards me. Her face isn't clear from this distance, but my heart lifts thinking she'll run back to say she didn't mean it. I take a step forward, ready to run to her too. But she vanishes into her building, like my hope vanishes into the cool autumn night.

I fall against a wall, clutching my chest, my breaths quick, my skin clammy. 'One thing I can see...' A red SUV parked across the street catches my attention. 'Two things I can hear...' I tune into the sounds of passing cars, the thump of music from inside the club. 'Three things I can touch...' I grab my shirt with a trembling hand, the fabric soft between my fingertips. I feel the bracelet around my wrist, the coolness of the silver. I run my hand over the wall, the brick coarse under my palm. My breathing slows enough that I can get myself back inside.

Stevie dashes over to me. 'Is Maya okay?'

I shake my head. 'No, she's really upset.'

'Then what are you doing here? Go!'

'I, erm, I can't. She – she ended it.'

'Ended it?' Stevie's brows furrow. 'You mean she broke up with you?'

I nod.

Stevie frowns and gestures to the stage. 'Because of what happened up there? That makes no sense.'

I pinch the bridge of my nose, a throb starting behind my eyes. 'She said something about not belonging here, and that she was stupid to think she did, and it'd been fun, meaning us.'

'Then you go after her,' Stevie urges. 'Talk to her.'

I throw my hands up. 'What's the point when she's decided she doesn't want to be with me?'

'There's a lot of fucking point because you care about each other and what you have is special.'

I open my mouth to respond, but Amber walks out from behind the bar and inserts herself into our conversation. 'Where's your girlfriend?'

I scoff. 'Fuck off, Amber.'

She pulls her head back in surprise. 'Easy. I was only asking.'

'No,' Stevie says, shooting her a glare. 'You were stirring, like you always do.'

'Did you say something to her?' I say to Amber, my tone accusatory.

'Me?' Amber says, pointing to herself. 'No!'

I narrow my eyes suspiciously, a realisation dawning. 'You were working the lights. Why did you set them so bright for Maya? You didn't do that for the other acts.'

Stevie turns to Amber, her face hardening. 'What the fuck?'

Amber holds her hands up. 'Hey, they were dull so I turned them up. We don't exactly have a top-notch lighting system. It's hit and miss. A professional would be able to handle that.'

'Except it's not a night for professionals, is it?' Stevie hisses. 'It's a night for people to learn, where we're kind and under-standing and help them out.'

Amber makes a face. 'It was some bright lights, for god's sake. And people need some level of professionalism to get up there. Not my fault she can't handle it. I mean, she's not exactly drag material, is she?' She reaches for my hand. 'Look, I'm sorry if—'

I snatch it away, glaring at her.

'Amber,' Stevie says. 'What part of *fuck off* didn't you understand?'

She gapes at Stevie.

'And you're on shift,' Stevie continues. 'Get back behind the bar, please. We'll discuss the lighting situation later.'

Amber's jaw tenses, but she does what she's told.

I clench my fists. 'She did that to Maya on purpose. I know it.'

'Ignore her.'

'I have to get out of here,' I say. 'I need to go home. I'm sorry. I know we're busy.'

Stevie lets out a heavy sigh. 'It's fine. Did you drive in?'

'No, I got the train because I was going to stay at Maya's.'

'Right. Give me a few minutes, I'll give you a lift.'

'No. You need to be here. I'll catch a cab.'

'You won't,' she says firmly. 'You need family around you. Besides, it's quietened down since the show ended. There's enough staff here to handle it.'

I nod. 'Okay. Thanks. I'll wait out the back. I can't be in here with her,' I say, jabbing my finger in Amber's direction.

Backstage, I wait by the exit to the car park, pacing back and forth, trying to make sense of what happened.

Stevie appears a few minutes later and guides me to her car with a supportive hand to my back.

I text Mum to tell her I'll be home after all, then stare out the window as we travel north, shocked and confused.

After a good five minutes of silence, I say, 'She was upset because I wasn't there for her.' I face Stevie. 'She was nervous and I promised I'd be somewhere she could see me. But I could tell she was thrown by the lights. I told her to put the sunglasses on if that happened, but she didn't, and she didn't look at me to give her a sign, so I went to adjust the lights for her. I was quick, but then I bumped into her in the corridor instead.'

'And she was still upset after you explained that?'

I glance out the window again.

'Callie? You did explain?'

'I told her I went to fix them, but she said something about not needing me to fix the lights, she needed me to support her and that she's tired of me running away all the time, and she can't be with someone like that. But I wasn't running. I was trying to help,' I say, my voice cracking. 'I don't know how to deal with this. She sounded certain, you know? Like it was all too much of a hassle, like *I'm* too much of a hassle.'

'You are not too much of a hassle,' Stevie says. 'This isn't about you. She's upset about what happened and needs someone to blame.'

I shake my head. 'I don't even know what happened. It can't have been that bad?'

Stevie pulls up at a red light. 'The nerves got to her, that's all. She couldn't do the performance and ran off.'

'You mean she just got the timing off – a few things didn't go to plan?'

Stevie looks at me briefly. 'She couldn't do any of it.'

My heart clenches. 'She didn't even start?'

Stevie shakes her head. 'No.'

'Fuck,' I groan. 'That was her biggest fear.'

'It's not that bad,' Stevie says. 'I did it a few times myself in the early days, and I've seen others do it, but it's tough to deal with when you're the one it happens to.'

'I tried to tell her it doesn't matter, but she has such high expectations of herself. And now she thinks she doesn't belong there.'

'Of course she does, whether she's a king or not. She's your partner and she's one of us now.'

'*Was* my partner,' I correct.

Stevie flicks on the indicator and turns into my driveway. 'Let's not past-tense the relationship just yet, hey? Is Aunty Donna home? I don't want you spending the night on your own.'

'Yeah.'

'Okay. Take tomorrow off. I'll get someone to cover your shift.'

I lean over to give her a hug. 'Thanks, and thanks for the lift home.'

'I'll call tomorrow.'

I head inside, my footsteps slow and heavy. It's dark except for a slim beam of light shining out from under Mum's bedroom door. I walk into my room and Maya's essence consumes me – her scent, her laughter, her clothing. I can almost see her sleeping, curled up in my bed, her hair strewn across the pillow, her chest rising and falling. My heart breaks all over again, and I quickly change into my pyjamas and leave, shutting the door behind me, trapping the memories.

I knock on Mum's door.

'Come in,' she calls.

I open it and lean against the doorjamb.

'Hey, love. Didn't expect you home tonight. Everything okay?'

I frown, my throat burning with unshed emotion.

Mum places her book on the side and sits up a little,

removing her reading glasses. 'What is it?' When I don't reply, she peels back the covers and says, 'Come on. I take it this has something to do with Maya?'

I crawl in beside her, a tear escaping, soaking into the pillowcase.

'Okay, tears, hopping into bed with me and not talking can only mean one thing,' she says softly.

'I really liked her, Mum.'

Mum's brows crinkle. 'What do you mean "liked"?'

I tell her the whole story, about Maya's nerves, my own worries about her performing too soon, disappearing to fix the lights, her jealousy of Amber, the reasons she gave for ending it, and what Stevie told me in the car about Maya's non-performance.

'Oh,' Mum says. 'The poor thing. She'll be so upset.'

'And she's all alone and won't let me be there for her.'

Mum frowns. 'Maybe she needs some time and will be more willing to talk about it in a day or so?'

I nod, but the look on Maya's face, her anger, her hurt, and the words she spoke – I don't know how we move past that.

Chapter 36
Maya

'Mason asked about you the other day,' Mum says to me in a sing-song voice.

I drop my cutlery onto my plate, the clatter causing alarmed expressions around the table. 'For god's sake, Mum, stop with the matchmaking!'

She flinches and Dad, Liv and Bella gape at me. Mum places her cutlery in the middle of her plate with an affronted sniff. 'Well, sorry for letting you know someone might be interested.'

'I don't want to know!' I can't keep it contained any longer. 'Stop trying to set me up with a man. Jesus, why haven't you worked it out?'

Dad's eyes narrow, but Mum looks at me with a blank expression.

'Worked what out?' she says. 'That you want to be single for the rest of your life?'

Liv places a hand on my back and Bella pats my thigh under the table. Right now, I don't care what comes out of my mouth, because nothing could be worse than the humiliation I experienced two days ago. 'No, Mum,' I say in a surprisingly even voice, 'that I'm gay.'

Dad huffs out a sigh and Mum's brows shoot up.

'Gay?' she says. 'Bisexual?'

'No. Bisexual would mean I'm interested in men, wouldn't it?' I say. 'I'm a lesbian.' The emotion escapes now and my voice wobbles. 'I only like women. I only date women. I have only ever been involved with women.'

Mum shakes her head, her brows creased. 'But you've had boyfriends.'

'No, I haven't—'

'Yes,' she says, determined to prove my heterosexuality. 'At high school, you had boyfriends.'

'I went on dates with guys because it was expected of me. Nothing ever went beyond a date.'

The dent in her brow deepens as she peers at me. 'But you lived with a boyfriend not so long ago, you and Arianne.'

'He was gay,' I say. 'And Arianne was my girlfriend.'

She falls silent, her eyes darting left and right, trying to make sense of this bombshell.

'I told you, Robyn,' Dad says, tossing his napkin onto his empty plate.

I glare at him. 'You *told* her? You knew and you didn't talk to me about it?'

He raises an unimpressed brow. 'You're twenty-eight, Maya, we're not going to treat you like a child. Besides, I wasn't certain. It crossed my mind because, well, like you said, you've never had a boyfriend and I've noticed you've had some close female relationships. I figured you'd talk to us when you were ready, if that was the case.'

'Ugh.' I throw my hands up and stomp into the house, tossing myself on the couch. Despite the discomfort of that conversation, a weight has lifted and I can breathe easier. They finally know, and I suddenly feel foolish that I didn't say that seemingly simple sentence years ago. *I am a lesbian.* But it's not simple; it's a sentence so loaded with connotations and societal expectations and stereotypes that I'm amazed anyone can say it.

Mum and Dad come inside and tentatively sit on the two-seater across from me, so I have no choice but to look at them.

Mum clears her throat. 'I'm sorry, darling. I didn't handle that well. It was a shock and I don't understand why you've waited so long to tell us, especially considering, well, considering how much I talked about you finding a male partner.'

Her remorse triggers my guilt because Dad's right, I'm not a child. I should've discussed this with them long ago. 'Why do you think, Mum?' I say, softening my tone. 'You've pigeonholed me into this person you think I should be: a heterosexual career woman who marries a man before she's thirty and has a family, who's then expected to continue on the career trajectory because being a mother wouldn't be enough. I'd have to be a CEO of my own or someone else's company by the time I was forty, while my children are being raised by someone else or fending for themselves.' Hurt flickers across her face and I breathe out a regretful sigh. 'Sorry, that wasn't a criticism of you.'

'We just wanted what was best for the three of you,' Dad says. 'We wanted you to have a good life and to be able to help you financially as adults. You know neither of us had much growing up; we didn't want that for our children.'

I hang my head. 'I don't take it for granted, but I always felt so much pressure from you both to live a certain way, like I didn't have the space to be me.'

Dad nods, his mouth a tight line. 'I'm sorry we made you feel like that.'

'It's only because we saw so much potential in you,' Mum says. 'And we thought we were nurturing that, but obviously it was misguided and it was hurting you, to the point that you felt you couldn't talk to us about your sexuality.'

I swallow back the lump in my throat. How can I refute that? Because they have nurtured me and I could want for nothing.

Mum continues, 'It's just that you're—'

'What?' I ask, jumping to conclusions about what she's going to say. 'That I *look* straight? You'll be disappointed if I marry a woman? That being a bookseller isn't ambitious enough?'

She sighs. 'I just want you to be happy, and you're so smart and beautiful and—'

'I can be a smart, beautiful lesbian who works in a book-shop. They exist, you know.'

'I know that,' she says quietly.

'The person you brought to the awards dinner,' Dad says. 'Callie, I think her name was. I take it she wasn't just a friend?'

Hearing her name causes a fresh wave of pain to roll through my chest. 'No, but we've broken up, so it doesn't matter anyway.'

'I noticed the way she looked at you,' Mum says in a quiet voice.

'Sorry?' I ask.

Mum nods. 'Mmm. You were dancing. There was such a natural flow between the two of you, the kind that only comes with being a couple. When you returned to the table, she passed you a glass of wine and she looked at you with such tenderness. And, I suppose, deep down I knew, given your father had planted the seed. But you said you were bringing a friend, so I let myself believe that.'

I swallow. 'She looked at me with tenderness?'

Dad nods. 'And it wasn't one-sided.'

I squeeze my eyes shut to stop the tears, but one escapes and I quickly wipe it away. 'I've been so stupid.'

'You didn't cheat on her?' Mum says, her tone sharp. 'We raised you to value loyalty and—'

'God, Mum, no. I'm not some player.' I sift through my thoughts, trying to work out the simplest way to explain. 'Callie is a drag king on Saturday nights at the club where she works. It's in that old theatre on Wickham Street that Grandma and Grandad used to take me to when I was little. Ash and I went there at the beginning of the year, and after a few weeks, I met Callie and we started seeing each other. Things were going well and we were happy.'

They sit quietly, listening to my story, so I continue.

'I really love their shows, and you know how much I love the theatre. Drag looked like a fun thing to try.' It's about so much more than being a fun thing to try, but it's too soon to have a conversation about expressing masculinity and challenging gender norms with my parents. 'They have amateur night every Thursday, and Callie is so passionate about drag, it's infectious. She could tell I was interested, so we came up with an act, just for me. Then I decided, foolishly, that I'd try performing at amateur night. I practised until I thought I had it right, but when I stepped onstage, I froze.' My skin burns, the humiliation raw, like I'm right back in the thick of what happened. 'I ended up running off less than a minute after walking on and' – I lower my gaze – 'I blamed Callie for not being somewhere I could see her. But the truth is, I was so ashamed about what happened and felt so embarrassed for her going out with me that it seemed better to end it.'

'Oh, darling,' Mum says. 'I'm sure it wasn't that bad.'

'Oh,' I say with a humourless laugh. 'Believe me, it was.'

Dad gives me a sympathetic smile. 'You've always been the same,' he says. 'Even when you were little. You'd do things over and over until you had it down pat.' He looks at Mum. 'Do you remember that time when she was in grade one and she had to do a show and tell? She used a model of a building from my office and wrote a little essay on it. She rehearsed day and night for over a week until she had it memorised.' He grins at me. 'And when you couldn't recall a line or said the wrong word, you'd grow so frustrated with yourself.'

'I do,' Mum says wistfully. 'Such a determined little thing.'

I remember that too, and I delivered the perfect grade one show and tell, setting me on a course of practise-until-perfect with no room for mistakes or below-par presentations.

'So, this theatre dream of yours,' Dad says. 'You're giving up that easy?'

I can't help but smile. I should've known they'd be more upset about me quitting something than being a lesbian. 'It's not exactly a theatre dream – I don't want to be a stage actor – but there's something about drag that resonated with me and I wanted it to work.'

'Why can't you try again?' Mum asks matter-of-factly.

'Because I made a complete fool of myself in front of the entire club, including Callie's colleagues and her cousins who own the club, not to mention in front of her, which is the most mortifying of all.'

'Then you get back up there and un-fool yourself,' Dad says. 'I don't know a lot about being on a stage or drag kings, but I do know that if I gave up every time I made a monumental error in my line of work, I wouldn't have a company, nor would half the buildings we construct be standing. And we certainly wouldn't be winning awards. Success comes with trial and error, and mistakes, lots of them.'

I hear Callie telling me the same thing. Her voice is so clear, like she's in the room. Every part of me aches for her, to have her hold me close and whisper soothing words in my ear that everything will be okay. 'I feel so stupid,' I say. 'Both about what happened onstage and how I handled it. It kills me that I hurt Callie like that, but I can't face people after what happened. I don't know how to do that.'

'What do you want, Maya?' Mum says. 'Do you want to be with someone? Be in a loving and committed relationship? Is that where this was headed?'

I nod. 'Yes, and I thought we had something really special. It certainly felt like it anyway.'

'Then you probably need to be having this conversation about Callie and your feelings with her,' Mum says. 'I think she gets to decide whether or not she's embarrassed by you. That's not your call.'

'That's wise advice from your mum,' Dad says, standing. 'I think we should give you some thinking space.'

'Can I stay here tonight?' I ask. 'The flat reminds me of Callie and I don't want to be alone.'

Mum walks around the coffee table and sits beside me, pulling me into a tight hug. 'That's a question you never have to ask.' She pulls back and gently grips my face. 'We love you so much, darling.'

I nod. 'I love you, too.'

She follows Dad out onto the patio. Liv and Bella rush in, smothering me in sisterly hugs, and I let the tears fall.

Chapter 37
Callie

I lay on the couch, twisting the plaque of my bracelet. It's only been two days since Maya and I broke up, yet it's as though I've been living in this strange reality for months. Like I'm in thick fog, pushing uphill, no sense of where I'm going or how long it's going to take me. I've shifted from the couch to my bed and my bed to the couch, apart from the one hour I sat in the backyard yesterday afternoon, letting the April sun dry my tears. Mum has tiptoed around me, gently probing to check that I'm eating and showering. I don't recall doing either.

I called Maya yesterday, holding a tiny spark of optimism that this was a simple misunderstanding caused by heightened emotions. She didn't answer, so I left a voicemail reiterating why I wasn't there for her and saying how sorry I was, and for the other times I ran from her. She hasn't replied.

I rub a hand over my chest, a futile attempt to soothe the pain. The house reminds me of Maya – dancing in the lounge room, eating at the kitchen table, loving me in my bed, nestled into me as we slept. It's torturous to be in here, but at the same time, it's all I have of her and a painful memory of a love lost is better than no memory at all.

The slam of a car door pulls me from my reverie and I sit up, hope rising that it's Maya, but then I hear a second door and deflate.

Mum pops her head through the doorway. 'Stevie and Krissy have just pulled up.'

'I don't want to see anyone.'

'I know,' she says. 'But they will want to see you.'

I don't reply. They'll come in whether I want them to or not.

Mum answers the door. There's an exchange of 'hellos' and 'she's in the lounge', then Stevie and Krissy appear, sitting either side of me. Krissy is the first to wrap me in her arms. I crumble, fresh tears falling.

'It's okay,' she coos. 'It's going to be okay.'

'I ... thought ... she ... was ... the ... one,' I sob.

'I thought she was, too,' Krissy says, her tone soothing.

I pull away and wipe my face with the sleeve of my pyjama top.

Stevie slips an arm around me and I lay my head on her shoulder. She's been there through all of my romantic dilemmas, but this is my lowest. Even Lacey's crap didn't floor me like this; that's because what Maya and I had was real. A healthy, functional relationship, so the loss feels so much deeper.

'How long since you've had a shower?' Stevie asks.

I lift my head. 'Do I smell?' She gives me a quick smile, and despite my melancholy, the corners of my mouth tug upward. 'Very subtle, Stevie.'

She pats my thigh, her smile widening. 'Go and have a shower and get dressed. We're taking you out.'

I shake my head. 'No. I'm not—'

'Callie,' Krissy says sternly. 'You need to get out of the house.'

'I sat outside yesterday,' I counter.

She arches a brow, unimpressed. 'Just come for a drive, then you can come back and fall apart if you want to.'

I give a resigned sigh and lift myself from the couch, my body sluggish, and head for the bathroom. The shower heats as I strip off, my nose wrinkling when the underarm body odour hits me. I wash my hair and scrub my body, then press my forehead to the cool tiles, breathing in the sweet scent of soap as the hot water massages my shoulders. Eventually, I get out, dress in track pants and a thin jumper, and head back into the lounge room.

Mum's face lifts. 'Well, this is a nice sight. Washed and changed.'

'Sorry I've been miserable,' I say, hugging her, clinging on, wishing she could fix this for me. I release her and say to Krissy and Stevie, 'Let's go before I change my mind.'

They jump up and hurry me outside.

In the backseat, my eyes water, remembering the night Maya and I shared kisses in this very seat when we caught a lift to Krissy's party. Our relationship blossoming, learning more about each other and sharing a bed for the first time. I choke back a small sob. 'Oh, god. I've been in this seat with her.'

Krissy flicks Stevie's arm without taking her eyes off the road. 'I told you to sit in the back.'

Stevie twists in her seat and grimaces. 'Sorry.'

'It's okay.' I pull a tissue from my pocket and dab at my eyes. 'She's everywhere anyway.'

Krissy comes to a stop, parallel parks and cuts the engine.

I glance out the window. 'Why are we at the beach?'

'We're going for a walk,' Stevie says, unclicking her seatbelt.

'A walk?' I whine.

Krissy turns to me. 'Yes, Callie. You're going to get some fresh air and sunshine and be near the water. It's healing.'

I respond with a sulky pout, but I get out and slip on my sunglasses to shield my sensitive eyes from the late-afternoon sun. I slot in between the two of them as we stroll the path that runs parallel to the beach. The sea breeze is strong, swirling through the trees and whipping the high tide into small, choppy waves that crash against the rocks. I glance out across the bay. What's Maya doing now? Working? At her parents? At therapy? Is she relieved to be free of me?

Stevie nudges me with her hip. 'Hey. Wanna talk about it?'

I look at her briefly, then return my focus to my feet. 'I don't understand how it went so wrong so quickly, or why she won't speak to me. I've messaged and called, explained why I wasn't there, but she hasn't replied, and it's like' – I swallow – 'it's like she died, you know, because she was there, and then she's gone.' I rub my chest. 'And it physically hurts, like I'm grieving.'

'You are grieving,' Krissy says. 'It's a normal emotion to feel under the circumstances.'

'I'm not just missing her. I'm sad about losing what we had. This beautiful relationship I've wanted for so long. I was happy, and I thought *we* were happy.' I shake my head. 'Why didn't I stay where I was so I was there for her? I should've listened to you, Stevie, because I knew she wasn't ready for this.'

Stevie sighs. 'Don't beat yourself up about that. This isn't your fault. Even if you had've been there, Maya still might've got stage fright and blamed you. People look for someone to blame when they mess up, and she's probably feeling really awful about that now.'

What Stevie says makes sense, but it doesn't cut through my regret. We reach the concrete stairs that lead down onto the sand and sit, squeezing in between the railings. The water splashes over the bottom step, sucks back out and rushes back in to splash over the concrete again. An old song I heard on the radio this morning plays in my head. I began to hum, then mumble a lyric.

'What's that?' Stevie says.

'"The First Cut Is The Deepest", you know that old song that's on the radio all the time? I heard it this morning and it's true. It *is* the deepest, and I'd like to love again, but I don't know how to do that, nor do I want to because no one will ever compare to Maya.'

Krissy slips an arm around my shoulder. 'Maybe let yourself get through this first before thinking about loving again, hey? Maya might just need some time. Being onstage is second nature to you now, but it's daunting and intimidating for most people. I'd feel exactly the same if I was her.'

'Why don't you have this weekend off,' Stevie says, 'and come back next weekend?'

I look at her. 'No. I need to work.'

'You probably won't be at your best tonight—'

'No,' I repeat. 'It's the only thing I've been looking forward to.'

'Callie,' Krissy says. 'You know what Saturday nights are like; we need bar staff who are on the ball and the kings to be at their best.'

'I will be. I can perform under any circumstances, you know that. And I can work the bar.'

Krissy looks at Stevie with uncertainty.

I've just lost Maya. I can't lose Tom, too. 'I'll be fine,' I say turning to Stevie.

Stevie sighs and says sternly, 'Okay, but if you're there, it's another staff member we don't call in, so you need to be on.'

'I will be. In fact' – I stand – 'I'm ready to work now. Let's go.'

Chapter 38
Callie

F our hours later, I'm pouring wine, pulling beers, mixing cocktails, darting around colleagues, keeping the bar top free of dirty glasses, and proving to Krissy and Stevie that I am *on*. The bar is lively; there's no time for remorse or reminiscing. Amber tries to talk to me, but I hold my hand up and say, 'Busy.'

'Callie, what are you still doing serving?' Stevie says. 'You're on at eight.'

'On it.' I take the customer's payment, then start to walk away, heading backstage, but Amber grabs my arm.

'Callie. Stop.'

I spin around. 'I don't really want to speak to you, Amber.'

'I know, but I've been trying to apologise all night.'

I fold my arms. 'Make it quick. I've got to get changed.'

She takes a deep breath. 'I'm sorry, okay? I didn't set the lights higher on purpose. What I said was true. I thought they were too dull for the earlier performances, so I turned them up. It didn't occur to me that might throw Maya off.'

I narrow my eyes at her, but she looks genuinely apologetic

and she's right that our lighting system isn't the best. Still, she was cruel, so she doesn't win my forgiveness that easily. 'It's Maya you should be apologising to, but she'll probably never step foot in here again because of what happened.'

Amber shifts her gaze to the floor. 'Sorry.'

I sigh, my defences dissolving. We have to work together so we'll have to sort out our differences eventually. 'We'll talk about it another time. I need to go.'

She nods and walks away.

I run to the dressing room, bumping into Krissy as she walks out of the office. 'Sorry,' I say, not stopping.

'Jesus, Callie, slow down!'

'Can't,' I call over my shoulder. 'Busy!'

In the dressing room, I quickly steam my outfit and hurriedly apply make-up. I don't bother taping my chest or wearing a packer. I can't be in here long. It's too full of Maya. A painful reminder of the place where we were last a couple. I check the time on my phone – 7.35 p.m. Twenty-five minutes until I'm onstage. I race back to the bar and start serving again.

'What the fuck are you doing?' Stevie says.

'I'm ready,' I say, pouring a measure of vodka into a cocktail mixer. 'I'll serve until I'm on.'

She rolls her eyes but leaves me to it and heads backstage to change for her own performance.

I serve a few more customers before Krissy gets the show started. She gives her usual opening spiel, then introduces me. I hurry out from behind the bar, giving the audience a wave, lapping up their applause, the high of performing already dulling my heartache. I jog through the tables and up the stairs, ready to put on a show, but the toecap of my left shoe catches on the top step. My body jerks forward and my arms flail, trying to keep me upright. Then my legs give way, and I land on the stage with a hard thud, crying out in agony from the stabbing pain in my ankle.

Krissy appears, bending over me. 'Fuck, Callie.'

I look up at her and start to cry.

She uses the microphone to ask the bar staff to call an ambulance, then announces, 'Short delay, folks, as we move Callie from the stage. Get yourselves a drink and our next king will be out soon.'

Krissy kneels beside me. 'We need to get you backstage to wait for the paramedics. Do you think you can hop on one leg if a few of us support you? How bad's the pain?'

'So fucking bad,' I cry. 'I don't think I can move.'

'Okay. I'll be back in a sec.'

She rushes away and I lie there, vulnerable and exposed. At least my back is to the audience so they can't see my tear-stained make-up. My thoughts shift to Maya being up here unable to perform, how vulnerable and exposed she would've felt, and I start to cry again.

Krissy returns with our bouncer, Kai, who scoops me into her arms and carries me across the stage. The crowd cheer and clap, and I give them a thumbs-up before I'm whisked through the side curtain.

'I've set up the sofa bed in the office,' Krissy says, rushing ahead.

'I finally get to carry you to bed,' Kai says to me with a wink. 'Thought it would never happen.'

I sniff back a small laugh. 'And have your wife on my case? No thanks.'

She grins and lays me gently on the thin mattress. 'Hope it's not too serious. I'll let you know when the ambulance arrives.'

'Thanks, Kai,' Krissy says.

Stevie walks in, dressed to perform. 'Jesus Christ, Callie.'

'Don't say it,' I warn.

She holds her hands up. 'I'm not saying a word.' She opens the bottom of my velcro pants and winces.

My ankle is swollen, my skin already a canvas of mottled reds and purples. Krissy wraps an icepack around it and props some cushions under my foot. 'Best we can do for now. I'd give you some painkillers but we should leave that to the professionals, just in case.'

'Thanks.' I glance between them and offer a sheepish, 'Sorry.'

Krissy covers me with a blanket and gives a 'what are we going to do with you' sigh. She kisses my forehead. 'We don't want to leave you alone, but we've got to get back to work.'

I nod. 'I don't suppose one of you could quickly grab my phone? I have no idea how long I'll be in here, and I can't deal with only my thoughts to keep me company.'

'I'll get it,' Stevie says. 'You go introduce me, Krissy. I'll be out in a minute.'

They both leave and a minute later, Krissy's muted voice re-starts the show and Stevie is back with my phone. 'There you go.' She lays my cosmetic bag and a small mirror on the bed. 'Thought you might want to take your make-up off.'

'Thanks.'

She points to my body. 'Got anything on under there that needs to come off?'

I shake my head. 'I didn't do any of that tonight. Didn't want to be in the dressing room long. Too many reminders of Maya.'

She nods. 'I'll check back in soon.'

There's a roar of applause as she takes the stage. I clean my face and call Mum to tell her what's happened with a promise to keep her updated. Next, I scroll to Maya's number, take a steadying breath and call, my pulse thumping as it rings.

Hi. It's Maya. If you want me to call you back, leave a message.

My heart sinks. I don't leave a message. There's only so many times I can say sorry.

∼

I spend the next forty-five minutes scrolling my phone and video chatting with my aunties. The show is almost over by the time Krissy brings the paramedics into the office.

'Hello,' the older of the two says. 'Heard you had a fall.'

I sit up a little. 'Yep. Sure did.'

'I'm John. This is Andy,' he says, pointing to his colleague. 'Let's have a look.' He carefully removes the icepack and winces. 'Ouch. Taken anything for the pain?'

'Not yet. We thought we should wait.'

He nods. 'What's your name?'

'Callie,' I say. 'Callie Johnson.'

His eyes shift from my ankle to my face. 'Callie Johnson? Donna's daughter?'

'Yeah,' I say, thinking nothing of it, given Mum has worked for the ambulance service my entire life. Then it clicks. 'Ah, you're *that* John.'

He laughs a low, gravelly laugh. He's handsome with his dark hair peppered with grey, stubbled smile and hazel eyes framed by deep laughter lines. 'That's right, I'm *that* John. It's nice to meet you, Callie. Didn't think this is how we'd be introduced, though.'

'Ready over here,' Andy says, walking over from the stretcher he's laid out. 'Okay, Callie, we're going to lift you onto the stretcher and get you to the hospital.'

They carry me with care and wheel me out to the vehicle. John sits in the back with me, administers pain relief and keeps me comfortable while Andy drives. I call Mum and tell her I'm in the back of a van with her boyfriend, which makes John laugh. By the time we arrive at the hospital, I've warmed to him and it's easy to see why Mum's interested.

They take me through to Emergency and lift me onto a bed in a cubicle. 'Back to work for us, Callie,' John says. 'A doctor will be with you soon, and hope to see you again.'

I manage a smile now that the pain relief has kicked in. 'Yeah, I hope so too.'

They head back out into the night and there is nothing else for me to do but try and sleep. Good news is that my ankle doesn't appear to be broken, so hopefully a week of rest and I'll be back at work next weekend. I lay my head back on the pillow and close my eyes.

'Callie...'

My eyelids open at the sound of my name. Someone with short, blonde hair is looking down at me.

'Hi. I'm Dr Taylor.'

I shift up the bed, looking around for a clock.

'You came in an hour ago.'

I nod. 'Guess I fell asleep.'

'That's a good sign. Means your pain isn't too severe at the moment.' The doctor looks down at my ankle. 'You've got some stellar swelling and bruising there, so we're going to X-ray and scan.' The doctor calls a colleague over for assistance and they wheel me along the corridors to the X-ray room.

The next hour is spent hobbling from bed to bed for the X-ray, being taken to another room for the scan and trying to manage the bathroom.

After another hour back in the cubicle, dozing to the chaotic background noise of a Saturday night in Emergency, Dr Taylor returns.

'Hi, Callie. How are you feeling?'

I nod. 'Pretty good on these painkillers.'

The doctor smiles. 'Well, good news is that nothing is broken.'

I breathe out a relieved sigh.

'Bad news is that you have a grade two partial tearing of ligaments, which is a good four to six weeks' recovery and no weight-bearing on that ankle.'

I shake my head, uncertain I've heard correctly. 'Sorry, did you say four to six weeks?'

'I did.'

'But I have to work. I perform and work behind a bar.'

Dr Taylor shrugs. 'Unless you want to do some permanent damage, you really need to stay off that ankle.'

I clench my jaw, trying to stop the tears that are threatening. 'Surely it won't take that long?'

'You might be okay after four weeks, but it wouldn't be wise to rush the recovery. But, hey, look at the bright side, a break would be much worse.' They give me a broad smile. 'We always look for the positive here in Emergency. We'll get you bandaged up and into a moon boot, some crutches, a care plan and you're free to go. Have you got someone who can collect you? If not, we can get you a bed until tomorrow.'

My head reels with my new reality. 'Um, yeah, I called my mum before. She's on her way.'

'Good. Go easy on that ankle, hey?'

I nod.

Dr Taylor leaves and I squeeze my eyes shut, not wanting to cry in front of the nurse. But when Mum arrives half an hour later to collect me, and I collapse into her car, I cry all the way home.

The one time I desperately need Tom to help me through and he abandons me as well.

Chapter 39
Maya

'Tell me more about what happened before you left the stage,' Dr Garcia says.

We're half an hour into the session, and I've skimmed over what happened at the club but talked at length about coming out to my parents. I suspected she'd return to the topic of my failed performance.

'It started as soon as I walked in,' I say, the night still vivid in my mind. 'I didn't expect the club to be so busy. It's usually quiet on Thursday nights. So that threw me. Then I saw Amber – you know that person I've mentioned before.'

Dr Garcia gives a single nod and writes on her notepad.

I take a sip of water as though it will wash away the bitter taste in my mouth. 'She's the one who doesn't like me and who Callie's had a ... something with. She wasn't supposed to be there. That's why I chose that night to perform for the first time.'

Dr Garcia's eyes narrow slightly but she doesn't comment, so I continue.

'In the dressing room, I felt sick with nerves and I couldn't shake the idea of Amber watching me. But I also knew that I'd be disappointed in myself if I didn't try.' I cross my legs on the couch, trying to get comfortable. 'When I walked onstage, everything felt heightened. The music was too loud; the lights were too bright; too many faces were watching me. I froze and my lips wouldn't move, so I couldn't even just stand there and lip-sync. Callie was supposed to be there, but she was gone.' I pause to catch my breath. 'But Amber was watching me, laughing. Like I was a complete joke.' I shake my head. 'I couldn't stay up there like that.'

Dr Garcia is silent for a beat, watching me thoughtfully. 'You and Callie didn't discuss what happened? You ended the relationship instead?'

I hang my head. 'It felt like the best option. I was humiliated, for both of us.' I lift my gaze. 'How can I face people in the club after that? How can I face Callie?'

Dr Garcia gives me a sympathetic frown. 'Humiliation is a difficult emotion to process.' She glances at her notepad briefly. 'I'd like to talk more about Amber.'

'Amber?' I say with a bitter scoff. 'I'm not wasting my therapy session on her.'

'I think there's something there, Maya, and if we can uncover what it is, it might help,' she says in an encouraging voice.

'I don't see how.'

'Well, you may not realise it, but you've mentioned her in a few sessions now,' Dr Garcia says, 'and you said her being present impacted your ability to perform.' She crosses her legs and places the notepad and pen on the table beside her. 'The behaviours in others that irritate us can often reflect our own self-beliefs. The comments you've made previously about how Amber has treated you and how she makes you feel are similar to the judgements you make about yourself.' She pauses to let that statement sink in. 'As though she's holding up a mirror to you,' she adds gently. 'So it's not surprising to hear that when you saw her watching you, you seized up.'

It's only because I trust Dr Garcia that I don't immediately disregard what she's saying. I cast my mind back over my interactions with Amber, the way I always felt inferior and unwelcome around her, wanting to keep myself small, and the only time I did confront her was driven by a deep insecurity on my part.

'That concept can be difficult to comprehend,' Dr Garcia says. 'Would you like me to explain further?'

I shake my head. 'I think I understand. So what happened onstage was a subconscious thing?'

'That was likely part of the problem, yes.'

'But how am I supposed to move past something like that?' I ask in a small voice, my body deflating. 'That feels too big to overcome.'

'The first step is awareness. Nothing can change without that, and now you're aware. Next, you take small steps to work on negative self-belief and other things that may impact you, and you're doing that. You've told your parents about your sexuality. You're coming to regular therapy sessions and you're open to listening. You embarked on what sounded like a healthy relationship, and you threw yourself into learning about performing because it's something you always wanted to do. These are things to be proud of, Maya. Things that help you grow and build confidence. Whether your performance went well or not is almost irrelevant.'

'It doesn't feel irrelevant,' I say. 'It cost me my relationship, and being with Callie was one of the best things that's ever happened to me.'

'But it doesn't need to cost you the relationship,' Dr Garcia says. 'You have a choice about how to deal with this. You can take your power back, own what happened on that stage and let it be an event you learn from. And if Callie made you happy, it seems a shame not to try and fix it.'

My eyes sting and a solitary tear rolls down my cheek. 'But how can I face her friends and colleagues when I humiliated myself so badly? Even if she didn't see what happened that night, someone would've told her.'

'You mentioned at the start of the session that Callie's called you several times and left messages. Doesn't that indicate she's not embarrassed by you?'

I give a sulky pout. 'Yes, but it's been over a week since she called, so I think she's given up.'

Dr Garcia gives me a small smile and says softly, 'Or maybe she thinks you don't want to speak to her since you haven't responded.'

I drop my gaze, the guilt rising.

'Is it more than being embarrassed?' Dr Garcia asks. 'Are you still angry at Callie for not being there for you? Punishing her somehow?'

I stiffen at the suggestion of intentionally punishing Callie. 'I'm not punishing her, but she always runs away when things get hard and she knew how I felt about that. If she'd stayed where she was, I might've been okay.'

Dr Garcia purses her lips, her gaze penetrating, and I look away because that expression tells me she's preparing a challenging question. 'How would seeing Callie in that moment have made a difference? Especially if you were already feeling overwhelmed and like you couldn't perform?'

'She would've given me a sign about how to handle it, or just knowing she was there would've helped.'

'But she was trying to make the environment better for you by adjusting the lights. Isn't that being there for you?'

I drop my feet to the floor and bounce my knee.

'It's natural to want to blame circumstances outside of ourselves when things don't go to plan,' Dr Garcia says. 'But given how you were feeling about performing and what you've told me about Amber, it's possible you would've seized up anyway, even if Callie was visible.' She softens the blow of the statement with a kind smile. 'Let's take everyone else out of the equation. What were your own expectations of how this would turn out?'

I shrug. 'I expected to remember the lyrics and to move my body. I didn't think I'd get a standing ovation or the reaction the other kings get, but I thought I'd get through the nerves to make it to the end of the performance, at least.'

'Okay, so the fact it didn't start perfectly threw you? Both from when you walked into the club and from when you stepped onstage? 'That's a lot of pressure to put on yourself, Maya.'

I frown. 'I know.'

Her eyes flick to the clock on the wall. 'We've covered a lot today, and there will be more to unpack next session. When you get home, maybe you could give yourself some rumination time and empty your mind of your thoughts about what's happened? Then work on forgiving yourself for being human. If you've downloaded the app I recommended last week, that has some helpful strategies.'

I manage a smile. 'I'll do that. Thanks, Dr Garcia.'

I leave the consulting room, book my next appointment and head out into the afternoon sunshine. I walk towards the river to catch the ferry instead of taking the bus. I need the calm of the river to help process the session, especially the part about Amber being my damn mirror.

Chapter 40
Callie

The days following my injury are long and slow. There is little I can do except lay around with my foot elevated. My family rally around me, keeping my ankle iced, bringing me food and drink, finding me shows to stream, playing cards, and doing what they can to make me laugh. They're reluctant to leave me alone, but inevitably they need to because they have jobs and lives to get on with. And when they do, I sit quietly, no choice but to let the thoughts and emotions flow.

Processing my emotions is something the therapist encouraged me to do after I cut ties with Lacey, and as a way to deal with my anxiety. In theory, it's a good practice, but in reality, when I'm in the thick of a situation, my brain doesn't function, and fight-or-flight is my default. But forced to sit still, I faced it.

I thought mostly about Maya and our relationship, about her comments that I ran away instead of talking to her. I thought about her jealousy of Amber and admitted to myself that it did worry me, but that I ignored it, because I didn't want to believe there were any issues between us. But it's obvious now that I should've talked to Maya about it and how the situation with her ex-girlfriend affected her.

I thought about her desire to perform, how in awe she was of drag, and Amber's insinuation that Maya was using me as a springboard. Given that Maya broke it off so swiftly when performing didn't work out for her, it's hard not to believe that's true. But there were too many other signs that she cared about me, weren't there? Spending time with me at every opportunity, wanting to know that it was me who liked her and not just Tom, caring about my family, inviting me to her dad's event, the very intimate and loving sex, making an effort on my birthday, and the comment she made that day – *for the most beautiful person.* How could all of that be false? But we're no longer together, so something changed for her that night.

The ache in my chest flares. An ache that hasn't dulled as the days have passed. Instead, it's intensified as I feel her absence more and more. I miss her. I miss her smile and bewitching laugh. I miss her mouth on mine and the softness of her naked skin. I miss the way she looked at me. I want it back. I want it all back.

Something else has bubbled up this week, too, something that has simmered underneath for an eternity, tucked away in the depths of my soul, a belief that underpins everything. And that is my view that love is temporary, yet on the surface, I've walked around with an idealised notion of what love is.

The realisation hit me when a memory surfaced a couple of days ago. It wasn't long after Dad didn't show for my seventh birthday. I was lying on the lounge room floor with a colouring book. Mum and Gina were in the kitchen, talking, their voices floating across the hall. I heard Mum say, 'Love is only temporary, Gina.' I repeated it to myself slowly as I concentrated on colouring between the lines, trying to get my mouth around the long word I hadn't heard before. 'Temp-or-ary. Love is only temp-or-ary.' It felt like a secret between adults, something I should tuck away for the future. Of course, I didn't understand what they were talking about, but on some level I knew it was connected to my dad and dissatisfaction with relationships.

The doorbell rings, dragging me from my busy mind, and I sit up, remembering we're having people over this afternoon.

'I'll get it,' Mum calls.

I grab my crutches and hop out into the foyer where Krissy, Stevie, Gina and Lisa pile through the door.

'Here she is,' Aunty Gina says. 'Up and moving around.'

'Yep, getting a bit sick of lying around now,' I say.

They file into the kitchen and I hobble behind them.

'How you doing, Callie?' Krissy asks, walking over to the table and pulling out a chair for me just as I'm ready to sit.

'Getting there,' I say. 'Pain isn't as bad and the swelling is down.' I rub my stomach. 'But of course I get my period in the same week.'

Stevie wheels over my make-up chair that has temporarily resided in the kitchen as my foot stool and gently lifts my leg onto it.

'Cheers, cuz,' I say.

She takes the seat beside me and Krissy sits across from us. 'And how are you doing with the other thing?' Stevie asks.

I shrug. 'We haven't spoken if that's what you mean, and I feel like shit about it.'

'You haven't tried to contact her again?' Krissy says.

I shake my head. 'Nah. I've left messages, and she would've seen my missed calls. She still hasn't replied, so it doesn't feel like there's much point in continuing to call her.'

Mum brings us over a cup of coffee each and moves back to Gina and Lisa.

I take a sip and say, 'You don't think she was only interested in me because of the drag stuff?'

Stevie's brows rise. 'What? No. Why would you think that?'

I frown. 'She was so into it, pushed to do it, then dumped me when it didn't work.'

'Callie,' Krissy says. 'I think the dumping you part might be a bit more complicated than that. She's bound to be upset by what happened that night. It's probably taking her a while to deal with it.'

'You think so?'

Krissy nods. 'Yeah.'

'She cared about you, Cal,' Stevie says. 'No question.'

I swallow, emotion edging up my throat. 'Then where is she?'

Stevie sighs. 'I don't know. Maybe you should call her again if you haven't for a while? Maybe she'll answer this time?'

I nod. 'Maybe. Or, I've been thinking about writing her a letter? She likes books, words on a page, right? It might give her time to process what I've got to say?'

Krissy smiles. 'I love that. It's a great idea.'

My heart lifts. 'Yeah?'

Stevie nods. 'Do it.'

The chime of the doorbell echoes around the kitchen. Mum smooths down her hair and checks her reflection in the window. The rest of us glance at each other with knowing smiles.

'That must be the new boyfriend,' Aunty Lisa says.

Mum blushes. 'Why do you say that? It could be anyone.'

We all laugh and she looks at us, oblivious to what's funny.

'I've never seen you so flustered over the ringing of a door-bell, Mum,' I say.

She tsks me and hurries off to answer it.

'It's very cute,' Krissy says.

'Mmm, it is,' I agree.

Mum walks back into the kitchen, carrying a gorgeous bunch of orange blooms, John in tow.

'Hello,' John says, treating us to his handsome smile. 'Looks like I'm late to the party.' By his side is a small scooter, which he wheels over to me. 'This is for you, Callie. A knee scooter I had lying around from when my son hurt his foot last year. Thought you might like to use it.'

'Oh my god. Thanks, John,' I say excitedly. He helps me to stand and fits my knee on the scooter. I take it for a spin around the kitchen, a laugh bubbling up from feeling so free. 'This is awesome. Why didn't I think of this?' I glance around at everyone. 'Why didn't anyone suggest this?'

'Because you needed to rest up for a good week first,' Mum says.

I scoot over to the fridge, grab myself a can of lemonade, put it in the little basket attached to the handles and wheel back to the table. 'I can get things myself!'

'Good. I can stop waiting on you,' Mum says.

'And, if you like,' Krissy says. 'You can come back to work on Monday and take charge of the office while you're recovering. Stevie and I will do more front-of-house stuff.'

'Really? Like, full-time until I'm back on my feet?'

Stevie nods. 'Yep. You're better at it than us anyway.'

I smile, my spirits lifting. 'I will be there first thing Monday.'

Feeling brighter, I join everyone as we spend the next couple of hours eating lunch, exchanging stories about the week and getting to know John more. He slots in well to our family dynamic, with his easy-going nature and genuine interest in everyone's lives. And the way he looks at Mum and places a gentle hand to her back while they're cleaning up warms my heart. I hope this is it for her and that she gets to lift her 'love is only temporary' curse.

Around four p.m., Stevie and Krissy leave to get the club ready for Saturday night. Gina and Lisa head home, and Mum and John retreat to the lounge. Mum invites me to join them, but I decline. Not only to give them space, but because I haven't stopped thinking about this idea of writing a letter to Maya.

I grab a notepad and pen from the kitchen bench, pop it in the basket of my knee scooter and wheel down the hall to my bedroom. I prop up a couple of pillows behind me, another couple under my foot and put the tip of the pen to paper.

Dear Maya...

Chapter 41
Maya

I pull my leg up, resting my heel on the edge of the balcony chair. Ash's face fills my phone screen as they eat a late lunch in the staffroom. 'Sorry you had to do my shift,' I say. 'I had a bad night's sleep and it was too much today.'

Ash shrugs and swallows their mouthful. 'It's fine. It's been a tough time for you. I'm sure I'll need the favour back one day. The session with Dr Garcia last week didn't help at all?'

I wrinkle my nose and look away from the screen, watching a pigeon land on the balcony balustrade of the next apartment block. 'Yes and no. Yes, it was good to speak to someone and she's always so practical. But no because she gave me a lot more to think about.' I face the screen. 'Including suggesting my issues with Amber are a reflection of my own self-beliefs.'

Ash's brows rise as they chew. 'Wow. Does it stack up?'

I give a slow nod and puff out my cheeks. 'Yep. I've spent a lot of time thinking about it, and I understand what she means.'

Ash grimaces. 'Never fun learning uncomfortable stuff about ourselves.'

'No,' I say. 'Amber wasn't nice to me, though. I didn't

imagine that, and she definitely had – or has – a thing for Callie. But I suppose it's true that her behaviour reflected my own views about myself, and what happened with Arianne triggered me to react the way I did. I wouldn't have let her get to me otherwise. I mean, even our jealousy mirrored each other's, right?'

Ash gives me a sympathetic smile. 'Self-awareness can only be a good thing.'

'Mmm, I suppose so.'

'So,' Ash says tentatively, 'nothing more from Callie? And you haven't called her?'

I frown. 'No and no.'

'You don't want to speak to her? Try and work this out?'

There's a stab in my chest and a fire in my throat. 'I miss her, so yes, I think I do. I'm just not sure how to go about it. I feel like such a fool.'

'Well,' Ash says. 'I reckon you pick up the phone and have a chat.'

I give a small smile. 'Easy in theory.'

Ash nods. 'Yep. It's always easy in theory.' They glance away from the screen, towards the clock on the wall. 'Need to get back to work. Probably see you tomorrow?'

'I'll be there. Thanks again, Ash.'

'Anytime.'

They hang up and I move inside. My laptop is still open on the kitchen table from where I spent an hour before Ash called, bashing at the keyboard, finally getting around to following Dr Garcia's advice. I hit a key to light up the screen. It's a jumble of words and sentences, a stream of consciousness.

It's only been eleven days since my epic stage fail. Eleven excruciatingly long days. With the passing of time, the humiliation has eased marginally, but the guilt over the way I treated Callie continues to grow and thicken, suffocating me. The anguish in her beautiful eyes and her confused, sweet face taunt me every day. She was the one person who had zero expectations of me, who welcomed me into her world and who believed in me. She thought I was an incredible human. She listened to me. She was loving and trustworthy. And my life is empty without her.

Her last call was nine days ago – the Saturday night before last at 8.30 p.m. That was the night I came out to my parents and my phone was tucked away while I spent time with my family, so I didn't see the missed call until the next morning. I didn't understand why she'd call in the middle of a show, unless she felt confident to do so since she was in drag. But I didn't want Tom. I wanted Callie. I didn't call back because I was still embarrassed and couldn't see a way forward. I thought she might've tried again, though, and it stings that she hasn't. But underneath my bruised ego, I know that she would've done that for me, thinking it was what I wanted. That's who she is.

I close the lid of my laptop and move over to the couch, flicking on the TV. As I scroll searching for something to watch, my eyes drift to the single sofa where the clothes I'd worn onstage are neatly folded atop a pile ready to take to a charity shop. Callie's words drift into my mind – *we've all messed up; that's how we get better.* Then I hear Dr Garcia – *forgive yourself for being human.* Over the past few days, as the humiliation has begun to dissolve, I've been able to tune into other thoughts and emotions. Despite my nerves and inability to get through the performance, I liked the feeling of being dressed and ready to perform. There was even a tiny part of me, I see with hindsight, that liked standing on that stage.

I let out an exhausted sigh and lay my head back. Who cares about all of that when I lost the one thing that really matters? Performing is something I can try again, if I really want to, but I'll never meet someone like Callie. People like her are rare, and I ran from her. I ran from her because it was easier than facing things.

I raise my head, my mouth falling open as something clicks. *I ran from her. I* was the one to run when it became too hard. I groan. What have I done?

I check the time. Where would Callie be on a Monday afternoon? At home? With Stevie and Krissy? In the office? I rush to my bedroom to change, my heart thumping.

Please don't let it be too late.

Chapter 42
Callie

I've been in the office since eight a.m. – placing orders, posting on socials, making new content, mending costumes, and doing accounts. It's my first day back at work since my fall, and it's good to be out of the house and to be contributing to the club again.

Now it's four p.m. and I'm ready to go home, delaying one final job as long as possible. But Stevie and Krissy have done so much for me, I don't want to leave it for them. Plus, they won't be here until we reopen in another two days. I prop my knee on the scooter, slip my bag across my body, grab the poster for next week's show and scoot through the empty club to the front entrance.

Outside, it's a bright, crisp, autumnal afternoon. The sun hangs low in the sky and I inhale deeply, filling my lungs with fresh air after being indoors all day. I tend to the task, sliding out the old poster from its plastic frame and slipping in the new one, resisting the urge to glance down Wickham Street towards Maya's. As I roll up the old poster, my eyes prickle and I swallow back the lump that's risen in my throat from the memory of our last encounter on this very footpath. I can't fight the urge any longer and my gaze drifts towards her apartment block. What would happen if I went down there? Pressed the buzzer for Apartment 805? Sat in the foyer until she appeared?

My gut stirs, a melting pot of jitters, excitement and hope. I slip my hand into my bag, my fingers brushing the folded piece of paper I've grown attached to and keep with me at all times. A sudden jolt passes through me, a desperate longing to fix this. I throw the old poster inside, lock up and start scooting. I'm moving too fast, I know I am, but now I've made my decision, I can't get there quick enough. My skin warms under my jumper and my good leg aches from the exertion.

Ahead, someone walks out of Maya's building and my heart skyrockets. 'Maya,' I breathe. She turns away and pats her pockets, then heads back inside.

'Maya,' I call, speeding up. *She's home. She's home. She's home.* I'm forced to stop to readjust my knee, then take off again. Minutes later, I press the buzzer, over and over.

The heavy foyer door swings open. I go to scoot inside and come face-to-face with Maya, making my heart leaping.

She gasps.

'Please give us another chance,' I blurt.

She blinks at me, her eyes turning glassy, then looks down at my knee scooter and gasps again. 'Callie, what hap—'

'I have something to say.' I fumble in my bag and pull out the letter, unfolding it with trembling fingers.

'Maya,' I say, my eyes fixed on the paper. 'When I first saw you, I knew you were going to be an important part of my life. I didn't know why or how, but my soul knew I had to meet you. And when I messed it up, you came to me, proving it was destiny. You were what I'd been searching for. Someone who liked me for me. But I was too scared to jump all in. Too frightened that if I didn't give you something more than just me, you'd walk away. Because if we didn't have that mask between us, then what did we have? But the truth is, although I always thought I believed in love, I never truly believed it was possible for me.'

I lift my eyes from the paper and look at her. Tears spill down her cheeks. 'And I don't understand how I haven't known you for a lifetime,' I continue. 'Because it feels like you've always been a part of me. How did I even exist before you? I'm sorry I wasn't there for you. I'm sorry that I hurt you. But I don't care what happened on that stage. It doesn't matter to me. *You* matter to me. What we had matters to me. We don't need Tom and Georgy, we don't even need the club, we just need each other, because' – I take a shaky breath – 'I love you, Maya, and you might not love me, you might not even want to talk to me, but I had to tell you. I had to try. And I'm not running away anymore. I'm here, facing it.'

Maya chokes back a sob, clutches my face and kisses me hard. Her lips are salty and wet from her tears, and I start to cry, too.

She breaks the kiss and rests her forehead against mine. 'I called Stevie to see where you were, and I was coming to find you,' she says. 'To beg you to give me another chance. Because I'm the one who messed up. I'm the one who ran away when it got too hard. I need to apologise, not you. I shouldn't have taken any of that out on you. And I shouldn't have put you in the position of needing to save me. I love you too and I was stupid to think I could be without you.'

'Y-you love me?' I ask.

She nods and kisses me again. 'Please can we try again?'

I laugh through my tears. 'Yes.'

Chapter 43
Maya

I'm sitting at the dressing table in my underwear as Callie applies my make-up. On top of the thick foundation and concealer, she keeps it simple – full, pencilled eyebrows and a five o'clock shadow with a dark bronzer.

It's been one month since Callie turned up at my door as I was leaving to go and find her, and she's spent most of that time living at my place. It made sense being so close to the club and meant she could scoot to work, rather than needing to get a lift or take the train. We got to know each other all over again. I confessed my true reasons for picking that particular night to perform and told her about Dr Garcia's mirror theory. Callie told me more about her very brief history with Amber, and it turned out that I didn't have much to be jealous of.

Liv and Bella have visited a lot; they adore Callie almost as much as I do. Ash and their partner have been over a few times for dinner, too, and I love that we've formed a couple friendship. We've been to Mum and Dad's a couple of times, and it was heartwarming to watch them make Callie feel part of the family. Callie and I also talked about my performing aspirations, and I discovered that I wanted to give drag one more try. I loved my secret time as Georgy, and I wanted to let him loose.

Callie digs into my bag with my drag clothes and pulls out my packer, which I bought a week ago. 'Are you going with this?'

'Yes,' I say with enthusiasm. 'I'm getting my big king energy on.'

Callie grins and helps me slip it on, stepping back to inspect me. 'Fits well.'

I check myself in the mirror. I've been wearing the packer at home as much as possible, but it still feels out of kilter to wear it under clothing. Callie assures me it gets easier.

'Are you okay?' Callie asks.

I turn to face her and twist my hips side to side so that the packer moves. 'Never been more ready.' Not entirely true, but I'm following Dr Garcia's advice and building confidence by taking action on the things I want to do. *Don't wait for the confidence to do the thing; do the thing to gain the confidence.*

Callie grabs my jeans and passes them to me. 'So I'm going to stand in the wings, okay? You get nervous, you look at me. I won't leave for any reason. If the lights are too bright, put the sunnies on. It's part of George's look, so it won't look odd.'

I step into my jeans. 'Firstly, you haven't been back on your feet long, so you're not standing.'

She smiles. 'I already have a stool ready and waiting.'

'That's okay then.' I zip up and grab my T-shirt. 'If I put the sunglasses on, then I won't be able to engage with the crowd.'

Callie shakes her head. 'That's not your priority tonight. Remember – keep it simple when you're starting out.'

I nod. 'Okay.' I pull my hair up to fit the wig and finish the look with a gold cross earring, boots and a leather jacket and hook the sunglasses over the neckline of my shirt.

Callie looks me up and down slowly. 'Wow.'

I step over to her and kiss her. 'Thank you for believing in me.'

Her face softens. 'Always.'

I take a deep breath. 'Let's do this before I change my mind.'

Her phone dings with a message and she taps her screen. 'You're up next, Georgy.'

I shake out my arms, dispersing the adrenaline coursing through me, then pick up the guitar, lift my chin and say, 'Ready.'

We head to the wings and watch the second amateur act of the night while I breathe through the queasiness starting to roll through my stomach. The performance finishes, the small audience claps and Amber walks onto the stage. *I belong here. I'm gay enough and I deserve to be onstage as much as anyone else. She's not my mirror anymore.*

Amber talks up the king who's just finished, then without looking my way, she says with surprising enthusiasm, 'Let's hear it for our next king, Georgy Michael!'

I glance at Callie.

'Go. I'm here,' she says, resting on the stool. 'I will not move.'

My heart hammers as I step out onto the stage. The crowd give me a welcoming round of applause, and Stevie and Krissy whoop from the bar. The music starts and I sneak a glance at Callie who is miming removing the sunglasses from her shirt. I scramble for them and slip them on. Shading my eyes instantly calms me and I look out into the crowd, my gaze landing on Amber, watching me with an unreadable expression. It's the fuel I need to begin. I shake my hips, pretend to strum the guitar, and start lip-syncing to 'Faith'. The audience reward me with a cheer and I keep going, focusing on the people who are singing along. I mess up a few moves and forget some others but

I stay focused on the lyrics. At the end of the track, I remove the sunglasses, open my eyes wide and soak in the applause, albeit small.

Amber jogs up the three stage steps and says into the mic, 'Well, we got there in the end. Thanks, Georgy Michael.'

The barb rolls off me and I rush straight into Callie's arms, feeling a buzz I've never experienced before.

'That was incredible!' she says.

I beam at her. It was far from incredible, but I got through it and I can improve. 'I forgot some of the lyrics,' I say. 'And the lights threw me at first.'

'Completely normal,' Callie says.

We walk back to the dressing room, chatting excitedly about the performance. I talk to Callie about the parts I feel didn't go well – getting my footwork off and forgetting to stride across the stage in the instrumental. She talks me through how to make that easier next time. *Next time.* I can hardly believe it.

By the time I clean my face, change back into my own clothes and we get into the bar, Amber is doing a solo performance. Apart from the slight dig at the end of my act, she's kinder these days, the cool gazes and brittle tone becoming less frequent. I sometimes still experience that shrinking feeling around her, but as Dr Garcia reminds me, Amber can only make me feel like that if I let her.

I turn away from the stage. Callie is grinning at me from behind the bar as she shakes a cocktail mixer. My heart expands with love for her. She's missed Tom, and she's so excited to perform this weekend, she can barely sleep. But I think it's been good for her to live without him for a while, and good for our relationship. I've loved having her all to myself.

Callie pours the liquid from the cocktail shaker into a salted margarita glass. She walks out from behind the bar and places it in front of me. 'I think you deserve a margarita after that.'

I slip off the stool and kiss her. She wraps her arms around my waist, letting the kiss linger. Every part of me, every atom, is fizzing. Because I finally performed. Because I feel like I belong. Because I found exactly who I want to be. And because I get to spend the rest of my life with this incredible human called Callie.

Acknowledgments

What a journey this novel has been! From a short story over two years ago, to a full-length novel today. I knew when I wrote the short story that these characters had more to give, but I wasn't sure they'd ever get the chance because I had other novels planned. But, as so often happens with characters, they took charge and *King Love* became my third novel.

Before I get on to the specific *thank yous*, a huge thanks to all the drag kings around the world who have created YouTubes and blogs and websites dedicated to the art of drag, documenting their experiences of being a king and what it means to them, providing costume tips and make-up guides. I spent many, many hours trawling all of it so I could ensure this book was as realistic as possible. Did I buy my own stipple sponges? Absolutely. Am I tempted to dress as a king for book promos? Also yes. But, for now, I reckon I'll stick with writing books.

Publishing a book takes a village, and I'm so pleased to have had the opportunity to work with the same people across several novels. A special thanks to the following people.

Penny Carroll – thank you so much for the invaluable manuscript assessment. It was exactly what I needed at the time to progress this story. I was struggling and you helped me work out the plot holes, find the conflict, highlighted character behaviours that I didn't see myself and inspired me to shape the novel into this published version. Thank you for believing in this story – probably more than I did at the time! Thanks also for the proofread and the blurb polish (and the inadvertent promo slogan that came from that).

Jess McFarlane – I am so grateful to be on this writing journey with you, Jess. You are always there for me, in my corner no matter what, and while I *could* do this writing thing without you, I never want to. You've been the bestest author mate, and I'm so grateful for you and for the excellent feedback on (and praise for) the very, very bad draft you read of this story. Promise me you'll read the published version one day so that I can redeem myself. And I'm ready for AR book four and the western!

Stephanie Davy – ah, Steph, I am still so thankful Casey led me to you. Thank you for the beta read, for the character insights, for appreciating that all of my characters have zodiac signs (and for guessing Callie and Maya's purely from the way they interact with the world), and for loving this story so much. The way you gel with my Australian characters from Brisbane is always a delight. You know the release of this book is going to lead to many Scorpio Moon chats and exchanging of petty queen TikToks, and I look forward to it.

Samantha Sanderson Marshall – Sam, another gorgeous cover where you brought my characters and my story to life! I'm so glad to have you on my team. I appreciate your continued support and your patience while I had you on hold most of the year as I sorted out this novel, and for throwing in some artwork for my spur-of-the-moment *Meet Me in Berlin* special edition in the middle of my booking. Like Jess, I hope you get to read the published version, because the draft you read was a little rough.

Sophia Blackwell – it was so nice working with you again on the copy-edit, Sophia! I'm so grateful *Meet Me in Berlin* led me to you years ago. I appreciate your insights, experience and support, and I am very grateful for your patience while I kept extending the deadline. I'm sure we'll work together again on a future novel.

Pip Landers-Letts – Pip! So glad our paths crossed. And how cool we're in a Sam-Pip-Sam-Sophia quad. Thank you so much for the super speedy beta read and the great feedback. Thanks also for your continued support and friendship. I appreciate you and love our online chats. Hopefully we'll meet in person one day and we can go and see A Midnight Summer's Dream – insert rolling on the floor laughing emoji. Apologies to Shan for introducing you to jam and cream lamingtons. Can't wait for your next book!

And as always, thank you to my wife who lets me sit at my computer every night and every weekend with my 'imaginary friends' (her words, not mine) and to my family for their continued support.

And to you, dear reader. I hope you love Callie, Maya, Tom and Georgy with a Y as much as I do.

Normal Functioning Adult
Chapter One

I stare at the glass doors of The Psychology Centre. I've been coming here since my wife died, since my soul cracked and shattered, but only for occasional one-on-ones with my psychologist. Now he's put me into a group therapy program that starts today, and the thought of reliving Mel's death for strangers makes my pulse thump.

A knock to my shoulder jolts me forward. 'Jesus!' I shout.

'Watch it, love,' grunts a man in a suit striding past.

I'm about to call him an arsehole when I realise I'm blocking pedestrians by standing in the middle of the footpath. I take a deep breath and walk through the sliding doors. My skin welcomes the cool air – a reprieve from the blistering January heat. A few people are scattered in the waiting area flicking through magazines or watching the morning news on the wall-mounted TV.

A gentle voice greets me as I slip my sunglasses into my handbag. 'Hello, Amy. I could see you out there. I wondered when you'd come in.'

The familiar face behind reception eases the tension in my

shoulders. 'Hi, Barb. Just trying to psych myself up. I'm here for the group session.'

She gives me a warm smile. 'It's in the end room on the left.'

I thank her and head down the corridor. Large black-and-white photographs of Brisbane landmarks decorate the walls: Story Bridge; Mt Coot-Tha; City Hall. The consulting room doors are all closed with the 'do not disturb' signs on display. My phone buzzes in my bag. I dig it out to find a message from Caroline, my best mate and colleague.

> good luck chat later x

I reply with an 'x' and slowly open the therapy-room door. Morning sunlight streams through a large window, and a few people are gathered on lime-green sofas, their voices a low murmur. I pick up a couple of pamphlets that are neatly stacked in a tall display rack by the doorway. The headings *Understanding grief* and *Coping with loss* make the constant pang in my chest burn. I quickly replace them and move towards the group, recognising a delicate floral scent as I get closer. My skin prickles. Oriental lilies. Mel's favourite. I want to believe they're a sign, but in reality they bloom year-round and are in every bouquet. I can't escape them.

I sit and the man opposite acknowledges me with a nod. Such torment in his eyes. Beside him is a young woman who's so vibrant I can only assume she's not one of the clients. Either that or she's dealing with the death of her spouse better than I am. Her bouncy, blonde curls frame a petite, youthful face, and her floral-print dress and bubble-gum pink nail polish fit perfectly with the brightness of the room. I attempt to smile but suspect the caustic taste she's left in my mouth plays out on my lips.

She does a quick headcount. 'Good, we're all here. Hello,

everyone. I'm Kylie. I'll be your therapist for the program.' The brightness fades as she gives a sympathetic frown. 'I know this is difficult, but you've taken an important step in your recovery by being here.'

My psychologist, Dr Sachdev, is the one who wants me to be here. I'm too *introspective* and *bitter*, apparently. Not progressing as I should. Attending group therapy will allow me to be with people who understand. I'd had the urge to shove him off the chair when he'd said that, but now here I am, on the Good Ship Lollipop with Shirley fucking Temple for a therapist. I silently snigger at my joke and picture Mel rolling her eyes and saying, 'Get some contemporary references, will you. You're so un-relevant.' Then she'd laugh and touch her finger to my nose and say, 'But you're very cute.'

Kylie continues, 'As your psychologists would've explained, this group is for people who are experiencing' – her voice takes on a sage tone – 'complicated grief.' She pauses, clearly pleased with herself. 'Of course, there's no time limit on grief, but when certain symptoms persist beyond twelve months it can put people at risk of developing serious mental, social and physical complications.' She pauses again as though we need time to process what she's said. 'Complicated grief therapy will complement your psychology sessions and help you connect with others who might feel the same.'

I cross my arms and focus on the lilies, willing myself to believe they're a sign I'm where Mel wants me to be.

Last week, Dr Sachdev spent our entire session covering complicated grief. He told me about the symptoms and treatments, and explained how some of my behaviour isn't healthy, such as my fixation on Mel's death, the belief I could've done something to prevent it, and my persistent yearning for her. But I hadn't been completely honest with him about my lifestyle over the past few months, so when he explained that not dealing with certain behaviours can lead to anxiety, sleep disturbances, difficulty at work and alcohol dependency, I told him he should be a psychic. He told me I had complicated grief disorder and that I needed group therapy, as well as weekly sessions with him.

'Let's start with introductions.' Kylie's melodic voice brings me back to the room and her gaze lands on me.

I raise my hand to wave, but quickly drop it and cross my arms again. 'Hi. I'm Amy.'

'Welcome, Amy,' Kylie says and looks to my left.

The woman beside me has cropped silver hair and gives off a strong maternal vibe that makes me wish she was the therapist. She pushes black-framed glasses up the bridge of her nose. 'Hello, everyone. I'm Trish.'

Kylie smiles warmly and turns to the man sitting beside her. I'm surprised to see someone so young here – he must only be mid twenties.

He has messy blonde hair and the dark circles under his eyes are prominent against his pale skin. He pulls the fingernail he's been chewing from his mouth. 'Um, I'm Steve.'

'Nice to meet you, Steve.' Kylie says and turns to the final person in the group – the man opposite me with the tormented eyes.

His dark-brown hair is lightly peppered with grey and his skin is tanned, as if he spends most of his time outdoors. I wonder if the fine lines around his eyes and across his forehead have deepened since he lost his partner. He rubs his hands up and down his thighs. 'G'day. I'm Luke. '

'Welcome, Luke,' Kylie says. 'So, the sessions will run for an hour and the program lasts for six weeks. I haven't planned anything specific today because I'd like you to share your stories. If you feel comfortable that is – there's no pressure.' She smiles kindly and continues. 'Over the course of the program, we'll talk about grief in more detail and look at strategies and resources that can help. But for now, we'll try and get to know each other a little bit and understand why you're all here.' She turns to Luke. 'Would you like to start?'

He stares at her. 'Oh. Erm...' After a few seconds, he says, 'I don't know what to say.'

'Tell us about your wife,' Kylie says softly.

Normal Functioning Adult is a story of grief, friendship and love told with heart and humour. Available in Ebook and paperback. See www.samvalentine.com.au for signed copies, or you can order from your local bookstore or buy on Amazon.

About the Author

Samantha L. Valentine is an author of contemporary sapphic fiction, both romance and life lit. She is passionate about diversity in fiction and would love the world to read more diverse Australian stories. She graduated with first-class honours in English Language and Linguistics and holds a Masters in Writing, Editing and Publishing. She lives in Brisbane with her wife and their two Boston Terriers. She is the author of three published novels, two published short stories and many unpublished drafts.

If you'd like to stay up to date, you can sign up to her monthly newsletter at www.samvalentine.com.au or follow her on Instagram, TikTok, Goodreads or Amazon.